· · · · · · · · · INTENSIVE CARE · · ·

ALSO BY FRANCIS ROE

Doctors and Doctors' Wives

Francis Roe

· · · · · *INTENSIVE CARE* · · · · · · · ·

A DUTTON BOOK

DUTTON
Published by the Penguin Group
Penguin Books USA Inc., 375 Hudson Street,
New York, New York 10014, U.S.A.
Penguin Books Ltd, 27 Wrights Lane, London W8 5TZ, England
Penguin Books Australia Ltd, Ringwood, Victoria, Australia
Penguin Books Canada Ltd, 2801 John Street,
Markham, Ontario, Canada L3R 1B4
Penguin Books (N.Z.) Ltd, 182-190 Wairau Road, Auckland 10, New Zealand

Penguin Books Ltd, Registered Offices:
Harmondsworth, Middlesex, England

First published by Dutton, an imprint of New American Library,
a division of Penguin Books USA Inc.
Distributed in Canada by McClelland & Stewart Inc.

First Printing, August, 1991
10 9 8 7 6 5 4 3 2 1

Copyright © Francis Roe, 1991
All rights reserved.

 REGISTERED TRADEMARK—MARCA REGISTRADA

LIBRARY OF CONGRESS CATALOGING IN PUBLICATION DATA

Roe, Francis J. C.
    Intensive care / Francis Roe.
        p.   cm.
    ISBN 0-525-93324-7
    I. Title.
PS3568.03489615   1991
813'.54—dc20   90-28658
                                                                     CIP

Printed in the United States of America
Designed by Eve Kirch

PUBLISHER'S NOTE
This is a work of fiction. Names, characters, places and incidents either
are the products of the author's imagination or are used fictitiously, and
any resemblance to actual persons, living or dead, events, or locales is
entirely coincidental.

*To Barrett and Rini Price, for their friendship,
forbearance, and encouragement*

Acknowledgments

I would like to thank the people who have contributed their expertise and advice to this book, in particular my talented and tireless editor, Michaela Hamilton, together with John K. Paine and the other members of her team.

· · · · · Prologue · · ·

Fran Dixon had several years' experience in the operating room, but only a few hours to prepare for the biggest operations she'd ever been involved in. Unfortunately, the person who could have helped her most to get everything right was dead.

Fran had scrubbed for Caleb Winter before, and knew about his requirements and the way he operated. She glanced at the clock and then at the large window that separated the scrub area from the operating room. One minute and he'd be here. He was invariably on time, she knew that.

Frank checked the instruments on her front tray one more time. Everything was ready. The patient was draped, and she could see the chest moving in time with the black diaphragm of the respirator. On the other side of the ether screen, Dr. Pinero, the anesthesiologist, fiddled with his syringes. Three gowned doctors stood around the operating table: Don McAuliffe, the silent, aloof senior resident; Ed van Stamm, the big, usually jovial junior resident with the square, boxer's face; and Porky Rosen, the intern.

"Why don't you start the operation yourself?" Ed van Stamm asked Don quietly, almost in a whisper.

Don McAuliffe shook his head. "Dr. Winter wants to take this one from start to finish." Fran glanced at him in surprise. There was no mistaking the bitterness in Don's voice.

"Here he comes," said Porky.

Through the window Fran saw Caleb Winter's green-clad

figure appear, and the already tense atmosphere in the operating room tightened even further.

"She okay?" Don looked over the ether screen. He spoke more to alert Pinero that Winter was here and things were about to start happening.

Nodding, Pinero made a quick adjustment to the respirator and pushed briefly on one of the syringes attached to the intravenous line.

The door from the scrub room opened and Caleb came in holding an untied mask in front of his face.

"Ready?" he asked.

Pinero and McAuliffe nodded simultaneously, and behind his mask Pinero felt annoyed; he'd nodded too fast. He wasn't a resident anymore, he was a senior attending, and he didn't need to kowtow to anybody. Winter took in the entire operating room at a glance before heading back into the scrub room. Fran straightened the heavy scissors on the Mayo stand, feeling sure that he'd noticed they were fractionally out of line.

There was a thump and a hiss of water as Caleb turned on the faucet in the scrub room.

It wasn't just Fran who was uptight, she knew that. Everybody was. They were all acutely aware that today's case was controversial. All kinds of rumors had been flying around the hospital for days.

"Check the suction," said Don. "Both of them." The circulator went around the table, and a moment later there was a hiss and the two clear plastic tubes quivered.

Ed checked the electrocoagulator. Exactly three feet of free wire; long enough to go anywhere it was needed on the operative field, not so long it could get tangled. "Set it at twenty," he said to Fran. That was the setting Winter invariably used.

Gabe Pinero fiddled unnecessarily with the intravenous line. Each person in the operating room was just marking time until Caleb Winter finished scrubbing his hands and came in to start the case.

Fran heard the metallic clank of the water being turned off and had a dry sterile towel ready when he backed through the door into the operating room. Caleb silently dried his hands and looked straight ahead of him while Fran shook out a rolled-up gown. She watched his solid muscles moving under the smooth skin as she held out the gown. Caleb stepped into it, pushing his hands through the sleeves, then through the elastic material at the wrists. In a moment he was gloved and adjusting the fingers to a snug fit. The circulator tied the gown behind him.

Don McAuliffe quietly moved around to join Ed on the patient's left. Dr. Winter preferred to operate from the right side, next to the scrub nurse.

All that could be seen of the patient was a large square extending from just below the breasts to the pubis. It was covered by a transparent, adhesive plastic film and surrounded by an all-covering green laparotomy sheet.

"I draped for a roof-top incision," said Don flatly, his voice devoid of inflection.

Fran watched Dr. Winter prod gently at the lower end of the patient's rib cage. She knew that the incision would be all the way across the abdomen, highest in the center, following the line of the ribs. What she didn't know was the extent to which Caleb Winter had geared himself up for this one, how he'd had to repeat to himself that this was just another difficult surgical case, to be dealt with like any other.

"Call my lab," he told the circulator. "Tell them I'll be making a decision in about an hour."

Don and Ed exchanged an astonished glance.

Caleb stepped back half a pace. He always did that before starting. It took him only a moment to check his patient's vital signs on the monitor, to see that Pinero was attentive and ready, that the suction was on, the cautery at the proper setting. He noted the Zeiss operating microscope, draped and ready if they needed it; Fran saw his eyes flicker over her instrument trays.

"You have the micros?"

Fran lifted a green towel to show him the set of microsurgical instruments on a separate table, and Caleb grinned briefly. "Just checking," he said, but Fran felt a bead of sweat form on her forehead.

After a final glance at the clock, Caleb stretched out his hand and Fran placed the broad-bladed scalpel in it, in exactly the right position, so he could grasp it between thumb and forefinger.

Caleb paused for a second, and in that moment the anonymous, naked belly before him became again part of a living, vibrant, and quite extraordinary person. With an effort, he firmly closed the shutters of his mind and memory.

"Everybody all set?" he asked in a perfectly normal voice. "Okay, let's go."

$\cdots\cdots\cdots$ **PART ONE** $\cdots\cdots$

The car wheels rattled on the metal grille of the Third Avenue Bridge, and Celine de La Roche looked up from her papers. They were moving slowly in a glutinous stream of traffic; on Celine's left four young black men in an old cream-and-aqua Plymouth shouted at her driver and tried to see through the dark windows of her limousine. When they reached the FDR Drive the traffic moved more easily, and when Trevor pulled up outside Celine's office building, it was seven minutes before the scheduled start of her first meeting.

Celine's publishing company occupied part of the fourteenth floor in one of the older buildings on lower Fifth Avenue, not a fancy address by any means, not like Random House or Simon and Schuster farther uptown. At this stage, Celine used her corporate budget to sign up carefully selected books and to assemble a team of the best editors, sales, and advertising people she could get; the elegance would come later.

As the elevator wheezed and groaned up to her floor, Celine felt eager and full of confidence. It was going to be a good day. She stepped through the shabby doors and nearly ran into Tom Pfeiffer, her second in command, who was waiting for her with a folder under his arm. His face was even paler than usual; with his dark suit, pear-shaped body, slicked-back dark hair, and impeccable manners, he looked like the maître d'hotel of a four-star restaurant.

"What's the matter, Tom?" she asked. "You look as if somebody'd stolen your coke stash."

"This is no time for jokes," he replied. "We have a big problem."

"So what else is new?" Celine led the way to her small office. "Why couldn't you take care of it?" she asked, sitting down at her work table.

Tom slapped the folder on the desk in front of her, and Celine flicked through the lease agreement for the space the company occupied. She had signed it two years before, and there were three more years to run.

"Well?"

Tom produced a folded letter from his jacket pocket and put it in front of her with a flourish. It had the name of a well-known firm of attorneys at the top.

"Frank Berwick," she said, before reading the letter. "I know him."

"Read the letter, Celine," said Tom. "Then you'll wish you'd never heard of him."

The letter stated briefly that the ownership of the building had changed, that it was scheduled for demolition, and that under the terms of the contract they had thirty days to get out. Yours very truly.

Celine fought her panic; how could she possibly find another place and move within a month?

She made an attempt to sound casual. "Tom, I thought it was something serious! Like you getting Marilyn pregnant, something like that."

Tom flushed. Marilyn, Celine's attractive secretary, *had* been doing a lot of Xeroxing and faxing for him, tasks most people in this small organization usually did for themselves.

"What does the contract say?" asked Celine.

"They're within their rights," replied Tom. "If the building changes hands, all present contracts automatically come up for renegotiation."

"That's negotiation?" She pointed at the letter.

"Well, if they're pulling the building down, there's not much point . . ."

"I suppose you're right. What's the cost of office space these days?"

"For a comparable place, around thirty dollars per square

foot, or about twice what we're paying now. But it's not only that. We'd have to shut down and open up again. By the time we got a suitable place it could be right in the middle of the Christmas rush. Celine, we're overextended as it is. Any more strain on our cash flow would kill us."

Celine sat back in her chair, trying to prevent the shock from showing on her face. This problem couldn't have come at a worse time. The rapid expansion of her company had cost a lot of money; like other publishing companies, she had to shell out large amounts of cash in advances, and it usually took a few years to recoup it. And as her husband Charles, who was on the board and did some of the legal work, had pointed out, they weren't exactly overcapitalized. A new thought occurred to her. Was it really a coincidence that this problem should arise now? Some people would be more than glad to see her and her upstart company in trouble, and those same people had enough clout to arrange it.

"Tom, leave me alone for half an hour." She looked at her watch. "I need to mull this over."

For several minutes after Tom had gone, Celine sat at her desk, immobile, until a thought lifted the corners of her mouth, and she reached for the phone.

At ten, Tom came back for the editorial meeting. When they'd sat down, all five of them, crammed together in the small office, Tom waved a slim manuscript, showing his excitement. "We have a chance to bid on this. The agent sent an outline and three chapters, and it's the best thing I've read since *Love Story*. It's about a disturbed Vietnam veteran who meets a woman jogging in Central Park. The kicker is that she's Vietnamese and less than half his age . . ."

Celine listened to the presentation; Tom had a convincing style, and he transmitted his enthusiasm to the others. "It's perfect for our list," he finished. "I recommend we make a strong bid for it."

After an animated discussion, Celine asked what else the author had written.

"This is a wonderful first novel," he replied, tapping the manuscript. "And of course if we get it, we'll have the option on her next work."

"I read the outline," said Celine, "and I agree it's wonderful. And the three chapters were pretty good, but I can't say the earth moved."

"Karl Linstrom is one of the best agents in town," Tom protested. "And I'm thrilled that Karl let us in on this one; it's the first he's ever sent us . . ."

"Right. So why do you think he sent us *this* one?"

Tom shrugged. "He knows that we're getting bigger . . ."

Celine grinned at him. "Yeah, sure." She pointed at the pages Tom was putting back in the Federal Express envelope. "What he knows is that neither Knopf, Viking, nor any of the power houses would touch it. So he sends it to us because we'll be so impressed that we'll snap it up. Tom, this author has no track record, and when I gamble, I want a much better chance of winning. Now, what's next?"

It wasn't until after eleven that the phones really started to ring in Celine's office, and by the time she'd taken several calls her eyes were sparkling with a mixture of controlled excitement and mischief.

"She's up to something," whispered Marilyn when Tom came back for his typing. The door was half open; just enough for them to hear Celine's silky, confident voice on the phone.

Just before noon, Marilyn put through a call from a Mr. Anwar Al-Khayib, the chairman of a large New York property development corporation. Celine had been expecting his call, but not quite so soon.

"I'm delighted to be speaking to you," he said. "I'm told you're the most elegant lady in publishing."

"Thank you, Mr. Al-Khayib, and I'm equally pleased to talk to such a nationally respected builder," replied Celine. She had never met him, but had found out a great deal about him in the course of the last few hours. She grinned to herself; it was like being back in France, where political and business back-stabbing was done with the most civilized refinement.

"I was just talking to one of our attorneys, Frank Berwick, who speaks of you in the most glowing terms," went on Al-Khayib, and Celine made the appropriate modest noises. "I am desolated to hear that your company is located in the building we recently acquired." He made clucking sounds of compassion. "But I have no doubt you will be able to find suitable alternative premises. Any building in New York would be honored by the presence of you and your company."

Celine wondered why he was putting on all this Levantine charm. She knew for a fact that Anwar had lived all his life in the States, had gone to Choate, and had taken over the huge building and real estate empire on his father's death two years before.

"We'll be really distressed to leave here," she said, tapping her pencil on the work table. "It's so convenient, and we've finished all the changes we needed to make it perfectly suitable for us."

"I'm really so very sorry."

A trace of enthusiasm touched Celine's voice. "Have you ever actually seen the building, Mr. Al-Khayib? It is really quite charming. If you ever have an opportunity to stop by, I'd be delighted to show you around."

"I know the building quite well." Al-Khayib sounded puzzled. "Did you say *charming?* I personally wouldn't have used that term."

"Oh yes!" said Celine, the enthusiasm clear in her voice. "Do you know who the architect was? It was Sturtevant Burr; he designed and built it in 1929, just before the Crash. I'm sure you've heard of Sturtevant, related to Aaron . . . no, it's a really fine building, Mr. Al-Khayib. Sturtevant Burr was the first to use strengthening cross-members in the external structure. It's a unique construction, almost a landmark, you might say."

There was a brief silence.

"Well, luckily there are plenty of his buildings around New York," said Al-Khayib, beginning to sound more American. "This is certainly the least remarkable . . ."

"Actually it's the only one," said Celine mildly. "That's what the *American Heritage* people told me, anyway. They were quite excited about it."

"Now, Ms. de La Roche, I know what you're saying, but don't think for one minute that you can get that dreadful edifice listed as a historical building. Why, if it had any real historical value, we'd be the first—"

"Mr. Al-Khayib," said Celine in her sweetest voice, "let's talk realistically. I'm well aware that it's unlikely that we could ever get this building listed."

"Of course not," purred Al-Khayib. "But if there's anything we can do to make your transition more comfortable, do please let me know."

"Well, that's most kind of you," said Celine. "As a matter of fact there is. I understand you own another fine building at Thirty-fifth and Lexington, and the fourteenth floor there is presently vacant. We'd like to take it, rent-free for a year, of course, then at our present rent here for the remainder of a five-year lease. That would be only if you could give us immediate occupancy and moving costs, of course."

The silence at the other end was palpable. Then Al-Khayib exploded. His voice was a complete contrast to his earlier unctuous tones.

"Are you joking? What the hell is this? Look, lady, I'm warning you, you'd better be out of those offices on the dot, or I'll have you evicted in the presence of all the TV networks in the city. Rent-free for a year? What do you take me for, an idiot? Or are you completely crazy?"

"Mr. Al-Khayib, now really!" Celine was enjoying herself enormously. Tom had edged into the room and was listening open-mouthed.

"I know how you like straight dealing, Mr. Al-Khayib," she went on. "Well, here it is. This morning we applied to have this building placed on the New York list of historic buildings. Now, I know it won't get through, but with the bureaucracy we have in this town, it may take years to settle. Meanwhile the building stays up. I happen to know what you paid for this building and how much interest you're paying. It's shocking, isn't it, the interest rates they're inflicting on us these days?"

There was no answer, so Celine went on. "If you have your pocket calculator handy, Mr. Al-Khayib, you will quickly see that I'm offering you a real bargain. Yes, of course, take all the time you need, just let me know within twenty-four hours."

Celine put the phone down, and a second later felt a sudden fluttering, a feeling of intense discomfort in her abdomen, just below the breastbone. It caught her breath, and she leaned forward, feeling faint.

Tom looked down at her with surprised concern, but he didn't realize that anything was really wrong until Celine raised her head. Her face was pale and drawn.

"Call Trevor on the car phone, Tom, please," she said, striving to keep her voice steady. "I think I ought to go home."

By the time the chauffeur arrived, Celine had drunk a glass of water that the distraught Tom brought her and was feeling better.

The drive out of New York was uneventful, but on the Connecticut Turnpike, near the Round Hill Road exit, Celine felt the pain again. She must have cried out, because Trevor called through the intercom to ask if she was all right.

"I think we'd better stop at Dr. Torrance's office," replied Celine, barely able to speak. "It's on Glenbrook."

"I know where it is, ma'am," said Trevor. In the rearview mirror he could see Celine huddled up in the seat, white-faced, clutching her stomach.

By the time they reached the Victorian house Ned Torrance had converted into a doctor's office, Celine was already feeling better.

Ned was his usual cheerful self when she came in, and after she had told him what had happened, he seemed quite ready to dismiss the whole thing as the result of too many publishers' lunches.

"I suppose you're still working as hard as ever?" he asked over the screen as she disrobed.

After examining her, however, Ned wouldn't look her in the eye. The nurse came in and drew some blood from her arm, and when that was over and she'd finished dressing, she came through into his office just as Ned was putting down the phone.

"You need to see a specialist in this kind of thing," he said, sounding unusually solemn. He fiddled with the long pen from his desk set.

"*What* kind of thing, Ned?" asked Celine, the first intimations of fear sliding up into her chest.

He ignored her question. "I want you to see a fellow by the name of Winter, at the New Coventry Medical Center," he said. "He's a bit young, I suppose, but I'm told he's one of the leaders in the field."

"*What* field, for heaven's sake, Ned?" A growing impatience was fighting with her apprehension.

"The field where your problem is, my dear, the pancreas," he replied. "I just spoke with Dr. Winter. He's seeing outpatients this afternoon, and can see you as soon as you get up there." He consulted a scribbled note on his pad. "Room 423 in the Harkness Building on Walnut Street. Here, I'll write it down for you. It's right opposite the hospital. Okay?"

He stood up, smiling reassuringly at her.

"Do I really have to go there *now*, Ned? Can't it wait until tomorrow?"

"No, Celine, I don't think you should wait, unless you want to get another attack."

Celine was about to argue when she felt a stab of the pain again. A few minutes later they were back on the highway, and Trevor's foot was hard down on the gas pedal as they flew toward New Coventry.

The limousine slowly turned into Walnut Street, and Celine peered through the dark windows. She hadn't felt any more pain, and was already beginning to feel annoyed with Ned Torrance for making her rush up here. And how silly of her to have agreed. This Dr. Winter would think she was crazy.

That must be the hospital over on the right, she thought, with the medical school on the left, just as Ned had said. The street was lined with parked cars and sickly looking sycamores. Celine's hands were sweating as Trevor drove slowly along looking for the entrance, and the mirror shook in her hand as she gave a final touch-up to her lipstick. She made a quick, nervous appraisal in the mirror. Her mascara was okay, and the tiny lines around the outer corners of her eyes weren't too obvious. Laugh lines, Charles called them. She certainly didn't look sick. Celine pulled her mouth into a momentary smile and turned her head briefly from one side to the other. The car slowed, and Celine's memories of hospitals and doctors came back in a rush. Professor Dupuis, who'd looked after her mother when she was dying. He'd had a thin face and black pomaded hair, smelt of garlic and insisted on holding Celine's hand while he told her there was nothing he could do. The too-busy Dr. Etienne, in Lyons, who'd taken care of her father, and never had time to see her, giving that tiresome job to one of his junior doctors.

Celine could feel her body tensing with apprehension. What

could possibly be the matter? She hadn't been feeling well for the last few weeks, and even Charles had noticed that she just picked at her food. Pancreas, Ned had said. Celine wasn't sure where that was, but guessed it would be where the pain had struck. She sat up very straight; whatever panic might exist in her mind, it would never show on her face.

When the car stopped, Celine took a deep breath and stared in front of her until Trevor came round and opened the door. She swung her long legs out, and two male medical students watching from the entrance looked at each other.

"Wow!" said one of them softly; it wasn't the gray stretch limo that had impressed them.

Looking up at the dreary-white flat-fronted five-story building, part of the sad architectural adventure the university had entered into in the sixties, her fear escalated. Why did she have to be taken care of in such a slum?

Celine went up the wide steps behind a large black woman pulling a child. The child swung back on his mother's arm, tears rolling down his fat, round face. Celine stuck her tongue out at him and his face froze with astonishment; she grinned for an instant, then walked past, head high. One of the students hurried to pull the door open for her. She smiled at him and went through into the main reception area.

A guard directed her to the surgical offices, and she walked briskly down the bleak corridor, her heels clicking on the plastic tiles. She tried to feel like a visitor, not someone who was there because she was sick. Horizontal streaks of black ran along the walls, all at the same level, about three feet off the ground. If she were in charge here, Celine thought, she'd soon have the place spruced up. It wouldn't even cost much; what it needed was some big, colorful wall decorations, plants at the corners, a bright carpet to replace this institutional tile. And it would be fun doing it.

A stretcher with a patient rattled towards her, guided by a pale young orderly. The stretcher's rubber bumper hit the wall as they passed her, leaving another black streak. Celine caught the barest glimpse of the patient, a young woman with a yellowed, tight-skinned, skeletal face and no hair. One hand was clutching at the blanket, a wedding band ruinously loose on her third finger.

Celine pressed herself against the wall to let the stretcher past, and the orderly grinned at her. "Jesu Marie," said Celine in a whisper after they had passed, and resisted the urge to cross herself. Suddenly she wanted to run back to talk to the woman. Was she a patient of Dr. Winter's? Who was she? What had happened to make her look like that?

Seized with panic, Celine forced herself to walk on. She felt her legs taking her faster and faster along the corridor, and waves of erratic impulses surged inside her, pressing her in different directions, to run away, to hurry and get this over with. Calm down, she screamed at herself, but it was as if all her senses were on the surface, like raw skin; she knew that if somebody spoke to her now she would shout instead of replying softly, strike when she should stroke.

The surgical waiting room was drab, with sickly orange plastic chairs around the walls, occupied by half a dozen people, most staring morosely into space. One wizened old man leaned forward in his chair, short of breath, trying to read a newspaper. Celine tried to pay attention, to calm herself and look around with her usual interest, but she was tight and shaking when she walked up to the desk. There was one nurse behind it. The name on her tag was Cathie Allen, R.N. Behind her another corridor opened into the doctors' offices. The black woman and her child came up to the desk behind Celine.

"New patient?" The nurse smiled at Celine.

"Yes, I am." Celine heard the sharp tone of her voice, but she couldn't do anything about it. She was wound up so tight that she thought she was going to explode.

The nurse's smile froze. She tore a form off a pad and pushed it toward Celine.

"Fill this out, please, with details of your medical history and insurance . . ."

Celine's lips tightened. She put a large envelope on the counter. "It's all here," she said. "This is from Dr. Torrance, my G.P."

"Sorry, but it's the routine, ma'am. All new patients—"

"Is that Dr. Winter?" asked Celine. She had just seen a slight flurry of activity behind the nurse. A door had opened, and a tall, well-built man in a white coat poked his head out and was talking to another doctor in a short white jacket. At the question, Cathie Allen glanced back, and her expression told Celine all she wanted to know. With complete assurance she stepped around the counter and walked toward them.

"Hey, you can't go down there!" The nurse grabbed for her arm, but with a quick twist of her shoulders, Celine evaded her. The black child howled, and the nurse hesitated. By the time she caught up with Celine, she had already stopped and was addressing the man in the white coat. From closer he wasn't quite so young, maybe around forty, and his brown hair was dark and thick with a touch of gray around the temples.

"Dr. Winter?"

There was a pause, while the man glanced at her. "Yes . . ." He looked at the nurse.

"She . . . she just walked right past me," said Cathie indignantly. "I—"

"Dr. Winter, Ned Torrance said you could see me as soon as I got here, and here I am. I don't want to keep *you* waiting."

Cathie Allen took a deep breath. "Mrs. ROCHE!" she said, "You must—"

"*De La Roche*, Nurse Allen, and it's Ms.," murmured Celine. She smiled, and after a moment Dr. Winter smiled too, and his eyes flickered clinically over her.

"Put *Ms.* de La Roche in room twelve, Nurse Allen, if you please." He turned to face the nurse. "That is, when it's her turn." His eyes came back to Celine, just for a moment, with the same impersonal, clinical gaze. "Meanwhile, she can wait in the reception area just like everybody else."

Cathie put a hand on Celine's arm, but she shook it off angrily. Tears of anger made her eyes glisten for a moment, but she turned before anyone could see them, and went back toward the desk.

As it turned out, she didn't have to wait long. Five minutes later, Nurse Allen, tight-lipped, led her down the corridor to room twelve. It was a bare, white, windowless cubicle, with a second door opposite the one she'd come in by. A folded sheet lay on the wooden examining table, and a green curtain shut off the end of the room. A small sink and a chair completed the furnishings.

"There's a gown on the hook behind there," said Cathie, pointing to the curtain. "Take off everything, and I mean *everything*, including bra and panties, and put on the gown. The doctor won't be long . . ." She turned at the door. "Oh, and Mrs. Roche," she said, "you'll find it much easier if you just go along with our routines. They were developed for everybody's benefit."

Celine was about to apologize for her bad manners, but Cathie had that smile on her face again, and Celine wanted to slap it right off her.

There was a single hook on the wall, next to a small square mirror. A faded gray gown with blue stripes that hung from the hook made her think of Solzhenitsyn's hero in *The First Circle*. Panic again. Celine opened the door and almost ran back up the corridor to the desk. Nurse Allen was listening to the black lady, trying to get a word in. The woman's voice was rising, and her child was now making a continuous whining noise. Even in her overwrought state, Celine could tell the child was ill, and that added to her panic.

"I need hangers, please," interrupted Celine. "These clothes . . ." A movement was enough to get her meaning across. She was wearing an Armani suit.

"Excuse me," said Nurse Allen to the black lady, and shakily pushed back a stray lock of blond hair off her forehead. Normally Celine would have felt badly for her, but in her present state of mind Nurse Allen was one of the enemy.

She followed the nurse back down the corridor. The girl opened several doors and finally came out with three triangular wire hangers, two with cardboard strips.

"That's the best I can do," she said, glancing back toward

the desk. She handed the hangers to Celine. The black woman was now calling down the corridor in their direction, and she had been joined by two men, one very tall and lanky. Nurse Allen smiled at Celine again. Lady, the smile said, God help you if you're ever my patient in this hospital.

Celine returned to her cubicle, shivering with tension. By the time she'd changed into the gown, sat down on the orange plastic chair, and waited for several minutes, her mood had consolidated into a silent seething fury, but she had it under better control when Caleb Winter came in. He knocked before opening the door, but still he entered like a whirlwind. His personality filled the room, and Celine, who would have felt equal to him under normal circumstances, felt at a terrible disadvantage in her bare feet and mean hospital gown.

Dr. Winter, who had the X-rays and the medical reports in his hand, didn't waste any time.

"I've looked at the X-rays, and they don't tell us anything," he said. "Neither do the lab tests they did down in Greenwich."

He sat down on the examining table, watching her. He noted in passing that Celine de La Roche was an extremely attractive young woman, aristocratic-looking and shapely, with masses of beautiful dark curls, but that wasn't what he was looking for. Automatically he scanned her face for signs of weight loss, the whites of her eyes for traces of jaundice, her neck veins for indications of heart failure; he watched her breathing pattern long enough to detect any hint of lung problems. Celine would have been astonished at how much information his trained eyes gleaned from her; she still thought that her carefully made-up appearance would give the confident impression she wanted to present.

Celine took a deep breath. "I'm sorry about crashing the line," she said. "It's only that—"

"No problem," interrupted Dr. Winter. He said it as if he was used to the way New York bitches behaved.

Celine's lips tightened again.

"You'll find it'll be much easier if you just follow the rules," he went on. His smile held no humor in it, and his voice was brisk and impersonal. "Now, Celine, tell me what's the matter with you."

"I got this sudden pain, right here." Celine put her hand on the middle of her upper abdomen. She repeated the exact words she'd used with Dr. Torrance, and wondered how many times she would have to tell the same story.

"And I've been having some kind of indigestion for about six months." Her large, dark eyes looked directly at Dr. Winter. He wasn't sure in the harsh light if her eyes were very dark blue or dark brown. Anyway there was a faint occasional greenish flash in the irises when she moved her head.

"What do you mean by indigestion?"

"Well, I'd feel very full after a meal, even when I hadn't eaten much, and I'd, well, burp a lot."

"Any pain?"

"Aside from this afternoon? Yes. Just the last few weeks, more of an ache, really, but sometimes it goes right through to my back." She watched to see if he believed what she was saying. Or did he think she was just another silly hysterical woman? He probably saw quite a few of those.

After finishing his questioning, he pushed a button near the light switch, and Celine could hear a distant raucous buzzer. A moment later Nurse Allen came in and motioned to Celine to get on to the exam table.

Close up, Dr. Winter had an almost electric quality about him, and to take her mind off the fear eating at her, Celine watched *him*. He moved with a quiet assurance, as if incapable of making a clumsy movement. His neck was strong, smooth-skinned, and when he leaned forward a vein ran up to the corner of his jaw. Examining her eyes with the opthalmoscope, his face was very close to hers, close enough for her to feel his body heat and smell his odor. There was an overwhelming sense of maleness about him that she couldn't avoid noticing, even in her agitation.

His hands on her belly were cool, probing, gentle, remorseless. He found the place in a second, and she could feel his fingers evaluating, questioning, checking from another angle. "Yes, doctor, it does hurt there."

And then he was finished. He washed his hands at the sink, and somehow this struck Celine as yet another insult. Had he washed his hands before examining her? She hadn't noticed.

Celine's hands shook when she put her clothes on, but they were steady again when she touched up her lipstick. Her next stop was Dr. Winter's office. The walls were covered with diplomas, but she didn't look at them. If Ned Torrance had selected Dr. Winter, the man presumably had the proper qualifications. He was sitting there calmly, his stillness emphasizing the impression he gave of confident, contained energy. His eyebrows, thick, curved, and slightly darker than his hair, now formed a straight line divided by a vertical frown.

"I think you have a tumor of the pancreas," he said after she sat down. "But that's about as much as I can say right now. We'll need to do more studies, an ultrasound, an arteriogram, a CAT scan, maybe an NMR. I'll make arrangements to get you into the hospital as soon as possible, and we'll take care of it." He stood up, sounding as unconcerned as if he'd been talking about a loose filling.

Trying to control her trembling, and furious that he seemed to be taking it all so lightly, Celine stood up too. For once she had nothing to say, and she was still silent when he showed her out.

From the desk, Cathie Allen saw Celine stumble coming up along the corridor. She's petrified, Cathie thought, and Celine's expression confirmed it. Celine stopped, and looked at Cathie with a dazed expression, remembering how unpleasant she'd been to her. She fumbled in her leather handbag and pulled out a big silk square with a large printed gold-and-black tiger encircled by a heavy golden chain. "I'm really sorry," she said. "There was no excuse for the way I behaved." She smiled, trying to regain her poise, and folded the scarf before putting it round Nurse Allen's shoulders.

Cathie was about to step back indignantly when she felt Celine's hands trembling where she touched her.

"It suits your coloring better than mine," said Celine. "Enjoy it." Then she turned and almost ran down the corridor.

Her eyes following Celine, Cathie slowly took off the scarf.

"Hermès," she read on the label; that didn't mean anything to her, but it was clearly an expensive scarf.

Celine's anger at Dr. Winter came back as she flew along the corridor. "Pig!" she muttered as she headed down the dingy corridor toward the exit. "What an arrogant, impersonal, condescending son-of-a-bitch!"

As Trevor brought the car round to the front of the house, Celine heard the tires crunch on the white gravel. She didn't wait for him to open the door, but climbed out as soon as the car came to a halt. The still-fierce heat of the late afternoon struck her as she emerged from the air-conditioned interior, and a spasm shot from her stomach right through to her back as she stood up. It caught her breath, but only for a second. Minette, her Blue Persian cat, met her at the door and twined herself around her legs in an unusual display of affection.

Celine bent down and gently scratched the top of Minette's head. "You know, don't you?" she murmured.

It was cool and dark inside the house. She walked through to Charles's study at the far end. It was a large room, with french windows that opened out over a rose garden and the deep end of the pool. He sat with his back to the windows; the table in front of him was covered with bound company reports, three telephones, and the computer with which he followed the vagaries of the stock market. He was dressed as usual in a white polo shirt and cavalry twill pants. He stood up, lean, spare, and muscular. Even without knowing it, one could have guessed he was a horseman.

"Well, how was it?" he asked. He tried to sound as if he hadn't been anxiously awaiting her return, but the long creases of his face seemed deeper than usual, and the look in his deep blue eyes gave him away. He came to her, his arms outstretched, and with a twinge of familiar sadness, he felt the reflexive stiffening of her body as he touched her.

"I need a drink," she said. Her weakness and fear were over for now, although they had left her drained and exhausted. Charles turned to the small bar opposite the door and reappeared in a moment with a glass in each hand, the ice clinking in hers. He smiled, watching the tension gradually leave her face.

"Why don't we just sit down for a few minutes?" he said. "Don't say anything for a little while, just get your breath back."

Celine flopped into an armchair; Charles was watching her with an expression of muted concern that she couldn't bear, and she closed her eyes. She couldn't object to his compassion, but it made her feel old and dependent; Celine imagined that he was looking at her the way people look at the inmates of a nursing home. He was probably wondering if she was going to die. And if she died Charles would be free to go off with that woman. She clamped her eyes shut, thinking about Marion Redwing. Marion, with her smiling gray eyes that became so sparkly and intense when she was with Charles. Maybe Marion could give him what he needed.

Charles watched her silently. He knew that it was better to wait, to say nothing until Celine felt like talking. He knew about her distance, her moods, and sometimes regretted having encouraged her to start her own business. Before that, they had been so wonderfully close, and at first, it had been such a game, looking for an office, then talking with agents, interviewing editors, convincing bankers, lunching with other publishers who wished they too could be as young and enthusiastic again. When they started the company, he'd done all the legal work of incorporation, drawn up the author contracts. Together they'd interviewed prospective employees, and even read manuscripts together. But as Celine became busier and more successful, she had less and less time for anything outside her company; like an invasive tumor, it had taken over her entire life. They'd planned to start a family after they'd been married a couple of years, but by then Celine simply didn't have the time.

Charles pushed that thought aside and moved in his chair to watch Celine's face. It had changed since he'd first met her: she was still as beautiful, but the childish softness and the aristocratic innocence were gone. Celine had fought many a battle since then, but still overreacted, still felt insecure, and never stopped trying to prove her worth. Charles's eyes moved to his desk, to the silver framed photo of Celine standing on the steps of the family château. When that was taken, Charles had been traveling in France with a couple of law school friends from New Haven. The father of one of them, Raymond Ansett, had arranged an introduction to Guy de La Roche, a publisher who lived with his family near Lyons.

All three of them were invited to the de La Roche château, about twenty miles from town, to help celebrate the *fiançailles* of his daughter, Celine, who was going to be married to a young aristocrat by the name of René Du Plessis. The party was held in the formal gardens of the château, and there the three young American law students encountered a luxury and a sophistication that left them open-mouthed. Celine and her father welcomed them; he was a sturdy, good-looking man with a thick mane of white hair, but Charles hardly noticed him. Charles's entire field of vision was taken up by the strikingly beautiful Celine, regal in a white organdy dress, with haughty dark eyes and a breathtaking figure. Despite the nature of the celebrations, the hitherto impregnable Charles was smitten. They talked, and she liked him, and he took her photo, after politely asking René to move out of the picture. Charles and his friends left, as planned, for Perpignan the next day, and with one thing and another, it was several days before Charles could call her. No one answered the phone, although he called several times. On their way back to Paris, Charles insisted that they make a long detour to stop at the château; by this time he was desperate.

The tall wrought-iron gates were locked with a huge padlock and chain; there was no one in the lodge, and nobody answered the bell. The great front lawn, so immaculate only three weeks before, was already overgrown and spotted with dandelions. And the tracks of heavy vehicles criss-crossed the lawn, cutting and crushing the formal flower beds as if they hadn't existed.

Charles came back from his reverie. Celine had opened her

eyes and was looking at him now with a peculiar, fixed expression. Her stomach was starting to tighten at the thought of what she had to tell her husband.

He stretched out his hands and took her unresisting ones in his. "You should have let me come with you to New Coventry." He watched Minette jump up into her lap. "Even the cat was worried about you."

"The news isn't good, Charles."

Charles took a deep breath. He couldn't imagine Celine being sick. "Tell me what happened."

Celine's earlier fury came back and her eyes flashed. "Ned Torrance really picked a winner!"

"Dr. Winter? He—"

"He's a pig, a supercilious—"

"Come on, Celine," interrupted Charles, who was interested in Winter's competence rather than in how he got along with his patients. "That doesn't matter. It wasn't a social visit."

Celine gripped the edge of her seat; her hands were warm again.

"God damn it, Charles. He was an arrogant, condescending, cocksucking son-of-a-bitch!"

There was a brief silence.

"Well, you seem to have found out quite a lot about him," Charles murmured. "And what did he find out about you?"

Celine stopped, her mouth open for a retort, then she smiled briefly when she realized what he had said.

She set her lips and moved her head so she could look him straight in the eye. "He thinks I've got a tumor on the pancreas," she said, and saw Charles's eyes widen with disbelief. "He said I need to come in to the hospital for more tests."

Charles was silent for a moment. "I suppose that's good news really," he said. "If they need more tests that means they don't really know for sure what it is, right?"

"I'm not going," said Celine.

"Of course you're going," said Charles sharply. "You can't possibly—"

"Not back there." There was a light in Celine's eyes that he knew well. "I don't like the place, and I didn't like him," she said stubbornly. "Ned can find somebody in New York. Surely there's somebody in that town who can take care of me, somebody I can get along with."

Charles walked toward the French windows and stood there for a moment before turning around. After the initial shock of what Celine had told him, a disbelief settled in his mind. How could she possibly be seriously ill? Celine had never been sick a day in her life.

"How did Corinthian do today?" Celine cut in on his thoughts, anxious to change the subject. It was ridiculous to go on about her medical problems, as if she were a sick old woman.

"Coming along nicely," replied Charles. He glanced out the window toward the stables, relieved to talk about his favorite horse. "He's still a bit unsure going around new jumps for the first time, but he's getting the hang of it." He almost added, "And he'll be on top form by next week," but Celine was there before him.

"He'll be ready for Atlanta?"

"Well, we'll see about that," replied Charles, almost brusquely. "Your health is a lot more important than any Olympic trials." He put his hand on one of the telephones. "Why don't I call Ned, or Dr. Winter? They must have come to some conclusions by now."

"Call Ned," said Celine. "Winter said he'd call him right away." Celine's eyes flashed with retrospective annoyance. "As soon as I was out of earshot, of course. After all, what business was it of mine?"

Celine stood with her feet apart and hands on her slim hips. The light from the window illuminated her face and made highlights on her dark hair. At that moment she had a dangerous and defiant look. In that challenging pose, she certainly didn't seem ill; on the contrary, she looked ready to take on the world. Charles watched her with the usual mild alarm he felt when she wore that expression. She should have been named Carmen rather than Celine, he thought.

Charles picked up the phone and flicked through a Rolodex file. "Right, here we are." There was a pause while he dialed. "Ned? Charles Forester here. Look, there's apparently a problem with your Dr. Winter. Celine wasn't too impressed with him."

There was a long silence while Ned talked. Celine could just hear his voice, and he sounded excited or indignant, or maybe both.

Finally Charles put the phone down. He turned to Celine and said, "Let's go for a swim."

Any discussion now would just harden Celine's resolve, he knew, and make it impossible for her to back out. Charles had every intention of finding a graceful way to allow her to reverse her decision. Ned was convinced that he'd sent Celine to the right man; if Winter has a problem at all, Ned had said, it was that he didn't much care for women.

Charles opened the French windows and they walked out into the garden. Celine scrunched up her eyes against the sunlight dazzling off the water and followed Charles around the pool. The water looked cool, blue, and inviting; the first half-dozen leaves of the fall floated on the surface, curled a golden brown, sailing slowly toward the filter. Charles's roses, planted out in beds to the right beyond the pool, looked languorous and exhausted. In an attempt to give them partial shelter from the brutal sunlight, Charles had constructed a kind of lattice roof over the rosebeds, but although the roses lasted longer, the dark, striated shadows destroyed the glorious effect of the hundreds of multicolored blooms.

"I'm going to have to do something about them," said Charles, looking over his shoulder as they walked round to the poolhouse. "Maybe an awning would be better. One of those heavy net awnings."

"I'd just dig them up if I were you," said Celine, still feeling generally destructive. "If you have to work that hard to make them grow properly, try something else. Put in some cactuses."

Charles grinned at her.

"You know, my dear, if you took your own kind of advice . . . remember that woman, the crazy one, Margharita something who wrote the book about Freud's women? How long did you work with her to get her on the best-seller list?

Couldn't you have just dug her up and planted another easier, saner author?"

Celine laughed, and some of the tension went out of her. "You're right, Charles, as usual." She *had* worked like a demon with that woman, because she truly believed in her. They'd seen her through her paranoid crises at the sanatorium, even after Margharita clawed at Celine's face thinking she'd come to assassinate her.

There were separate changing rooms for male and female visitors on each side of the central patio. Behind that was the sauna, and at the poolside, an open veranda with a bar and bright-cushioned raffia chairs. It was cool and dark in the poolroom. Celine changed into a dark swimsuit that felt a little loose on her, but Charles said it looked terrific. Celine, remembering the hunt for clothes hangers at Dr. Winter's office, told Charles the story. Listening to her, he could imagine how Celine would have stormed in there, frightened out of her mind, attacking whoever was nearest.

Charles put on a pair of red, white, and blue trunks. He had a tanned, muscular physique without any extraneous fat on him. Celine went up to the springboard, then thought better of it. She didn't want to risk getting that pain again, so she went sedately down the steps at the shallow end. The water was deliciously cool, and the goosebumps crept over her again, but this time they felt tingly and pleasant.

Swimming lazily across the pool, Celine felt the anxiety and anger leave her body; they seemed to diffuse right out into the water. Charles was doing laps, using his customary workmanlike and tireless stroke. He looked as if he could go on doing it forever.

Celine kept an eye on him, staying out of his way, and reviewed her situation as the sun went behind the trees and the shadows crept up toward the edge of the pool. The old whitewashed clapboards on the side of the house still shone painfully bright in the sun, but were now tinged with the faintest dappling of evening pink.

Dr. Winter . . . maybe she'd been a trifle hasty about him. She had acted like a spoiled brat, she now admitted to herself, up in New Coventry, crashing past that nurse, what was her name, Cathie Allen. And if the truth be told, Dr. Winter had been rather nice to see her when he did; there had been others in the waiting room when she was called.

Charles always did twenty laps, no more and no less, rain or shine. Without consciously counting, Celine knew when he was on his last lap and got out of the pool ahead of him.

While he was drying off, Celine said in a subdued voice, "You know, Charles, you could get shade trees, poplars. They have them at Harrow's, I think, already a good size, like twenty feet, and they'll come and plant them. You could put them on the south side away from the house, and put in sprinklers along the rosebeds."

Charles understood. He gave her a long, wordless hug, and although he was still wet and she was already dressed, she didn't resist. On the contrary, she felt the distant stirring of feelings she'd almost forgotten.

There was a strange, strangled noise beside them, and Celine looked down. Maggie, Trevor and his wife Catherine's retarded eight-year-old daughter, was standing beside her, eyes full of tears, holding a small bunch of dead flowers.

"What's the matter, lovie?" Celine got down on her knees and put her arms around the child, then wiped the tears from her chubby cheeks with one finger. Maggie, still weeping and snuffling softly, held up the flowers.

"They're dead, Maggie," said Celine. Then she understood. "Let's go and see what happened." She stood up, and with a quick, almost apologetic smile at Charles went off toward the back of the house, Maggie trotting along beside her, clutching a single finger of Celine's hand with a fierce intensity. Charles watched them until they disappeared around the corner of the house; Celine would have made such a wonderful, caring mother.

Celine and Maggie went around the house, past Catherine's vegetable patch to Maggie's own little garden. It was all dried up, with gray stalks and faded geranium and chrysanthemum blossoms all flattened on the ground.

"Oh my," said Celine. She squatted down and hugged Maggie. There was no point trying to explain to the child that flowers had to be watered regularly. "Okay," she said, "let's forget about those." She took Maggie's hand and they went in the house, up the stairs and into Celine's dayroom. Maggie looked about her, open-eyed. On the sofa table was a royal blue Sèvres pot containing a splendid bouquet of wild flowers, red and white poppies, bluebells, goldeneye and vervain, wild roses and irises. Celine lifted them out of the pot. "Here, Maggie. These don't need any water, they're made of silk." Maggie looked at her with big eyes and kept her hands behind her back. "All right, then," said Celine, "let's go down to the kitchen, and we'll find you a pot for them." They went back downstairs, Maggie hanging on to one finger again, but now vastly reassured by Celine's loving attention and smiling happily.

A few minutes later, Celine went back up the stairs to the room she used as an office. There was a small pile of papers extruded by her fax machine. There was nothing unusual on the next day's schedule; a breakfast meeting at eight, marketing meeting at eleven, lunch with an agent at twelve-thirty, cover proofs ready on the latest Hollywood revelation. A Mr. Didier Franchet had called from Paris, leaving no message. Celine laughed. Good old Oncle Didi; she wished he'd call her at home, but Charles and he didn't get along, and that bothered Celine because Didier had been a friend of her father's, and remained close to the family. Feeling tired again, Celine went along the corridor to her bedroom and sat down in front of the mirrored dresser, taking care not to look into it. Without a sound, Minette came and jumped up on her lap. As usual there was no expression on that elegant creature's face, but she seemed to be aware that something was the matter. She rarely came up on Celine's lap, and that was the second time that day. Celine stared into Minette's eyes, but apart from a slow, luxurious blink, they showed nothing.

"Well, my Minette," said Celine, looking at the two of them framed in the mirror, "you know I'm in a fix, don't you?" Minette stared back, but only for a moment, as if she wished to avoid any kind of emotional involvement.

"In fact, I'm in two fixes." Celine stroked Minette's back all the way down to her tail. "I'm sick, and I'm also losing my husband." Minette purred contentedly. Celine's voice went up with self-exasperation. "I know it's my fault, and I'd probably feel the same way. Maybe I'm just self-destructive, what do you think?" Minette arched her back and pushed up against Celine's hand, and Celine picked her up and rocked her against her breast, her head full to bursting with despairing thoughts.

Charles went down to the stables and spent the next two hours with Jeremy, his stable boy, putting up a set of mercury arc lights in the big paddock, the same kind that would be used in the jumping ring in Atlanta. By the time they'd finished, it was almost dark, but they had set up a series of new jumps and Charles decided to take Corinthian around them before dinner. Corinthian, a big, powerful, and normally placid roan, was restless and made an unusual fuss about being saddled.

"What's bothering him?" asked Charles, holding Corinthian's head.

"The heat, I guess," replied Jeremy, cinching up the saddle girth and keeping a wary eye on the restive animal's hoofs. "And he hasn't been out since this morning."

Charles got a leg-up from Jeremy and vaulted lightly into the saddle. Corinthian bucked mildly and started to prance sideways until Charles quieted him down and guided him gently into the paddock. The new lights glowed orange, making everything look strange; the shadows seemed blacker than black. Charles let Corinthian walk around for a minute to get used to his different-looking surroundings, then rode him back to the start. There they paused for just a moment, then off they went for the first gate, Charles feeling a surge of excitement at the strength and confidence of his mount. Charles was concentrating on positioning Corinthian exactly right for the first jump when out of the corner of his eye he saw a movement. A stray black cat had slipped under the fence, and now, frightened by the noise of Corinthian's hoofs on the hard dirt, was darting right across their path. Spooked, Corinthian slid, reared up, crashed his hindquarters against the first fence, and panicked. He took off for the other end of the paddock like a bolt of lightning, and Jeremy, sitting on the fence by the gate, almost fainted because there was no way Charles could avoid a serious accident. The tall paddock fence loomed up directly ahead of Corinthian as he pounded along, the white bars gleaming ghostly against the dark of the unlit grassy field beyond. Charles, who was hanging on to Corinthian for dear life, saw the fence getting bigger by the second. In a moment, the horse was going to realize that it couldn't possible make it, would stop dead, and Charles would go over the top for sure. Feeling the irresistible momentum of the animal under him, Charles had only a fraction of a second to make up his mind, and he decided to try the impossible. He set the horse at the fence, slackened the reins, and urged Corinthian on at full tilt. He could feel the stallion gather himself, the huge muscles tightening and preparing for the mightiest jump he'd ever attempted; Charles leaned forward, rose a little in the saddle, and then he was sailing up, up . . . Charles closed his eyes, knowing that he'd be lucky if he survived when Corinthian crashed; then the horse was over, his rear fetlocks clipping the top board, but he was over, now plunging downward out of the bright lights into the darkness, nothing indicating the level of the ground. Corinthian's forehoofs hit the ground, he stumbled, and Charles slid around his neck as the horse struggled to regain his footing. With only one foot still in the stirrup, Charles hung on grimly, only the strength of his arms and shoulders keeping him from being flung to the ground. He knew that if Corinthian started to gallop now, he was gone, as he wouldn't be able to get his other foot out of the stirrup and he'd be dragged until the horse tired. But Corinthian, no doubt amazed by his stupendous jump, and also not able to see where he was going in the dark, stopped as soon as he recovered his footing, and waited, docile as a hack, while with a huge effort Charles swung himself back up into the saddle and very gently rode back around the outside of the big paddock to the gate. Jeremy, pale as a ghost, opened the gate for them and was tremblingly readjusting the girth when Celine appeared, coming from the house. Charles, still white and shaken, gave Jeremy a warning look not to say anything, then trotted Corinthian round the ring a couple of times to settle him down. Back at the start, he grinned and jauntily touched the brim of his hat to Celine, then took his mount around the jumps as if nothing had happened. It was a splendid performance, and Celine clapped when it was over.

"He's coming right up to his best," said Charles as they walked back to the house. "I think I'll get Denis Devereaux to ride him in Atlanta. You know I can't go with all this hanging over you." He put his arm through hers. "Anyway, Denis's mare's been off form for almost six weeks now, and he doesn't think he can get her ready in time."

"That's ridiculous," said Celine quickly. "For one thing, Denis isn't strong enough for Corinthian, and for another you're going to be riding him." An uncharitable thought came into her mind. "Why don't you get Marion Redwing to ride him? She'll be there, won't she?"

"That's really ridiculous," replied Charles sharply. "She could never hold him. She'd probably come off and break her neck."

"Exactly," said Celine.

The silence lasted until they got into the house.

"I think you should concentrate on what you're going to do," said Charles coldly. "I'm going up for a shower and a change. We can discuss your plans at dinner."

Celine went to the kitchen where Catherine was preparing the meal. She was a quiet, pale woman with short, graying hair and large capable red hands, which were at that moment stirring some sweet basil into a wonderfully aromatic stew. Celine came up and sniffed the pot.

"Mmmm. Smells wonderful."

"It should," said Catherine. "It's one of the recipes in your book." She gave Celine a curious glance. "Thank you so much for Maggie's flowers," she said. "She went off to bed holding them."

At dinner Celine seemed withdrawn and said very little. Charles deliberately poured himself a glass of Cosd'Estournelle after Celine put her hand over her own glass.

"Well, have you decided what you're going to do?" he inquired.

"There's this great faith healer I heard about in Mexico City," murmured Celine, glancing at him.

"Luckily you won't have to travel that far," said Charles.

His voice was firm, but he knew better than to try to tell Celine what she should do.

"You guys are ganging up on me," said Celine. "You and Ned and Winter."

"We are the collective voice of reason," replied Charles, smiling. He raised his glass. "And this time it's too important for you to ignore it."

"But I can't just stop everything I'm doing," protested Celine, beginning to feel desperate. "I have the Fortman and Carfield deal to finish, just for starters."

"That reminds me," said Charles, putting down his glass. "Old Dan Carfield called earlier. He said his lawyers have the option on his shares all drawn up and ready to sign. Any time, he said."

"Well, I'm not ready," replied Celine. "I still need to get about four percent of the stock before exercising that option. Damn!" Celine shook her head with frustration. There was so much she had to do; and she certainly didn't have any time to be sick.

"Maybe I should never have got you that illuminated manuscript," said Charles, watching her face.

"Oh no! Then I'd have never met Dan. Damn it, Charles! Why did this have to happen now?"

"Well, that's beside the point," said Charles. "The first thing you need to do is get yourself taken care of." Watching her, he thought how wonderfully sexy and attractive Celine looked in the light from the chandelier.

"I'll make a deal with you," she said. Charles took a slow sip of wine. It was usually wise to give Celine's "deals" careful consideration.

"You go to Atlanta," she said, "and I'll go to the hospital and get the tests and stuff done. Okay?"

"Fine," said Charles immediately. "If it's just tests, and if you're home by Tuesday. Otherwise no deal. And in any case I'll send Corinthian down with Jeremy so that Denis has a chance to work with him."

"Okay," said Celine. "By the way, I was just assuming that Marion is going? To Atlanta, I mean?"

"I'm sure she will," said Charles steadily. "After all, she's the leading female jumper in this country."

"You don't have to tell me her qualifications," Celine snapped. "I just wondered if there would be somebody there to warm your bed."

Charles shrugged. They had been through all this many times before, and this was not the time for another row.

Celine pushed her plate away; she felt very tired, and could feel the place where the pain had been. "Okay, I'll have the tests done," she said. "But there's only one thing."

Charles waited resignedly. Celine sat very straight in her chair. "No Dr. Winter. Ned has to find me somebody else."

That night they went to bed early and lay awake next to each other, acutely conscious of the places where their bodies touched. In her head, Celine reran everything that had happened in New Coventry, and felt terribly afraid, but a voice in the back of her mind told her that whatever happened to her she deserved it all, and worse, that her illness was a punishment for having let her marriage slide into such a precarious condition. But she couldn't help that, she answered herself, she'd certainly tried. Charles moved, and slid his hand down her back, then, very tentatively, around to her breast, touching her with a concerned tenderness which made her grit her teeth.

She rolled abruptly on her side. "I'm not dead yet," she said, her tone fierce. Celine grabbed him, and pulled him against her.

"Feel me," she said, pushing her breasts hard into him. "I'm still all here. Everything works."

Still concerned, Charles hesitated, but only for a second. He rolled swiftly over her, one elbow on either side, and stared hard at her face, a few inches away in the darkness.

Celine's legs opened and she pushed up fiercely as he entered her. "Just one thing," she whispered angrily, "Don't ever let me think you're pitying me." She wrapped her legs around him and squeezed so hard it pushed the breath out of him.

They had made love in anger before, each knowing they fueled and liberated the other's animosity and resentment. Charles felt Celine's desperate fury as she pounded against him, but realized that this time it wasn't directed at him.

Afterward, they lay panting in the warm darkness. A faint

breeze stirred through the partially open window, and he could see the red star Antares winking balefully at him in the dark sky. He moved his head to see the rest of the constellation. Scorpio . . . beautiful, cold, and always with that fearful sting in its tail. Celine was a Scorpio, he hardly needed to remind himself.

Celine's breathing became regular and her whole body quivered a couple of times, as it often did just before she fell asleep. Charles felt her conscious presence recede, then fly silently off on owls' wings. He sighed and turned on his side, but wasn't able to fall asleep until it was almost dawn.

· · · · · · · · · · · 4 · · ·

The pale yellow of the early sun filtered through the window, shadowing the curtains and settling on the big rosewood armoire, but by the time Celine came out of the bathroom the sun had lost its hesitancy and was showing its mailed fist over the roof of the stables. It was going to be another scorcher. Charles was still asleep, but he must have subconsciously realized that she was gone, because his breathing pattern had changed and his arms were extended as if reaching out for her.

Celine padded rather aimlessly around in her slip, feeling numb, lethargic, unable to shake her brain into action. Working on reflexes alone, she selected a suit from the walk-in wardrobe, but by the time she finished making up and was applying her eyeliner, she couldn't help feeling that she looked great. She stared into the full-length mirror. Could anybody tell from her appearance that she had a tumor inside her? She turned sideways to see if it showed up in profile. Not yet, anyway. But how much longer would it be before it started to bulge, and when would her cheeks start to go yellow and cave in, and her hair start to fall out?

Stepping softly out of the bedroom, she walked down the wide stairs and ten minutes later she was in the car. They had just reached the entrance ramp on to I-95 when Celine felt a fullness in her stomach, and within seconds it had turned into an agonizing pain, much worse than the one she'd had the day before. Trevor saw what was happening in his rearview mirror and pulled the limo over immediately. As soon as he'd stopped, he looked over his shoulder, and what he saw made him reach for the car phone.

"Take her to the emergency room at the New Coventry Medical Center," Charles told him, sitting up in bed, clutching the phone hard enough to crack it. "I'll call ahead and tell them she's coming. Just get her up there as fast as you can make it."

Trevor didn't wait to discuss it with Celine; the limo's tires squealed all the way around the ramp and in a minute he was on I-95, staring fixedly at the road in front of him, afraid to look in the mirror.

"I think it should come out easily enough now, Red," said Caleb Winter, looking at the clock. "But I can stay if you want."

The intestinal tumor was large, the size of a baseball. Dr. Red Felton, one of the staff surgeons, had got into unexpected trouble when the tumor started bleeding and he wasn't able to control it. Caleb happened to be in the operating suite when Red called for him, and he'd scrubbed and gone in to help him out. Even so, it had taken Caleb almost an hour to control the hemorrhage and free the tumor to a point where it could be removed.

"I think we can manage now, Cal. I sure appreciate you coming in to help." Red still looked a bit shaken, but Caleb was confident he wouldn't have any trouble finishing the case.

Caleb put on his white coat as he came out of the operating room; he was fifteen minutes late for his weekly research meeting.

Every Wednesday morning at nine, Caleb Winter's research group met to review progress and discuss their work. Caleb insisted that the meeting start precisely on the hour whether he was there or not. Otherwise people would drag in late and time would be wasted.

Milo Zagros, an immunologist and Caleb's second-in-command, looked at the clock and brought the meeting to order with a loud "Humph!" They got down to business right away. Milo had just come back from a meeting in London, and he summarized the highlights of the conference. By nine-fifteen, Maureen Spark, who was in charge of the technical side of the transplantation program, was describing a new laser-based technique for joining pancreatic ducts. The others in the room, a total of a dozen postdoctoral fellows, technicians, and the residents on Caleb's surgical service, were all listening interestedly to what she was saying, but she could feel the undercurrent: everybody was waiting for Dr. Winter to appear.

Then the door opened, and he came in. Porky Rosen, the intern on Dr. Winter's clinical service, jolted awake; he'd been dozing between Ed van Stamm and Don McAuliffe, the junior and senior residents. There was a faint buzz of anticipation, and everybody sat up straighter in their chairs.

Maureen watched Caleb as he stood for a moment in the doorway. There was something so assured, so uncompromising in the set of his shoulders and the way he stood, that it never failed to affect her. Caleb Winter had eyes that nobody could lie to, eyes that reflected excitement, driving energy, intellect, and passion. Passion for work, thought Maureen acidly, the only thing he'd ever been truly passionate about.

From the door, Caleb scanned the group, then he made his way to the front, squeezing between the chairs. He had a possessive feeling of pride in his team—they were his professional family. He had taken six painstaking years to bring them all together, but it had been worth the effort, because now he had what was recognized to be one of the finest transplantation teams in the country.

Caleb sat down next to Maureen's empty chair and nodded to her to go on with her presentation. In this context he saw himself as a sort of scientific sheepdog, keeping his team pointed in the right direction. The scientists working with him were imaginative and occasionally went off on wild-goose chases, but Caleb made sure they did that on their own time. What he wanted was quite specific; to solve the problems of transplanting the pancreas from other animals into humans.

The overall project fell into three main categories. First was control of rejection: when the host recognizes that a transplanted organ is foreign, a chain of events is started that ultimately destroys the graft. Milo Zagros, the immunologist, headed up that side of the project. The problems of joining the donor's tiny blood vessels and pancreatic ducts to those of the recipient were primarily Maureen Spark's responsibility. The third category, in which they all shared, was the problem of keeping the donor pancreas alive and functioning until it could be placed in the recipient's body.

The two biggest problems Caleb had to face, however, had nothing to do with science, and he had no training for them. One was getting a continuous supply of money to pay for his research: the salaries, space, animals, equipment, and supplies. The other, and often the biggest of all, was overcoming the professional jealousies and political intrigues that threatened him, as they threatened any medical pioneer.

Caleb glanced over at his surgical team. As usual, Porky looked half asleep, but the others looked alert enough, although Caleb knew they were tired. He expected his house staff, the surgeons-in-training, to come to the research meetings when they could. It gave them a different slant on the practice and study of medicine and showed them that not every problem could be dealt with by surgery or improved drugs.

In front of the residents sat the four technicians, all women, and Caleb could see that at least two of them were casting occasional glances at Milo. Milo was some stud, Caleb knew that. A brilliant researcher, Milo wasn't particularly handsome: small, dark-skinned, with hairy arms and muscles that showed right under the skin. But he certainly had something that certain women simply couldn't resist.

Porky *was* asleep. Ed and Don both saw Caleb's glance, and two elbows jabbed hard into Porky, one from each side. They were all having trouble keeping awake in the stuffy atmosphere; the three of them had spent the night working on a taxi driver whose abdominal aneurysm had ruptured, luckily for him, while he was picking up a patient at the emergency room.

At that moment the phone rang in the seminar room, and Porky jumped up. The phone was on the wall by the door, and several people were nearer to it than Porky, but as the junior person there, it was his job to answer it.

"He's in a meeting right now," he said, trying to catch Dr. Winter's eye. "Can I give him a message?"

Don appeared beside him. "Is it about a patient?"

Porky nodded.

"Give it to me." Don spoke into the phone briefly, then put it down. He nodded to Ed to join them and headed for the door. Outside, he said, "Porky, you know better than that! If it's a clinical matter, we deal with it first. Christ, I don't mind telling you everything once . . ."

"What's up, Boss?" asked Ed, joining them. "Did you fix that call so we could get out of there?" He grinned. A big, rather lumbering individual, Ed was easygoing and friendly, but a hard and meticulous worker. Unlike Don, who always wore a white shirt and tie when he wasn't in operating room greens, Ed wore a brightly colored open-necked shirt and loose slacks. He always looked as if he were about to go off on a vacation.

"It's a private patient of Winter's," said Don. "Acute abdominal pain. She's in the emergency room. We'll see her down there and report back to him."

They walked quickly along the corridor. All the residents who worked with Caleb Winter soon learned to walk fast. Porky trotted behind Don and Ed, feeling abashed. He never seemed to be able to do anything right. Passing the surgical suite where Dr. Winter and the other professors had their offices, they heard Dr. Brighton, the department chairman, talking in his loud, rather braying voice.

"Wonder who he's yelling at," said Ed.

"Isn't he supposed to be in outpatients this morning?" asked Don, looking at his watch.

"Yes, but he never goes," said Porky, panting along behind them. "Too many other things to do, he says."

Don and Ed glanced at each other.

"Porky, why don't you concentrate on what you're supposed to be doing," said Don. "When I want your opinion I'll ask for it."

They went down the back stairs in silence, and hurried toward the emergency room.

They found Celine in a curtained booth, being interviewed by a woman from the insurance office. Her bout of pain had almost passed, but it had left her shaky and weak, and she put up no argument about going to the hospital. Porky's eyes opened wide; he was struck by her beauty and elegance.

Don's gaze fixed on the insurance woman, who instantly became flustered. "I'll get the rest of the information later," she mumbled to Celine. She stood up and held her clipboard in front of her like a shield. "Excuse me."

"Hi," said Don when she had left. His eyes flickered dispassionately over Celine. "I'm Don McAuliffe." He introduced the others. "I'm the senior resident, and we work with Dr. Winter. What's the matter?"

His manner was cold, aloof, and professional in the sense that to him Celine was a patient and that was all. If she happened to be nervous or scared, that was no concern of his. That she happened to be young and beautiful was irrelevant. She was a patient, and that immediately stripped away any feeling of human fellowship he might have had for her.

"I was just telling the nurse a minute ago," said Celine.

"Well, she's not here to repeat it to us," said Don stiffly.

Celine took a deep breath. There was no point in antagonizing this impersonal young man. What was it that little nurse had said over in the Harkness Building? *You'll find it easier if you go along with us . . .*

What was worse, Don McAuliffe was much less gentle in his examination then Caleb Winter had been. When he pressed, it really hurt, and he didn't ease the pressure; Celine noticed that while Dr. Winter had watched her face to see her reactions, this Dr. McAuliffe looked in front of him at the wall.

And he kept on prodding, pushing, asking stupid questions. The big one with him just stood there, looking about as intelligent as a cop on point duty, but the fat little fellow with the grubby white jacket with pens, stethoscope, and a notebook spilling out of the pockets smiled and sidled up to her and put an unobtrusive comforting hand on her shoulder and squeezed when he saw the other doctor was hurting her.

When Don finally straightened up after examining her, Celine felt as if he'd been prodding at her for an eternity.

"She's got some kind of abscess in her belly," he said, addressing Ed. He turned to Porky. "Call Dr. Winter, tell him his patient, Mrs. ..." He looked at the E.R. sheet, "de La Roche is here." He pronounced her name "Della Roach."

A few minutes later, they heard his footsteps. Ed straightened up as if for an inspection, and Don cleared his throat. Porky stood at attention by the examining table, looking, Celine thought, like a plump piglet on roller skates. To her surprise, Celine felt her own heart beating fast.

The curtain was pulled aside, and Caleb came in like a gust of wind. He nodded to Celine. "What's the story?" he asked Don.

"This is a thirty-one-year-old married woman." Winter glanced at Celine but didn't smile. Halfway through Don's stilted presentation a technician appeared holding a basket full of syringes and tubes. Not wanting to interrupt, she crept in, tied a piece of rubber tubing around Celine's forearm and stuck a needle in the crook of her arm. Celine flinched, but not until the girl put on a Band-Aid, bent her elbow to stop any bleeding, and crept out again did Celine realize there hadn't been any by-your-leave, no word of what she was doing, no permission asked or given. She bit her lip. Don finished his presentation with his diagnosis and paused. Caleb raised his eyebrows.

"An abscess? Hmmm." He turned back to Celine, who was lying on the exam table with a sheet over her.

"I didn't expect to see you back quite so soon," he said, pulling the sheet back. His voice was friendly enough, but there was a distance, a dissociation from her as a human being.

"I was just passing through," she said, trying to sound unconcerned, but his level look made her feel as if she'd said something inexcusably flippant. His fingers moved over her belly, pausing here and there. His questioning fingers seemed to have a life of their own; and somehow they gave Celine the information that the thing inside her belly had suddenly become bigger. She also understood the difference between Winter's and Don McAuliffe's examination; Winter was the unquestioned master, the expert. For the first time, Celine appreciated the idea of quality in this context; it was easy enough for her to recognize quality in a book, to distinguish literature from merely clever writing, but it had never occurred to her that that kind of distinction could be made between surgeons.

"Don, come over here." Winter moved to make room and his closeness made her uncomfortable. "Put your hand here." Celine felt Don's hand. It was cooler, rougher, less assured. "Can you feel the outlines of the mass?"

Pause.

"I . . . think so."

"Ed, come and feel this." Don moved away and Ed came up. His hands were warm, huge, and somehow irresolute. Celine could tell he wasn't getting much information from them.

Suddenly she sat up abruptly. "Would you mind telling me what's going on? What's this about an abscess?"

"Take it easy, Celine," said Caleb in that same impersonal tone. "We're figuring out what's the matter with you." But he didn't make Ed continue, and stepped back from the table.

"What makes you think it's an abscess?" he asked Don.

Again Celine felt like a schoolgirl who'd done something vaguely naughty that was being tolerantly overlooked.

"It's a painful, tender swelling," replied Don. "It's come up quite suddenly . . ."

"It's enlarged suddenly, I agree. Did she tell you there was already a mass there?"

Don looked accusingly at Celine. "No, she didn't."

"You didn't ask," said Celine sharply, but she was looking at Caleb. There was a dull aching feeling where they had been poking and prodding, and she was tired of all this. She wanted to get this pain taken care of and wished Caleb would do his professor bit some other time.

There were more footsteps outside, then the sound of Charles's voice. Celine had never been so happy to hear it. A nurse's voice said, "Yes, she's in there, sir, but you can't go in yet. The doctors are examining her."

Charles's head appeared around the curtain. Paying no attention to the doctors standing around Celine, he looked questioningly at her, and his expression quickly changed to one of relief.

She smiled up at him. "I'm feeling a lot better," she said.

"Good. I'll be back as soon as they're done examining you."
His head vanished.

Winter went on with his teaching as if there had been no
interruption. "If that was an abscess, and it was that size,
you'd expect her to have a fever, chills, signs of a major infection, wouldn't you? But her temp's normal, so what else
do you think it might be?"

"An aneurysm?" asked Porky unexpectedly.

There was a pause, and Caleb looked at him as if he'd just
appeared. "Does it pulsate?" he asked Porky.

"I don't know, I didn't feel it," replied Porky, looking at
the floor and feeling abashed.

"Then don't give unsupported opinions," Caleb said, annoyed. Don looked daggers at Porky, who decided he had
other things to do elsewhere.

"Get the CBC on her," Ed whispered to Porky as he left.
"It should be ready by now."

Porky went to the desk to find the nurse, but found only a
young, scared-looking aide.

"Is the CBC back on Mrs. de La Roche?" he asked her.

"I'm sorry," she said, looking flustered. "What's a CBC?"

"It stands for Complete Blood Count," replied Porky, picking up the lab slips on the counter.

"I'm just here for the phone while the nurse went to the
bathroom," said the aide. She had a round, pink face with a
lot of acne, and looked ready to burst into tears. Porky grinned
sympathetically at her. He knew how she felt. He called the
lab and they gave him the results, which he wrote down on a
scrap of paper.

"By the way, what are you doing about those pimples?" he
asked the aide in a low voice. She took a quick, shocked
breath, and her face went a bright blotchy pink. She put up
her hands to hide it, and Porky saw a tear roll down between
her fingers.

"Hey, don't get upset!" Porky smiled at her. "I used to have
it a lot worse than you." He scribbled something on a pre-
scription pad. "What's your name?"

The girl mumbled something almost inaudible, and Porky
made her repeat it.

"Here, Gloria," he said, giving her the paper. "This is for

tetracycline. Take one every eight hours for three weeks, don't eat any chocolate, and you'll have a complexion like . . ." He bent down and whispered close to her ear, "Like the lady in that booth there. You take a look at her when she comes out."

Gloria smiled uncertainly and watched him go back behind the curtain, and Porky could feel her gaze on him. He grinned at his tiny feeling of accomplishment. At least one person thought he was a real doctor.

"CBC's normal," he announced.

"Just give us the values," said Caleb briskly. "We'll do the interpreting."

Celine wondered why everybody was giving Porky such a hard time; she didn't realize that was the way the system worked. The surgical intern is at the bottom of the hierarchy, and if he has the ability to withstand the pressure, the hassling, the long hours, the tedious and often unrewarding work, then maybe he will be selected to go on to a higher grade. And Porky wasn't doing well. His colleagues didn't think he had the right attitude or enough zeal. Then too, Porky was fat, and who ever saw a fat surgeon? The skids were already placed under Porky, although as yet he was unaware of it.

Porky read out the values. Everybody seemed to agree that they were indeed normal.

Caleb looked at his watch. "Makes it unlikely to be an abscess, don't you think, Don?"

"What do you think it is, Dr. Winter?" asked Don, obviously puzzled. What could give a young, otherwise healthy-looking young woman these symptoms?

"Well, it's obviously a tumor, located in the stomach or pancreas," said Caleb. "Most likely the pancreas. And she's had a hemorrhage into it today. Not a major one, but enough to make the swelling suddenly get bigger and give her a lot of pain."

"Ah . . ." It was obvious that Don hadn't even considered that possibility. Ed shook his head and tried not to look astonished. Porky couldn't hide his shock, though. How could such a beautiful woman have something so awful going on inside her?

Caleb hesitated on his way out. Normally he would have

let the house staff talk to her, but he already knew that this was going to be a very unusual and important case, and he sensed she might be a difficult patient.

"Ms. de La Roche," he said, "you heard what I think is the matter. You need to be admitted to the hospital now for more tests. I'll let you know how things progress, but I can tell you now that we'll probably need to operate."

"Excuse me, Dr. Winter," Celine retorted. "But if you don't mind, I'll make that decision, as it happens to be my body we're talking about."

Caleb stopped dead, and Celine heard Don draw in his breath with surprise. After giving her a long look, Caleb said "I'll see you later, up in your room."

Then he was gone, and the other doctors glanced at each other and relaxed; then they, too, left. Only Porky looked back; he smiled encouragingly at her, but guiltily, like a warder giving forbidden encouragement to a condemned prisoner.

5

Caleb hurried back to the seminar room. He'd spent an entire fifteen minutes in the E.R. with that woman, much too long. He felt concerned that Don McAuliffe hadn't had the faintest idea of Celine's diagnosis. Don had only a few months to go before he finished the training program and was let loose on the unsuspecting public.

And today Don had seemed even more uptight than usual. He'd positively flinched when he found he was completely on the wrong track with the de La Roche woman. Caleb decided to talk to Henry Brighton about him. As chairman, it was Brighton's job to keep tabs on the residents and make sure they were properly trained by the time they finished the program.

Back in the seminar room, there were two newcomers, visitors from other labs, sitting in the chairs vacated by the residents. Caleb nodded affably to them; they had been over in the animal facility during the earlier part of the meeting.

Milo was at the podium, presenting some results of his recent work. His English had much improved in the last few years, but his residual Yugoslav accent had been strangely combined with a Brooklyn twang; when he first came to New York, he'd taken lessons in spoken English from a retired Brooklyn schoolteacher.

Milo looked up when Caleb came in.

"I was just saying that we now have eighty percent survival at three years with the current series of pig-to-monkey transplants," he said. "and that should speak good for us next week."

Caleb looked at him steadily. How could Milo be so indiscreet? Had he *told* the group and the visitors what was happening next week? The expressions on the visitors' faces revealed nothing, except that they were listening very attentively to what was being said. Hans Salzman from Bern was sprawled in a chair near the front, taking notes in a small leather-covered notebook. He was a big man with a leonine mane of prematurely gray hair, waved and pomaded in the European style. And Paula Muldrew from the Transplantation Unit in San Francisco—damn, that must be it, Caleb thought. Milo always had to show off for any attractive woman. That was probably why they'd sent her; everybody knew about Milo. Difficult, suspicious, and aggressive with men, he was the epitome of charm, generosity, and kindness to women, any women, and always with the ultimate purpose of getting them into his bed.

Christ, thought Caleb, looking at Paula, I hope I never have to resort to using beautiful undercover agents to find out what's happening in other people's labs.

Paula, like many scientific visitors these days, had a small voice-activated tape recorder mike clipped unobtrusively to her blouse. And Paula was no dumb brunette; last year her transplantation lab had come up with a simple method of detecting graft rejection in its earliest stages, when there was still hope of recovery; it had been a real breakthrough. But the last thing Caleb wanted the visitors to know about was the meeting scheduled for next Monday in the hospital boardroom. Always ready to share data and swap ideas with colleagues around the world, he drew the line at disclosing plans that might provoke other researchers into trying to get a jump ahead of him.

"I was asking him if the monkeys were now grunting!" Hans Salzman said, and his big frame shook with ponderous laughter. The techs sitting in the back looked at each other; they didn't know about Swiss humor.

"We're more interested in function than just survival," said

Caleb, taking charge again. "Did you show them our insulin data?" he asked Milo.

Milo shook his head.

"Okay, let's have the slides . . ."

Somebody pulled the blinds down, and the slide projector flickered on. Hans pulled out a long cigar and was about to light it.

"Sorry, Hans, not here." Caleb grinned. Hans flushed, and slowly put the cigar back in its case. Probably the first time in ten years anybody's told him what to do, thought Caleb. At home he's a tyrant.

After the slides there was a brisk discussion, and they all compared findings from their various labs. Caleb knew that Hans Salzman's lab in Bern was having huge technical difficulties, the kind that strike even the best labs from time to time. Hans was Swiss; he didn't like to give away too many of his own secrets, but that didn't prevent him from trying to find out all he could about the details of Caleb's work. Paula, on the other hand, was very open with her data and was anxious to set up a joint project with Caleb's group. Milo was pantingly in favor of that. But one thing emerged clearly from the discussion, and that was best put into words by Paula.

"You're way ahead of us," she said.

Don, followed by Ed and Porky, reappeared just as the meeting was winding up. They waited until Caleb finished talking, then came up to him.

"We got some abdominal X-rays on Della Roach, but they didn't show much," reported Don. "Her amylase was up. I guess the hemorrhage started up some inflammation." Don sounded vague, unsure of himself. His eyes were puffy, and he looked as if he hadn't slept in a long time. But then every senior surgical resident looks like that, Caleb reflected. It goes with the job.

"We got her a bed in the Harkness Wing," said Ed, glancing at Don. Ed was a good guy, smarter than his lumbering gait and wide boxer's face suggested. He was taking up the slack, backing up his senior. "Don's ordered an ultrasound of her belly, and a CAT scan whenever they can get it on the schedule."

"Did you give her anything for her pain?" asked Caleb.

"I gave her 75mg of IM Demerol down in the E.R.," said Porky. "I'll stop by later and make sure she's okay."

Hans and Paula were hovering near the door, waiting to say good-bye when Caleb called Milo over. "Take them back to their hotel, Milo. And no funny stuff," he added in an undertone. "Paula's married to a friend of mine, okay?"

Milo grinned wolfishly but kept silent.

Caleb went over to say good-bye to the visitors, and Milo ushered them out. Caleb turned back to his residents.

"Do you have a room number for Ms. de La Roche?"

Porky shuffled through the cards in his hand. "Room 427," he said. Caleb suppressed his impatience. When he had been an intern, he remembered everything without carrying pieces of paper around with him. Porky unwittingly gave a lackadaisical impression that in another context might have been fine, because Porky was clever and the patients liked him, but he didn't have the gung-ho attitude expected of a first-year surgical resident, the new title for interns. Porky did his job, but he just wasn't "surgical material." One couldn't quite pin down why that was, but almost everybody agreed.

"What else do you have in the house?"

Porky consulted his cards again. "Two new patients came in through the E.R., a possible appendix and an incarcerated inguinal hernia. There's also a scheduled gallbladder."

"Good. I'll meet you all at six, on Harkness, and we can do rounds before supper."

Caleb walked toward Maureen, who was sitting by the podium. She became very still when he came close.

"Let's go over to your office," he said. He didn't wait for her, but walked straight out the door. The seminar room was at the far end of the research floor, and Caleb's block of three labs was down at the other end. Some people still called them the C.V. labs, because they had previously belonged to the cardiovascular group. Caleb usually walked by himself, because few people could keep up with his pace, and he didn't slow for anybody, even Maureen, not even in the old days when things were going better between them. Maureen's corner office, separated from the main lab by a big window and a glass door, contained a desk with a computer terminal and a telephone, two chairs, and three large filing cabinets with all the old lab records. Now, of course, everything went on the computer, all the protocols, all the experimental data, all the grant applications.

By the time Maureen arrived, Caleb was sitting on the edge of her desk going through an envelope of photos taken at a lab party a couple of weeks ago.

"Milo's still got his eye on you, hasn't he?" Caleb asked, pointing at one of the photos.

"Nothing new, is it?" replied Maureen coolly. "He's been looking for an opening ever since you used me as bait down in Atlantic City."

Milo had come over from Yugoslavia to give a paper at an international meeting that Caleb and Maureen had attended. Caleb had instantly seen the outstanding quality of Milo's work, which meshed perfectly with his, and tried to get him to defect. He was unsuccessful until he had the brilliant idea of bringing Maureen over to talk to him.

And so, for the sake of Maureen's cornflower-blue eyes, Milo abandoned a promising career at the University of Belgrade and threw in his lot with Caleb's tiny group. Strangely enough, Milo's defection set Caleb on the way to his own success. At the time, Caleb's work was not fashionable; the hot subject was cardiovascular surgery, with open-heart procedures and heart transplants making the headlines. To most people, the pancreas just meant sweetbreads, and to surgeons, it was bad news, one of the most difficult organs to operate on, and often with pitifully bad results. But when the media heard about the defection of a top Yugoslav scientist, and learned how Caleb and Maureen had smuggled him back to New York to join in their work, they were invited to appear on radio and television programs all over the country. Caleb told the world that his research could provide the key to curing diabetes and offered hope in pancreatic cancer. This led to his first large National Institutes of Health grant, which also provided Milo with a salary. Until then, Milo had lived in Caleb's bachelor pad, sleeping on the sofa, listening to rock-and-roll music, and learning English. The rest of the time he set up an immunology lab in the hospital using borrowed, recycled, and discarded equipment.

What was on Milo's mind most during this period, though, was sex. Caleb thought it was maybe the change of food, or the climate, but actually Milo had been like that since the age of thirteen, when he lost his virginity to an older woman of fifteen while on holiday with his parents up in the mountains near Vir-Pazar. Since that time, sex had colored Milo's every thought, forming a backdrop to his waking hours and probably the others as well.

Caleb grinned to himself. The group's early days had been heady, exciting, full of brilliant ideas, and everybody had worked like hell to get the lab started.

"How did you get on with Hans?" asked Caleb, his voice casual.

"Okay ..." Maureen hesitated. "He was very nice, but ..."

"He was snooping, wasn't he?"

"Exactly. There's a difference between being professionally interested and what he was doing. What's he up to, do you think?"

"No idea. His own transplant project's in deep trouble, but I don't know exactly what went wrong. Bob Rankine at Mass General says Hans may pull out altogether and become some kind of consultant. Bob's trying to find out exactly what's going on. Oh, and he said there was a lot of hardball politics going on there."

"Politics, huh? *Everything's* political. Look at next Monday's meeting. Do you think it'll be decided on scientific merit? Not on your damn life!"

"You're getting cynical in your old age, Maureen," Caleb said. "You'll be knocking apple pie next—or maybe even matrimony!"

Two spots of color came into Maureen's face. "If you were anybody else, Cal, I'd call you a bastard, but with you, the word loses any kind of meaning."

Caleb put out one hand and placed it very gently on

her left breast. He held it there for a moment, feeling the fullness, the warmth of her, and they looked at each other silently.

Caleb took his hand away and went on as if there had been no interruption.

"The meeting's on Monday, but I only got the list of who's on the committee today." He pulled a sheet of paper from his coat pocket and unfolded it.

"Why is it such a big deal?" asked Maureen. "I mean, this particular project?"

"Come on, Maureen, surely that's obvious," Caleb said, irritated. "Putting animal organs into humans is an explosive topic. You've got the animal rights groups to contend with, and the old ladies in sneakers who feel it's unethical."

"I know that," said Maureen calmly. "What I'm worried about is what happens if they turn the application down."

Caleb's face went grim. "They won't. That could only happen if the hospital and the university were to totally reject our entire research program."

Maureen was gazing at him with a steadfast look that said "Don't bullshit me, Caleb Winter," and he fell silent for a moment.

"All right, Maureen. We'd lose all our research grants and have to shut down the lab."

Maureen's eyes widened for a second. "You mean we're at the mercy of that bunch?" She pointed a finger at the letter in Caleb's hand.

"That's the way it goes, these days," replied Caleb, shrugging. He sat down behind the desk. "Our job is to make sure the project gets approved." He flattened the letter out on the desk. "Now let's go over this list."

Maureen came around and stood behind him. "Dear Dr. Winter," she read. "This is to inform you that the Ethics and Public Welfare Committee will be meeting on Monday, August 24th, at 9 a.m. in the Board Room, New Coventry Medical Center, to discuss and consider your proposal to carry out pancreas transplantations from animals into human patients. The names of the Committee members are as follows:

Foster B. Armuth, M.D. (Chairman)
Anna Lynn Page (Hospital Board representative)
L. Graham Benson, M.A., B.D. (University chaplain)
Leroy Williams (Ombudsman, community representative)
Chauncey Milford Roper (Hospital Board representative)
Henry Brighton, M.D. (Chairman, Dept. of Surgery)

Facilities for slide projection, chalkboard, etc. will be available. No other proposals will be considered at this time. Yours sincerely."

"Henry Brighton, huh?" said Maureen. "Do you expect any problems from him?"

Caleb's eyes clouded momentarily. "Henry? I can't really believe that he'd go against me. But then, who knows?"

Maureen smiled. "Henry's like an unsuccessful gambler, always looking for a hot tip, but not smart enough to know when he has one. But he must have gone through the same sort of committee evaluations himself, surely?"

"Him? Not on your life. The only research Henry Brighton ever did was some dumb thing on bowel disease, ulcerative colitis, I think, but nobody's ever heard about his work since. Scientifically, Henry Brighton's a zero."

"How did he ever get to be chairman?"

Caleb shrugged. "He was just a lackey to the last chairman, Terence Oldham, who promoted him way beyond his capacity. When Terry retired, nobody else wanted the job. Anyway that's all history. What I'm concerned about is Monday."

"Caleb," she said, very seriously, putting a hand on his arm, "watch out for Henry Brighton. You know he can't stand you, he's green with envy at your success." Maureen looked to see if her words were having any effect. "He'll do you in, Caleb," she said in a louder voice. "In any way he can."

Caleb shook his head in an irritated way and started to say something.

"Listen to me," said Maureen, shaking his arm. "Brighton

is your *enemy*. Or do you still think that all doctors always back their colleagues, the way you do?"

Milo Zagros was turned on, a kind of crazy heating up of his entire system, a condition over which he had little control. Two kinds of stimuli had this effect on him; one was the white-hot bolts of inspiration that had put him among the world leaders in immunology; the other was women.

The one in his sights right now was Paula Muldrew, the researcher from California, and Milo's senses were crackling like drops of water on a hot skillet. He could see nothing else; nothing else existed. Caleb had warned him not to fool around with her, but Milo was beyond advice. He was an addict whose fix was smiling right in his face. Even while Caleb was talking to him, he already had her in his bed, her legs apart . . .

The three of them, Hans Salzman, Paula, and Milo went down in the elevator together. On the way down, Milo held Paula's elbow, the first step toward intimacy, toward total physical and mental control. A surge of sexual potency almost lifted him off his feet when she turned and smiled up at him, a trusting, ingenuous smile.

At the door, Milo asked the visitors which hotel they were staying at, praying with all the force of his desire that they were lodged in different hotels. Hans hesitated, then said he was going to the Hilton since he had an appointment there. He went off after a hurried good-bye to both of them. Milo was left on the steps alone with the focus of all his nervous energies, near her, touching her. He felt his whole body swelling; he thought he was going to burst. Paula was staying at the Carleton, only two blocks away, and without further ado Milo took her elbow again (it was still too soon to take her hand) and they crossed the road, Milo still talking and planning. Work was obviously the topic to start with, as she knew a fair amount about immunology. Milo's English was far removed from the halting, disconnected pidgin he had once sprayed out like a malfunctioning Gatling gun; now he was fast and fluent, and when he couldn't find the exact words his hands took up the story.

Milo timed it perfectly. When they reached the hotel after a few minutes' brisk walking, he had reached a crucial
stage in his explanation of a new type of immuno-
electropheresis system he was introducing into the lab, and
Paula was very interested. She had come to find out what was
happening in her field of research, and here she was, privileged to get the latest scoop from one of the world's leading
experts.

"Why don't we go on with this up in my room?" she
said, her eyes shining with enthusiasm. "There's a sitting
room, and they can bring up some coffee."

In the elevator and all the way to her twelfth floor suite,
Milo was brilliant. He wove ideas, juggled them, made
wonderful, dazzling patterns in the clear uncharted air of
future science. He was like Yehudi Menuhin playing for a
promising Juilliard student, and Paula was properly overwhelmed.

Milo's eyes swept around the comfortably appointed sitting
room. Everything he did, everything he saw now was interpreted only in terms of the approaching seduction. The sofa,
upholstered in shiny, ivory-colored brocade, was too high, too
small, and too hard to roll around in. A brass-and-ebony standard lamp stood behind it, the switch uncomfortably high,
just below the bulb. The sofa faced two similarly upholstered
chairs across a low rectangular table. Two doors led off the
sitting room; one presumably to the bathroom, the other to
the bedroom. Milo knew instinctively which was which; he
could feel the heat of his glance flashing across the room; it
could have burned a hole in the bedroom door and melted
the doorknob.

"Why don't we sit here?" he said, indicating the sofa. Paula
sat down, adjusting her skirt. Milo caught a flash of silky thigh,
and his mind instantly continued the process, undressing her
in his mind's eye, staring boldly at her curly pubic triangle,
then nuzzling up to her soft, firm, pink-nippled breasts. . . . It
was going to be like leading a lamb to slaughter.

"Shall we send for some coffee?" Paula had her hand on
the phone. Milo licked his dry lips.

"No. Let's not. Now, look here . . ." He took a piece of

paper out of his inside pocket and leaned forward to put it on the table. His pen waved over the paper.

"Normally the radioactive marker is carbon 14, and it attaches to these sites here." Milo's hand was trembling visibly as he sketched it in. "But if we use radiophosphorus, *here*. It shows up an entirely different . . ."

Milo stopped. He simply could not go on. Paula was leaning forward to see his diagram and he could see the swell of her breast as her blouse billowed slightly forward.

His voice cracked. "Paula, I can't stand it."

She turned her head to look at him and her mouth opened slightly in surprise. He dropped the pen and his hand came up gently to her breast, pressed it tenderly, and drew her close to him, just as his feverish mind had preplayed it. Only it didn't go as he planned. Paula grabbed his wrist firmly and pulled it away. But Milo was already launched and beyond recall. He pulled her toward him, roughly because of her resistance, and strove to reach her lips with his, as she moved her head from side to side to evade him.

"Stop! Dr. Zagros, please . . . !"

Milo, approaching frenzy, didn't even hear her. His hand tore the button off her white silk blouse. The clear sight of her breast, enveloped in a light lacy bra, was like a spur in his groin, and his hand fumbled to rip it off.

Suddenly he found himself on the carpet, flat on his face, his arm bent behind him, and he was shouting with the terrible pain that seemed to be ripping his armpit open. Paula was straddling him, but there was nothing sexy about her position. He gasped, unable to speak, just hoping she wouldn't put that dreadful pressure on again.

She stayed there for what seemed to Milo an eternity, then got up quickly, pulled down her skirt, which had ridden right up during the scuffle, and drew her torn blouse across her chest. Milo struggled to his feet, panting. His right arm felt numb from the shoulder down.

"You sure play hardball, Paula," he said, trying to smile.

"I think you should go now, Dr. Zagros," said Paula quietly. "Thank you for your explanations. And I'll send the bill for a new blouse to Dr. Winter."

"Oh God," muttered Milo. "I wish you wouldn't do that. I'll be happy to pay—"

Paula opened the door.

"I shall," she said. "Not because I'm vindictive, I can assure you. But you're a menace to women, Dr. Zagros, and that's why. Now get out!"

6

Celine stared at Charles as he sat down on the edge of her stretcher, seemingly unconcerned. "What did Dr. Winter say?" she asked. "Did he tell you I'm going to die?"

"Good Lord, no!" said Charles, airily. "He talked about the tests you were going to have. He mentioned you might need surgery."

Celine couldn't make up her mind whether Charles was being deliberately callous or just covering up his anxiety. Charles looked around the tiny cubicle, and Celine could sense his claustrophobia. He stood up abruptly and started to pace up and down in front of the stretcher. Obsessive about health and fitness, Charles detested hospitals. The mere idea of illness repelled him.

"I think you should go on home, Charles. There's no point in your hanging around here. Anyway, Minette needs to be fed."

Charles hesitated. He knew as well as Celine did that Catherine would feed the cat, but the vet was coming to check Corinthian before his trip to Atlanta, and Charles wanted to talk to him about a new travel sedative that had been used on horses in Europe.

He glanced at Celine. She didn't look sick at all now, and they knew where to reach him if he was needed.

"Okay," he said, relieved. "I'll phone you when I get home, and I'll come up tomorrow." He leaned down, kissed her on the forehead, and was gone. He walked swiftly down the corridor toward the exit, thinking, "My God, our marriage has come to this, where I'm glad to get away from her. If this had happened just a few years ago, I wouldn't have left her side for a second."

Celine listened to his footsteps on the tiled floor, and when she couldn't hear them anymore, a slow, sad heaviness spread through her, although she was glad Charles had gone. She noticed that she was shivering, and saw an air-conditioning vent directly above her head. When she came in they had made her change into a hospital johnny, a thin gray cotton garment. Celine lay back on the stiff pillow and pulled the sheet up around her neck. At least she wasn't hurting now, although the poking and prodding had left a dull ache that went all the way through to her back.

The curtain rings scraped, and a different technician came in holding a basket in one hand and a piece of paper in the other. "De La Roche?" she asked without looking at Celine. She had short, thin dark hair and wore no makeup.

"Yes," said Celine.

"Roll up your right sleeve," said the tech, putting her basket on the chair. She had a syringe already in her hand, and a line of test-tubes of different colors peeped out of the top pocket of her coat.

"What for?"

The girl stopped for a second and looked at Celine with surprise. "Blood tests," she said briefly. "Straighten your arm, please."

"Damn it," said Celine, smiling bemusedly, "what kind of blood tests? A girl came in and took some already, not twenty minutes ago. Why do you need more?"

"That was just a CBC and FBS," she replied. "They ordered a whole bunch more."

"More what? What kind of tests?"

"I don't know," said the tech, tying a rubber tube around Celine's upper arm. "All I know is two red-topped tubes and two whites. Now you're going to feel a little needle-stick . . ."

She filled up the colored test-tubes with blood and departed with her basket, leaving Celine with a piece of cotton wool jammed in her second elbow, presumably to prevent her from bleeding to death.

The emergency room was very quiet now, and Celine could hear the sound of subdued voices coming from the desk. What was she waiting for now? For more tests? For the doctors to come back? Her back was really beginning to ache, and she hoped that awful pain wasn't going to start up again. Somebody had given her a shot just after the doctors had gone; she felt warm, woozy, and a bit nauseated. Celine turned her head, trying to hear what they were saying at the desk. It was just a murmur of voices.

In the next booth a voice started to say in a monotonous, chantlike voice, "Muthafucka, muthafucka, muthafucka . . ."

Somebody giggled. A metal pan dropped on the floor with a loud clang from the direction of the corridor where the other cubicles were. The curtains around her booth were a faded green; one of the rings was twisted and made a high-pitched scraping noise when the curtain was pulled. The ceiling tiles were a grayish white, pitted with hundreds of holes. Celine tried to find a pattern in the location of the holes, but her eyes wouldn't focus on them for more than a second or two. She realized that was from the pain medication, which was also making her mouth dry; Celine licked her lips, but it didn't help. She called for a nurse and asked for some water. The girl hesitated, said "Yes, sure, I'll be right back."

"You Roach?"

The aide, a thin youth with long, straight blond hair and a gold earring in one ear, poked his head around the drapes. Something inside Celine struggled, then gave up. For the correct pronunciation of her name, it just wasn't worth making a fuss.

"Yes," she said.

"We're going for a ride," he said, unlocking the wheel locks on her stretcher.

"Where to?"

"To our destination, lady." He pronounced each syllable separately, des-tin-a-shun.

Everything snapped. Celine sat up and shouted at him, although the sudden pain made her sick. "Where the fuck are you taking me?" Even as the words came out of her mouth, she knew she was in the wrong. Charles would have dropped his crop if he'd heard her talking like this.

The boy looked at her, scared. Then, deliberately, he pulled back the curtains. Celine could see at least three pairs of eyes staring at her from behind the long desk. She must have been very loud. The boy went over to the desk and said something to one of the nurses. She handed him a piece of paper but didn't take her eyes off Celine.

The boy read the paper out loud, for everybody's benefit. "We are going to the Exeray Dee-partment where you will have . . ." Here he paused for effect, "an ultrasound! Of the abdomen!"

Having thus restored his pride, he fastened a belt around Celine, grinned at her, dropped her pocket book beside her on the stretcher, cheerfully grabbed the end bar, and maneuvered it with insolent skill out of the cubicle. Celine could imagine how he would drive a car; that boy would leave skid marks at every traffic light.

Celine closed her eyes as they trundled past the desk. She felt thoroughly embarrassed, and didn't want to see those nurses staring at her.

The boy hustled the stretcher along the corridor, the wheels rattling. Celine opened her eyes again, but the ceiling was going past so quickly she became dizzy. She remembered that dreadful-looking bald young woman when she had first gone to see Dr. Winter. Were the people in the corridor looking at her like that, pressing their backs up against the wall to avoid being contaminated? Probably not this time, but how about a week from now? A month?

Celine closed her eyes again, trying to control the fear that rose like bile inside her. As the walls and ceilings and people passed by along that interminable corridor, she realized that her flashes of anger were a kind of antidote against fear; when she was angry, like with this kid who was piloting her stretcher like a Maserati, she couldn't at the same time be afraid about her disease or wonder how far away death might be.

Celine realized that she hadn't eaten anything since breakfast, and that had only been a cup of coffee. She wasn't hungry, but felt the lack of sustenance. Everything seemed so distant. With an effort she remembered her conversation with Anwar Al-Khayib. He had promised to call back some time today. She'd need to tell Tom to expect his call, and what to do if the sly bastard tried to wriggle out of the situation. Tom, Al-Khayib, the office . . . that part of her life already felt hopelessly remote.

They turned a corner so sharply that her body was jammed against the seat belt, and then the stretcher stopped in a waiting area. It looked like a parking zone, with a half-dozen empty stretchers lined up against the wall, silently waiting, straps dangling. Celine craned her head around. The boy had gone, and there wasn't anybody there. Silence. Where was she? It didn't look like an X-ray department—it looked more like the waiting room of the morgue. Why hadn't that boy told her where she was, how long she'd have to wait? Surely he wouldn't have abandoned her in some remote part of the hospital that nobody ever visited, just because she had been rude to him?

"It's easier if you do it our way." The ghostly voice of Nurse Allen came back to her. Fighting off the beginning of panic, Celine forced herself to think about the world outside—if there still *was* a world outside. Charles. Food. There was plenty in the freezer, and, anyway, Catherine would take care of him. She thought about the house. Would someone remember to water the indoor plants? She always used a mister on them in the summer, it kept the edges of the leaves from curling. Damn it, Celine thought, why am I lying here thinking like a dumb hausfrau? I have better things to worry about than that. What's happening to me? What are they doing to my mind?

Without warning, the stretcher began to move. Startled, Celine let out a cry.

"It's okay, ma'am, I'm right behind you." She twisted her head back, but couldn't see anybody there. This time she really panicked and made a noise that was half gurgle and half scream. The stretcher stopped, and beside her appeared the figure of a dwarf wearing a tiny white jacket. His forehead was domed forward and he had the square face of an

Irish fighter. "You in pain, ma'am? I'll go slower if you like."

He vanished again, and the stretcher started its slow forward progress. Celine was sweating, and the feeling of panic was still there. This whole thing is like a nightmare, she thought, something Hieronymus Bosch or Goya might have dreamed up. She was about to ask the invisible dwarf where they were going when she saw the sign. ULTRASOUND. An arrow pointed the way they were headed. Of course, that's what the blond boy had said.

Why was she going there? Ultrasound. She remembered seeing a program on television where they had showed a fetus moving inside its mother's womb. Did they think she could be pregnant? Celine smiled grimly.

"Hi, I'm Candy." The white-coated girl looked down at her, smiling. She had a kind of routine blonde prettiness, with stiff hair and too much makeup. In half an hour, Celine thought, I could make you look great, and the first thing we'd do is wash all that stuff off your face. The girl checked the wrist tag. 'Ms. de La Roche? That French or something?"

Celine nodded.

The stretcher had stopped next to a big, complicated-looking console. It was making a low humming noise, and a display glowed in small letters on the screen. The girl pressed some buttons and a bright, wedge-shaped green image appeared, replacing the previous display.

"Let's see now . . ."

The girl undid the strap around Celine's waist and pulled the sheet off her stomach, leaving it exposed.

"I'm going to put this jelly on your belly." Candy grinned, as she had a thousand times at the same words. She held up a white plastic tube with a nozzle. Celine could feel the goosebumps rising. Candy picked up the sensor, a heavy cylinder the size of a shampoo bottle with an angled tip. It started to whirr softly.

"This won't hurt, Mrs. . . . What's your first name, hon?"

Celine wasn't going to answer, but Candy waited, sensor poised.

"Celine," she said finally.

"Yeah, nice," said Candy. "Nice name. Is that French too?"

Again she waited for an answer. Celine would have preferred being at the dentist, where at least one didn't have to answer when they talked to you. Candy pressed another switch and the room lights went out. Celine could see only her outline against the screen, but after a few minutes, her eyes grew accustomed to the gloom. For the next forty-five minutes Candy prodded, turned, and poked at Celine with the sensor, which seemed to have acquired an aggressive life of its own. The only interesting thing that happened was when the door opened momentarily and Celine felt the draft on her skin. A man came in and stood beside Candy, looking over her shoulder at the screen. Candy moved suddenly, and Celine knew that he had touched her, or done something to her under the cover of darkness. He left a few moments later.

"Can you show me what all that was about?" asked Celine when Candy finished the study and was wiping the jelly off with a terry towel.

"Sure," replied Candy. She pointed at different parts of the screen, where the image was now frozen. "Here, that's your gallbladder, up here's your liver, and that dark streak on the left is your aorta."

"What about the tumor, the thing they said is on my pancreas, can you see that?"

"You'll have to ask the doctors about that," said Candy, her voice changing. "Sorry, but I'm not allowed to discuss it."

Ten minutes later, the dwarf, who told Celine his name was Albert, trundled her through innumerable corridors and elevators up to the private wing. The Harkness Wing, they called it, after Mary Harkness, who had distributed millions to various medical facilities around the East Coast, including the New Coventry University Medical Center.

It was the visiting hour, and Albert couldn't find a nurse, so he parked Celine against the wall near the elevator, made sure her belt was fastened, bade her a cheery good-bye, and waddled off with his peculiar stiff-legged gait.

Celine lay back and watched the people go by. They

collected around the elevator and looked at her without curiosity. She laughed wryly at herself, imagining what she must look like by now, her hair messed up and all her makeup gone.

Where were her clothes? Still in the emergency room, presumably. Did they expect her to stay in this gown? She'd forgotten to ask Charles to bring in a few nighties, underwear, the things she'd need. He wouldn't have the faintest idea where these things were, but Catherine could pack them all into a small suitcase for him. She decided to call Charles at home; then he could bring it with him tomorrow.

After about half an hour, a nurse came up to her and said, "Hi, I'm Cindy."

"Well, hi, Cindy," she replied with a smile that was maybe a shade too bright. "I'm Celine."

Cindy paused for a second, looking at her. "Sorry to keep you waiting, but your room's being cleaned right now. You'll be in room 427."

It's being cleaned. Cleaned from what? Blood on the walls? Colostomy leak on the mattress? Celine shuddered. A sudden thought struck her.

"Did the patient in that room die? Because I couldn't—"

"No, of course not." Cindy sounded indignant at the idea that anybody would be inconsiderate enough to actually die there, in the expensive Harkness Wing, of all places.

Cindy pulled the pen off her clipboard. "I might as well admit you right here," she said. "Tell me why you're in the hospital."

She waited, pen poised.

"Before we go through all that again, do you think I could have something to eat? I haven't had anything since this morning."

Cindy looked at her watch. "Gee, Celine, lunches are over and the kitchen's closed now. I'll see if I can get you a sandwich or something, but let me get the information I need first, okay? Now why was it you came to the hospital?"

Just do it our way, it's easier if you just go along with us, our routines are for everybody's benefit. The words resounded in Celine's brain.

Celine was beginning to hurt again by the time she was installed in her bed. The room itself wasn't bad, and she could make the bed go up and down at the press of a button. She experimented a bit with it. Another button made the middle come up, bending her at the knees. The position was actually quite comfortable. There was also a big, complicated-looking panel behind her bed with lights, switches, a green-painted sign that said "oxygen."

Christ, she thought, if she got really sick she might need that. She tried to visualize herself attached to an oxygen mask, fighting for breath. They'd had one on her father when he died. She remembered the strange way he was breathing; a rapid intake of air, when all the muscles in his neck would tense up, then a long pause when nothing seemed to be happening, then another jolting breath. A few times it had seemed that he wasn't going to breathe again, and Celine held her own breath watching him for what seemed like an eternity, and then he breathed again, and she breathed, and sighed with relief even though she knew it couldn't go on much longer.

And now here she was, maybe also suffering from a fatal disease. She thought of people she knew who'd cheerfully checked into the hospital for tests and never come out. When her mother and father were in the hospital, at least they had her to hold their hands when the going got rough, but here, she was on her own.

Celine was the last person to succumb to self-pity, but now the combined effect of all her insecurities struck her all at once and left her breathless. Their effect was much worse here, in the hospital, because she couldn't work or cajole or bargain her way out of them.

She forced her thoughts back to her office, where there was so much to do. Tom was fine as long as things were going smoothly, but this was not the time for her to be out of touch. It wasn't the problems themselves that troubled Celine as much as the frightening sense of not being able to do anything about them. As long as she was in control, she could deal with just about anything, but here she felt devoid of any bargaining power, and entirely at the mercy of the impersonal hospital system. Feeling thoroughly frustrated, Celine punched her pillow hard, then fell back on it. But even when she lay there with her eyes closed, everything kept going round and round inside her head until she thought she couldn't stand it any longer.

After the research meeting, Caleb went on ward rounds with Don, Ed, and Porky; then they all went to the O.R. lounge for a cup of coffee. This once-a-week informal chat had become a tradition on Caleb's service. Porky, as the junior doctor, was in charge of the coffee, and he listened from the vantage point of the coffee machine. Caleb was talking about early days in pancreatic research.

"Have you guys ever heard of Banting and Best?" he asked.

"They were the first to produce insulin," said Porky instantly.

"In Canada," added Don, not to be outdone.

Caleb sat forward, his eyes bright. "Right. Imagine yourselves up there, in Toronto, about seventy years ago," he said. "Those guys knew that diabetes followed the removal of the pancreas, and Langerhans had discovered that certain cells in the pancreas disappeared in diabetics."

"Beta cells, in the islands of Langerhans," said Ed, stirring his coffee and listening carefully. He enjoyed Caleb's method of teaching, because it made everyone think and participate.

"Right. Hence insulin, from *insula*, Latin for island. Now, try to visualize their problem. They were trying to isolate the stuff coming from these little islands of Langerhans, but when they made an extract from the pancreas, the material from the digestive part of the pancreas always destroyed the insulin.

"They were under a lot of outside pressure, too," Caleb went on. Don, Ed, and Porky grinned. They knew that Caleb was familiar with that kind of pressure. "Other groups were trying to be the first to isolate and purify insulin, and rumors were always flying around that one group or another had found a technique that worked."

The phone in the lounge rang, and Porky went over to answer it.

"How did they get around the problem?" asked Ed.

"They came up with an absolutely brilliant solution," said Cal, his enthusiasm so obvious it made the others smile.

"It's for you, Dr. Winter," said Porky, holding the receiver.

"Think about it," said Cal, getting up. "It was brilliant, utterly logical, and it worked."

Cal's call was about a patient in the emergency room, and they all trooped off to see him.

Later, while they were waiting for the patient to come up to the operating room, Don asked Caleb how Banting and Best had managed to overcome the problems of isolating insulin.

"They tied off the pancreatic ducts," he replied. "That killed the digestive cells of the pancreas, so their enzymes didn't destroy the insulin when it was later extracted. Simple, huh?" He grinned at them. "All the most brilliant discoveries are simple," he said. "Unless you're trying to make one yourself."

It was late before he got up to see his private patients on the Harkness Wing.

"Well, Celine, are you settling in all right?" Caleb's tone was pleasant enough, but she was feeling tired and irritable, and objected to his use of her first name. She didn't call him Cal.

"It hasn't been the greatest day in my life, Dr. Winter," she said, knowing that she sounded rather curt. Caleb smiled and shook his head for a second, thinking, lady, if you could have seen the day I had! Celine misunderstood his smile and her lips compressed into a tight line. "I think I must have lost my sense of humor when I came in here," she said stiffly, "because I didn't think what I said was particularly funny."

"Lots of people lose their sense of humor in here, but it's

usually temporary, and rarely fatal." He grinned at her. "Don't worry, it'll come back."

"What I meant was . . . never mind. I'm here, hungry, bad-tempered . . ."

"Hungry?"

"I missed lunch because I was having that ultrasound so I asked for a sandwich, just a measly sandwich, but it never came. Then I suppose I fell asleep and they didn't bring any supper. I haven't had a thing to eat all day."

"Didn't you ask the nurses?" Caleb's expression seemed to say that wasn't the kind of problem he was normally expected to deal with.

"Yes, damn it, I did." She glowered at him, and for the first time Caleb felt the strength and stubbornness of her. "Am I not supposed to complain? Don't your patients ever complain if things go wrong? Or are they all too scared of you and the system?" The words came out before she had time to cancel them; her frustration had frothed over the top.

Caleb's smile was hardening around the edges when there was a knock on the door and a very young-looking aide came in bearing a tray with a carton of milk and a couple of plates, one with a metal cover over it. "I'm so sorry, ma'am," she said to Celine as she put the tray down on the bed table. "The kitchens were closed, so I got this from the cafeteria for you. I hope it's all right." She gave a scared glance in Caleb's direction, and he gave her a big, amused smile.

"Thank you so much," said Celine, smiling also, but she knew that she must seem very foolish in Caleb's eyes. After the aide had filled her glass with water and gone, Celine looked under the lid on the plate, then quickly replaced it.

"I'm not really hungry after all," she said, getting more and more angry. Everything she did or said now just made her look even more ridiculous. She pushed the bed table away, feeling certain that he was enjoying her embarrassment.

Caleb sat down on the chair by the bedside.

"What did the ultrasound show?" she asked coolly, in an effort to regain the ascendancy.

"Celine, I just this minute got out of the operating room.

I haven't had time to go over it. First thing tomorrow, though, I promise."

"Could you please tell me what's going on? Nobody's really told me anything about the tests, or even what you're looking for."

"So far, there isn't really much to share with you." Caleb smiled. "Around here, if people don't tell you, it's usually because they don't know." He sprawled in the chair, suddenly feeling expansive and relaxed, maybe because he felt that Celine's annoyance was evaporating. She was the last patient he had to see before leaving, and he could feel himself unwinding. Celine was a most attractive woman, and her prickly personality intrigued him. To his surprise, he realized that he'd been thinking about her, somewhere at the back of his mind, for most of the day.

Celine watched the tiredness spread over him. It was like a boxer's weariness; the footwork was slower, but the guard never came down.

"You looked pooped," she said.

It was the wrong thing to say. Instantly Caleb got to his feet, confidence and strength jolting defensively back into his system.

"No, I'm fine. I'd better be on my way—I'm operating first thing in the morning." He smiled, all his power back. "You have a CAT scan scheduled tomorrow afternoon, and I'll have gone over your ultrasound by the time I see you next, okay?"

The door opened, and Porky Rosen poked his head in, looked from Winter to Celine, then came in.

"Hi," he said, addressing Celine. "I was wondering if you need a sleeping pill."

"Good night, Ms. de La Roche," said Caleb, walking to the door. "Sleep well."

Caleb made a phone call from the nurses' station, then went straight down to the parking area. He looked at his watch. He had arranged to meet Maureen at Benno's for dinner in twenty minutes and he'd just make it. But as he drove on to the expressway, it wasn't Maureen's blue eyes he was thinking about.

* * *

"He sure has lots of energy, doesn't he?" Porky sat down in the chair Caleb had vacated, and stretched his legs out in front of him. He looked exhausted, but unlike Caleb, he didn't have any inhibitions about showing it. He unbuttoned his white jacket, and his stethoscope clattered to the floor. He grunted, reaching for it.

"God, what a day!" he said, then remembered that Celine was the patient, and it was her that he should be concerned about. "Gee, I'm sorry," he said. "I should be asking how *you* are." He smiled, his round cheeks giving him a cherubic, puckish look.

"Do you know what the nurses call you?" he asked.

"Nothing very nice, I bet." Celine smiled back, warming to this odd, untidy young man who looked more like an apprentice ice cream vendor than an intern.

"Oh, it's nothing bad. They call you Della, Della Roach. That's all."

"I've been called worse, I can assure you," laughed Celine. "When I was at school in France they called me the 'grenade,' so be careful!"

Porky stood up. "I'd better be going," he said, "or the rumors'll start. Not that I'd mind, of course."

There was an odd kind of defiance in his voice, and Celine had a sudden feeling that things were not going too well for Porky.

"What's your real name?" she asked gently. "I know what they call you, but I don't think they should call you that, as if you were still in junior high."

Porky reflected for a moment. "Ambrose," he said. "After my great-uncle Ambrose who was named after a lightship or something. But I don't mind Porky. In fact I prefer it. That's what I've always been called, and it really doesn't bother me. I'd probably call myself that if nobody else did."

He smiled, and Celine thought it was a lovely smile, guileless and open, and very vulnerable. She had a sudden desire to hug him, followed by a feeling that Porky didn't belong in this environment, among these dedicated, chilly, unforgiving technicians.

"What made you decide to be a surgeon?" she asked curiously.

"It was written in the stars," said Porky. "I have an uncle who's a surgeon, my father is an orthopedic surgeon, and my brother David just finished his training at Mass General. I think I was born a surgeon, but they wouldn't let me operate until I was more grown up."

From somebody else, that might have sounded presumptious, but not from Porky. It sounded more as if he wanted to believe in his own surgical destiny. He smiled self-consciously, then realized that he was about to unload his problems on this beguiling woman, and quickly changed the subject. "Did Dr. Winter tell you about your ultrasound?" he asked.

"He hasn't seen it yet. He'd just come out of the operating room."

"God, yes. What a case we had." For a second he wondered if it would be a breach of professional confidence if he told her about it. Well, he'd tell her anyway without mentioning any names. "Just about supper time, this tall kid, he must have been about nineteen, came into the Emergency Room holding onto a knife handle. No big deal, normally, but the rest of the knife was stuck in his neck. Well, the head nurse saw him come in, thought he was some kind of a nut, that he'd done it to himself, but of course the kid was just holding it steady, keeping it from moving around. They were very busy down there and she shouted at him, something about wasting their time with this kind of nonsense when they had really sick people who urgently needed attention. Anyway she went on like that for a bit and finally the kid just pulled the knife out, right there, standing in front of her, and the blood shot out like a fountain, all over her."

Celine's eyes were like saucers. "My God!" she whispered.

Porky was enjoying the effect his story was having.

"Well, go on! What happened?"

"It's hard to believe, because it all happened so fast, and he was losing so much blood, still grinning away at the head nurse, and spouting over her. She was screaming. He'd have been dead in a minute or two. Luckily for him, Dr. Winter was there, he'd just finished seeing a patient in the booth opposite the desk."

To her astonishment, because she didn't like the man, Celine had a strange feeling of pride when Porky mentioned Dr. Winter's name, a kind of remote pride, as if a stranger had said something nice about a member of her family. Maybe it was because of Porky's obvious admiration for him, but also she was his patient, and felt relieved that she was in good hands.

"Anyway, Dr. Winter came out when the nurse screamed, saw what was happening, came up behind the kid, quick as a flash, put his hand on his neck, pressed hard, and bingo, the bleeding stopped, just like magic."

"Then what?" asked Celine, anxious to hear the end of the story. "What happened?"

"Well, there was a wheelchair up against the desk, and Dr. Winter sat the kid down in it, still keeping the pressure on. Then he told Connie Davis, that's the head nurse, who was still standing right there, her front all covered in blood, he told her to put her fingers on the kid's neck—he showed her how to keep up the pressure—told the desk clerk to call Don McAuliffe, that's my senior resident, and warn the operating room. Then he went on his way, not a hair out of place, as if nothing had happened. Half an hour later he was showing Don and me how to fix the cut in the kid's carotid artery, and we've been there ever since. I guess that's why he was late coming to see you."

"Oh, right. Well, in that case I guess I can excuse him."

"I tell you, Ms. de La Roche, you couldn't be in better hands than him," said Porky, his enthusiasm getting the better of his grammar.

"Why don't you call me Celine?" she said.

"Okay, Celine it is."

"Porky, my CAT scan's tomorrow. What exactly is it supposed to show?" Celine sat straight up in bed, and Porky could see her outline through the thin hospital gown. His mouth went dry, and he stared hard at the oxygen outlet behind her head as she went on. "They already know the tumor's there, so why doesn't he just go ahead and cut it out?"

"He needs a lot more information, like how big it is, if it's stuck to other organs like the stomach."

Celine was silent for a few moments, and a cold wave of

fear washed over her at the thought of being cut open and having pieces of her body hacked out. She shivered, and Porky felt great compassion for her. She wasn't much older than he was, and already her body was invaded by a tumor that would probably kill her within a year.

Spontaneously, he placed his hand on hers where it lay on the sheet. His hand was pudgy and warm, and he patted hers with a kind of gentle clumsiness. After a moment he got up.

"I'd better get going, I still have a couple of histories and physicals to do. See you tomorrow."

He left, then came back a few seconds later.

"I'm sorry, Celine, but did you say if you wanted a sleeping pill?"

As soon as Porky left, Celine pulled the table back and reexamined the food on the tray. She had just started to eat the bread roll when the phone rang. Celine picked it up, but because it was placed awkwardly on the bedside table she dropped it with a clatter on the floor.

"Sorry," she said into it. "I just dropped the phone."

It was Charles, but her pleasure at hearing his voice evaporated with his first words.

"Are you behaving?" he asked.

Celine took a deep breath. "Behaving? What do you think I'm doing? Here, do you want to speak with Cal Winter? He's here in bed with me; he can tell you if I'm behaving."

Charles laughed, and Celine got the impression that he wasn't really taking her hospitalization very seriously. Her hand tightened on the phone, and she could hear her own voice becoming chilly.

"The reason I called is because your Oncle Didi phoned this evening from Paris." said Charles. "I had to tell him that you were in the hospital, and he said he's coming over. He said he had to be in New York anyway."

"Good old Oncle Didi. What did you tell him?"

"Just that you were up in New Coventry. He wanted to know what was the matter. I suppose he'll stay at the Plaza and drive up."

"I wish he felt comfortable enough to come and stay with us in Greenwich," said Celine.

"Well, he doesn't, and nor do I," said Charles. "Tom Pfeiffer called, by the way. He has some manuscripts he wants you to read, but I told him you needed a rest, and you'd call him tomorrow."

Celine felt a fresh twinge of irritation at Charles's protectiveness.

"Okay. I'll call him."

Celine hung up, shaking her head, upset with her own feelings of irritated hostility toward Charles. It hadn't always been like that, not by any means. When he wasn't there, she could see him as she knew others did, handsome, intelligent, capable, a man she didn't appreciate and didn't deserve. I'm not the creature I'd like to be, she thought sadly; if I redesigned my own emotional self the way I wanted, I'd be very different; I'd be warm, loving, the way I was when we were first married. And I suppose I wouldn't let the business run my life to the exclusion of everything else.

Celine lay back in the bed; she'd never in her life felt as tired as now. It was like a huge dead weight that seeped all the way into her bones. She felt too tired to move, too tired even to put the light out, although the switch was only a few inches from her hand. She slept uneasily, her body making little twitches of which she was barely aware. She dreamed the most vivid dreams, and Caleb Winter was in all of them, always frightening, always dangerous, fighting bloody battles with her two dragons, Grobochus and Jagragousse, who had protected Celine in her dreams from early childhood.

Caleb and Maureen were in the habit of having dinner together about once a week, although they'd only managed a couple of times in the last two months.

They went to Benno's, an Italian restaurant a few minutes away from where Caleb lived and where he was well known. Benno himself conducted them to a corner table and spread the linen napkins on their laps. Both Caleb and Maureen felt slightly uncomfortable with each other, but neither could have said precisely why.

"I hear you admitted a potential graft patient," said Maureen, glancing at him over the menu.

"You mean the de La Roche woman? How did you happen to hear that?"

"Well, you know I keep an eye open for anybody who might fit the bill. How was the osso bucco? I remember you had it last time."

"Excellent; try it. Yes, she might be our first. I think she might do very well. She's in a good age group, no intercurrent disease. As long as her tumor hasn't spread, and so far there's no sign of that."

Maureen always liked to watch Caleb order in a restaurant; he wasn't a man who ever had a problem making decisions. In fact, she often preferred that he order the meal for her since he knew her tastes well, and she had an irrational, instinctive feeling that somehow he would choose better.

"They say she's quite a ticket, your Ms. de La Roche—beautiful, egotistical, difficult to get along with. But I don't suppose any of these things were a problem to you, even if you noticed them."

He looked up, irritated that Maureen was slighting his powers of observation. "You seem to know more about her than I do," he said, his tone sharp. "Depending on the tests, I'd like to operate on her next week, as soon as we have permission from the committee." Caleb caught himself, realizing that he was sounding a bit pompous. He put the menu down. "That would make it Tuesday at the earliest."

"Fine." Maureen was smiling at him and he didn't know exactly why. "That'll give me time to get the donor and everything else ready."

"Are you going to have the osso bucco?"

"Yes. Caleb, do you remember the first meal we ever had together?" Caleb frowned at this saccharine turn in the conversation, but Maureen's eyes were shining in the candlelight, and the highlights caught her hair. She looked as beautiful as the day they'd first met.

At that time Maureen had been taking an elective evening course in experimental biology, and on this particular evening a visiting lecturer was expected to discuss xenografts, which meant, as Maureen found on looking it up, grafts taken from one species of animal and placed in another.

Doug, her fiancé, called to say he'd meet her at ten, when her class finished, then they'd go and have a pizza together before going home.

The lecturer was a doctor, a young man, good-looking in a stern kind of way. At first, he wasn't particularly interesting. He talked about the history of grafting, showed a slide of two saints, Cosmas and Damian, reputedly the first to transplant a leg from one human to another. The follow-up studies were not convincing, the lecturer noted dryly, and after a moment there were some scattered giggles from his audience.

But once he got going, it was magic. The lecturer not only came to life himself but took his audience with him. A crackling excitement developed around him, and as he talked, explained, and theorized, his personality seemed to grow to proportions quite beyond the dimensions of the rather mean little lecture hall.

Like the others, Maureen was hypnotized, overwhelmed. Later, during the lab part of the session, when Maureen was sewing a tube of skin from an anesthetized guinea pig to a rabbit, the lecturer paused to watch what she was doing, and Maureen almost stopped breathing, overcome by the sheer power of his presence.

"That's really beautiful," he said appreciatively. "You must have learned to sew when you were very young."

Maureen raised her eyes to ask him about a point in his lecture. Maureen's eyes were a stunning cornflower blue, and when combined with her red hair and other attributes, the overall effect was dazzling. Understandably, the lecturer found her question profoundly challenging, and spent much of the rest of the session answering it.

They were still sitting on the bench when the late-night cleaners arrived with their mops and buckets. And when the lecturer asked Maureen if she'd like to go for a pizza somewhere, Maureen put her hand to her mouth. She had totally forgotten about Doug.

"You were thinking about our first pizza?" asked Caleb. He smiled suddenly at her over the single candle. "Those were the days, Maureen, when we were young and poor and determined to save the world whether it wanted to be saved or not." Hearing a note of sadness in Caleb's voice, Maureen thought, how typical, he thinks of his work, and I think about how we fell in love.

"I fell for you so hard," she said quietly, shaking her head. "I wouldn't have believed it was possible."

For months, Maureen had forgotten about everything except Caleb Winter. He couldn't stay over at her apartment because of her two roommates, but Maureen went to the hospital when she could and spent the night with him. Often enough, she'd let herself into the tiny, white-walled room, and wait. Usually he'd call from the emergency room or the intensive care unit or wherever he was, but often she'd be asleep by the time he got back to his room, exhausted but never showing it, and nearly always the phone would ring within a few minutes and he'd have to leave again.

But Maureen didn't let any of that bother her. Their brief

times together were enough to keep her fires burning at white heat.

"Bring us a bottle of that fine Barolo," Caleb was saying.

"The Giacomo Borgogno you had last time, Signor Winter? Of course." Benno hurried off on his flat waiter's feet.

"You're looking tired," said Maureen, stretching out her hand across the table to him.

"That's exactly what Celine said a little while ago," replied Caleb with a laugh. "Actually, I'm not tired; I'm just getting old."

"*Celine?*" Maureen's hand returned quickly to her side of the table. Caleb rarely used patients' first names, but it was more the way he said her name, as if he could taste it.

"You need a vacation," she said, her blue eyes fixed on him. "You're getting edgy and you're losing your sense of humor. And we've never had a real vacation together." Maureen was speaking a little faster. "I was thinking we really deserve one. How would you like to go to Bermuda for a week?"

Caleb looked up, a forkful of meat poised in midair. "Now? Bermuda? Maureen, you're out of your tree! Just when we've got a candidate for our first pancreatic xenograft? You know as well as I do we couldn't go now." He shrugged and went on eating.

Maureen hid her disappointment behind her napkin. There had always been something. Either there was a deadline to meet for a grant application, or too many surgical cases lined up, or somebody else was on vacation. When Maureen first became Caleb's official assistant, she'd suggested a weekend away to celebrate, but they'd just started a new antirejection program and he couldn't leave the animals for even half a day.

Becoming his assistant had been a mistake, as after a short time Caleb began to think of her only in terms of work and the laboratory. He was so caught up in the developments of transplantation and immunology that they talked about little else. They slept together when they could, occasionally grabbed a couple of hours to go and eat dinner, and for a long time Maureen had been content just to have him there, to

share in his excitement at a successful experiment, to participate in writing papers for the medical journals. Caleb was
authoritative in his attitude toward her, but she didn't mind,
because from the very beginning he'd been the boss and he
knew best. But finally Maureen woke up to the realization
that all she and Caleb shared was work.

"You know, Caleb," said Maureen, taking a sip of wine,
"you're the exact opposite of most people."

Caleb went on eating. He didn't especially care for that
kind of evaluation, but had learned to tolerate them.

"My father, for instance," Maureen went on. "He likes his
job as much as most people. But when he comes home he
relaxes, and he feels that that is his *real* life, at home with the
family, working on his car, going out to a restaurant with
Mom every Friday."

Caleb looked at her with a slightly cynical smile as she went
on. "But you're the other way around. You're only really at
home when you're working, and the rest of the time is just
in between, a pause, until you can get back to it."

"It's not just me," smiled Caleb. "Most men are like that.
Madame de Stael said it best: 'Love is only an episode for a
man, but for a woman, it's the whole history of her life.'"

"I wish you wouldn't quote stuff at me like that," said Maureen, annoyed and feeling speared by the baroness's words.
"Two hundred years ago, women didn't have much else to
think about."

They'd had this kind of conversation before, but just as
Maureen was thinking that it had been a mistake to go out
to dinner, Caleb suggested that she come back to his apartment for a nightcap, and Maureen hesitated for only a second
before agreeing. As always, her willpower simply evaporated
when he was around.

After Caleb had sipped his way through a small cognac and
she'd downed a sizable cherry brandy, he smiled, took her
hand, and led her into the bedroom. Caleb loved to watch
Maureen undress, and he sat on the bed while she quickly
slipped off her blouse, then turned for him to undo the hook
on her bra. When she faced him again, the sight of her perfectly shaped breasts made him catch his breath, and she

cupped them with her hands and stroked them, watching his eyes. There was a kind of intimate eroticism in the way he stared so directly at her breasts. Even at this charged moment, however, it occurred to Maureen, and not for the first time, that sex with Caleb was like a wonderful but temporary dressing on the raw burned surface of her life. Caleb's gaze moved up to her face and he stretched out his arms, put his hands on her waist, and drew her close to him. He put his face between her breasts and gently pressed them with his hands so as to enfold himself within them. Smiling with an almost motherly pleasure, Maureen's fingers slid down and started to undo the buttons of his shirt.

Then they lay naked on their backs, Caleb as always on the left side of the bed. With his surgeon's perfect touch, his index finger lightly traced circles around her right nipple, then he turned on his side and touched Maureen's left nipple with the tip of his tongue. Her breathing became deeper, and she felt subterranean forces starting to lift her as she prepared to surrender to him.

Caleb felt it all differently; he knew Maureen's body exquisitely well, and had an instinct for what gave her the most pleasure, but he didn't let himself go until their mutually aroused passion reached a level even he couldn't resist. And when he did finally let himself go, Maureen became the center of a whirlwind of incredible force that pulled and sucked them up to the top of the precipice and over the edge . . .

After they had fallen back and lay panting together, Maureen put her arms around Caleb and held him tight. But within moments his other, separate concerns flowed irresistibly back into his consciousness; the intense absorption of making love with Maureen slipped through his fingers like water from the receding tide. Lazily, Caleb put an arm around her, but from his touch she knew that he was gone already. He lay there, staring at the ceiling, thinking about all the things he'd briefly managed to exclude from his mind, but soon a sleepy contentment came over him and he dozed off.

When he awoke thirty minutes later, Maureen had gone.

Henry Brighton carefully locked his car door and walked toward the entrance of the New Coventry Hilton. He was about six feet tall, slightly stooped, and walked in a fussy, preoccupied way that suggested he was busily engaged in some vitally important activity. He had a round, boyish face, with small eyes and a lock of once-blond hair that kept falling rakishly down over his eye. Somebody once said he looked like a pink balloon with a Magic Marker face dotted on it.

Henry was excited about the meeting he'd been summoned to, although he had no idea of what it was about. The phone call from Chauncey Roper had come a few days before. Roper was a man he knew only slightly, very wealthy and an important member of the hospital board, so Henry wasted no time taking the call.

"Brighton?" Roper had a gruff, commanding voice. The man was obviously used to giving orders.

"Yes, sir." Henry pitched his voice to an appropriate mix of deference and firmness as he pulled a legal pad toward him. He might have to take notes, and wanted to be ready. You didn't keep somebody like Chauncey Roper waiting.

"There's a meeting next week I want you to attend," said Chauncey. "We're going to discuss certain matters which pertain to your department."

"A hospital committee, Mr. Roper? Because—"

"Not a hospital committee, Brighton. A private group of people in the pharmaceutical field. They may wish to offer you something to your advantage."

Henry scratched his head with the pencil he was holding.

"To my advantage, Mr. Roper?" he said, puzzled. "Do you mean for the department, or—?"

"The Hilton, next Tuesday afternoon, at three. Suite 538." There was a moment's pause. "That's on the fifth floor."

"Yes, of course, Mr. Roper. Thank you, I'll most assuredly be there. Is there any material you'd like me to bring? Departmental statistics—?"

But Chauncey had hung up. A very busy man, thought Henry. That would explain his brusqueness. For the next few days Henry wondered what the summons could be about. Something to his advantage, Mr. Roper had said. Maybe they were going to offer him a job, as a kind of ambassador between the pharmaceutical industry and academic medicine.

Henry was full of anticipation as he entered the hotel lobby. He tried to get a glimpse of himself in the glass doors, just to be sure he was quite presentable, but somebody was coming out, so he went to the men's room and examined himself in the spotless mirror over the sinks. Not bad; clean collar, nice striped tie, not too flamboyant; Henry knew that these upper-echelon businessmen were conservative in their dress, and he didn't want to look out of place. Hair combed over the forehead . . . there was still quite a lot of it, and some was still blond. Combed like that it gave him a nice, boyish, enthusiastic look. Henry looked at his watch. Eight minutes to go. Too early to go up to the suite—they might still be discussing the terms they were going to offer him—but he couldn't just hang around here; somebody might get the wrong impression. Henry went into one of the stalls and bolted the door. He sat there for exactly five minutes, his briefcase on his knees, then stood up, let himself out, and headed for the elevator.

He paused outside suite 538 and took a deep breath before knocking. He could feel a light beading of sweat on his forehead.

Chauncey Roper opened the door. "Dr. Brighton!" he checked his watch. "You're the man of the hour!" His voice was loud but jovial; he sounded much more friendly than over the phone. There were two men in dark business suits standing behind him, one tall and cadaverous, the other big, bluff-looking, with a thick mane of gray hair. Both were foreigners, Henry decided instantly, judging by their clothes and general sleekness. They greeted him with proper deference, Henry was pleased to note, bowing when they were introduced.

"Herr Ortweiler, from the Pharmaceutical Consortium in Basel," said Roper, beaming jovially as he introduced the thin one. "And this is Professor Doctor Hans Salzman, recently of Bern University, and now our newest link with the medical profession." Henry then learned to his surprise that Professor Salzman had spent the better part of the day visiting Caleb Winter's lab.

"Let's sit down," said Roper, indicating the comfortable easy chairs around the low glass-topped table. "Henry, you're the guest of honor, why don't you sit here. Drink, anybody?" He waved toward the sideboard.

Henry glanced ostentatiously at his watch. "Not during working hours, thank you," he said, hoping to raise a small laugh and break the ice. He sat back in his chair; it was important to look confident and at ease in the presence of powerful men such as these.

"Thank you for taking the time to meet with us," started Roper, his eyes twinkling in the friendliest fashion. "We all know how busy you doctors are."

The others nodded, and Henry started to relax. He'd obviously misjudged Chauncey Roper.

"You're the guest of honor," Roper repeated, "so most of our comments will be addressed to you."

Henry nodded, then pushed an errant lock of hair back off his forehead.

"Herr Ortweiler, why don't you start?" Roper addressed him with obvious respect, and Henry focussed his full attention on the man.

Kurt Orweiler flashed a cold, mechanical smile. He was unusually tall, with a dark, lean face, black hair combed straight back, and a thin neck. He looked at the three men, one after the other, reserving the longest look for Henry, as if he were gathering them all into his fold.

"As most of you know, I represent a small number of corporations whose annual trading volume is in excess of five billion dollars," he said. "And all that, I may say, in the service of humanity."

Ortweiler went on, his voice clear, lightly accented. "Our group manufactures a large range of life-saving pharmaceuticals," he went on. "Antibiotics, tranquilizers, other psychoactive drugs. The list is long, but one of our main interests is hormones, including, of course, insulin." He paused, looking around at the three men again. "I would like you to consider the economics of diabetes, just for a moment. There are around eighty million diabetics in our range of operation, excluding, for the moment, China, the U.S.S.R., and Third World countries. Of these eighty million diabetics some twenty million are unfortunately severe enough to need insulin." Ortweiler paused. "And that, gentlemen, is a pretty big captive consumer group, I'm sure you'd agree."

"I've never heard that expression before, have you?" whispered Henry Brighton to Chauncey Roper, who ignored him. But Ortweiler had heard the comment, and turned courteously to Henry. "I use the word *captive* in a purely economic sense, Dr. Brighton," he said. "Nobody's forcing them to buy our product."

He went back to his prepared speech. "Now, diabetes is not curable, but treatable, generally for the remainder of the patient's life. It is permanent, requiring daily injections. Each treatment costs an average of ninety-six cents not including syringes, needles, and antiseptic solutions, which we also supply through subsidiary corporations. We are talking, gentlemen about a business that brings in, year in and year out, a total of well over a billion dollars."

Well over a billion, thought Henry. It was hard even to conceive of all that money.

"Of course, we take this vast human responsibility very seriously," went on Ortweiler, as if he were addressing an audience of thousands. "Every year we spend huge sums of money on our own research and in subsidizing research in various centers of learning, such as right here in the New Coventry Medical Center."

He glanced at Henry, who nodded with a show of forced enthusiasm. His department had a grant of twelve thousand dollars to evaluate infection rates at insulin injection sites. Hardly worth all the paper work it involved, but it was money, and it had to be picked up where he could get it.

Herr Ortweiler paused, and suddenly Henry realized that the man was using the silence like a drumroll. He was about to make a major announcement. Ortweiler placed the tips of his long fingers together and looked at each man in turn.

"I am authorized to tell you of a major breakthrough our industry has been working on for many years," he said. "Of course this information is absolutely confidential; the world press and other media will not be informed of this until a later date."

At that moment, Henry noted that all three men were smiling and looking at him as if he were about to receive an award.

"Our major research facility in Basel has finally perfected a preparation of insulin that can be taken by mouth, not by injection."

Henry gasped out loud. He realized instantly that this was a medical breakthrough of gigantic dimensions; an oral preparation of insulin meant that diabetics could throw away their syringes, forget about the pain, the infection, the dangerous drop in blood sugar that could follow injection of insulin. Henry could hardly believe that Ortweiler had divulged such a piece of news to him. Inside information of this kind from the secretive pharmaceutical industry was rare as hen's teeth, and in this case, also priceless.

Henry understood immediately that he had been presented with a gift that could be worth hundreds of thousands of dollars, as purchases of stock made now in the huge foreign corporation would be unlikely to attract attention when the news came out officially and the share value rocketed. Henry repressed an urge to leave the room immediately to call his broker.

Ortweiler smiled, showing his very large teeth. "That was just a little background, gentlemen, which I feel was important for you to know."

"Is that all you wanted to tell me?" asked Henry, hoping that he could leave and place his order before the market closed.

"Not quite." Herr Ortweiler's English was clipped, over-correct, and held a slightly condescending tone that didn't offend Henry in the least. After all, the man was used to dealing with heads of vast corporations.

"This new oral insulin has cost us many tens of millions of dollars to develop," went on Ortweiler, staring at the far wall. "We are investing several more millions to set up manufacturing and production facilities." He paused and his eyes focused once more on Henry. "As you can appreciate, we are talking here about a really gigantic program."

Henry looked at Ortweiler and tried to imagine what it would be like to control an organization that size. *Billions*, he'd said.

"It will take many years to amortize this investment, as I am sure you understand. And, of course we cannot afford to have any product or process that might compete with it."

"Do you mean Caleb Winter's transplants?" asked Henry, and a wide grin appeared on his face. "Because it would take all the surgeons in the world *years* to make any real differences, even if all they did was put in pancreatic transplants twenty-four hours a day, seven days a week."

Henry sat back contentedly, but not for long.

"Perhaps Professor Doctor Salzman would be kind enough to address that matter for us," replied Ortweiler.

Hans stood up, his face glowing. What he was going to say would surprise at least some of them.

"I had a most interesting visit at Dr. Winter's lab," he started in his ponderous way. "Most interesting." He looked around the group, enjoying his moment. "Winter and his colleagues have apparently perfected the transplant model. I saw primates, macaques who had their own pancreases removed, living happily with pig pancreases inside them."

"A great technical accomplishment," said Henry with polished sarcasm. "But it doesn't answer the point I just made. Even if all the surgeons—"

"No, no, no, Dr. Brighton," interrupted Salzman, a triumphant smirk on his face. "You don't understand."

Henry was about to make a cutting remark when Ortweiler spoke up, so softly that Henry had to lean forward to hear what he was saying. "It's the future, Dr. Brighton," he said. "It's not what Dr. Winter is doing now, it's what his laboratory will be doing next year and the year after. You see, at some point, if he continues the caliber of work he is putting out now, there will be a major breakthrough from his lab. We will welcome that, of course, in the interests of humanity, but not quite yet." He looked at Salzman, and Henry suddenly understood that the consortium had bought out Salzman's research program too.

"And of course we applaud those early efforts of Dr. Winter's," cut in Chauncey Roper smoothly. "But we must realize that they are indeed early. Obviously it would be unethical and irresponsible to allow any such transplantations into human subjects at such an early stage."

The three men were now gazing steadily at Henry, and he felt that they were waiting for him to say something. A thought came into his head. "Dr. Winter's projects bring a great deal of money into the department," he said, trying not to sound too apologetic. "And if the Ethics and Public Welfare Committee doesn't approve his application to put animal pancreases into humans, it may well result in the loss of all his research grants."

"We are ready and willing to react promptly to such a tragedy, Dr. Brighton," replied Ortweiler quietly. "I believe there is a major research effort in your own department that is currently stalled because of lack of funds."

Henry thought for a moment, puzzled, then caught his breath. "You must mean the ulcerative colitis project? Yes, that is very important work ... and yes, it is stalled, temporarily, at any rate." Henry's voice faded, and his eyes moved questioningly around the group.

Again there was a silence, broken by Ortweiler's clipped voice.

"My board of directors has suggested that in view of the importance of that work, we might fund it to the extent your department would suffer by the loss of Dr. Winter's transplant project," he said, sounding bored.

"That would be ..." Henry swallowed. He saw the carefully blank expressions of the other men around the table, but he didn't care. If he could get that money, it would be worth any temporary humiliation; once he got his research career back on the rails his pride would come back automatically.

Henry suddenly realized there was a point Ortweiler obviously hadn't considered. "I would like to remind the group that although both Chauncey and I are on the committee, that doesn't mean we can convince the other members. And there are four of them in addition to ourselves."

"I'm quite sure your opinion will have a great influence on the other members," said Ortweiler. "And if there are any incidental expenses, we will of course be happy to cover them."

Henry smiled at him. These big businessmen didn't always know how things worked in the groves of academe. "I don't think so," he said. "I don't believe that any of these committee members can be bought, if that's what you're suggesting."

Ortweiler's mouth opened for a second, then closed instantly. "In that case," he said, "I will leave the matter to your own discretion."

A faint twitch came from the region of Henry's atrophied conscience. "If the committee turns down Dr. Winter's application, that will probably mean the end of his research career," he said. "None of the funding agencies will ever renew his grants."

Henry found every eye in the room fixed on his.

"Precisely," said Ortweiler.

Then to Henry's surprise Ortweiler said something that seemed more blunt than was really necessary. "As I'm sure you must be aware, Dr. Brighton, our group pays for results, and for results only. We will resume our discussion when your committee has turned down Dr. Winter's proposal and the official notification is in our hands. And now, gentlemen," he said, standing up, "I think we have completed our business."

"Right," said Chuancey. "The meeting is adjourned. Thank you all for coming."

Henry looked at his watch. It was too late to call his broker. He turned toward Chauncey with an expression of respectful familiarity. "Let's go and have a drink downstairs, Mr. Roper," he said. "We have a lot of arm-twisting to do before next Monday."

When Porky gently closed Celine's door, he stood outside it for a few moments, thumbing through his little stack of dog-eared six-by-four cards. There was a card for each patient on the service, and on each were the results of tests, date of operation, the medications they were on, and other details pertaining to their care.

He slid the rubber band back around the cards. That was it for today; Della Roach was the last one. Porky walked back along the corridor. The name Della Roach sounded so funny it made him laugh out loud, it was so totally unsuited to a lady with such class. Porky looked at his old Mickey Mouse watch, still surprisingly accurate, which he had worn since high school. He didn't mind that his colleagues, who leaned more toward Rolexes, found his timepiece odd. On the contrary, the battered old watch was a talisman; and it neatly got around the possibility that they might find him odd whatever kind of watch he wore.

It was getting late, not that it made any difference to Porky; he was going to be staying in the hospital all night anyway. He wondered where Don and Ed were; if they hadn't already gone home, they'd probably be down in the emergency room. The E.R. doctors' lounge was the place where the late-nighters eventually wound up. There was a kind of subdued late-night euphoria about the place, especially after midnight; the people who sat in the armchairs around the coffee machine had usually been up for twenty-four hours or longer, and usually somebody had a story to tell.

Sure enough, Don and Ed were there, in the lounge, laughing at the story that Bob Aminoke, the Nigerian E.R. doctor, was telling about Sonja Blake, the evening supervisor. They all knew her, a tough, man-hungry blonde whose mission in life, besides finding a doctor who would marry her, was to keep all the neighborhood bums and drunks out in the street where they belonged, and not in her nice clean emergency room. Sonja was merciless. She watched the entrance door from the raised nurses' station, and if one of these street people was brave enough to come in, she'd scream at him until he lost his nerve, turned tail, and fled. Most of the local bums had figured out when she was on duty and steered clear.

"Anyway, there was Sonja," said Bob, his long legs over the arm of his chair, "sitting at the high desk, deep in conversation with Morrie Weinberger, the derm guy, who was covering for internal medicine." Bob had a deep melodious voice like a singer's. "You know Morrie—he knows he's pretty good-looking and really likes his women. So there he was, sitting next to Sonja and gazing into her eyes."

They heard a crash of glass from out in the E.R., then a man shouting, but nobody in the lounge paid any attention, except for Porky, who looked uneasily at the door.

"Right about that time the outside door opens, but nobody comes in. At least you can't hardly see him as the guy's on his hands and knees to avoid being seen, because he knows Sonja's at the desk. It's the one they call Mal, the dirtiest one of them all. He's got a deep cut on his head and he's really foul, with his beard and hair all matted with God knows what, in his filthy smelly rags and everything."

A siren swelled outside, then died. Footsteps sounded. A thud, another shout. Porky noticed that Bob Aminoke's forehead was beaded with sweat, although it wasn't hot in the lounge. He must be on something, he thought. Certainly Bob was hyperactive, telling his story with lots of jerky hand movements and wide gestures.

"Sonja doesn't see Mal, because she's so engrossed with Morrie. Mal keeps creeping along, and finally gets to the desk, and still Sonja hasn't seen him. He's still on his hands and knees when he comes around the corner of the desk. A few seconds later Sonja feels a hand on her thigh, and think it's Morrie, and she stares even harder into his eyes. The hand moves. . . . This goes on, better and better until after a while Morrie gets up to leave. But of course the hand is still there. And that's when Sonja lets out a scream you could have heard clearly in Hoboken, New Jersey . . ."

Porky, standing by the door, had been thinking about Celine and lost track of the last part of the story. His colleagues' laughter jolted him back to where he was.

"What happened in Hoboken?" he asked.

They looked up at him expressionlessly.

"Go and see if you can find us something to eat," Don told him. "Maybe there's somebody in the kitchens."

"If anybody can find food, it has to be him." Porky heard Bob Aminoke's comment and the laughter that followed as the door closed behind him.

The kitchens were locked and in darkness, so Porky decided to go and get some sleep. The on-call room was on the eighth floor, the same as the O.R., and he wearily headed toward the elevator. When he finally got to the on-call room and opened the door, the telephone started to ring as if on a signal.

They were admitting a couple of people who'd been injured in an automobile crash, the E.R. secretary told him, and at least one was hurt bad and would have to go to surgery. So get your ass down here fast, she said, and hung up quickly.

Porky turned and walked back slowly toward the elevator. He vividly remembered Ed van Stamm under the same kind of circumstances, when Ed had been an intern and Porky was still in medical school, doing his surgical rotation. Ed had run for the stairwell, shouting that the elevators took too long. Porky had followed him, puffing and blowing as they ran down the concrete stairs, while Ed shouted about airways and blood pressure cuffs, all the things he'd need to remember about resuscitation and what he'd need to do when they got to the patient. That one had been shot in the face with a shotgun, Porky remembered, and a DOA had come in in the same ambulance with him.

Walking toward the elevator, Porky was aware that he

wasn't living up to the high standards set by Ed and generations of other surgical residents before him, but he couldn't help it. It was too far to run, and in any case he knew he'd be so breathless by the time he got to the E.R. that he wouldn't be able to function properly.

Porky was different from the rest of his family; the only other fat one was a distant cousin, and all the others laughed at him because he was not only fat but a poet, of all things. He earned a meager living teaching English somewhere in Arizona, and in return he didn't give a damn for any of them, with their dedication to humanity, their Mercedes, and their high social standing.

Porky's father was a distinguished orthopedic surgeon, one of the first in the U.S. to put in artificial hip joints. His dedication to his patients was legendary, to the point where Porky as a child barely recognized him when he came home. It occasionally worried Porky to think that he might owe his entry into the surgical program to his family's surgical heritage, and during his occasional periods of depression he suspected that he might not have got in without it.

But Porky knew that things would improve. The first year was always the worst, and as he got more experience and better organized, he'd find his feet all right. But instinctively he knew that he was an outsider in the surgical fraternity. He just didn't think or function in the same way, although academically he was as bright as any of them.

The elevator was taking ages to get up to his floor. Following its progress by the little lights that winked hypnotically above the doors, Porky swayed on his feet. He was dead tired. There wasn't anybody around, so he decided to sit on the floor opposite the elevator until it arrived. He leaned back against the wall, and by the time the elevator arrived Porky was fast asleep. He didn't hear the door open or see the bright light that flooded over him until the doors closed again. And of course he couldn't hear the telephone ringing in the on-call room—and Ed had borrowed Porky's personal pager because his wasn't working.

Porky slept for one and a half hours, and almost fainted when he woke up and realized what had happened. He stumbled down to the emergency room, but everything there was quiet.

"Jesus Christ, look who's here!" Bob Aminoke stared at him. "Where were you? All hell's been breaking loose. They had to call somebody in from internal medicine to help out when they couldn't find you. They're all up in the O.R. You'd better get your ass up there and fast."

Sick at heart, Porky made his way up to the operating suite and changed into a scrub suit in the deserted locker room. As he walked along the corridor into which the operating rooms opened, he saw that only one room was lit, and he could hear the murmur of voices from inside. He planned to slip in unobtrusively, help write the postop orders, and make himself generally useful, but when he opened the door the talking stopped and five pairs of eyes swung on to him. Porky recognized one of the medical interns holding a retractor; he must have been the one they'd brought in.

"We're just closing," said Don. "We won't need you. Get lost."

Porky opened his mouth to say something, but changed his mind, turned about and left. Even though he was still feeling numb from sleep, the contempt in Don's voice stung him painfully. He went to the on-call room, still in his greens, fell on the bed, and went to sleep again almost instantly.

After Porky left, there was a brief silence in the operating room, broken only by the intermittent sigh of the anesthesia machine.

Don looked up at the clock. "What's on the morning schedule?"

Ed had to think for a moment. He was so tired that his thoughts and reflexes had slowed down to a walking pace.

"Dr. Winter's got a common bile duct, then we have the hernia we put off from yesterday, then a gallbladder. I was going to help Porky do the hernia."

"You can do it yourself. Porky's off this service as far as I'm concerned. I'll talk to Dr. Brighton first thing in the morning, and see if he can get us a replacement. I know there's a loose body out at the V.A., a guy called Cormack they can maybe spare."

Ed shrugged. He was a kindly soul and didn't think Porky deserved to be fired, but he knew better than to argue with Don, especially at two in the morning. He was pretty sure this wasn't a sudden decision and that Don had picked his moment carefully. No senior resident in his right mind would fire his first-year resident unless he was certain of a replacement. There was simply too much work for the remaining two docs to handle.

Ed helped Don with the closure, holding the tissues together while his senior stitched up with a stout curved needle and a heavy suture material.

"Skin clips."

The scrub tech handed the instrument to Don while Ed took two small forceps with little teeth in them and held the cut edges of the skin against each other. Don put in the staples so fast Ed had trouble keeping up with him.

"Your hand's shaking," said Don. "You've been spending too much time screwing that new nurse, what's her name, Collie Zintel."

"If that did it," retorted Ed, "I'd have enough of a shake to work a road drill with the motor off."

Everybody laughed; the case was almost over, and they could all relax. Don put the skin dressing on, pulled the drapes from the patient, and he and Ed stripped off their latex gloves, soaked with sweat on the inside.

From the operating table there was a gurgling noise, then a spluttering cough as the anesthesia resident took the endotracheal tube out of the patient's windpipe, then stuck a suction tube in his mouth, getting rid of the collected mucus.

"He's okay," said the resident. "Temp's down a bit, no big deal. What do you want to hang up next in his IV?"

"Ringer's lactate," replied Don, without taking his eyes off what he was doing. He was squatting on the floor with the patient's chart on his lap, writing the postoperative orders. He was so tired he had difficulty writing, and he had to go back and check he wasn't writing everything down twice.

"He'll need some more blood, but he can get that later. Let's get a stat CBC in recovery."

The ruptured spleen they had removed was in a jar on the

windowsill. Though normally the requisition sheet that went with the specimens to pathology would be filled in by the intern, Ed picked up the form, borrowed a pen from the anesthetist, and wrote down the patient's name, hospital number, clinical summary, all the tedious details the pathologists required. If the form wasn't filled out completely, if the surgeons tried to cut corners and send the specimen with only the patient's name on it, within an hour the pathologists would be on the phone complaining to Dr. Brighton, who'd bitch and moan about it forever. It was easier to fill in the damn form and be done with it.

Don had better find a replacement for Porky, Ed thought grimly, or it'll kill us both.

He followed Don back to the locker room. They didn't speak; there was nothing to say. They changed out of their bloodstained greens.

"I'll check him," said Ed. "Why don't you go home for once?"

Don didn't answer. The two of them stopped by the recovery room. Their patient, a middle-aged man, was the only one there, looking isolated and forlorn in the big room that could hold twenty postop patients in the middle of a normal day's operating schedule.

"He's okay," said the anesthetist, sitting at the desk. "Pressure's steady, temp's coming back up."

"Good. We'd better leave him on the monitor for a while. Take care of him. I'll be in the E.R. lounge if you want me. Ed, you're going home, right?"

"Damn right," said Ed, although he knew it was hardly worth the effort. He'd barely have time to get to sleep before he'd have to get up again, but it was still better than spending a couple of hours trying to doze in the E.R. lounge. You had to be a bit of a fanatic like Don, even a touch masochistic, to do that, night after night.

But of course Don didn't have Collie Zintel waiting for him, nice and warm in bed. When he got home, Ed tiptoed in to the bedroom, feeling his way in the dark. He was so tired he hoped Collie wouldn't wake up.

She was awake, and as he climbed stiffly into bed Ed could

feel the tension and excitement in her naked body. She rolled over toward him, and he felt the heat of her as she stretched out her arms to draw him in.

"Oh, honey!" Collie's voice was husky, rough with desire. He felt her hand stroke his stubbly face, but that was just for orientation. In a moment he was lying flat on his back and she had straddled him and was guiding him into her. Ed felt her urgency, her wetness, and in the dark he heard her groan with an animal satisfaction when she had him firmly inside her. Collie never said much when they made love, and when she did, he couldn't understand what she was saying. Sometimes he had the weird feeling that she wasn't even talking to him.

She rode him like a horse, fast and deep, her arms outstretched. He could feel when she was about to come, and at the last moment, Ed pushed back up into her, hard, and felt her nails bite deep into his shoulders. Collie put her head back, and let out a long animal noise that was half scream, half howl.

She sat there, impaled, motionless, for what seemed a long time. Ed could feel the sexual energy draining from her like out of a pool. But even when she rolled off him, still without a word, Ed knew she still wasn't satisfied, that somewhere inside her lurked a wild desire he would never understand, let alone fulfill.

Celine woke in her hospital bed feeling hot and dry-mouthed, and with a grumbling discomfort in her belly. She sat up and pushed the covers off her legs and feet. From the light coming through the window opposite the bed, she guessed it must be about six. A quick look at her watch showed twenty minutes past.

She heard laughing outside the room; then the door opened suddenly and a boisterous voice shouted at her from the doorway.

"Hi, Della. Sleep good?"

A large, grinning woman in nurse's uniform came in, carrying a round tray on which were a dozen medications in small paper cups. Turning her head, the woman said something to someone in the corridor, and that was followed by more raucous laughter.

"You're in the wrong room," said Celine coldly, and the grin evaporated from the woman's face. She checked her list, and a stubborn, unpleasant expression came over her.

"Waja mean, wrong room?"

"My name isn't Della."

"Yeah, right, okay, Mrs. . . . Look, I can't pronounce that so I'm just gonna call you Della, okay? That's what they called you in report, anyway."

"No," said Celine calmly, "you'll call me by my proper name, just as I'll call you by yours, Mrs. . . ." Celine leaned forward to see the name on her badge, ". . . Koslowski."

The nurse poked a finger at her list. "That ain't no normal

American name," she grumbled. "If you don't like 'Della' I'll just call you by your room number, 427."

She placed a small paper cup with a thick whitish liquid in it on Celine's bedside table.

"Drink it," she said. "I gotta stay here until you get it down."

Celine picked it up and examined it. "What is it?"

"Looks like M.O.M. to me."

"M.O.M.?"

"Yeah, milk of magnesia, for your bowels."

"I'm sorry, but I'm not taking it." Celine put the cup back on the bedside table.

Mrs. Koslowski gasped, and her face took on a look of sheer outrage. "It's ordered for you, and you gotta take it," she said loudly, sounding quite threatening.

"Who ordered it?" asked Celine. "Nobody told me about it. And my bowels are just fine, thank you." Celine tried to make it sound light, but she was beginning to feel stubborn herself, and annoyed, too.

"Well, I don't know!" said Nurse Koslowski loudly, at the limit of her patience. "The doctors don't have time to tell everybody what their medications are. You have to take it."

Celine folded her arms.

Nurse Koslowski stormed out, saying that when she came back she'd bring the head nurse with her, or even one of the doctors.

Celine looked calm enough, but her heart was beating fast. She knew what Charles would have said: don't make such a fuss, they know what they're doing and wouldn't order something you didn't need.

Celine waited, but nothing happened, so she opened one of the two manuscripts she'd had with her in the car and read until the trolley with the breakfast trays came by.

"Sorry, Della, nothing for you today!" said the aide brightly. "You're N.P.O. for a test."

"Oh," said Celine, who could smell the coffee. "Will you keep it for me? I'll be famished when I get back."

"Sorry, Della. It all goes back to the kitchen. They'll get

you a sandwich or something when you're through." She giggled. "We've never lost a patient from starvation yet."

"What's N.P.O.?" called Celine after her retreating figure.

"Nothing by mouth," replied the girl promptly, pulling another tray out of the rack.

"Wouldn't that be N.B.M.?" cried Celine, trying to see the funny side of it but feeling rather desperate.

"Dunno," came the cheerful answer, "but that's what it means."

Celine flopped back on the bed, bemused by all this hospital jargon. N.P.O., she said aloud to herself, then turned and punched her pillow viciously. She'd show them N.P.O.!

She listened to the fading clatter of the breakfast carts as the procession made its way slowly down the corridor, with shouted greetings to the patients as they were presented with their meals. Celine slammed back on her pillows, hungry, angry, and ready for trouble, but then she must have dozed off, because she was startled when the doctors came in.

"Good morning," said Ed, standing by the bed, looking down at her. His voice was cheerful, but he looked exhausted.

"Did you sleep well?" Don looked even grimmer than he had the day before. He hadn't shaved, and the dark stubble didn't improve his appearance.

"Yes, fine, thanks." She looked through the open door, but saw no tubby intern. "Where's Porky?"

Don and Ed exchanged a quick, almost furtive look.

"He's off today," replied Don.

In fact, at that moment Porky was on the carpet in Dr. Brighton's office.

"You fell asleep *after* you were called to the emergency room?"

"Yes, sir," answered Porky miserably. "I didn't mean to. I just sat down while I was waiting for the elevator."

"You were waiting for the elevator?" Dr. Brighton's face was a picture of disbelieving contempt. "You take the elevator to emergencies these days, do you?" He wrote something on a piece of paper in front of him, then held the pencil in the air for a few moments, thinking.

"You are aware that Dr. McAuliffe has asked that you be removed from his service?"

"No. I mean yes, but I didn't know until this morning. I never explained . . ."

"This kind of situation happens only rarely, thank goodness," said Dr. Brighton angrily, chewing on the eraser end of the pencil. "But when it does, it creates havoc with the surgical rotation, not that I expect you would lose any sleep over that."

Porky, in his misery, looked up to see if Dr. Brighton was trying to make some kind of a joke, but evidently he wasn't.

"Dr. McAuliffe tells me he's been dissatisfied with your work for some time," Dr. Brighton went on. "I keep a close watch on what you people are doing, and I haven't been too pleased with your performance either."

Porky sat there, feeling unhappier than ever before in his life. It was like being under the guillotine, only the knife was coming down slowly. He mumbled something unintelligible.

"Aren't you from a medical family?" asked Brighton abruptly.

Porky nodded dumbly.

"They're going to be real pleased about this, real proud of you, aren't they, Dr. Rosen? Well, aren't they?" he repeated more loudly when Porky didn't answer.

Brighton shrugged and looked at his watch. "There's nobody I can replace you with right now, so you'll just have to go back on service," he said. "Tell Dr. McAuliffe I said so, okay?"

Porky looked at him like a whipped dog. He didn't know which of the two options was worse, being fired on the spot, or having the execution delayed. At least, with the delay, he could try to make up lost ground, work harder and try to rebuild his reputation. Maybe if he did well they might keep him on. The thought of having to go home and tell his father that he'd been fired made him feel physically ill.

Porky stood up. "Ah . . . thanks, Dr. Brighton."

"Yes, right." He watched Porky turn and head for the door. With an expression of acute distaste he said, "One more thing. I suggest you spruce up your appearance. Your obesity must make the active life of an intern difficult, and it's also unappetizing for the people working with you."

Brighton turned back to the papers on his desk.

With a leaden heart Porky walked away from the chairman's office. Now he had to go back and face Don's contemptuous expression.

He looked at his Mickey Mouse watch, then with a sudden angry gesture tore it off his wrist and stamped it into the floor. He was going to do better, make them *want* to have him on their team, and he was going to start that very moment.

Porky went up to the Harkness Wing and decided to look in on Celine. He straightened his jacket with its bulging pockets, knocked on her door, and walked in.

Celine was sitting up in bed, reading a magazine.

"Oh, Porky! I'm surprised to see you! They told me you were off today."

"I had to see Dr. Brighton, the chief of surgery," replied Porky, but his bravely horizontal gaze dropped. Celine gazed at him thoughtfully for a moment.

"By the way, Porky, did you order M.O.M. for me?"

"No. Oh dear, was I supposed to?"

Celine told him what had happened with Mrs. Koslowski.

"Let me go and find out," said Porky with unaccustomed briskness. "I'll be right back."

A few minutes later, Celine heard the sound of footsteps and Porky came in, followed by Etta Pringle, the head nurse, who was looking concernedly at the medication sheet in her hand. She asked Celine what had happened, and Celine gave her a very plain recital of the facts.

"There's no medication ordered for you," said Etta. She was obviously puzzled. "Not since your sleeping pill last night, and you didn't even want that." She eyed Celine for a moment. "I'll look into this," she said. "I'll be back in a minute."

Porky sat down in the chair.

"Won't they be looking for you?" asked Celine. She was happy to have him there, but not if it got him in trouble.

The footsteps returned, and Mrs. Kowlowski came in, red in the face and obviously furious; Etta Pringle followed right behind her, making placatory noises.

"She says she never gave you anything," said Etta hesitantly. "She just came in to say good morning. You didn't have any medication ordered, as I thought."

Celine took a deep breath. "It happened exactly the way I told you," she said.

"No it did not!" exploded Mrs. Koslowski. "I didden say nothing to her cep Hello, Good Morning, and that was it!"

"You didn't give me a little paper cup with stuff you said was M.O.M.?"

"No way. That was for Mrs. Magnusson in 429, for her bowels. She has terrible problems with her bowels. *You* don't, do you?"

"No, I don't—"

"There, you see, that proves it!" said Mrs. Koslowski triumphantly. "That proves it!"

Etta Pringle looked at Celine, and Mrs. Koslowski put her hands on her hips. She knew she had won.

"I read recently that thirty percent of all hospital medications are given wrongly," said Celine, speaking to Etta. "Do you think there's maybe the faintest chance that's what could have happened here?"

"Thirty percent!" said Etta, shocked. "Not here, not in this hospital!"

"Nationwide," said Celine, looking at Mrs. Koslowski grimly.

Mrs. Koslowski snorted and went out. Celine could hear her heavy footsteps slapping all the way back to the nurses' station.

Etta was almost in tears. "We have such a problem getting nurses," she said. "If one of them gets offended, they just leave. They don't care, they just go across town and get a job at St. Jude's Hospital."

"I'm not really worried about getting somebody else's M.O.M.," said Celine, trying to be reasonable. "I can take care of myself. What bothers me is that you're covering up a problem, and a much more dangerous mistake could happen to somebody else."

"I think it was just a misunderstanding, but I'll put it in Report, if that'll help," answered Etta, quickly recovering her poise.

At that moment Charles came through the door carrying a suitcase with the things she'd asked him to bring. He looked at Etta, then at Celine.

"I'm leaving," said Celine, making a sudden decision. "I'll explain it all to you on the way home."

"I don't think so," said Charles in a quiet, noncommittal voice. He turned courteously to Etta. "Would you mind leaving us for a few minutes?" Etta was out of the door faster than Celine thought her capable.

Charles put the suitcase on the bed and sat down on the chair by the window. "What happened?" he asked.

Celine told him. Charles shrugged angrily, incredulously. "You let that kind of trivial annoyance interfere with your treatment? Don't you realize you're ill? Seriously ill?" He paused for a second, as if he couldn't believe Celine's willfulness. "You're behaving like a spoilt, irresponsible bitch," he went on quietly but very distinctly. "You're in the hands of a surgeon with a worldwide reputation."

"I'm not complaining about him," interrupted Celine, with an ominous calm. "Anyway, whose side are you on, Charles? Mine or the hospital's? Why don't you want me to come home? Has Marion Redwing moved in already?"

Charles's movements were always smooth and unobtrusive, but the speed at which he got out of his chair surprised even Celine. He was quite obviously at the end of his patience as he faced her down.

"I don't want you to come home until you're cured," he said in the quietest of voices, but the sight of his furious, compressed lips stirred a fresh devil inside Celine.

"It's perfectly obvious," she said, her voice getting louder. "I leave, she moves in. I bet she's a better fuck than me, isn't she? After all, it must be years since anybody went into that cheesy—"

Celine never saw his hand move, but the slap across her face made a noise like a gunshot. Charles stared at her for a moment as she fell back and sat heavily on the bed, holding her hand up to her cheek, which was already bright red.

He went to the door and opened it. "Call me if you need anything else," he called back in an entirely normal voice. "I'll be home."

Wiping the floor with Porky made Henry Brighton feel a little better, but there were weightier matters on his mind than having to deal with one fat, incompetent intern. He sat at his desk for a few minutes, chewing the end of the pencil, then got up and went across the corridor to Red Felton's office. Red, an associate professor in the department, was reading the financial section of *The New York Times,* his feet up on the desk, which was clear except for a telephone and a battered, sweat-ringed old Stetson. Henry leaned against the door post and watched him for a moment, shaking his head.

"For God's sake, Red, don't you have anything better to do?"

Red pulled his paper down a couple of inches and peered at Henry over the top.

"Don't have a darn thang else, Henry. No cases, no rounds till eleven. If I'd known, I'd have stayed in bed this morning with ma honey."

Red Felton was a general surgeon who'd somehow managed to get himself on the faculty several years before. He was a perfectly capable individual, liked by the residents because he didn't bother them and revered by the students because of his cool, laid-back Texas humor and calm common sense. He was a real, down-to-earth doc who took care of patients, didn't fill the students' heads with the highfalutin cardiac electromechanics or fluid and electrolyte balance that some of the other professors talked about to demonstrate their superiority. Red could just as easily tell anecdotes about hunting bighorn sheep in Arizona as about patients he'd saved single-handedly from a grisly death.

The problem was that Red did no research and had no intention of doing any. From the beginning that had been a major source of irritation to Henry. Red took up a place on the academic payroll, but contributed nothing academic. Henry had been trying to get rid of him for years, but Red could always rally the students and the residents to his support, and Henry had never done more than bluster and finally capitulate. Now, with the likelihood of money coming in from the consortium to support his big project, Henry had a new weapon; if he couldn't get rid of this Texas buffoon, he could at least put him to work.

"Red, I had some really good news yesterday." Henry came into the room, sat in the visitor's chair, and put on an expression of forced bonhomie. He pushed a thin blond lock of hair out of his eye. Red recognized the signs and slowly put his paper down.

"You got offered a job in California?" Red's face broke into a slow grin. 'I can't tell you how pleased—"

"No. Come on, Red, be serious."

"I'm sorry," said Red, contrite. "Of course *nobody* would offer you a job in California."

"Of course not!" said Henry, irritated by Red's going on about California. "Why should I ever move? I've got everything I want here, Squeaker, the kids . . . even the lobster pots are doing well this year. Look, Red, you and Charmaine should come over for a cookout, how about Saturday? We have a whole bunch of frozen lobsters from last year we need to use up."

"Sounds great, Henry," said Red, now full of suspicion. Brighton was renowned for his stinginess, although it wasn't because of poverty; his wife, Squeaker, so named from childhood because of her voice, came from a wealthy Connecticut family. The Brightons lived in a fine old house by the water, but in an unnecessarily penny-pinching style, and never entertained unless there was someone important to impress, or something major to be gained. In fact, Henry had once been heard to tell the chairman of medicine that once the freezer was full, he'd rather give the extra lobsters to his cats than invite his staff to eat them.

"Does Squeaker know about your plans?"

"Sure, no problem. She'll go along. Okay then, for this Saturday?"

Red reached for his Stetson, sat back in his chair, and stuck the hat on the back of his head. He watched Henry with piercing, pale-blue eyes.

"Well, Henry, you sure know how to take a guy by surprise," he drawled. "I'll have to check with the little ol' woman 'fore Ah can say yea or nay. Meanwhile, why don't y'all set back and tell me what's exercising them brains cells o' yourn."

Red took a round box of Red Man chewing tobacco from his desk drawer and stuffed a wad between his cheek and gum in approved cowboy style. He knew it disgusted Henry, and that added immensely to his enjoyment.

"Well, Red, it looks as if all the work I've been doing over the last ten years on ulcerative colitis is finally coming to fruition."

"Nice choice of words, Henry. You make it sound like yo're about to have your very first bowel movement in a decade."

Henry ignored the comment. Red really was disgusting, a real purebred Texasshole.

"There's a group, a consortium, I suppose you could call it . . ." Henry explained about the huge influx of money that would be coming in to revive his long-deceased research project. "And this is something I want you to be totally involved in, Red. You're the very best here at rectal and colon biopsies, and of course you'll be coordinating with the pathology people. I'm counting on you to put this show on the road, Red. I'm sure you'll find it exciting and a real challenge. And, of course," Henry smiled knowingly, "the word gets around pretty quickly in the fast lane, Red, and your fame will spread in surgical circles all across the land."

"What's coordinatin', Henry? Isn't that what you said, coordinatin'? I don't know nothin' about that kina stuff, Henry, really."

Henry's lips tightened. He'd known Red would be no pushover; the man hated to do anything that wasn't purely clinical, but that was just too bad. He was going to have to lay down the law, show his strength and determination as head of the department.

"Red, I'm going to be quite serious now. This is a big project, and it has to be done right. I need your help because all the other faculty members are gainfully employed in other directions. I know how you feel about research, but it's an integral part of your job."

Henry paused to see what kind of effect his words were having, but Red's face was expressionless; all Henry could see was his jaw tensing rhythmically as he worked on his chaw. Henry's face deepened to a blotchy, unattractive shade of pink.

"Red, I'm not kidding. If you decide not to cooperate, I'll take your job away, so help me. There are lots of bright young surgeons out there who'd give their eyeteeth to be working here in your place, especially on a new and promising avenue of research."

"Right you are, Henry," replied Red cheerfully. "Point me in the right direction, tell me when to start, and I'll make you rich and famous, see if I don't."

He raised his paper again and resumed his perusal of the bond market reports. Henry hesitated, then left, trying to restrain his annoyance. Getting this project off the ground was going to be even more difficult than he'd anticipated. But, he realized, there was one thing in favor of a fast takeoff: there wouldn't be any NIH teams snooping around asking embarrassing questions about the usefulness and validity of his research. All he needed to do now was make sure Caleb Winter's project was turned down by the Ethics and Public Welfare Committee.

Back in his office, Henry pulled out the list of committee members. Might as well start at the top. He called old Dr. Armuth, who had been the chairman since these committees were started. He was known to be a wise old bird, but he didn't have a high opinion of surgeons, from what Henry had heard.

"Dr. Armuth?"

"Yes, this is he."

"Hi, Dr. Armuth, this is Henry Brighton."

There was no sound of recognition from the other end.

"I'm chairman of the department of surgery." That title always sounded so formal and official that Henry followed it with a short deprecatory laugh.

"Well?"

"I wanted to talk to you about Dr. Winter's application to perform pancreatic transplants on humans. Your committee will be reviewing it next Monday. There are a couple of things I'm concerned about, and I thought we might have lunch and discuss them."

"If it's that important, I'd rather you sent me a letter about it. I could then distribute it to the other members of the committee, if you don't mind."

"Actually, Dr. Armuth, what I have to say is rather confidential, and I don't want secretaries and . . ."

"Bring it over yourself, then. What was your name, did you say? Brigham?"

"No, Dr. Armuth, it's Brighton, Henry Brighton. I'm chairman . . ."

"Yes, I heard you the first time. We don't hear much in the research line from your department these days, except for that young chap Winter. He must be the light shining in the wilderness, eh?"

"Well, I wouldn't call it a wilderness, exactly," protested Henry.

"No, I don't imagine you would, would you?" Old Dr. Armuth cackled at the other end. "Well, I don't want to keep you from whatever branch of your blood sport you happen to favor, Dr. Brigham. I'll be expecting that letter."

"It's not something I could easily put in a letter," said Henry, beginning to feel desperate. "I . . ."

"I know it's hard for you surgeons to put pen to paper," said Dr. Armuth understandingly. "Get somebody to help you. Now I really must go. I have patients waiting."

Henry slammed the phone down. That patronizing old buzzard!

He was about to go down the list, call everybody he could get hold of, when his secretary came in with a message that his wife was on the office line and there was something wrong with the extension, so he'd have to take it in her office.

"Hi, Squeaker," he said querulously. And all she wanted was for him to pick up some margarine on his way home. They were having broiled fish because of his stomach, and she always put a little dab of margarine on the top.

"Please, for God's sake, don't call me here for things like that," he told her wearily. "You know how busy I am." He looked suspiciously at his secretary, but she was putting something away in a filing cabinet. "By the way," he said, "the Feltons are coming over for a cookout on Saturday. No, I'm not joking. You know those lobsters at the bottom of the freezer, the ones left over from last year? Yes, right. Well, it's not certain, Red has to talk to his wife."

Henry put down the phone and turned to what he called his operations center, a specially constructed cork-backed chart that almost filled the side wall of the outer office. On it, in various colors, were the assignments of all the residents and interns on the surgical service. This wall chart was one of Henry's proudest achievements. Each resident on the surgical service, including the affiliated Veteran's Administration hospital in nearby West Coventry, was represented on the chart by a different-colored square. The time frame on the board was four years, so the entire career of each resident could be traced; every rotation, vacation, research assignment was recorded in Henry's meticulous, tiny script. Each colored rectangle was crafted with agonizing precision, and Henry looked forward to the last week of each month when he would spend several hours standing on a chair, with his colored pencils and eraser in hand, updating the chart and posting the next month's assignments. Very rarely, and usually when other things were intruding into his mind, he would make an error, which could usually be erased, but if it was more serious, he would take a scalpel and wholly excise the offending square, then glue in an exactly matching area of blank squared paper.

In the last days of the month, the residents and interns made their way up to the office to find out from the board what their next month's assignment was.

Henry stared at the board for a full ten minutes, while his secretary did some typing, answered the phone, walked around him.

"Windsor and Newtons, please," he barked finally, and she sprang up, hurried to a filing cabinet and pulled out a long tin box of colored pencils, then stood at attention beside him.

"Emerald Green." His voice was powerful, commanding. He didn't look at her, just stuck out his hand for it. She quickly selected the right color, took out the green pencil, and slapped it into his hand, just as she imagined an operating room nurse would hand him a scalpel.

He worked for several minutes, so absorbed that the tip of his tongue stuck out of the right corner of his mouth. Then he made a faint, irritated clucking noise.

"Eraser."

Twenty minutes later, he stood back and admired his hand-iwork. It was a wonderful system, and Henry always made a point of explaining it in detail to visiting professors. He'd heard that his method was now being used in a department of surgery somewhere in Minnesota, and Henry was seriously thinking of applying for a patent.

"Well, that takes care of that," he said with satisfaction, tearing his gaze away from the brightly patterned chart. The secretary put the pencils back in their box in the order Henry insisted on, starting with the reds, going through the yellows, greens, and blues and finishing up with the violet, in the same order as the spectrum of the rainbow.

With a considerable amount of creative juggling and imag-inative reassignment, Henry had been able to eliminate Porky Rosen's Chrome Yellow. As of next month, Porky's position would be take by a new Emerald Green square that repre-sented Dr. Denis Cormack, presently an Aquamarine at the Veteran's Administration hospital.

Henry pulled himself away from the chart only when his secretary told him he was wanted on the phone.

Porky walked toward the operating room, mulling over what he was going to have to do. Of course he'd have to lose weight, but that should be easy, he'd done it before. More important

was to learn to recognize problems before they became problems, the way both Don and Ed did. For instance, on the day
before Grand Rounds, they always remembered to collect
X-rays of patients to be discussed the next day and put them
safely away in the locker room. Porky, on the other hand,
would suddenly discover that he didn't have any of them and
didn't know where they were. He'd rush around, pestering
the ward secretaries and the people in the x-ray department,
and of course whatever he was supposed to be doing at the
time didn't get done.

His memory was another problem. Porky certainly tried to
remember what he was supposed to do, order tests, check on
pathology reports, and collect information for rounds, but
somehow he always forgot something. In an effort to coerce
him into better habits, Don had started to make out a list,
which he handed to Porky every morning. Even that didn't
always work, at least in part because Porky was slow in his
work. It took him longer to draw blood, start an IV, or do a
lumbar puncture than it should, partly because he wasn't
technically very adept, but also because he didn't have the
God-given ability to do things both well and fast.

Anyway, things are going to be different from now on,
thought Porky, full of new resolve. He'd try to stay ahead of
the game instead of tagging along behind as he'd done up to
now.

Don and Ed were in the locker room, changing into their
greens.

"Hi," said Porky, feeling embarrassed. "Dr. Brighton said I
had to stay on the service because he doesn't have anybody
to replace me. Sorry."

Don shrugged. "That's okay with me. Why don't you help
Ed with that hernia." He turned to Ed. "I'll go dictate some
discharge summaries," he said. "I have a stack of them so
high I can't even see over the top."

"Don . . ." said Porky faintly. Don paused at the door and
turned to look at him. "I'm really going to put in the effort,
Don. Really. I think I know what I'm doing wrong, and I'll
correct it. I promise."

"Good. We'll try to help you make it work." Don didn't

sound very positive about it, but he could hardly be expected to under the circumstances.

But Porky was absolutely determined to show him.

"Well, don't just stand there like a limp dick," said Don brusquely. "Get changed into your greens and help the nurses position the patient."

Porky hurried to his locker. That was exactly the kind of thing he had to learn to do, go and position the patient before anybody reminded him. He had to learn to see ahead, do things before he was told to.

Ed grinned and threw him a pair of large O.R. green pants and a large shirt.

"Welcome back, Porks."

"Ed?" Porky asked tentatively, expecting criticism. Sometimes when he had a question, Don or Ed would laugh at him incredulously as if they couldn't believe he didn't already know the answer. "Ed, what's a Whipple?"

"It's the biggest operation in general surgery," Ed replied, attaching his watch to the shirt of his greens with a safety pin. 'It's usually done for cancer of the pancreas."

Porky stooped, waiting for more information.

"Aside from taking out the pancreas, you have to remove the gallbladder, a good part of the stomach, the duodenum . . ." Porky's eyes grew bigger as Ed went on with his description.

"It sounds awful," he said. "How on earth do you ever get the patient back together again?"

Ed explained how parts of the intestine were rerouted and how the ends were joined in a complex anastomosis.

"I think I'd rather die of the cancer than have that done to me," said Porky.

"The results aren't even that good," confessed Ed. "They nearly all die within a year." He hesitated, then went on, "You see, Porks, a Whipple's a kind of badge of manhood for a surgeon. Every senior resident dreams of doing at least one before he finishes the program. If Don doesn't get one soon, he probably won't get an opportunity to do one for years after, maybe never."

"Isn't there any other way? I mean to treat cancer of the pancreas? Isn't there any treatment that's less destructive?"

"Well, funny you should mention that, Porks," said Ed. "The first person to do that will probably be our own Dr. Winter, and the word is he's about ready to go. His idea is to take out the tumor, radiate what's left of the pancreas with high-frequency microwaves to kill off any residual tumor cells, then put in a transplant to take over the function of the destroyed pancreas."

"Wow!" said Porky, awed.

"Yeah, transplants from monkeys." Ed looked suddenly thoughtful. "I wonder if he has Della Roach in mind." He twisted the padlock on his locker, securing it firmly. "Now will you get your ass on deck and go help move that patient?"

"Bakke dilators, please, Collie."

Collie Zintel passed Caleb a slender instrument with a flexible, olive-shaped tip.

"Let's start with the smallest size, Collie, if you don't mind."

"Sorry."

How could he tell? she wondered. There wasn't even a millimeter's difference between the one she'd passed him and the smallest size.

From across the table, Ed grinned encouragingly at her without reducing his pull on the retractors. Dear Ed, he was so unflappable, so unwaveringly good-natured it sometimes made her want to scream. And their relationship should have been so completely perfect—Edward van Stamm represented everything she could have ever wanted, the three S's every unmarried female nurse dreamed about, Security, Status, and Sex. Well, she wasn't so sure about the Sex.

In just about every way the two of them got on beautifully together, and, although she didn't really dwell on it because it wasn't too important, as a doctor's wife she would immediately leap up several social levels. Her own parents were so in favor of Ed she could hardly believe the two of them had actually agreed on something. Collie couldn't even remember when that had last happened. From the time of her earliest memories her parents had fought, and Christ how they fought! Not just verbally either, although they shouted enough for the police to make the Zintels' place almost a routine stop. Her father was not very big, not big like Ed, for instance, but he had strong muscles and a kind of dark, wiry, quick toughness about him.

"Let's have that probe again, I can't feel the stone."

Caleb had one hand inside the belly and the other was manipulating a long curved instrument designed for the removal of stones inside the common bile duct. He knew the stone was there from the ultrasound and the X-rays; about the size of a pea, it was blocking the passage of bile from the liver to the intestine, and the patient was getting progressively more jaundiced as the bile backed up.

Collie had the probe in Caleb's hand almost before his words were out, and his eyes crinkled appreciatively behind the mask.

"You're okay, Collie, I don't care what Ed says about you!" Caleb didn't stop working when he talked. Collie let out a little gasp and stared hard at Ed in simulated indignation. Little mimes of this kind were part of the secret life of the operating room; everybody enjoyed them because they were a sanctioned relief of tension. But she couldn't explain that to her nonmedical friends; they all imagined that working in an operating room was quite different from the reality of it, and they remained in some awe of her.

Now followed a quiet, rather relaxed part of the operation, and although half of Collie's brain kept second-by-second track of what was going on, of what Dr. Winter would be needing next, whether she'd need more sutures or an instrument not on the table, the other half slipped back to thinking her private thoughts. She frequently did this during long and uneventful operations, and usually her thoughts slipped back to her childhood years.

Life at home hadn't been easy for her, but it had been a lot worse for Sandra, her little sister, who got beaten a lot more than she did. Collie wasn't sure why, but her father seemed to want to take it out more on Sandra, and many were the mornings when Collie went to school without her sister because of her bruises. Neither of the children thought too much about it: Life was just the way it was; they had nothing better to compare it with, as they weren't allowed to visit other children in their homes. It wasn't until much later that Collie realized that her father wasn't just *beating* Sandra . . .

"I think I have it," said Caleb, looking at Don across the table, but Don could tell from his eyes that Winter didn't see him; all the sensory input at the moment was from his fingertips. "If this were your case, Don," said Caleb, "what would you do now?"

"Irrigate the duct, make sure there aren't any more stones," said Don promptly.

"And check the gallbladder," chipped in Porky, "because that's where the stone came from originally."

"Right," said Caleb. "But of course this man had his gallbladder taken out five years ago."

Porky blushed violently under his mask. He'd spoken without thinking again. Porky had taken the patient's case history last night when the patient came in, and knew it was out. He shook his head with self-despising frustration.

"There's one additional thing I always do," Caleb went on. "I check the stump of the cystic duct. Sometimes if it's left long a stone can develop in the remnant, then travel down into the common duct." Like a conjurer, Caleb pulled a small smooth brown stone out of the wound and opened his hand.

"Porky, how can you tell from looking at this stone that it hadn't just come out of the gallbladder?"

Porky shivered at the thought that he might be about to make an ass of himself again. "It doesn't have facets," he replied hesitantly, "the way they do when a bunch of them get compressed together in the gallbladder." He looked at Caleb with a mute appeal, and his lips moved. Please God, he was saying silently, let me be right, just for once.

"Correct," said Caleb. "Porky, we'll make a surgeon of you yet."

Porky caught Don's eye. "Don't count on it," was its unspoken message.

Collie held the specimen jar out for the stone, and Caleb dropped it in. Collie screwed the lid on and handed the jar to her circulator. Next he'd be needing the irrigation, then a T-tube. She had a selection of sizes ready. The 0000 silk sutures were also ready, the tiny curved needles of the first two already on their needle holders. That was the gauge size Dr. Winter always used, so there was no point cluttering up her Mayo stand with stuff she knew he wouldn't need. Collie was set for the next several minutes, barring accidents, and these rarely happened when he was operating.

Collie had always been jealous of Sandra, maybe because her father never paid as much attention to her. Collie would have dearly loved to be the one in the locked bedroom, not for what was happening, because that was gross, but because she would have had his full attention. Once, outside the bedroom door, Collie had tried to hammer a nail into the side of her head. Her mother smacked her really hard for that when she came out. "You'll die if you do that!" she screamed at Collie, who hadn't realized people could actually kill themselves. Since then the whole idea of death had intrigued and attracted Collie. And she thought about it a lot. There were a lot of different ways of dying.

Dr. Winter stepped back to wash his gloves in a metal bowl of warm saline, and Ed took the opportunity to smile at Collie and make a kissy-face under his mask. All that affection! It was hardly a criticism she could levy against him, but although she knew how ungrateful she was being, it did make her feel irritated and, yes, bored.

Caleb came back to the table. He started to move fast, now that the stone was out, and Collie was kept fully occupied for the next half-hour. Then they had to wait for the X-ray. The hospital still had an old-fashioned system where a portable machine was wheeled in, and X-ray plates were pushed into a slot under the operating table. It was tedious, and wasted a lot of time while it was being set up. Finally the pictures were taken, and the tech brought them back into the operating room and flipped them up on the fluorescent screen. Caleb, Don, Ed, and Porky gathered around it, their hands clasped in front of them to avoid contamination.

"Looks okay to me," said Caleb.

"No residual stones, and the contrast drops right into the duodenum," said Don.

"If it's okay with you guys," said Ed, "it's okay with me."

They all looked at Porky in a joking kind of way.

"Well, I'm not so sure . . ." he said, peering at the films. Everybody laughed, and Porky grinned happily to himself. Maybe some day he might really be accepted in this magic circle.

After the case was finished, Porky stayed to write the post-op orders. He took a pen from the drawer of the anesthesia machine.

"Let's see," he thought. "Pain medication, fluids . . ." He turned to the anesthesia resident, a tiny, fragile-looking Asian woman.

"How much fluid did you give him during the case?" he asked her.

"Two liter, Pokky," she said, smiling at him. "One Ringer's, one nommal saline." She pronounced "Ringer's" as "Ling-er's."

"IV 5% dextrose in water, 1 liter," wrote Porky. "Run at 125 mls per hour . . ." Pain medication. He'd almost forgotten that. "Demerol," he wrote, "100mg IM q3h prn." That was the shorthand jargon for one hundred milligrams of Demerol to be given not more often than every three hours by intra-muscular injection, if the patient needed it. Antibiotics had been started the day before, so Porky just continued them. He had finished writing the orders into the order sheet when the orderly came in pushing a stretcher, which he lined up next to the table.

"Hands, please!" cried Collie, and every available person, about five of them, grabbed the edge of the sheet lying under the still-sleeping patient.

"One, two, three, up!" The patient went up and on to the stretcher, light as a feather under their combined lifting power. Porky accompanied the patient to the recovery room. Once he had been safely handed over to the staff there and Porky was satisfied that he was stable, Porky headed toward the O.R. lounge where the rest of the team would be having coffee.

There was a visitor in the lounge, sitting on the old sofa; it was Milo Zagros, who occasionally visited to talk to Caleb, drink the coffee, which was better than the lab brew, and generally to check out the scene. Sometimes he brought a box of doughnuts with him; he didn't belong to this group, and he had an Eastern European sensitivity about eating other people's food. Milo was telling them about a talk on immunology he'd once given a group of pig farmers back in Yugoslavia, and the kind of questions they'd asked him. The mood was cheerful; everyone seemed relaxed until out of the corner of his eye Milo saw Collie Zintel staring at him. She was new on Caleb's service, and he'd only glimpsed her a couple of times before, but now there was something so primitive in the way her gaze was fixed on him that Milo recognized the contact instantly. He had this effect, an instant animal attraction, on certain women, and when it happened it was unmistakable. This time, Milo felt the jolt of it right through his system. She came a little closer, as if drawn by a magnet; Milo kept on with his story, not even looking at her, but he could feel the invisible electricity that crackled between them. Nobody else had noticed. Milo's gaze traveled over to Ed, who was laughing at his description of the pig farmers who'd got up in a body halfway through his talk to watch a huge boar mount an equally gigantic sow. But now, Milo's senses were screaming at him as if he'd had a massive injection of amphetamine. Collie was edging imperceptibly closer, but he calmly continued his pig-farm story. Without even looking at her Milo knew that he was gradually, unmistakably reeling her in.

Porky came in, and had been in the lounge only a few moments, pouring himself some coffee with a spoonful of Coffeemate, when he sensed what was happening between Milo and Collie, and he had to hold back a gasp of surprise. Porky liked Ed, who'd always been good-natured with him and overlooked many of the awful things he'd done. For God's sake, Ed, he wanted to shout, don't you see what's happening to your girl? Porky kept his eyes away from them, and looked at the faces of the others. Nobody seemed to have noticed anything. Maybe I've got it all wrong, he thought. He swallowed his coffee and ran. He looked in the recovery room to check the man they'd just operated on. Everything seemed to be under control. The nurse had just taken his blood pressure, and the monitor showed nothing in his cardiogram to get excited about, just a few extra beats from time to time, no big deal.

Back in the lounge, Collie Zintel gulped down her coffee, unable to keep her eyes off Milo. There was something about his maleness, his sexual arrogance, that stirred a memory from far back in her childhood. She sensed an undercurrent of violence in his restless smooth movements that affected her in the most basic, instinctive, animal way. She went to drop her empty Styrofoam cup in the garbage can under the coffee machine, which was right next to his chair. Close to him, Collie could almost feel the tension between her body and Milo's, and it drained the willpower out of her like current out of a battery. She knew he felt it too. He looked up, just for a second, and stared at her, then almost imperceptibly he moved his head. Get back into the O.R, the movement said. I'll come right after you.

Collie turned, shaking, and saw Ed flash his open, cheerful smile at her. It felt almost like a blow. He was suddenly a stranger, gone forever. Collie expected to feel some kind of compassion now for him, but there was none. All she felt was a hot, aching desire. She wanted Milo, she could feel him ramming into her without mercy, she could hear her own screams ... Collie almost ran out, frightened by the strength of her reactions. As she hurried back to the operating room she was aware of the sliding of parts of her anatomy she hadn't even realized moved when she walked.

Caleb stood up, and the others followed suit. Caleb never liked to stay in one place for very long. He turned to Don McAuliffe.

"Rounds at five, okay?"

Don nodded. Caleb had noticed a kind of unwillingness about him recently, a sullenness he tried to disguise. Caleb was not one to tolerate that kind of nonsense; there was too much work to be done.

"Is that a problem?" he asked sharply, and Don made a small, surprised movement.

"No, sir," he said, standing to attention. "We'll be there, ready, willing, and able."

Caleb looked around to see if Milo was going back to the lab, but he had already left.

Milo was heading fast toward the operating room. His eyes flickered around, noting the rooms leading off the corridor, the autoclave room, the equipment storage area.

Collie had taken the pads off the operating table before washing them and she was facing the window on to the corridor, as he knew she would. He made a small, imperious sign at her to come out. She glanced around guiltily, but none of her coworkers had noticed. Her heart beating fast, she came out into the corridor.

"Get in there," he said, pointing at the door of the instrument room. He followed her in and closed the door.

"You're not wearing a scrub suit," she said in a small voice. "You can't—"

He put out his hand and pushed her against a tall glass-fronted cabinet full of shiny instruments. His hand slid all the way down the front of her thin green scrub shirt, and he grabbed her hard. Collie gasped, and felt her knees buckling.

"I'd take you right here," he growled, his face right up against hers. He called her a name that made her gasp. "But I'll just make you wait till tonight. Don't wear any makeup or underwear. Where d'you live?"

Collie told him.

"By yourself?"

She nodded, not trusting her voice.

"Be ready at eight." His hands slid up, felt through the thin cotton of her shirt for her nipples, and he gave them a hard, simultaneous twist which passed like jolting electric shocks right through her.

"Now go back to your work," he ordered, stepping back. Collie leaned against the cabinet, shaking like a leaf. "Okay," she whispered, "I'll be ready."

Collie stumbled back into the operating room and spent the next hour tidying up, in such a daze that she didn't even hear the other nurses speaking to her.

Celine walked into the bathroom adjoining her room and looked at her face in the mirror. Charles's finger marks showed up red, and her cheek was already puffy. Well, that was it. The end. Good-bye Charles. A fury grew in her. He'd never struck her before, never. As soon as she was out of the hospital, she'd see her attorney and start divorce proceedings. Then she remembered that Charles was her attorney, and laughed in spite of herself. Could he represent her against him? No, she'd get somebody from New York, maybe a woman. Celine knew a couple of feminist lawyers who'd take up her case as if they were going on a crusade.

Celine shrugged that thought aside and looked at her watch. It was a good time to call the office. Her face still stinging, she picked up the bedside phone, read the instructions on how to get an outside line, and dialed the number of her office.

"Marilyn? I'd like to speak to Tom." She looked at her blue slippers up on the bed in front of her while she waited. "Tom? I'm in the hospital. Yes, New Coventry. I may be here a while. No, I don't know how long. Listen, what's happening with our friend Anwar Al-Khayib?"

"He says he'll give us free rent for six months," replied Tom, "as long as we sign a five-year lease, then the rent will be ten percent above what we're paying now, and going up by twelve percent a year."

Celine smiled. "How about the moving costs?"

She heard Tom hesitate for a second. "He wants to discuss

that with you in person. He says you're one tough cookie and wants to take you to lunch."

"No way," said Celine firmly. "Get back to him and get an answer. Tell him your boss delegates details like this. If he agrees to pay moving costs the deal's on."

"And if he doesn't agree?"

"Of course it's still on! Where could we ever get a deal like that again?" Celine reached over for a thick folder on the bedside table. "Now, about Jay Wiseman's manuscript. I finished it this morning. You can tell him it's terrific but a little sloppy. Like when Sir Desmond Crane is late for Queen Victoria's coronation and jumps into a hansom cab, he wouldn't lean forward to shout at the driver, because in a hansom the driver sat behind the passengers. There are too many things like that; he needs to do his homework."

Tom promised to call the author and tell him. "There's a couple of new manuscripts you have to read," said Tom. "And a new biography of Giovanni de Seingalt; Virago wants to sell us the U.S. rights."

"Send them up by messenger," said Celine. "I don't have much else to do here."

After putting the phone down, Celine lay back on the bed, feeling the energy draining out of her. Her anger was gone already, and she felt the fear of the upcoming operation crawling back into her bones. Charles wouldn't be coming back to visit her, she felt sure of that, and the thought of being alone in the hospital made her shake the tears angrily out of her eyes. She thought about Charles going off to Atlanta with Marion, and in spite of her anger, she felt the sadness diffusing gradually through her. She'd been married to him a long time.

There was a firm knock on the door. After a short delay, and to Celine's utter surprise, Dan Carfield walked in, dressed as usual in a brown woolen suit and carrying his heavy ironwood stick. A candy-striper came in with him and installed the old man in the window chair.

"What's the matter with you?" he asked gruffly, looking at her from under his thick white eyebrows. "Charles said you had something on your pancreas."

Celine told him what had happened. Dan, founder of the publishing house of Fortman and Carfield, was a particular friend of hers. She'd first visited him in his reclusive Greenwich estate about a year ago to ask his opinion of a medieval manuscript Charles had given her, and had seen the old man again on several occasions. Once he took her to see his collection of ancient manuscripts on the top floor of the Fortman and Carfield building in Manhattan, and when they got back, Dan was ready to talk business with her. He sat her down on her favorite window seat in his home.

"You've heard of Derek Krueger, the present CEO of Fortman and Carfield," said Dan. "Well, he's an accountant, doesn't know a damn thing about books, and he's driving the company straight into the ground."

Celine was aware of the present sorry state of Fortman and Carfield, and felt badly for Dan, who with Simon Fortman had built it up into a model publishing house forty years before.

"What the company needs is to be taken over by a class outfit and have it restored to its rightful place," Dan went on. "And that could be done by a much smaller corporation. The key here would be leadership, not size." He stopped his pacing, and faced Celine. "And if you're interested, this is how you could go about it."

He put the whole thing in a nutshell. "I own thirty-five percent of the voting stock," he told her. "The only other big shareholder is Astrid Fortman, Simon's widow. She has around thirty-nine percent, maybe forty percent. The rest is in small holdings all over the place. What I will do is give you an option on all my shares, at today's market price." Dan laughed, not a friendly laugh. "That damned fool Krueger, he's so busy publishing pornographic rubbish he doesn't even know the assets of his company. Just after the war I spent a summer going around abbeys and monasteries in Europe and bought all those illuminated manuscripts for almost nothing. At that time, they didn't have enough money to buy food. Anyway, the collection belongs to the company, although I'm the only one who knows anything about its value. Every year Krueger reports it in the balance sheet as Miscellaneous Assets, value $100,000, about twice what I paid for it. It's worth now, conservatively, around 18 million."

Celine's mouth opened slightly but she didn't say anything.

"And that's not all. We own the copyright to many of the books we published, bought them outright from some very famous authors. Now that Krueger's busy putting out that rubbish, he doesn't even know he's sitting on a gold mine."

"Why didn't you and Mrs. Fortman get together and put in your own man?" asked Celine. "Between you, you'd have around seventy-five percent of the stock."

Dan shook his head angrily. "She takes no interest in the company at all. When Simon died, she upped and went off to England with her clock collection. Clocks! Can you imagine?"

Dan's contempt was so open that Celine wanted to laugh, but she didn't dare. "I even called her up to make an offer for her shares," he went on, "but she just hung up on me. Actually, we never did get along." Dan grinned, and Celine could see that he never cared much about who liked him and who didn't.

"Anyway," he went on, "the stock is selling dirt-cheap now. You should be able to get the additional sixteen percent you need easily enough on the open market. When you're ready, you take up the options on my stock, and you'll have fifty-one percent."

When she got home, amazed at her good fortune, she recounted the entire story to Charles and to Oncle Didi, who happened to be visiting on one of his regular trips to the U.S.

"Just be careful, my dear," growled Oncle Didi, sitting by the pool in a cane chair that creaked under his weight. "Are you quite sure you can trust this man Carfield?"

"I can vouch for him," said Charles. "He has an impeccable reputation."

"Imagine that old woman being interested in clocks," murmured Didier, almost to himself, at the very moment Catherine appeared through the french doors to announce that dinner was served.

Dan was smiling at her from his chair by the window, and Celine thought he looked relieved. "You can't look so attractive and be very sick," he said. "How long do you think you'll be in here?"

They talked about that for a while; Dan had a few funny anecdotes about hospitals, and he amused Celine with them.

Just before getting up to leave, Dan said, "Sorry to intrude business at this time, but I think you should hurry your stock purchases in Fortman and Carfield; I know you're still short about three percent of what you need, but Gottlieb Ludman tells me that certain stock movements are causing him some concern."

"There's not much I can do," Celine replied. "I know Mr. Ludman's doing his best. I imagine it'll all be settled in a couple of weeks."

Dan looked at Celine's face. "Is everything all right with you and Charles?" he asked abruptly, getting out of his chair.

"No, it isn't," replied Celine. "We're getting divorced."

"Does he know that?" Dan looked shocked.

"If he doesn't, he will soon."

Dan looked at her for a few moments. "These are difficult times, my dear," he said, and bent down stiffly to kiss her. Then he smiled and picked up his stick. "And now I'm leaving. Don't worry, I'm sure everything's going to work out all right for you."

· · · · · · · *PART TWO* · · · ·

Collie Zintel's stomach was a tight ball of fear and anticipation when she opened the door for Milo. He pushed past her into the living room, and suddenly Collie felt short of breath, and her heart was pounding as if she'd had three cups of coffee too many. Since early that afternoon, her every thought had been of Milo, his body, his hands, his fists. They were not very big, but hard, sinewy, and hairy. She didn't have to be told what he was going to do with them. The thought made her weak at the knees, and she bit the side of her own hand in an ecstasy of sexual terror.

"Take off your clothes," said Milo, not even looking at her. He already had his shirt off, and stood there for her to see, his pectorals flexing, his tight abdominal muscles separated by a hard central furrow lined with black hair. Now his eyes were fixed on her body, staring at it with a kind of possessive insolence, as if she were a slave and he was deciding whether to buy her or not.

"Hurry up!" he warned, coming toward her with his hand raised. She had slipped out of her blouse and had both hands behind her back when he slapped her face hard, smack, smack, the second time with the back of his hand. Collie first felt the sting of pain, then a surge of wild, primitive excitement. Milo stood back and slipped out of his remaining clothes. His expression made the fear rise in her like the mercury in a thermometer, but it was a fear mixed with a fierce exhilaration.

He came toward her and she heard the ripping noise as her skirt came off. She had obeyed his instructions and worn no makeup or underwear, and in a moment she was standing naked, feeling the freedom, the vulnerability of exposure and then a yearning desire for him to punish her for all the bad things she'd ever done in her life.

Now he was calling her dreadful names, and she thrilled with the shock of hearing the words. He made her repeat them, shout them back at him, tell him what kind of filth she was.

He caught her by the hair and pulled her roughly down on to the bed.

"Louder, I can't hear you," he shouted, his face right next to her. He sank his teeth into the soft tissues of her neck, and she knew what it would look like in the morning, but she didn't care, she wanted more. And now she was shouting too, and writhing and twisting with the delicious pain of him inside the farthest depths of her. And then she felt his fingers coming around her neck and she took a deep breath and shouted to him to kill her, now, because this was how she wanted to die, in the wildness of her ecstasy. He started to put on the pressure, and he couldn't stop. Something was driving him to some ultimate orgasm where she would finally lie still with him in the never-ending bliss of death.

When he came, Collie's lips were blue and her eyes were bulging. She finally managed to take a breath, and wheezed and choked for several minutes. Grabbing him hard she pulled herself up against him as soon as she was able to breathe properly.

"Next time," she said, her voice so hoarse she could hardly speak, "next time, Milo, I want you to go all the way."

Collie struggled out of the bed and tottered to the bathroom, her breathing rattling and wheezing so hard that she had trouble even coughing. Lying there in the disordered bed, Milo started to shake uncontrollably. He was afraid—afraid of himself, terrified of what he had almost done. He was no stranger to passionate sex, and was used to knocking his girls around a bit from time to time, but that was as far as it had ever gone. Nobody'd ever got more than a few mild bruises or a bite mark here and there. Nobody'd ever got hurt.

But Collie . . . with her, a red-rimmed passion, a fury, had swelled up inside him, and almost consumed both of them. Milo recognized now that he had almost killed her, and that she had egged him on to destroy her. At the thought, Milo started to shiver again. He could hear Collie coughing in the bathroom, great retching coughs, and he felt a faint residual ripple of that homicidal passion.

He got out of bed and dressed quickly. Common sense urged him to get out, but the memory of Collie's firm, rounded breasts and creamy thighs kept him there in thrall, caught between his hot sexual urge and his fear about what he might do to her. What was it about Collie? Had she really wanted to die right then, at the moment of orgasm? Or had she been like him, merely caught up in the heat of the moment? Milo knew from the sounds coming from the bathroom that she would be coming out very soon, and found himself wanting her again. The desire he had for her was frightening; he wanted to crash into the bathroom, drag her from wherever she was sitting, from whatever she was doing, pull her by the hair into the bedroom, and throw her bodily on the bed. This time he would really . . .

Milo sat down abruptly and put his head between his hands, and his inner voice shouted, *Get out of here! Run! Get away from her!*

The toilet flushed. Milo scrambled into his shoes. Luckily they were loafers—he'd never have managed to tie the laces.

"I have to go," he said through the door. His voice had an unnatural tone. "I'll call you."

"Wait a minute." Collie's voice was an unrecognizable croak. She came out, still naked, and Milo's insides did a complete somersault. Her body was beautiful, but it was the purple bruises on her neck and breasts that turned him on again. Just looking at them gave him a surging sense of power, the power of a master over a slave.

"Collie, I have to go, I can't—" Milo was stuttering.

"That's all right, Milo." Collie smiled. She seemed serene, completely at ease. "It was beautiful." She coughed harshly again, and Milo felt the surge returning.

"I'll call you," she said when Milo was at the door, and he knew he would never be able to resist her summons.

He stood still once he was on the other side of the door, gradually realizing that he was no longer the aggressor but the potential victim. His heart was beating so loudly he was sure it could be heard at the end of the corridor.

"What am I going to do? What the hell am I going to do with this situation?" He asked himself the same question again and again, all the way back to his apartment.

"Here is a perfectly good Whipple," said Don, referring to Celine de La Roche. He was sitting glumly in the doctors' lounge off the emergency room, waiting for the casualties from an automobile accident. "And of all the hospitals in the U.S. of A. that I could have worked in, this is the one that's developed an alternative procedure."

"If Dr. Winter decides to do a Whipple," said Porky, trying to be helpful. "I'm sure he'll get you to do it with him. I feel it in my bones."

"I'd want to hear from something nearer the surface," snapped Don. He was in a thoroughly bad mood at the prospect of losing his Whipple. He'd spent the lunch hour at the computer unsuccessfully hunting through the medical admissions to find another potential candidate. He'd done just about every kind of case in the general surgical repertoire, total thyroidectomies, colectomies, abdomino-perineal resections, everything except the highest and hardest peak of them all, the Whipple.

Bob Aminoke came into the lounge, glowing with joviality. His movements were quick, hyperactive, and Porky again noticed a fine beading of sweat on his forehead.

"Well, you all look as if you're going to a wake," he said. He grinned at Don. "Or is it because you won't be doing that Whipple?"

"How the hell do you always know everything that's going on?" asked Don, irritated. "Down here, you're not even really part of the hospital."

"Did you ever tell your boys about Graham Porter?" asked Bob, grinning and nodding at Ed and Porky.

"No, I didn't," snapped Don.

"Well, chickens," said Bob, "just you gather round and lis-

ten to Mama Hen tell you a story." Bob sat down with a
thump in an easy chair, and Ed and Porky exchanged glances.
The wall of a siren was heard for a moment in the distance,
and Don moved restlessly.

"Once upon a time," said Bob, in that musical singsong
voice of his, "in fact about three years ago, there was this
senior resident called Graham Porter . . ."

Don stood up and walked toward the door. "Page me when
they come in," he said to Ed. "I'll be in the library."

Bob ignored him and went on. "When he was a junior, this
guy Porter boasted he'd do three Whipples before he finished
his residency, but of course nobody took him seriously. A
month before he was due to finish, he'd done two, and let me
tell you, chickens, that was some stupendous achievement."

Porky pulled the stack of patient cards out of his pocket
and started to go through them as he listened.

"Porter wasn't satisfied with that," went on Bob, "no sir. A
week later, this wrinkled old woman with a CA of the pancreas suddenly appeared on his surgical floor, complete with
X-rays to prove her diagnosis. Faster than a speeding bullet,
they had the old broad flat out on the operating table, and
five hours later Porter had his third Whipple under his belt."

"How did she make out?" asked Porky without looking up.
Bob shrugged.

"Who cares? Anyway, all was well until the whole story
came out." Bob got up and strode restlessly around the small
room for a few moments, while Ed and Porky watched him
with clinical interest.

"Porter had a friend over at St. Jude's, downtown," went
on Bob, "a medical resident who'd happened to mention they
had a CA of the pancreas who was to be operated on in a
couple of days. That same evening, Porter and his junior resident drove downtown to St. Jude's wearing their white jackets. They got there just before eleven, when the nursing shifts
changed and the nurses were in report. Porter left his car
outside, telling the cop on duty he'd be back in five minutes
as they were transferring a patient. Then the two of them
went calmly up to the surgical floor, found the old lady in her
bed, told her politely that she was being transferred, and put

her in a wheelchair. Porter even remembered to pick up her clothes, her X-rays, and the stuff in her bedside table." Bob grinned. "Now that really showed class. Anyway, he covered her knees with a blanket they'd brought with them, and wheeled her off down the corridor. The old lady was a bit confused, but apparently not frightened, and the cop helped put her into the back of Porter's car. They admitted her through the emergency room, and before you could say 'Lindbergh Baby,' they had her all cozy in a bed on the surgical floor."

The sirens were closer now, and Porky checked the big intravenous catheters he now always carried in his top pocket. Bob was oblivious to all the noise and seemed totally immersed in his story.

"Then Porter called the St. Jude's nurses, who'd of course panicked when the old lady turned up missing. He said he was her son, and that the old lady didn't want no surgery and he'd taken her home. The St. Jude's doctors were mad at losing their Whipple, but the fuss would have died down and all would have been forgotten. Unfortunately," Bob grinned his bright wide teeth at Ed and Porky, "Porter's junior resident boasted about it to the guy who'd told Porter in the first place."

A nurse opened the door. "They're here," she said. "One head injury, one pelvis."

"Go take care of them, Porky," said Ed. "I'll be right with you, I want to hear the end of this story."

Porky went off and Bob sat back in his chair. A muscle was twitching in his right eyelid. "The St. Jude's resident put two and two together and blew the whistle. There was a huge furor but somehow the administrators kept it out of the papers. After all, possession is nine points of the law, and the old lady'd already been operated on."

Ed got up. "I'd better go and see what Porky's up to," he said.

Bob grinned at him. "You can see why that isn't Don's favorite story."

Don came in at that moment. "Go help Porky," he said.

After they'd taken care of the head injury and the fractured pelvis in the emergency room, Don, Ed, and Porky walked wearily back toward the elevators.

"Do you think Bob Aminoke's on something?" Porky asked Don. "He seems really hyperactive."

"Of course he is," replied Don. "Everybody knows about it except you."

"Shouldn't we do something?" Porky sounded agitated. "I mean, get him some counseling, or some kind of help?"

"Counseling?" asked Don contemptuously. "What kind of shit is that?" He grinned at Ed. "Actually, Bob gets all the help he needs, doesn't he, Ed? It's just that he sniffs it up his nose." Don laughed, pleased with his quip, and Ed joined him dutifully but without enthusiasm.

Henry Brighton was on the Harkness floor when Celine came back from having tomograms in the X-ray department. He had just seen one of his few private patients, a woman from a nursing home suffering from a large hernia, and was standing at the nurses' station writing a brief note on the chart in his thready, backward-leaning handwriting.

"My goodness," he said, suddenly very attentive after Celine had been pushed past the desk in a wheelchair, "who was that?"

"Trouble, Dr. Brighton, that's who it was." Mrs. Koslowski followed Celine with narrowed eyes.

Henry liked to keep in touch with events on both the ward and private services, although his actual involvement was minimal. He relied on several people to keep him informed. One was the operating room supervisor, another was Mrs. Koslowski, whose gruff, uneducated speech gave her, in his eyes, the stamp of directness and honesty.

"What sort of trouble, Mrs. Koslowski?" Henry kept glancing at Celine's receding back, thinking it would be nice occasionally to have a patient who looked like that.

Mrs. Koslowski told him that "her" arrogance and demanding attitude had in the short space of one day made her universally hated by all the nurses, and she had even managed to antagonize her, Mrs. Koslowski, by calling her a liar in front of witnesses.

Henry raised his eyebrows.

"She called you a liar?"

"Yes she did, can you imagine?" Mrs. Koslowski straightened her back indignantly.

"Whose patient is she?" he asked.

"Dr. Winter's." Mrs. Koslowski sniffed. Then a malicious idea came to her. "He spends an awful lot of time with her, Dr. Brighton."

"What's wrong with that?" Henry looked up in surprise.

Mrs. Koslowski had an air of conspiratorial cunning. "She's a very pretty woman, very attractive, Mrs. Roach, wouldn't you say?" Her little eyes blinked, rhinoceros-fashion. "And that's all I'm saying," she said, standing up. "I've got work to do, Dr. Brighton, unlike some."

Henry grinned. A real character, Mrs. K., salt-of-the-earth kind of person, and not one to cast unwarranted aspersions. Although she wouldn't know an aspersion if she picked one up at the vegetable counter, he thought smugly. Those Polacks don't have that kind of vocabulary.

He looked at his watch; he had a committee meeting in a few minutes. Mrs. Roach. That was an odd name for a woman who looked so elegant and attractive. Henry went to the mobile rack where the patients' charts were kept. It took him a few moments to find Celine's chart, and he smiled when he saw the name, de La Roche. That was more like it, he thought, Celine de La Roche. She sounds like some kind of French royalty. He browsed through the chart. Why was it that Winter always seemed to get the big cases like this one? It had to be from all the publicity when he first came to New Coventry—Dr. Caleb Winter, the big transplant expert with his new laboratory and big grants and staff.

Well, all that was about to change, and soon, he thought grimly. Then *he* would be the one in the limelight, *he'd* be giving the interviews to the press, the TV spots. Henry's heart lightened at the thought, and he went off to his meeting, whistling under his breath, and wondering if there was anything to what Mrs. Koslowski had hinted at.

Caleb was in the outpatient building seeing patients with a group of five medical students. He'd worked with them before, and knew them quite well.

"How many of you have read Sherlock Holmes?" he asked while they were waiting for the next patient. They all had except for one, it appeared.

"Did you know that Conan Doyle was a physician?" Again, four of them knew.

"The point Conan Doyle always made was that careful observation can tell you many things about a person that completely bewilders anyone else," Caleb went on. He was sitting on the corner of the examination table; the curtain of the booth was pulled open so they all had an unobstructed view of the waiting room and the desk where the patients came to be checked in.

"A lot of that was exaggerated, surely," said Anne Fraser, a studious-looking young woman with round glasses and straight dark hair. "Like Holmes being able to tell from the color of the mud on a man's boot which part of the country he came from."

"I quite agree, Miss Fraser," said Caleb. "But the principle still holds, and a good physician still has to be a good observer."

He glanced into the waiting area. It was filling up with patients and he could hear the murmur of voices. A baby cried.

"But, Dr. Winter, that was before laboratory medicine," protested Phil Brooks, who was going to be a pathologist. "With ultrasounds, tomograms, NMR scans, chemical analyses, I mean, you can know more about a patient now, and without even seeing him, than Holmes ever could with his deductions and his magnifying glass."

He looked around at his colleagues for approval, but they were waiting for Caleb's response. Caleb grinned, and his eyes twinkled at them.

"Okay," he said, "let's see how much useful information we can get just by sitting here and keeping our eyes open. I want you all to look carefully at the next patient who comes through. We won't talk to him, and we'll only have a few seconds to get our impressions."

The students looked at one another. During sessions with most of the professors, they were used to taking notes, writing lists of symptoms and signs of various diseases, but Caleb's enthusiasm and novel approach interested them.

Somebody at the desk called out a name, and a few moments later a young woman passed in front of Caleb and the students before vanishing behind the curtain of one of the cubicles. Heavily built, she wore flashy but ill-fitting and shabby-looking clothes. She looked uncomfortably at them, stumbled in her high heels, and as she passed, she coughed and a spasm of pain crossed her face.

Caleb closed the curtain of the booth they were in. "Okay," he said. "Who wants to start?"

The students hesitated, not sure how to respond.

"First, has anybody seen that patient before?"

The students all shook their heads.

"Nor have I. Miss Fraser, why don't you start?"

"Well, uh, she's a young woman. She's got a cough, it sounds maybe like bronchitis?"

"Go on."

Miss Fraser looked around helplessly. She had nothing more to say.

"Phil?"

Phil just shook his head, looking annoyed. Like the others, he'd heard so much about the great Dr. Winter, and yet here he was wasting their time playing detective.

Miss Fraser added that she seemed breathless, and Caleb said, "Right! Good for you." He turned to Phil again. "Phil, what did she see that you didn't notice?"

Phil shrugged.

"Nothing you couldn't have detected with a three-hundred-dollar pulmonary function test, huh?"

Phil reddened.

"Miss Fraser saw her accessory breathing muscles working," explained Caleb. "Right?" The girl smiled and nodded, caught up in Caleb's enthusiasm. "You probably all saw it but didn't notice. Her neck muscles tensed up with each breath she took, and her nostrils dilated. I'm sure you've all seen that before."

That was as much as Caleb could get out of them.

"Okay," he said, settling back more comfortably, "then let me tell you about that woman." He grinned, for even Phil was looking expectantly at him.

"She's twenty-eight, had a baby about ten days ago, but

she was quite sick during her pregnancy. She developed a lot of fluid retention, her blood pressure was elevated, quite severely toward the end, to the point where her obstetrician decided to do a cesarean section."

"I thought you said you didn't know her," said Phil, aggrieved. "You said—"

"I have never seen her, spoken to her, or heard about her in my life," said Caleb firmly.

There was a silence.

"Will you tell us afterward how you know all this?" asked Miss Fraser timidly.

"Yes, of course. And when I'm done, I'll want you to check everything I said with the patient. I'm sure you all noticed that she's seriously ill, and will have to come in to the hospital as an emergency."

The students stared at Caleb, shocked. How could he possibly know all this, just from a quick glance at a woman he'd never seen before?

"Now, this girl worked as a waitress until she was fairly far advanced in her pregnancy, but unfortunately she hadn't saved any money, and being a single mother, she was in a lot of trouble."

A disbelieving snort came from Phil, but the others hung on to Caleb's words. "Luckily her mother was around, and that helped. She didn't have much milk, although she was breast-feeding."

"Dr. Winter, I really object to all this. You're trying to make fools of us." Phil was so angry he was ready to stamp out of the cubicle.

"Phil, just hear me out. I am not in any way making a fool of you, not that you'd need any help from me."

Miss Fraser stifled a giggle.

"Right," went on Caleb. "Where were we? A few days ago, she started to have some pain and swelling in her left leg. She tried putting it up, but that didn't work. Then she started to have chest pain and breathlessness, and coughed up a bit of blood. So her doctor told her to come here, and here she is."

"That's just too much," said Phil, gritting his teeth. "How could you possibly tell she'd been to see a doctor or what he said to her?"

"Shut up, Phil," said Miss Fraser firmly, and the others, spellbound, muttered their agreement.

"Okay, let's take it step by step. The first point, her age, is easy if you think about it. I can usually tell a person's age within a year or two, but then I've been doing that for years. Now, I said she'd just had a baby. That's easily explained. I heard the infant, and so did you, up in the waiting room. We saw everyone who came in, and she's the only one of child-bearing age there. Also—"

"There was a milk spot on her blouse," said Miss Fraser excitedly.

"Right! And that told us she'd been breast-feeding, and the rings around her eyes told us the baby hasn't let her sleep, and that's usually from hunger."

Phil laughed. "I apologize for what I said a minute ago, Dr. Winter," he said. "But I still don't see how you could tell she'd had a cesarean section unless you have x-ray vision."

"Well, there were a number of things that suggested that. First, when she coughed, and you all saw her do that, she winced with pain and put her hand low on her belly. Just ask anybody who's had abdominal surgery what hurts the most, and they'll tell you it's coughing or sneezing."

Miss Fraser started to write everything down in her college notebook.

"And the poor woman's all swollen. Did you see her face, her ankles? That's most likely the result of pre-eclampsia, which you must have heard of in obstetrics."

"Fluid loading, sodium retention, rising blood pressure. We could have guessed that, Dr. Winter." Phil sounded less impressed than he had been.

"Of course you could. While we're on that, I said she was a single parent?"

"She had no wedding band," said one of the other students, a small, mousy girl with bright brown eyes.

"Yes. And the woman at the desk called for Miss Coughlan. Now tell me about her mother."

Silence.

"Who do you think's holding the baby up there in the waiting room? If that woman had just come with a friend, she'd have taken the baby along with her, don't you think?"

They nodded, beginning to feel numb.

"Dr. Winter, how do you know what's in her bank account?" asked Phil, hoping that Caleb had overstretched himself on that one.

"Well, I don't, of course, but I can make a fair guess that there isn't much in it. Look at what she's wearing—a waitress's uniform, short black skirt, white blouse, high heels. But the waistband was so tight, it was almost cutting her in half. She obviously can't afford to buy even the simplest of new clothes."

Phil was shaking his head in unwilling agreement.

"You said she was very sick," he said accusingly.

"Right," said Caleb briskly. "Now that should be easy. What's the matter with her?" Again there was a long silence. Caleb started to feel irritated. This was not exactly the brightest group of students he'd ever had.

"Didn't you notice how she walked, and how much more swollen her left leg was? She developed a thrombosis in her leg veins, probably starting up in her pelvic veins, and pieces of the blood clot are coming off, getting into her circulation and causing . . . ?"

"Pulmonary emboli," said Miss Fraser, looking up from her notebook. "And that's what's making her cough. And these emboli can be fatal if they're big enough."

"Yes, that's exactly correct. So you would treat it with . . . ?"

"Heparin, bed rest, leg elevation," said Phil, who had seen a case of pulmonary embolism before and knew what the treatment was.

"Okay, that about covers it," said Caleb, getting down from the table. "Now go and talk to her and find out whether I was right or wrong. While you're doing that, I have to make a couple of phone calls. I'll see you back here in ten minutes, okay?"

Phil was looking pensive. "There's just one more thing, Dr. Winter, that you didn't explain. How do you know she went to see a doctor, and how do you know what he said to her?"

"Not too difficult, Phil; you could have figured it out yourself. The only way a patient can get to this clinic is by referral from a physician, so obviously he must have told her to come here."

Phil blushed, but didn't answer. He hurried over to the cubicle the young woman had gone into, closely followed by the others.

Ten minutes later they all got together again.

"Dr. Winter," said Miss Fraser, giggling, "you were wrong about one thing. She's twenty-nine, not twenty-eight!"

"That's the second time I've got the age wrong this week," he smiled. "I'll have to reset the computer."

"Thanks, Dr. Winter," said Miss Fraser. "You really made us think about medicine in a different way."

"Good. By the way, did any of you look carefully at her high-heeled shoes?"

There was a blank silence.

"There was a curious color of mud caked on the heel . . ." He looked at them solemnly as they tried to recall if they'd seen it.

"Yes, and therein lies the solution to the mystery," he went on. "That mud, unbeknown to you and Inspector Lestrade, comes from an abandoned clay pit in North-Eastern Devon . . ."

"You're kidding us, Dr. Winter," said Phil with an uncertain smile.

Two days after Celine's admission to the New Coventry Medical Center, Didier Franchet settled back in the window seat of the Air France Concorde and allowed the stewardess to fasten his seat belt around him. Didier was a big man, and for years had booked two adjacent seats when traveling by plane.

He had put this trip forward by a couple of weeks. The news of Celine's illness had taken him by surprise, and he wasn't sure how it would affect his plans. He had known Celine since her childhood, and was really sorry that she was sick.

He eased his bulk in the seat and glanced around, not without difficulty. The plane was about two thirds full, he noted. Business types mostly, equipped with hard jaw and fearless gaze in the best American tradition. Didier's gaze swept down the narrow aisle. One or two of his fellow passengers were also equipped with extremely beautiful companions; talented and highly trained secretaries, no doubt.

He had heard the news of Celine's illness only the day before, and from Charles' somber tone, it sounded as if she had something very seriously wrong with her.

Didier opened his briefcase and took out a packet of material neatly labeled "Fortman and Carfield." On the top were the annual reports for the last five years. He flipped rapidly through the reports, pausing only long enough to check a number here and there or make a comparison from one year to the next. He shook his head at the evident ineptitude of the company's management, and turned to a letter under the reports. It was from a well-known firm of Wall Street attorneys informing him that the sale of stock from Mrs. Astrid Fortman to one of his holding companies, Redi-Tech of Bermuda, Ltd., had been completed and paid for. Didier paused on that for a second, and laughed, remembering poor old Mrs. Fortman and her clocks. It had taken him some intensive homework and a couple of weeks on the spot to soften the old lady up before she would sell him her shares. How she'd wept when he showed her the kind of books her late husband's publishing company was selling now. Didier wondered if anyone would ever figure out that "Redi-Tech" was an anagram of the last four letters of his own name, Di*dier* Fran*chet*.

In accordance with his instructions, the letter went on, the actual transfer of the stock would be delayed, but would Mr. Franchet please instruct them as soon as possible to register the transfer, to avoid violation of Securities and Exchange Commission regulations. The letter was signed, Didier noticed, by one Greg de Vito, a very junior partner, a man he'd met for about one second some six months previously. That was typical of Gene Metscher, the partner with whom Didier dealt. If anything went sour, Metscher's name would not be found in the correspondence.

Didier checked the date on the letter; it had been sent just over three months before, a couple of weeks after Didier's last visit to Simon Fortman's clock-crazy widow, and there were two faxed follow-up letters clipped to it. Two more dealt with the purchase of Fortman and Carfield shares on the open market. Didier knew that Celine was also trying to buy those shares, but as Mrs. Fortman's block had been bigger than Dan Carfield's, he didn't need as many, only eleven percent of the total.

Didier picked a colorful folder out of the briefcase. It was Celine's latest company report. Didier turned the pages, then shrugged. It was a good little company with great potential, but seriously underfinanced, and only able to meet its day-to-day obligations by the skin of its teeth. It was a pity that it would go down the drain because of the Fortman and Carfield business, but there wasn't much he could do about that. A thought crossed his mind. Maybe she'd come and run Fortman and Carfield for him. He laughed aloud at the idea. Celine would be more likely to gouge his eyes out once she figured out what had happened. Of course it was her own fault, discussing Dan Carfield's proposal in front of him. Didier was a businessman, after all, and this opportunity was far too big to turn down. He had no interest whatever in Fortman and Carfield as a publishing house. To Didier it was simply a collection of assets which he would liquidate as soon as he had a majority position in the stock. The manuscript collection would go to auction, probably at Sotheby's in London, and the book copyrights would also be sold at auction, author by author. Then computers, furniture, real-estate leases, all that would go on the block. Didier figured that after all expenses, he should walk away with over twenty million dollars clear.

Before closing the briefcase, Didier took out a small jewel box and opened it. On the white silk lining was a diamond-and-ruby pin in the shape of a flag, the Stars and Stripes. It had been a gift from Celine many years before to commemorate Didier's U.S. citizenship, an honor he had practically forgotten about; Didier had addresses in Andorra, the Seychelles, Paris, and the Bahamas, and paid taxes to no one. He looked at the pin for a second, admiring the workmanship, then stuck it into his lapel, fastening the back with a little gold clip.

Yes indeed, he thought, settling back in his seat and preparing his mind for the landing, America is truly a wonderful country.

Caleb returned to his office, feeling drained after his hour with the students. It was fun when the group was clever and enthusiastic, but sometimes the way he approached the subject was simply too different. He wondered if they had learned anything from his rather simple demonstration, or whether they thought it was all just showmanship.

As he passed Red Felton's office, two doors along from his, Caleb was surprised to see Red's Stetson still on the desk, together with a pair of pointed cowboy boots with Red's feet inside them.

"Hey, Red, what are you doing here? Don't you know it's after five?"

The feet scrambled off the desk, and Red drawled to him to pull up a loose stool and park his ass awhile. Caleb had the distinct impression that Red had been waiting to talk to him.

"What's the matter, Red? Is your honey getting migraines or something?"

Red had recently married a young medical student, and told whoever would listen why it was important for him to get back home as early as possible in the afternoons.

"I'm worried, Cal, I confess to you that Ah am real worried."

Caleb waited. For Red to be worried could only mean one thing; somebody was trying to get him to do some work.

"Our distinguished chairman has been in and out of this here office, on my ass the entire day, and I'm telling you the truth, without a word of a lie."

"Get on with it, Red. I've got patients to see."

Red leaned forward, his long, horselike face serious. "He tells me he's finally got hisself some money for that project he's bin talkin' about for years, the one on ulcerative colitis."

"So? Good for him. I didn't think he knew how to write a grant application."

"That's it, ole buddy. That's the big Q. He ain't done no such thing. Somebody, some con-sortium, he says, give him the money all of a sudden, without any kind of warning."

"And he wants you to work on the project? Good for you too. You must be getting bedsores on your ass from just sitting on it."

"Cal," said Red in a disappointed voice, "you ain't as quick as I always thought you was." He reached for his tin of chewing tobacco. "He's going to need lab space for all them projects, a lot of it. He's got it in his haid to be doin animal work, endoscopies, all kind of stuff."

Caleb took a long, deep breath and eased back slowly in the chair. He was beginning to get a glimmer of what Red was getting at.

"After the last time he came in, all swole up with pride like he'd been bit by a poison toad, he said to me, an' I quote, 'You can have the small second-floor lab, Red,' he says, 'an' I'm going to put histology and the electron microscope in the big one.'"

Caleb listened silently. Red was watching to see if he was taking it all in.

"So I says to him, 'Henry,' I says, 'Henry, that lab belongs to Caleb Winter and his transplant team.' And he says back to me, with that prissy look we have all come to love and respect, 'Things change very rapidly in the fast lane, Red.' And off he goes with his yellow pad all covered with diagrams and plans for his new lab."

For once Caleb was at a loss for words. Red thoughtfully packed his chaw and started his rhythmic chomping.

Finally Caleb said quietly, "Red, right now my lab is fully funded by the National Institutes of Health and several other foundations. I have every indication that this funding will be renewed."

"When does the grant come up for renewal?"

"The main one comes up on October twenty-second," replied Caleb promptly. "The application went off two weeks ago."

"October twenty-second . . ." With unerring accuracy Red squirted a brown jet of tobacco juice into the plastic-lined litter can a few feet away. "Yeah, Cal, that's what he said. October twenty-second is the very day he plans to move in. It sure looks as if he knows something you and me don't know."

"Well, thanks for telling me all this, Red. Now don't you lose any sleep over it. I have a bunch of old reprints on ulcerative colitis in the office. I'll get them over to you—you'd better get started doing your homework, huh?"

Caleb went across the corridor looking for Henry, but both he and his secretary had already gone home.

Back in his own cramped sanctum, Caleb sat and thought. How was it that Henry Brighton, his research career long forgotten by the academic surgical world, was apparently getting what sounded like an unexpected and certainly undeserved windfall? Had something exciting happened to make ulcerative colitis the flavor of the month? Had anybody important like Queen Elizabeth or Saddam Hussein contracted it? Not that Caleb knew of, but he should be able to find out. They'd know at NIH, or possibly at the Ford Foundation.

Sitting at his desk, Caleb put it all together and gradually realized that he'd better start talking to the members of the Ethics and Public Welfare committee, and fast.

Caleb was passing through the outer office on his way to the recovery room when Donna, his secretary, pointed to the telephone in her hand, then to him. Caleb went back and sat down in his chair to take the call.

"Paula!" He leaned back in his chair, smiling, but a moment later he was sitting bolt upright again and the smile wasn't even a memory. His mouth tightened into a hard, unyielding line as he listened. He asked a couple of brief questions, and his face became steadily grimmer until he slowly put the phone down again, slamming it into the receiver hard enough to make the bell ring.

He pressed the intercom. "Donna, would you ask Dr. Zagros to come up here, please? Yes, right away."

Milo appeared in his white coat about five minutes later.

"Come in, Milo," said Caleb. "Close the door. I've just had Paula Muldrew on the phone."

Milo's dark eyes flickered, then stared at the floor. One look at Caleb's face and Milo knew she'd told him the whole story.

"Yes . . ." said Milo, walking slowly up to Caleb's desk. "I did something really stupid with her, Caleb. I've been meaning to tell you."

"You'd better tell me your side of the story, Milo."

Milo gave him a quick, embarrassed summary of what had happened at Paula's hotel.

Caleb's mouth tightened again as the tale developed. There was essentially no difference between Paula's story and his.

Caleb had hoped that she might have been been exaggerating, that she'd misunderstood Milo's overenthusiastic approach. By the time Milo finished, Caleb had to make an effort to keep the distaste out of his voice.

"Did she lead you on in any way, Milo, or make you think she wanted to go along with you?"

Milo hesitated. It would be easy to say yes, and then say she'd changed her mind and turned on him at the last minute. But Milo had too much respect for Caleb to lie to him.

"No, not really. The thing is, I got sort of carried away, and well, I figured she knew what was going on and, well, you know, was being agreeable."

"You didn't actually hurt her, or do anything, Milo, did you?"

Milo thought about his shoulder, which had ached ever since.

"No, well, her blouse got torn a bit, nothing much . . ."

"God damn it, Milo!" Caleb exploded. "I told you her husband is a friend of mine! It sounds as if you tried to rape the woman!"

"No, I swear, Caleb." Milo could see how angry his boss was. "Actually she almost killed me."

He told Caleb how it had ended. Paula had glossed over that part on the phone.

Caleb pointed to the chair. "Milo, sit down."

Milo sat down.

"I want you to understand that if anybody else but you had done this, I would have fired him on the spot." Caleb spoke unemotionally, as if they were discussing a shared problem, which of course it was.

Milo kept looking at the floor.

"I can't afford for us to get a reputation for this kind of behavior. We're a relatively small lab, and its good name doesn't only depend on the quality of our research." Caleb paused, his eyes searching Milo's face. "Milo, damn it, what gets into you? Why do you keep getting yourself into trouble with women? It's not as if this was the first time." Caleb was doing his best to contain his anger. After all, Milo was the key man of his team.

Milo raised his eyes and looked at Caleb without expression.

"I don't know, Cal," he said. "I know what I should do, but I simply can't resist them. I get swept up on this kind of crazy wave. And I can't seem to do anything to prevent it." He threw up his hands in a typically Slav gesture.

"Maybe in Yugoslavia you could lead your private life the way you wanted," said Caleb, "but here, there's a kind of moral code you transgress at your own risk—and I mean professional as well as personal risk."

Caleb looked to see if Milo was taking in what he said, but the dark eyes told him nothing.

"What I'm telling you is that you can't do both things. You can't keep on being an internationally respected immunologist and at the same time get yourself into situations like this. If you want to reach your potential as a scientist, I'll do all I can to help you. But if you want to go on being some kind of Don Juan, that's another situation altogether."

Caleb stood up to emphasize his final point. "Milo, I want you to listen very carefully to me. You have to make a conscious decision about this. It's up to you, I won't try to influence your judgment. But you have to realize that you can't have it both ways. Do you understand that?"

The phone in the office rang, sounding very loud in the small space, and Milo jumped. Caleb picked it up, thinking it might be Basil Mudrew saying he was on his way to New Coventry to tear Milo Zagros limb from limb. But it was the evening nurse on Harkness.

"Yes, of course," he said. "I'll be up in about half an hour."

Caleb put the phone down. "I'm going to eat over in the cafeteria," he told Milo. "Want to come?"

Milo, who wasn't feeling hungry, hesitated but said yes. He wanted to be around Caleb for a while, maybe just to be convinced that they were still friends.

The vast cafeteria was almost empty. A couple of servers in white hats and aprons stood behind the long stainless steel counter, and steam was rising from under the food containers. Three ICU nurses ahead of them in line looked tense and tired, and didn't speak to each other as they carried their trays to a nearby table.

Milo's courage was returning, and he brazenly examined the three nurses as he followed Caleb to a table halfway down the cafeteria.

"Two things I want to tell you," said Caleb, not missing Milo's look. "First, we're most likely about to do our first pancreas transplant."

Milo's eyes widened. "You have a patient? When?"

"Now you're the key man on this, Milo. I'll get you her height and weight so you can calculate the dosage and frequency of her antirejection drugs. I don't need to tell you how crucial the accuracy's going to be on this."

"It's all on my computer, Caleb," said Milo proudly. "It'll take about an hour to work out all the variables, then some time calculating different programs depending on her response. I'll do it this weekend."

Milo sounded pathetically happy to be so essential to the transplantation procedure.

"Good. Now, for the second thing." Caleb leaned forward, his eyes gleaming. "I've got our next big research project in mind." His voice was elaborately casual, and Milo gave him a swift, searching look.

Milo picked at his shrimp salad and waited expectantly. For Caleb to say something like that meant he'd already been thinking about it for some time, had researched the relevant literature, and knew exactly what he wanted to do.

"Did you do much embryology back in Belgrade?"

"Like everybody, I suppose."

"Do you remember how the pancreas develops?"

"More or less. It starts as a small bud of cells growing out of the foregut."

"Right," said Caleb, his eyes beginning to glitter with excitement. "It all starts off as just a few specialized cells that develop a system of ducts, and some of them develop into beta cells that produce insulin."

Milo listened, but Caleb could see that he hadn't yet grasped what he was getting at.

"The thing is, Milo, that these cells are born with that

potential for development, and if they can do it *inside* the embryo . . ."

Milo dropped his fork and smacked a fist into the palm of the other hand, his eyes suddenly alight with excitement.

"I know what you're saying! We can make them develop outside the body, as a tissue culture in the lab, or . . . oh my God, Caleb, you mean—?"

"Keep your voice down, Milo," said Caleb, smiling, as the three nurses looked over at them curiously. "Basically the idea is to implant a few embryonic cells through a needle into the wall of the patient's stomach, let the cells develop there, grow their own duct systems, their own insulin-producing cells. I don't need to tell you of the huge potential if we can get such a procedure to work reliably."

Milo was almost jumping with excitement. "And the embryonic cells don't stimulate much immunological response," he said, "so rejection should be much less of a problem."

"What we don't know," said Caleb, "is how much the response increases as the embryonic cells develop inside the host. It's an entirely new field of research."

Caleb gave Milo a couple of references to look up; somebody in Bologna had done some work on antibody production in fetal pigs, and a researcher at Addenbrooke's Hospital in Cambridge, England, was working on antigen identification in fetal sheep.

"All this will take a while, Milo, but if it works, we're talking potential Nobel Prize material."

Milo quickly finished his dinner and hurried over to the university's medical library as soon as possible to start work. He knew in his bones that Caleb was right about the potential for major scientific recognition, and he also knew that nothing, absolutely nothing could be allowed to get in the way of this stupendous project, not even Collie Zintel.

At this unbidden, unwelcome thought, Milo felt a stirring in his groin, and he struggled with a frightening sense of inevitability, a feeling that certain things, even when they concerned his survival as a scientist, were beyond his control. He remembered how close he'd come to a dreadful accident with Collie, and the thought made him break out in a cold sweat.

She'd egged him on, she'd begged him to kill her, strangle her at the moment of climax, and she was planning on having him come back. All Caleb's words came back to him; *you can't do both,* he'd said. *Either a world class scientist or a Don Juan.* . . . And now, Milo finally understood what that decision would cost him.

Caleb left the cafeteria soon after, feeling very good about having straightened Milo out, and excited about the new research project, which he knew instinctively would put his name in the scientific history books forever. And everything else would work out, just the way his major problems always had in the past. He was glowing with confidence and pleasure when he reached the Harkness Wing elevator.

After Dan Carfield left, Celine put all business matters out of her mind. She touched her cheek and thought angrily about her row with Charles, but finally she allowed herself the luxury of thinking again about Caleb Winter. Porky's story about the boy with the knife in his neck had mesmerized her, and she tried to visualize the scene when Winter's swift and decisive action had saved the boy's life. Celine was beginning to recognize how totally dependent she was on him. While she was mulling over this discovery, a momentary twinge of pain made her place her hand on her abdomen, and she slid further down in the bed. Thinking of Caleb, a feeling of excited warmth spread through her body, and unconsciously, her hand slipped down between her thighs. For the next few moments she fantasized about what it would be like to go to bed with Caleb Winter.

And then he came into her room. She sat up quickly, and pulled her white nightie around her neck.

"I hear you had a run-in with the nurses," he said, sitting on the bed. He had such a sparkle, such confidence, Celine felt weak by contrast. She looked at him and thought, I wonder what you'd say if you knew what I've just been thinking about. Maybe he did know. Those gray eyes didn't miss much.

"I've been having run-ins with *everybody* today," she said, thinking of Charles. "I guess I'm just scared and that makes me overreact."

"Being scared isn't a familiar sensation for you, I don't suppose," he said, smiling.

"Not this kind of scared," she said.

Seeing a shadow of her fear passing across Celine's face, Caleb said, with an odd, gruff kind of sympathy, "I'll try to make it as easy for you as I can."

She changed the subject abruptly. "Porky was telling me about your transplants. He said you were coming close to using them on patients."

"That's a hot topic," Caleb smiled. He looked down at her, unable to ignore the shape of her under the nightie. "We should know about that in a few days. In fact ..." Caleb hesitated for the briefest moment, "depending on the results of the tests, I may want to talk to you and Charles about that at some length."

Celine slid out of bed and stood up, facing him. "Talk to me about it now," ordered Celine, and put both hands out to him. He took them and stood up. He was now right up against her, and her feeling was so strong that she put her hands up to his face and stared silently into his eyes. After a second's hesitation, Caleb put his arms around her and held her close to him, excited by the pressure of her breasts on his chest. His hands slid down to the roundness of her buttocks, and she pushed in to him, breathing fast, feeling him growing against her. He reached down under her nightie and his hand traveled slowly up her thigh.

The door opened suddenly, and they both heard a gasp of surprise before it was quickly and silently closed. Caleb gently disengaged himself.

"That was really a bit silly of us, wasn't it?" He smiled, apparently quite unconcerned. "Now you go and sit over there," he said, pointing at the chair in the corner, "and I'll sit on the bed. Much safer, don't you think?"

Celine was shaking, but did as she was told.

"Where were we?" Caleb sounded and looked so relaxed standing by the bed that Celine felt a moment's astonished annoyance. Had he felt *anything?* Or was this how he handled all his female patients? "Oh yes. Transplants . . ." He told her briefly about the status of his work, but their encounter was too recent and too powerful for him to say much to her. Caleb got up, went over to where Celine was sitting, and put his hand so gently on her cheek that she could barely feel it.

"I'll see you tomorrow," he said. "Sleep tight."

Early the next morning Milo left his lab and walked down College Street to keep an appointment he'd made at the Medical Arts Towers, where many of the "town" doctors had their offices.

"So you work for Cal Winter, do you?" asked the urologist, Dr. Caldwell, scanning Milo's "new patient" form.

"Actually Caleb works for me," Milo said jokingly, but his joke misfired, and the doctor didn't crack a smile. Instead he sat back a little farther in his chair, watching Milo through the half-glasses perched near the end of his nose.

"So what can I do for you?" he asked. Usually when any of the university people came to see him, it was for something they didn't want their academic colleagues to know about.

Milo told him what he wanted done. Caldwell, shocked, took off his glasses and started to polish them vigorously with the fat end of his tie.

"How long have you been in this country?" he asked, without looking at Milo.

"Just over four years," answered Milo, puzzled.

"Well, my friend," said Caldwell, getting up from behind his desk, "maybe they do things like that back where you come from, but not here. No sir." Then he grinned. "Where is it you're from again?" When Milo told him, Caldwell's face lit up for a moment. "Right. I had some Yugoslav Riesling only last week. Damn good, for the price, but not quite like the stuff they brew in Riesling, Germany, right?"

Milo shook his head, not sure if Dr. Caldwell was joking.

Even after four years, he still had problems understanding Americans and their peculiar brand of humor, and it seemed that they had as much difficulty understanding him.

"Have you thought about hormone treatment?" asked Caldwell, getting back to the subject. "There was a time when they used it a lot here for sex offenders." He saw Milo's expression change, and went on hurriedly. "I'm not suggesting ... it's just that it worked pretty well, for some of them." His words faded into the air, and it occurred dimly to Caldwell that he could have made his suggestion with a little more tact.

Grim-faced, Milo said, "Tell me about it."

"About what?"

"About the hormone treatment."

"Well ..." Caldwell put his glasses on again. "Estrogens seem to have a fairly potent dampening effect on the male libido."

"Dampening?" asked Milo, puzzled.

"I mean it reduces the sexual urge," said Caldwell sharply. He didn't feel too comfortable with the topic or with Milo.

"Then maybe that is what I want," said Milo. "In fact I *know* that's what I want."

It was Caldwell's turn to shake his head. "It has side effects, as I'm sure you're aware." Milo's glossy dark eyes showed his ignorance. "Estrogens increase breast growth," went on Caldwell heavily, "and tend to put on fat, around the hips, you know, like where women carry it."

Milo's eyes widened. Breasts? Fat? He didn't need any of that. "How about vasectomy?" he asked. "Doesn't that have the same effect?"

They were getting back into an area Caldwell was more familiar with, and his voice reassumed its note of authority. "Not at all," he said. "For some people, vasectomy actually increases libido, but for most it doesn't make any difference. Not to what they feel or want, and I gather that's—"

Milo got up. He obviously wasn't going to get anywhere with this man. "Thanks, Dr. Caldwell," he said, and left the office.

Milo came out of the Medical Arts Tower almost at a run. Now he really didn't know what to do. He had spent two consecutive sleepless nights mulling over his predicament; it was clear that if things kept on the way they were going, he was headed for disaster.

Milo walked down College Street, back toward the hospital and medical school buildings. He passed a new parking garage, but he was blind to its innovative design and massive scrolled terraces. A police car howled past as he crossed the bridge over the connector; Milo didn't hear it. He was steeling himself, trying to make up his mind. It was part of his personality to undertake tasks with a Slavic bravado, but what he was contemplating would take all his courage and all his resolve, and even in the warmth of the day he felt chilled at the thought. But before he got back to the lab Milo had made his decision.

Caleb arranged to visit Anna Lynn Page and her husband, Larry, over on Fisher's Island, where they spent the summers. Anna Lynn was a member of the hospital board and was also on the Medical Ethics and Public Welfare Committee. Both had been friends of Caleb's for years.

They were waiting for the small plane when it landed on the airstrip. Anna Lynn hugged Caleb as soon as he got off the plane, and Larry held out his hand. They both looked tanned and healthy, and were delighted to see him.

Larry drove them back to the house for lunch. Caleb had been there once before, but he'd forgotten how pleasantly luxurious it all was. Lunch, made by their cook and served by a maid on a modern Wedgwood service, consisted of crab bisque followed by a fresh lobster salad and strawberries and cream.

After lunch they drove down to the dock. Their motor cruiser was captained by a sunburned young man with a curly red beard. He was busy polishing brasswork on deck when they arrived. Within a few minutes, everything had been secured and the boat was nosing cautiously out of the harbor. Just beyond the entrance they passed the ferry coming over from New London, and they swayed briefly in its wash. The air felt suddenly cooler, and a breeze picked up as soon as they were away from the land. Larry busied himself at the bar.

"So you're on the menu for next Monday," said Anna Lynn, her beringed hand on the teak railing. She was looking over at the mainland, her white hair blowing in the breeze.

"You mean I'm going to be eaten alive?" smiled Caleb.

"Could be," answered Anna seriously. She turned to face him. She was a handsome woman, direct and confident. "They say you're not ready to start transplanting into humans." She raised an imperious hand. "Don't bother telling me," she went on before Caleb had a chance to speak, "I know you, and you wouldn't apply for permission if you weren't ready." She put a hand on his arm. "And I also know them, maybe better than you do."

"Who precisely do you mean by *them?*"

"Dr. Brighton phoned me yesterday," said Anna Lynn. "Full of praise for your work, of course, because he knows you and I are friends."

"So?"

"He said it would ruin your career if we allowed you to extend your work to humans prematurely. He sounded most concerned about your career."

"Yes, I imagine he did."

"He also said the other members of the committee had persuaded him to call me, so that I would know."

"What do you think, Anna Lynn?"

"I think he's out to get you, Cal. Have you done anything to put his nose out of joint?"

"I don't think so, but you never know for sure."

Caleb had an urge to tell Anna Lynn about Henry Brighton's incompetence, his treachery and petty-mindedness, his efforts to replace Caleb's transplant unit with his own pet project, but he felt a strong, ingrained reluctance to bad-mouth his colleague.

Anna smiled at him, understanding his hesitation.

"I don't care for that man at all," she said in her forthright way, "and I don't trust him. There's something false and underhanded about him."

Larry came with a tray of drinks, and they sat on the rear deck and chatted about other things for a while, enjoying the sea air and the gentle motion from the swell.

Caleb, who was wearing a short-sleeved shirt with wide yellow and blue stripes, felt the beginnings of a sunburn on his forearms and moved his canvas-backed chair a foot or so under the awning.

"Don't think Anna Lynn's just been sitting around," said Larry, while Anna Lynn went off to get some sunblock cream. "She's been on the phone ever since that fellow Brighton called. She's on your side, one hundred percent."

Caleb made a sudden quick movement with his hands. "I'm really sorry it's become a political issue," he said. Larry noted his annoyance.

"It's no different from when I was at Loeb Rhoads," Larry said. "Except there it was maybe worse. After you get to a certain level, it gets harder and harder to do things because there are too many people who'd like to see you fall."

"There's a big difference, Larry," Caleb said. "You had a bottom line. If you were successful it showed on the balance sheet. In my line of business, it's a lot harder to show when things are going well."

"You'd be surprised at some of the things I had to fight for," said Larry, smiling. "I always tried to follow my old boss's precept: first decide what's really important, then fight to the death for it, whether it's a new desk for the secretary or underwriting a bond issue by the Kingdom of Jordan."

Larry's message was not lost on Caleb.

Charles spent most of the morning with Mort Perkins, the veterinary surgeon who took care of his horses, preparing for Corinthian's scheduled trip to Atlanta that afternoon. He'd known Mort for years, since he'd first come into the area as a young man straight from veterinary school. Mort whistled softly as he walked around Corinthian, checking his condition. "He's beautiful, Charles, I don't see anything . . ." He picked up the horse's rear leg, examined the fetlock, then the hoof, but both men knew he was just doing it for form. "No, he's in perfect shape, I would say." He looked at the fence around the paddock. "If I didn't know you better, Charles, I just wouldn't believe that he ever cleared that fence."

"Yes, he did," said Jeremy breathlessly. "I seen him do it. It was like magic."

"Well, I hope he does as well in Atlanta." He glanced mischievously at Charles. "If he doesn't win, it won't be his fault."

Charles grinned happily. His natural cheerfulness could not be suppressed for long. "That'll depend on how well rested he is after the plane ride, and that'll depend on what you give him."

"Is the missus going down with you?"

"No, not this time." Charles' good humor evaporated with the question. "I'll be flying down some time around the middle of next week. The Trials start on Saturday."

Mort glanced quickly at him but said nothing. What a pity, Mort thought. He remembered how inseparable Celine and

Charles had been the first few years they'd been married. Perhaps the rumors about Marion Redwing were true after all.

After Mort left in his pickup, Charles wandered back into the house; it seemed to echo emptily without Celine. Minette accompanied him, walking so close to his feet that he was afraid of stepping on her.

"You know she's away, don't you?" he said quietly. "Don't worry, she'll be back. Maybe." He picked up a pair of Celine's shoes from beside the bed; they felt strange and extraordinarily light. He stroked the gray lining of one of them, where her instep went, and looked at the heel, trying to imagine what it would be like, balanced up on two of these. Slowly he put them in the closet with the others.

Celine had been wearing high heels the first time he'd seen her, and they'd helped to give her that haughty, aristocratic look—"You make me think of 'liberté, régalité, fraternité,' " he'd said, feeling rather clever to be making a joke in French. He'd managed to separate her from her fiancé long enough to interest her, and when René returned from his search for a nonexistent brand of Scotch that Charles had asked him for, Celine understood instantly what Charles had been up to, and laughed, delighted with him. When the three young Americans left, Celine's eyes followed the car long after it disappeared through the gates.

While Charles was doing a year's stint in the Justice Department in Washington, D.C., he read in a small notice in the foreign news section of *The Wall Street Journal* that the firm of Librairie LaRoche had gone into bankruptcy. Through contacts at the French embassy, Charles found that Celine was now living in Lyons, working with a small publishing firm in the rue du Tertre.

Celine wanted nothing to do with anyone from her old life, and when he appeared, Charles had to convince her that on the contrary, he was the first wave of the new life. Finally she agreed to have lunch with him. Celine was as beautiful as ever, but she'd grown up a lot, and already there were flashes of a new toughness in her attitude. But, as Charles discovered later, she still wasn't the best judge of character. Her opinion of people depended too much on her emotional reactions to them.

At that time, Charles was rapidly making a name for himself in the equestrian world, and was as handsome and dashing as any Tolstoyan cavalry officer. He was also lighthearted, funny, and clever, and soon cajoled and teased Celine until she was able to laugh, relax, and be happy again.

Slowly he got the story of her father's financial crash out of her: the bailiffs, the trucks lurching across the lawn to take away the furniture, the cars, even the statues in the garden. The telephone service was cut in mid-conversation. For several days they'd lived in the château on bottled water, sardines, cheese, and the grapes that miraculously had been overlooked in the conservatory. From the time the first truck came lumbering through the rosebeds, Celine had found herself in charge. Her father simply couldn't handle the trauma; he sat in shock on a red velvet-covered chair in the center of the ballroom of the château while the bailiff's men took everything around him—furniture, rugs, paintings, even pulling some fine old silver sconces from the walls, leaving gaping holes and clouds of plaster. Then one of them said "Excuse me, sir," and removed his chair.

Celine organized the meals, got a lawyer (her father had left his family affairs in the hands of an elderly *notaire*, an old friend of the family, who turned out to be honest enough but totally incompetent). Oncle Didi visited quite often, bringing presents of food, blankets, and other necessities until they moved to Celine's grandmother's big, rambling farmhouse a few days later. The only good thing out of the whole dreadful nightmare was that within a week, her fiancé, René Du Plessis, sent her two dozen yellow roses (he knew the language of flowers) and a short letter regretting the unavoidable termination of their *fiançailles*. Celine threw the roses into the farm midden and followed them up with her Cartier diamond engagement ring. Then she sat down and wrote René a brief note saying he was welcome to go hunting for it.

Two weeks later, Celine's father, who had barely spoken a word in the interim, was taken sick and was taken by ambulance to the Hôpital Edouard Heriot in Lyons, where he later died.

By the time Charles had been in Lyons a couple of weeks, he had won more than her confidence, and they spent as much time as they could together. Celine discovered an unsuspected talent for cooking, and she put together delicious meals from odds and ends of meat and vegetables, and cooked them on her leaky and dangerous gas stove. She was very independent and wouldn't accept any assistance from Charles or anyone else. But they did talk about what she could do to get out of her crippling financial situation.

One evening Celine was making a leek-and-potato soup with garlic and finely chopped parsley, to be followed by an *escalope* that had been marked down by half because it looked a little gray after a few days on the shelves. She knew that the meat had simply aged and become more tender, and actually tasted better and took less long to cook than the brighter red meat preferred by less knowledgeable shoppers.

The weather was very warm, there was no air-conditioning, and Celine was wearing a flimsy little housedress and no underwear. Restless, Charles watched her as she cut the garlic up into small pieces. "I don't grate it," she said, deliberately misinterpreting his look. "The soup'll taste better this way. Now if you'd like to set the table . . ."

Charles had brought a couple of candles, but Celine firmly rejected the idea of using them at dinner.

"My father taught me two things about food when I was little," she told him. "One was *never* to serve anything *flambé* at the table; there is a room specially designed for cooking, called the kitchen. The other was to avoid candles or dim lights at dinner, otherwise the guests might think there's something in the food you don't want them to see."

"Write a cookbook for poor students!" said Charles suddenly. "You could call it *Food for Thought,* or *Raunchy Recipes for Starving Students.* We could do it together."

Celine stopped with her ladle in the air, delighted by his idea.

They hurried through dinner, then cleared the dishes off the table, and in the next four hours the two of them put together a six-page outline for a cookbook aimed at students, single people, and others who wanted to eat well but didn't have enough money to do it the conventional way.

First thing in the morning, Celine took the outline to the editor-in-chief of the company she was working for.

"*Oui, c'est une bonne idée, certainement, ma petite,*" he said, absently scratching the inside of his well-fed thigh. "But if they're too poor to buy good food, what makes you think they'd have the money to buy your book?"

Charles made Celine persevere with the idea nonetheless. She wrote the recipes, and he discovered he had a talent for writing humorous anecdotes to go with each one. Six months later, the two of them had a finished manuscript complete with wonderful pen-and-ink drawings; Charles had gone to the Institut d'Art Commercial and asked the principal for the name of their most brilliant student. Celine knew Charles had paid Emile, but could never find out how much. Then Charles had taken the book to New York and sold it for a small advance to a paperback house, and that was the last either of them expected to hear about it. But it was kindly reviewed, did well, was translated into French and six other languages, became a cult book everybody wanted to own, and a year later, to her utter astonishment, Celine had made more than enough money to clear her debts.

During this time Charles had entered his family's Wall Street law firm but was more interested in developing his expertise as a show jumper. Any time he could snatch away, he came to Lyons to be with her.

They celebrated her second royalty check by having dinner in the old flagstoned courtyard of Le Cygne Noir, one of the best restaurants in Lyons, a city with more fine restaurants to the square kilometer than any in the world.

"I'd like to go to New York," said Celine. "I want to finish my degree there."

Charles put down the wine list, leaned back in the wide cane chair, and looked at her in the still, pink light of the sunset. He had difficulty keeping his voice steady. "I quite agree with you," he said. "I think we should get married and go back together."

Celine smiled back at him. "Yes," she said. "I was going to suggest it if you didn't."

Charles was about to come around to kiss her when he saw bright tears in her eyes.

"I'm just sorry you couldn't formally have asked Father for my hand," she said.

They were married in the Eglise du Saint Père in the Place Perrache some weeks later, and at Celine's insistence, she was given away by her father's old friend and confidant, Didier Franchet.

Charles closed the shoe closet with a bitter sense of finality. A lot had happened to their marriage since then. He had to accept the fact that it was all over now, and he'd better start getting used to the idea.

Leroy Williams was next on the list of committee members, with the title of "Ombudsman and Community Representative." Caleb laughed. Some handle for a guy who'd made his living renting girls and cracking the heads of anybody who got in his way. Caleb still read about Leroy in the papers from time to time, although he didn't appear in the police courts any more. Earlier in his career Leroy had been arrested on charges of armed robbery, living off immoral earnings, as the law quaintly put it, and various other crimes. But right from the beginning he'd been smart enough to hire Moe Isaacs, a clever New Coventry lawyer who had successfully beaten the rap for him until the police got tired of trying and went in search of easier convictions. Now Leroy was a notable public figure who led the annual Martin Luther King Day parade with his arms linked to the mayor's and was in demand for TV spots when racial trouble threatened. He had mediated when there was a riot at the prison, at the prisoners' insistence. In Caleb's mind, also, was the image of Leroy, looking angry for television, supporting an antivivisection demonstration a year ago.

When Caleb called, Leroy was home. Unlike many successful blacks who fled the ghetto as soon as they had enough money for a down payment on a suburban house, Leroy lived in a walk-up fourth floor apartment on Washington Avenue, right in the most decrepit part of town. Cynics said that he had to be there to watch over his girls, but that was a foul, malignant lie. He had long since delegated that task to his two sons, now aged twenty and twenty respectively. They had been born within a week of each other, Maxie to a white girl who used to serve at the Elephant Grill and Leroy Two to Leroy's wife, who came originally from Jamaica.

"Yeah?" said Leroy.

"Hi," said Caleb. "This is Caleb Winter. I'd like to talk to you."

There was a pause while Leroy shouted at somebody on the other end. The Williams household sounded like a lively place.

"Yeah?" said Leroy again. "What about?"

"You're on the Ethics and Public Welfare Committee at the hospital."

Leroy laughed, a rich bass laugh, full of the joy of life. "Yeah," he said once more. "Ain't that a title? I'm gonna put that on my business cards, whaddya think? I wanna be chairman next year."

"I want to talk to you about next Monday's meeting. You'll be discussing—"

"Yeah, I know. Talked to one of your guys already today, Henry something. What's the big deal?"

"You busy now? Why don't we meet for a drink?"

"Come on over to my place. Washington Avenue, number 1444, fourth floor. Easy to remember. Leave your car right outside so they'll know not to take the wheels off, okay?"

Caleb paused for a moment before agreeing. A white man walking on Washington Avenue would stand out like a robed bishop in a massage parlor. Still, he didn't think anything would happen while he was visiting Leroy Williams, as long as Leroy remembered to tell his neighbors.

Twenty minutes later Caleb drove slowly down Washington Avenue, past the junked cars propped up on red milk crates. He felt the tires occasionally crunching a bottle or a can, and every few yards his vehicle jolted into a pothole. Half the houses on the street were boarded up, and lanky blacks strolled around slowly, hung out listlessly in the doorways, or sat nodding on the stoops. Skinny cats swaggered across the street as if they owned it. There were no recognizable numbers on the doors. Caleb passed a new white Cadillac with a fringe around the rear widow. It was almost the only vehicle with wheels in the street, and Caleb figured it must be parked outside number 1444.

He stopped, reversed, and parked in close behind the Cadillac, right on its bumper. Anybody would know that whoever left their car that close must be visiting Leroy.

In the lobby, layer upon layer of colored graffiti screamed at him from the peeling walls, and the ammoniacal stench of old urine was enough to make him cough. With some trepidation Caleb started up the worn wooden stairs. One of the second floor apartments had a steel door, also covered with graffiti, protecting the inhabitants. It looked as if it could withstand a tank. Caleb picked his way through the empty beer cans and Styrofoam hamburger containers, some still containing partly eaten food. On the gloomy second floor landing, he heard a sudden noise and scurry, and his hair stood on end, but it was only a rat.

A fair amount of noise was coming from the fourth floor apartment as Caleb stood outside, panting slightly. Below there came a sudden clattering, and what sounded like loud male teenage voices coming up the stairs. Caleb hurriedly knocked on the door, which was opened by a small, skinny black boy aged about ten with a frizz of hair and big suspicious eyes. He took one look at Caleb, slammed the door shut, and Caleb could hear him shouting inside.

The door opened again after a few moments, and Leroy appeared. Leroy was big. He was wearing a string vest and a pair of jeans. His feet were bare, splayed, and hard, and he wore a leather thong around his neck with a yellowed canine tooth from some large carnivore dangling from it.

"Come on in, Doc. The kid ain't used to seeing white faces around here."

Caleb squeezed past. On his right was the living room, and a young black woman in a shapeless print dress was watching television.

"Hi," said Caleb, smiling at her.

"Go down and watch his car," said Leroy to the boy, who vanished around the door like an eel.

Leroy led the way into the bedroom opposite. Inside was a

huge unmade bed backed by an ornate gilded headboard. Clothes, socks, stockings, and underwear, both male and female, were scattered around. Caleb noticed a fair amount of flimsy black lacy stuff and a black garter belt flung across the back of the single yellow wicker chair.

"Your pal Doc Brighton never made it here this morning," said Leroy, sitting on the bed and pointing to the chair. "I know he came by, but later he called and said he couldn't find the address."

He laughed, a loud, engaging, happy laugh. Two smaller children appeared silently at the door, looked at Caleb with big, serious eyes then vanished.

"You want a cup of coffee? Coke?"

Caleb shook his head, smiling, not sure if he was being offered Coca-Cola or cocaine. Leroy, watching him with an amused, wary grin, was very relaxed, totally in control.

"So what brings you to nigger-town, Doc?" Leroy leaned back and picked his feet up until he was sitting in a relaxed lotus position. The soles of his feet were dark gray and looked as if they didn't spend much time inside shoes.

"Why do you live here, Leroy?" Caleb asked quietly.

"Where else?" replied Leroy. "In some nice honky suburb? Westpark? No way. Out there, I couldn't stand out on the street and drink a can of beer with my friends. Couldn't make too much noise there neither, might disturb my upper-class neighbors. Me and her . . ." He jabbed a wide thumb in the direction of the front room, "me and her, we make a lot of noise sometimes." Leroy sat up. "Anyway, everything I got goin' is here."

"That makes sense," Caleb replied. "About the committee meeting, Leroy. I wanted to give you some background."

"No need," said Leroy, lifting his hand. "I'll ask you what I want to know."

"Go ahead. Ask whatever you like."

"Okay. Question number one. What's in it for you?"

"If you mean, do I get personal benefit out of it, the answer is no. What I will get is the ability to help a lot of people with diabetes and other diseases of the pancreas."

"Question number two. How many pancreases does a monkey have?"

"One, just like us."

"Does that mean a monkey dies every time you do one of these transplants?"

"Yes." Caleb shifted on his chair. "But thousands of cattle die every day for beef, and pigs die all the time to make pork. Nobody gets too excited about that, except maybe the cows and the pigs."

Leroy shook his head.

"Personally," he said, "I don't give a rat's ass for any of this, one way or the other. My pancreas is just fine. It's my image, man. I gotta keep a certain kind of, well, aggressive image around here, just to keep the pot boiling, if you see what I mean. A year ago we did the thing with the antivivisectionists. I don't give a shit for that either, but it was real good, man, good for morale an' we had a good shoutin', stompin', and singin' parade."

Leroy smiled. He had teeth that looked as if they could bite a piece out of that steel door downstairs. One of the small children slid into the room, put herself between Leroy's legs and stared at Caleb.

"You see, Doc, I know what my people need here. They need to get out, have a few beers, make a noise, have a parade, let off steam from time to time. And you can think what you like, man, but down here it's always a battle, every day, between the honkies and us."

Leroy stretched and got up. The little girl scrambled behind him.

"If I vote for you, Doc, it's a vote for the honkies. I can't do that. You understand. Nothing personal . . ."

Caleb drove back towards the hospital from Washington Street. He wasn't really surprised by the outcome of his meeting with Leroy Williams, and felt a new respect for him as a man. Caleb was used to the circuitous politics of the medical center, and Leroy Williams, with his direct and good-natured honesty, was a refreshing change. At least Caleb knew where he was with Leroy, and there was no point trying to change his mind.

He switched his thoughts back to the hospital. Old Mr. Montague, the patient he'd operated on that morning, the common bile duct; he'd been quite badly jaundiced before his surgery, and Caleb hoped that Don or Ed had remembered to put him on Vitamin K. There was always a risk of internal hemorrhage in this kind of case.

Don had muttered something about Porky being taken off the service because he'd fallen asleep on the job; Caleb knew they hadn't been happy with Porky, and nor for that matter was he, but Caleb avoided interfering in that kind of situation unless he was forced to. It was better to let the residents sort it out themselves, and in any case it was Henry Brighton's responsibility, not his, to maintain good order and discipline in the ranks.

At the thought of Henry Brighton a cold anger crept over Caleb. It wasn't so much what Brighton was doing that offended him; the idea that Henry, completely devoid as he was of research ability, might supplant him and take over his lab was so preposterous that Caleb laughed out loud in the car. No, it was the sneaky, treacherous way he was trying to do him in. Damn it, Caleb thought, we're a big part of his department, he should be rooting for the transplant team with all his might.

What troubled Caleb even more, although he hadn't put it into words, was that Brighton's behavior was a blatant breach of the ancient tradition of medical loyalty. The profession had enough political and legal enemies on the outside without betrayal from within.

He slowed for the lights at Elm Street. Ahead of him was a young woman driving a sports car, and the way she held her head made him think of Celine. Now that's a dangerous situation you're getting yourself into, he reflected. Particularly as he would be having to make difficult, clearheaded medical decisions about her, decisions that wouldn't allow for any kind of emotional involvement on his part.

A few minutes later, Caleb drove past the uplifted barrier of the doctors' parking lot and found a place near the back entrance.

He looked at his watch as he got into the elevator. Don was supposed to be starting an abdominal aortic aneurysm with the rest of the team. Normally, at his stage of seniority, Caleb would have let Don do it by himself, but he didn't have enough confidence in his skill or judgment, so he'd decided to scrub in with them. Don might take it as an insult to his professional ability, but that was just tough. As far as Caleb was concerned, the patient's interests came way ahead of Don's.

Caleb said, "We'll be ready to clamp the aorta in about three minutes, Gabe." Gabriel Pinero, the anesthesiologist, whispered to his assistant, who went out to get some more blood. Don's fingers were working around a large abdominal aortic aneurysm, a thinned-out dilatation of the aorta, the largest artery in the body, gently separating it from the surrounding tissues.

Caleb didn't take his eyes off Don's hands. He felt tense, as he often did when he was assisting the residents; he preferred to do the work himself, particularly when it was very delicate or dangerous, but the residents had to learn somehow. And Don would be finishing in another few months, and by that time he had to be ready for anything he might encounter. The next time he did an aneurysm like this he might be operating on his own, with only an inexperienced assistant to help him.

"Remember it's paper-thin, right there."

Don's fingers probed the structures around the pulsating aneurysm, trying to find a plane of dissection. In the middle of the abdomen, the aorta was normally the thickness of a standard candle, but this one had expanded into a bulge the size of a wine bottle.

"A little more tension on that Deaver, Porky," muttered Don. "I can't see."

Porky was gray with fatigue. The team had been up a good part of the night before, and when he finally had got to bed he was so tired he couldn't sleep. Porky eased back on the flat blade of the retractor, trying desperately to keep his eyes open. Both his feet seemed to have gone numb.

Don had been up too, and was just as tired, but he was doing the operation, and the pumping adrenalin kept him from feeling sleepy. But his reactions were noticeably slower, he could feel that as he worked; it took longer for the signals to pass from his brain to his hands.

Collie Zintel wasn't at her best either, but for quite a different reason. Her mask and hood covered most of the bruises, but her left eye was puffy and almost closed. Caleb had noticed, as he noticed everything, but hadn't said anything. He felt pretty sure Collie hadn't just walked into a wall. Maybe she'd had a fight with Ed. He'd certainly been looking daggers at her since the case had started.

"Hemoclips, large," said Don, encountering a large arterial branch behind the aneurysm. He would clip it in two places, and cut the vessel between the clips.

Collie didn't have them ready and fumbled putting the clip into the holder. The tiny clip dropped, and she had to put in another while everybody waited. The tension built up suddenly, but nobody spoke. If there was to be any criticism, it would have to come from Caleb, but he said nothing, merely waited for her to get it together. Collie's hand was shaking when she passed the long instrument to Don.

"No hurry," murmured Caleb. "Take it easy, huh, Collie?"

She glanced gratefully at him. It was nice that he'd handled it that way; Collie knew that if Dr. Winter hadn't been there, Don would have shouted and yelled in his frustration and anger at her.

Everybody relaxed just a little.

At that moment the aneurysm burst. Nobody knew for sure what did it. Maybe Porky had moved the retractors, or Don's tired fingers prodded clumsily or too far. Anyway, Caleb felt it tearing a fraction of a second before the blood spouted out of the wound like a fountain. Don's eyes showed his panic, and the sweat popped onto his brow like magic. Caleb plunged his hand into the wound, located the normal aorta above the aneurysm, pressed firmly with his fingers on the aorta above the tear, and the bleeding slowed down abruptly. Don had instantly taken on the role of assistant, and had both suction tubes removing the blood from the cavity of the abdomen as fast as the equipment could handle it.

"We've got a slight problem here," said Caleb calmly to Gabriel Pinero. "We just lost about two units, if you'd like to replace it."

Pinero understood exactly what had happened. It was one of the recurrent nightmares of surgery, the kind that woke even experienced surgeons in the middle of the night: the rupture of an aortic aneurysm while they were operating on it. Gabe hung up a second blood bag and started to pump the blood in with a pneumatic pressure cuff.

"Aortic clamp, Collie." Collie had it right there, a long curved clamp specially designed to compress the aorta without damaging its delicate walls.

It took Caleb three long minutes to get the situation under control. He had instantly taken command, but as soon as the situation was no longer an emergency, when the bleeding had stopped, he let Don take over again.

But Caleb felt deeply concerned. At the moment of decision, that split second when instant action had to be taken, Don had failed. If Caleb hadn't been there to take over instantly, the patient would never have made it off the table alive; he'd have bled out right there in front of them, with Don making desperate but ineffectual attempts to stanch the bleeding until the heart, starved of the blood it needed to keep pumping, finally stopped. And in a few months he's going to be out in the world, doing this kind of surgery on his own, reflected Caleb grimly. Collie got some fresh sterile towels to put around the wound, and they unclipped and discarded the blood-soaked ones. Once the operative field was cleared Don was able to get on with the operation.

After that the case proceeded without any major complication; they sewed in a Y-shaped Dacron tube graft to replace the thinned-out, dilated aorta. While they were putting the graft in, of course, the circulation to the lower part of the body had to be stopped, and they had some difficult moments getting it going again.

Caleb noted, to his surprise, that Porky was the one who

had responded most efficiently during the crisis. Galvanized into action, he not only kept his head, but retracted with might and main, understanding where his efforts were needed the most, making the work of the others that much easier.

The entire operation lasted almost four hours, and the room was silent during most of that time. Occasionally Caleb said something to encourage them when spirits seemed to flag, but a kind of depression settled over the rest of them after the emergency was over. Don recognized that he had been out of his depth, and that worried and frightened him. At this stage in his career he knew he should be able to deal competently with just about any surgical crisis that could come up.

When the aneurysm burst, Ed forgot his fury with Collie, but it came back when the emergency was over, redoubled. Positioned on the patient's left, opposite Collie, he was forced to see her black eye every time he looked up. She'd changed more than he could imagine anybody changing, all in the space of a couple of days. In spite of her bruises, or maybe because of them, she had an extraordinary look about her. It wasn't exactly contentment, although there was some of that too, but more an inexplicable aura of fulfillment, as if she'd been waiting all her life, actually *waiting*, to get bashed about by this animal Milo Zagros. Ed would have thought Collie would be too embarrassed to look at him, but no, she eyed him now quite calmly, as if there had never been anything more than just a working relationship between them.

"Ed, tighten up on the suture." Caleb was looking at him with a strange expression, and his voice was sharp. When operating with Caleb Winter, it was unwise to let one's mind wander. Ed took up the strain on the suture Don was using to sew the graft into position. He knew the importance of keeping the tension steady while the stitches were being put in. Otherwise the graft could leak when the circulation was opened up again, with disastrous results.

Collie was working on marginal efficiency also. Every bone of her body ached, and every time she made the slightest movement it reminded her of the evening before. Just thinking back made the blood rush through her body like a tidal pulse. Luckily she knew her job well. While Caleb and Don were checking that their operative field was dry and no small vessels were bleeding unchecked, she threaded the thick, curved Mayo needles with nonabsorbable sutures and clipped them on to a needle holder. These sutures would be needed to close the abdominal muscles, and although they weren't at that point quite yet, it was always wise to have things like that ready ahead of time. You never knew when you'd get another free moment.

Meanwhile she thought about Milo. She rolled his name around her head, lovingly. She was already planning the next meeting with him. They'd have the most wonderful dinner she could make, then she'd dance naked for him, before they went to bed for their final cataclysmic orgasm. Collie shivered, and Cal's eyes moved curiously to her for a fraction of a second.

After the graft was in, Caleb took the clamps off the blood vessels and checked that the blood was once more coursing through the lower part of the patient's body. Then, when Caleb was satisfied that everything was stable, he stepped back from the table and pulled off his gloves.

"I'll be on the pager if you need me," he said to Don, and headed for the door, untying his gown as he went. The circulator flew to untie it for him, but it was already off by the time she reached him.

"Thanks for your help, Dr. Winter," said Don as Caleb opened the door to leave. He was feeling thoroughly humbled. He knew that in a hundred years of surgical practice he would never get close to being the kind of surgeon that Caleb Winter was.

Caleb nodded at him over his shoulder, and then he was gone.

"He's quite a guy, huh," said Don quietly after a long silence. Nobody answered. Nobody had to.

Ed said nothing throughout the remainder of the case, but his fury gathered until he thought he would burst every time he saw Collie's black eye. A resolve grew in him as they put the final skin-clips into the patient, and was fully developed by the time they'd changed out of their greens.

"I'm going down to Winter's lab," he told Don. The tone of his voice was enough to let Don know why he was heading for these unfamiliar premises. "I'll meet you on Harkness."

"Don't do anything rash," said Don warningly. "Remember, you have a career to think about."

Ed's career was the last thing on his mind as he ran down the stairwell to the lab floor. He wasn't clear about what he was going to do. Milo would probably be in the lab, and Ed saw himself picking the little runt up by the scruff of the neck and pounding him to a pulp while the shocked techs watched the massacre.

Ed had almost reached the lab when a door opened ahead of him, and the wiry figure of Milo Zagros came out and started to walk up the corridor in front of him. The sight of Milo galvanized Ed. Light on his feet, he covered the ten yards of deserted corridor between them like a linebacker and caught the researcher by the shoulder and spun him around. Milo, startled, saw the fury in Ed's face and opened his mouth to say something, but Ed put a hand on each lapel of Milo's white coat and yanked them together, tight enough to squeeze the breath out of him.

"Listen to me, you little shit," said Ed, his voice growling in the back of his throat. He shook Milo as he spoke until Milo's teeth rattled, and he barely controlled his desire to smash his fist into Milo's face. "You just touch Collie Zintel again, and I'll make you sorry you ever saw her."

Ed pulled the terrified researcher toward him until they were nose to nose. "I can't stop her going out with you," he grated, "but I sure as hell can stop her getting hurt." Ed tightened his grasp, and Milo found he couldn't breathe. Milo was wiry and tough and could have got out of Ed's grip, but he felt paralyzed, partly by fear, but also because he knew that Ed was in the right, and that he deserved everything he got.

Ed changed his grip slightly, and Milo felt himself being lifted into the air and slammed against the wall. His head snapped back and struck the wall with a loud crack. Milo saw stars and thought Ed was going to kill him right then. Ed's big square face was still close up against his, the flat, boxer's nose, tight lips, and the eyes slitted with fury. Milo could feel

Ed's breath coming hard on him. Ed smashed him against the wall one more time, then let him go. Milo slid halfway down the wall, dazed, unable to get his breath, but he still had a strange, defiant expression on his face.

"Next time, you little fuck," whispered Ed, enunciating every word slowly, "if there is a next time, there will be a serious accident during which your neck will be broken."

Ed turned and walked back along the corridor, feeling only a little relief from the anger still seething inside him.

When Caleb left the operating suite, he checked over the things he still had to do that morning. The aneurysm had taken far too long, but he couldn't have left Don and his team any sooner. He looked at his watch. He had a meeting scheduled with L. Graham Benson, the university chaplain, in twenty minutes. Luckily he wouldn't have to go across town; to Caleb's surprise, Benson had insisted on coming over to the medical school.

"Your time is so much more valuable than mine," he had protested silkily on the phone, quite obviously not believing a word of what he said. "Fear not, Mahomet will be happy to make his way to the mountain."

"Pompous ass," thought Caleb. Anyway, he still had time to look in on the lab, and maybe there would be an extra minute or two to visit Celine. But first he'd need to find out the results of her CAT scan, he reminded himself, smiling. He now knew better than to visit her without due preparation.

At the door of the lab, he almost bumped into Maureen, and in a strange way the encounter surprised him, probably because his thoughts were elsewhere.

Maureen put a hand lightly on his sleeve. "I'm glad I saw you," she said. "Basil Muldrew called from San Francisco. He wants to talk to you urgently. I told him you were operating, and you'd call him back." Maureen hesitated. "He sounded really upset, Caleb."

"Did he say what he wanted?" asked Caleb, who had a pretty good idea. Paula must have told her husband about the episode with Milo.

"No. He said you would know. It wouldn't have anything to do with Milo, would it?"

"Could be," he said, evasively. Then reminding himself there was no point in keeping his most loyal and loving co-worker in the dark, he said, "Yes, it probably does." He told Maureen the whole story, and after he finished, she laughed.

"You know, Cal, maybe you're overreacting." Maureen's eyes were twinkling, just as they used to in the old days. "Milo makes a pass, she sits on him and almost breaks his arm, both go home. No bones broken, honor intact. End of story."

"I'm sure you're right. But tell that to Basil, not me." Caleb grinned, and his face seemed so open and boyish that Maureen could have wept with all the emotions he aroused in her.

That was when Caleb realized that there was something disturbing about the way Maureen was acting. "What's the matter, Maureen?"

Maureen hesitated. "Cal, I'd rather not talk to you out here."

"Let's go into your office, then," he said, and pushed open the door of the lab. Maureen followed him in.

"What's on your mind?" he asked as she closed the door of the office behind her.

"I've decided to leave, Cal," she said. She had practiced her speech, but even so her voice was unsteady.

Caleb sat down in Maureen's chair and stared at her. "Why, for God's sake?" he asked. "If you need more money . . ."

"Caleb Winter, you know better than that," she replied sharply, hurt that he could say something so crass. "It has nothing to do with money, as you must damn well know. Cal, don't you remember when we had no money at all? Before we got the big grants, when we used to go snooping around trying to borrow equipment, celebrating with a bottle of Gallo red every time we got a paper published, just one bottle because we couldn't afford two? Oh Cal, when we were all poor, it was so great, don't you remember?"

Impulsively, Maureen came around the desk, grabbed him by the shoulders, and shook him gently, her eyes full of tears. Caleb couldn't help being affected by those blue eyes; the tears made them glow with the same passionate radiance they had the very first time he saw her, that evening when he'd lectured to her biology class.

Of course he remembered. It had been the most frightening, the most insecure, and without question the happiest time in his life. He smiled, hoping he'd be able to make her change her mind.

"Do you remember the time we got that salesman drunk? The rep from Davis and Geck? On the last of our lab ethyl alcohol and some orange juice from the biochemistry refrigerator?" Caleb smiled at the recollection.

"It was a good investment, though. He gave us enough suture material to last us almost three months." Maureen's hands slipped down the lapels of Caleb's jacket.

"So what was that about leaving?"

Maureen let go of his lapels and stepped away from him. "It's all so different now," she said. "You're successful, your career is going well, the research is really taking off, and you don't need me any more."

"That's just nonsense," said Caleb. "You know perfectly well how much the whole research effort depends on you." He looked at Maureen, his eyes narrowing. "Okay, Maureen, out with it. What's the real reason?"

Maureen looked right back at him with a challenging stare.

"All right, Caleb Winter, if that's what you want. The real reason is that you're totally egocentric, you don't give a damn for anybody else's feelings, you just use the people around you, and I've had enough of it."

Caleb leaned back in his chair and folded his arms in front of him; Maureen could feel him withdrawing into himself. When he spoke, his voice was clipped, defensive.

"You know that's not true," he said. "I fight for what we're all doing, not just for me. I agree that sometimes people get hurt, feelings get ruffled, but I have to do that occasionally to keep everybody on track, to keep the momentum going." Maureen knew that she'd got him where it hurt, and she derived a certain guilty satisfaction from it. Caleb went on in the same tone, "I'm at least as hard on myself as on anybody on the team, wouldn't you say?"

"And not only that," said Maureen as if she'd heard nothing. Her voice quavered for a second, and she was furious with herself for her weakness. "Now I hear rumors around the hospital about you and Celine de La Roche."

"Well? What else do you hear?" Caleb's voice sounded disbelievingly amused, as if he'd stepped into a play he didn't belong in.

"That you were seen up in her room last night, holding her in your arms. The only thing that makes me believe it, Caleb, is that you *have* been acting different. That's why I'm leaving, finally. Only I'm doing it several years too late."

Caleb bounded out of the chair.

"I've never heard such absolute shit in my life. If that's the only thing that's bothering you, I suggest you get back to work, and right now. There's plenty to do before . . ."

"I don't think you're listening to me, Caleb," said Maureen gently. To her own surprise, his anger didn't seem to be having any effect on her now. "I'm leaving. If you really have to have a reason, it's a combination of all the things I mentioned. If you're not in love, I'm sorry. You should try it."

"Damn it, Maureen! You really know how to pick your moments! Of all times, you choose this one when we're about to do our first transplant." He glowered at her, and she almost quailed at the depth of his anger.

But his fury liberated her, in a way she didn't understand.

"There never would be a right time," she said. "Just like the vacation we never took. There would always be some experiment, some grant application, some presentation that had to come first. No, Caleb, this is the moment. And please, just do me one favor, don't start telling me that I'm letting you down."

Caleb banged his fist on the desk, once, very hard. He didn't look at her. It wasn't often that anyone had the temerity to stand up to him like this, but the worst thing was that Maureen should be the one to betray him, of all people.

"You have two more betrayals before you catch up with St. Peter," he said bitterly. "Why don't you go to work for Henry Brighton? He's looking for help, and I'm sure you could think of a third."

"That's not worthy of you, Caleb. You're simply too used

to getting your own way about everything. At some point you'll have to learn to deal with that." Maureen spoke seriously, her eyes on his face. Anybody with as strong a character as Caleb's was bound to get used to having his own way; that was how such people got results in their work. And the older he became, and the more his influence and power increased, the harder it would become for anyone to challenge him.

"I'll clear out my desk this afternoon," said Maureen. "Milo and you know where the records are, and where all the data's kept. There's no point in prolonging the agony."

She opened the door and went out, leaving Caleb alone.

"Fucking women!" he said several moments later, his voice loud in the empty lab. How could she leave now? She'd really screwed him this time. He'd have to get Milo and one of the techs to prepare the graft. Luckily Milo had had some surgical training in Zagreb, and he'd helped Maureen in the past with the animal experiments, so he knew what to do. But Milo still had to do all the work on the antirejection protocol that Celine would be on. Well, they'd manage somehow. Cal got up, feeling a huge wave of anger and resentment against Maureen. And all because she thought he was in love with Celine de La Roche. Caleb shook his head as he opened the lab door. How could she possibly have come to that conclusion?

Celine pushed away her unfinished dinner. Chicken breast with peas and mashed potatoes followed by bright red Jell-O with bits of banana suspended in it wouldn't have done much for her at the best of times. She wasn't hungry, and she had a nasty feeling the pain might be coming back.

The CAT scan earlier in the day had been an anticlimax; she'd got herself all mentally prepared for something more alarming than it turned out to be. They slid her into the hole of this huge doughnut-shaped machine, then the doctor told her to hold her breath, there was a whirring noise for a few seconds, and that was it.

There was a knock at her door, and Caleb came in. She hadn't heard him coming. Celine felt her heart leap, and wondered if he knew the effect he had on people when he appeared so dramatically, like Hamlet materializing on a hushed stage. Caleb paused in the doorway and Celine twisted her head around to look at him.

"Before you ask," he said, "I'm ready to talk to you about your CAT scan results."

Just from the sound of his voice, Celine had the feeling that he was treating her somehow differently now, but at the same time a sudden fear fluttered in her breast; she sensed she was about to hear more bad news. "Come in," she said. "I can't talk to you with my neck turned around like this."

This time Caleb sat on the edge of the bed, against hospital regulations. His energy danced like St. Elmo's fire around him.

Aha, she thought, looking at him anxiously, trying to get

an advance warning of what he was going to say, it's your eyebrows that give you away, my friend, more than your eyes or that mouth that so rarely smiles. The curve of Caleb's eyebrows had vanished, making a hard ridge above his eyes, separated by a deep furrow.

"So what do you have to tell me?" Celine looked into his cool, unembarrassed eyes, and for the first time had an inkling of how much information he extracted from that momentary inspection he always subjected her to.

She pulled the bed sheet up around her neck. Her heart was beating so hard she wondered if he could hear it.

"It's what I thought," he replied calmly. "The tumor is in the pancreas, it's about six centimeters across, roughly spherical." He looked at Celine, and a faint smile creased his lips. "A small tangerine," he explained. "It doesn't seem to have spread, but of course I can't be sure until I actually look at it."

Even with the news he was giving her, Celine felt like cheering. "Well, that sounds like good news, doesn't it?" she said, finding herself wishing he'd slide up the bed a little closer so she could feel the warmth of his leg.

Caleb's honesty made him hesitate. "Yes, in a way," he said.

There was a long pause while Celine tried to think of something to say that wouldn't break whatever it was that she felt so strongly was developing between them.

Caleb cleared his throat, and moved slightly. Celine could feel that he had come fractionally closer. His words brought her back to her underlying fear. "I think we should operate some time next week, probably around Tuesday. I don't know quite enough about that tumor yet."

"What more do you want to know? Its social security number? The color of its hair? Is it faithful to its husband?"

All these words came spilling out and she was aghast when she heard them. He'd think she was out of her mind. But her outburst didn't seem to faze Caleb in the slightest, and for a second Celine wondered if he was just humoring her.

"No, I know all that already. Here, this is what I need to know . . ." Caleb pulled a pen from the top pocket of his white coat, then a black, leather-covered notebook, which he opened to a blank page.

"Look." He edged along the bed nearer to her and started to draw something that looked like an elongated pear on its side. "Here's the tumor." He pointed to a place near the thick end of the pear and drew a circle there. He quickly drew some straight lines at right angles to the pear. Watching the smooth and accurate movements of his hands, Celine could imagine his fingers holding a knife, cutting into her with the most exquisite precision.

"And here is the portal vein, and these are the superior mesenteric vessels." He glanced sideways at her and laughed. "I know you don't understand a word of what I'm talking about, so I won't go on. It's simply this. If the tumor involves these blood vessels, I can't remove it. If it doesn't, and it hasn't spread to other places, there's a good chance."

"It doesn't," said Celine, again to her astonishment. "You'll get it out, I know it."

Caleb went on as if she hadn't said anything. His expression became very serious again. "It's not just a matter of taking the tumor out." He hesitated for a second, then stood up. "We're talking about what's called a Whipple procedure, Celine. Even if the tumor's operable, it means removing a lot of tissue, a good part of your stomach, some of the upper intestine." As he went on to describe the extent of the operation, Celine felt a cold and awful fear spread through her.

"Is that the only way you can treat this?" she said when he'd finished. Her voice was only a whisper. "I think I'd rather just die."

Caleb sat down on the bed again. "There is a possible alternative." His voice remained dispassionate, as if he were discussing two different ways of tying a shoelace. "That would consist of just removing the pancreas, radiating the area with microwaves, and putting in a pancreas transplant."

"Sounds a lot better to me," said Celine when he finished explaining. She put her hands under the bedclothes so he wouldn't see them trembling.

"You have to understand that I'm talking about an experimental procedure, Celine. We've never done one of those before, and nor has anyone else, so I can't tell you the chances of success."

"This is what you've been working up to, isn't it?" she asked. "I mean your research and everything. This isn't just something you dreamed up last night."

"We've been working at this for ten years, Celine, and I feel we're ready."

Normally, Celine would have felt an acute need for Charles's presence at this time to share the fear, to feel that he was there, on her side. But now, she felt that the only person she needed on her side was Caleb. Even if she didn't quite understand what he was talking about, Celine felt she knew enough to make the choice between the Whipple and the graft.

"I'll need to talk to Charles, of course," said Caleb.

The mention of his name seemed to place a barrier between them, but only for a moment.

"Anyway, before we can make any decisions," said Caleb briskly, "we need an arteriogram. That means injecting some stuff into the arteries that shows up on X-rays. Then I'll know what I want to know, and as soon as that's done, we'll decide, okay?"

"On one condition."

Caleb sat down on the bed again. "What's that?"

"That you're there when they do it."

"Do what?"

"The arteriogram."

Caleb didn't hesitate. "I'll be there," he said. "I promise."

Celine took a big breath. "About last night," she said.

Caleb sat very still, his gaze fixed on her. "Yes?"

"I just want you to know that I don't enter easily into relationships," she said, and after a pause she went on. "Caleb, I am a very serious person. If you're taking this lightly, I'd rather know about it now."

Caleb put his hand up very gently to touch Celine's cheek, and he held it there for a long moment, looking into her eyes with an expression she couldn't fathom.

"Celine, I'm a serious person too. Right now, you're my

patient, and I'm taking that more seriously than you could imagine."

Without another word, Caleb got up and left, leaving Celine trying to figure out exactly what he meant.

Within seconds of Caleb leaving, Mrs. Koslowski was back, poking her head into the room. "Ya need anything?" she asked, her big, honest smile wide on her face, but by the time Celine started to ask her to bring a glass of soda, she was already closing the door behind her.

"That woman," said Mrs. Koslowski when she got back to the nurses' station, "she thinks us nurses are some kind of slaves, or something. 'Do this, do that, fetch this, get me that,' she says, all the time. Never satisfied, there's always something else she needs."

"Yeah, she's a real bitch," said the aide, the one who had put Celine's clothes away. "She's scheduled for surgery next Tuesday. That'll make her change her tune."

The room buzzer sounded, and the light corresponding to Celine's room went on, a dim, yellow glow on the panel. The aide leaned across Mrs. Koslowski, turned it off, and went back to her magazine.

In her room, Celine saw the little yellow light go out on the panel, and it seemed an apt metaphor for her own existence. She lay down, feeling a wild need for Caleb's presence. As long as he was physically there with her, she felt invulnerable, but in the chilly solitude of that moment she was gripped by so many fears that she didn't even know where they were all coming from. She pulled the top sheet over her head so that if anyone came in they wouldn't see her tears.

"Basil, what can I tell you? You know I'm really mortified about what happened."

Basil Muldrew's angry voice rose again. "I want an apology, Cal, from this creature Zagros to Paula. She was so upset when she got back here, I wanted to come East and kill the bastard."

Caleb visualized Basil for a second, every slender inch of him. If Paula was half as tough as Milo had said, it was surprising that little Basil was still alive.

"You'll get it, Basil. I've already hauled him over the coals."
Basil was sounding so tough and protective, it almost made
him laugh. Only it was serious, and his anger at Milo flared
again. Maybe he should bite the bullet and get rid of him.

Instantly he felt angry at himself for such a disloyal thought.
Milo was his protégé. Hadn't he stolen him out of the jaws
of the Yugoslav KGB or whatever they called their spooks
there? If Caleb gave up on him, nobody would give him a job,
because they'd figure if he was still any good, Caleb Winter
would never have let him go.

Donna, Caleb's secretary, came in and indicated to him in
sign language that the Reverend L. Graham Benson had arrived and was waiting in the outer office.

By the time Caleb replaced the phone, he had been able
to calm Basil down. Having made his point and established
himself as the protector of his wife's virtue, Basil had reassumed his usual deferential attitude toward Caleb.

Feeling more than usually cynical, Caleb buzzed Donna to
bring in the Reverend Benson.

Benson was in his late thirties, not at all dismayed by his
developing monsignorial rotundity. His pink cheeks and the
large bald patch at the back of his head strengthened the
impression of membership in a monastic order committed to
the production of fine after-dinner liqueurs. His handshake
was limp and moist, and when he sat down his knees spread
because of the size of his paunch. He sat facing Caleb, a
benign smile on his face and his palms together in a prayerful
pose.

"May our deliberations meet with success, amen," he said
quietly, almost to himself. It was evident that God and he
chatted frequently together, in an unofficial kind of way.
Caleb watched him with a grudging amusement. That little
charade was certainly calculated to put any adversary at a
disadvantage.

"Good of you to come," said Caleb. "I suppose the committees you're on get you into strange places."

"Indeed, indeed," replied L. Graham. "From the hovels of
the poor to the palaces of the fortunate." His voice left no
doubt as to where his preferences lay.

"And talking about palaces," he went on, "I was privileged to meet with a mutual friend of ours just a day or two ago." His twinkling blue eyes didn't leave Caleb's face. "Anna Lynn Page and Larry are such wonderful people, aren't they?"

Caleb listened and said nothing; Benson was evidently used to keeping up a monologue. Eventually he got to the point. Caleb didn't need to convince him of the rightness of his cause. The rights of animals were important, there was no question about that, but those rights had to be subordinated to those of human beings. There was more than enough justification for that in the Scriptures, he went on, evidently ready to quote Caleb chapter and verse.

Caleb was surprised by Benson's perspiring, beaming pleasantness, for he knew of the chaplain's militant attitude concerning animal rights and had not expected his support. But his surprise didn't last long. As he left, Benson was fulsome once again in his praise of the Pages, and rather naïvely mentioned that they'd undertaken to finance a two-month visit to Jerusalem for him, during which time he would be given access to some extremely rare early Judeo-Christian documents that would almost guarantee the acceptance of his doctoral dissertation.

Good old Anna Lynn, Caleb thought. She knew how to get things done, and certainly didn't hesitate to spend money when that was the way to do it.

Didier Franchet sat at the sturdy Sheraton-type table in his suite at the Plaza. The white telephone had been in his hand almost continuously for the past two hours while he talked with brokers, his Wall Street attorneys, and a succession of dealers, liquidators, and auctioneers who would handle the sale of Fortman and Carfield's assets as soon as he had his hands on them. His strategy was simple; once he had fifty-one percent of the voting stock, he would call an extraordinary meeting of the board and make a limited offer to buy back the outstanding stock, most of which would be owned by Celine. But much as he liked Celine, Didier had no intention of sharing the profit with her. Didier knew she had financed the stock purchase through the bank, largely on the strength of her ability to revive Fortman and Carfield. But when the bankers discovered that the company was to be liquidated, and when they saw the trouble Celine's own company had got into, they would be forced to foreclose on her. Didier genuinely felt badly about having to sabotage Celine's publishing house, but there didn't seem to be any other way around the problem.

Meanwhile, it was time to go up into the wilds of Connecticut to find out how Celine was. At that moment a call came from the front desk, telling him his car was waiting. Didier put some papers in his briefcase so the traveling time wouldn't be wasted, and a little over two hours later he was at the hospital, tapping on Celine's door.

"Oncle Didi!"

With a cry of pleasure Celine put out her arms and hugged him. It was wonderful to see him; he smelt of the same after-shave, the same tobacco, and still had that bristly place on his chin where the razor couldn't get around the corner.

"Eh bien, ma petite," he said, wheezing a bit as he lowered himself into the chair, "I must say you look pretty well, for a woman with one foot in the grave and the other on a banana peel!"

Celine told him what had been happening, the tests, the choices she had to make. It was so nice to have Didi there; he gave her such a sense of her childhood, of safety and un-questioning, undemanding love.

While she was talking, Didier took his presents out of a large orange Hermès bag and placed them separately on the bed. Celine really did look well, and Didier was confused; surely all this couldn't have been just a false alarm? But he knew that Celine was no hypochondriac; she was far too busy and far too stable.

"Who is your doctor?" he asked, taking a cachou from a round gray-green box and putting it in his mouth. "Do you like him? Does he know what he's doing?"

Perhaps his tone was too skeptical; Celine felt an instant urge to come to Caleb's defense, although she resisted the impulse.

"Everybody says he's very competent," she said cautiously. "He comes across as a bit arrogant at first, but then show me a surgeon who doesn't." She smiled, but felt Oncle Didi's observant, cynical eyes on her, so she tried to sound cynical herself. "I'm being as nice as I can to him," she said. "Talk about life insurance!"

"Good, good," said Didier, nodding vigorously. He held the cachou between his front teeth and thoughtfully sucked air in around it. So Celine was getting emotionally involved with her surgeon. Well, that was very interesting, but not of im-mediate importance to him. Later, if the relationship sur-vived, and if Celine herself survived, that situation might have to be reappraised.

Didier was well aware that many women fall in love with their surgeons; he was also aware that very often the affliction is transient. He smiled at Celine with a conspiratorial grin. "Falling in love with your surgeon is perfectly all right," he said. "But remember, it's like mumps, hard to ignore while it lasts, but usually gone without trace after two or three weeks."

Celine laughed, not entirely happy with the comparison.

"What about the other doctors? How are the nursing staff and aides?" asked Didier. Having already understood about Dr. Winter, he felt no need to go on about him. People often mistook his quickness for tact.

Didier peered at the pile of manuscripts on Celine's bed table, and was asking how the publishing world was surviving without her when Mrs. Koslowski came in.

"This isn't visiting time," she said in her harsh monotone, looking Didier and his gifts over carefully. This woman Della Roach, she was something else again, with all those men creeping around her like maggots wriggling in an eye socket.

Didier gave her a cold stare, but almost at the same time noticed Celine's drawn expression. She was tired, and the last thing he wanted to do was overstay his welcome. So he got out of the chair, grunting and struggling.

"I'll be back tomorrow, if you can stand it," he said, leaning over to kiss Celine on one cheek, then the other.

Mrs. Koslowski stood by the door, her heavy arms held slightly away from her body, disapproval oozing from every pore.

"Whipple, Whipple, Whipple," muttered Didier to himself as he walked back along the corridor. On the ground floor he followed the signs that pointed to the medical school, and found the medical library without too much difficulty. The surgical section was up on the balcony; Didier creaked up the wooden stairs, too preoccupied to feel breathless. He wasn't sure where to start, so he went over to the shelves of general textbooks. In Sabiston's large tome he found all he wanted to know, and more.

When Caleb tried to reach Chauncey Milford Roper at his office, he was told that he was out of town and couldn't be reached. Caleb didn't know much about the man except that he was high up in the pharmaceutical industry and had made a great deal of money at it. Caleb had met him a couple of times, but since Chauncey was interested only in people with whom he could do business, their meeting had been cordial but brief. All the same, Caleb had no reason to think that Chauncey Roper would vote against the transplant project. He was known as a person who went along with anything that sounded reasonable.

As for Foster Armuth, the chairman, Caleb had decided to say nothing to him. Armuth had been around for a long time and knew what was what, and if he had any questions he would ask Caleb himself. The last name on the list was Henry Brighton, who seemed to have developed an incredible ability to avoid Caleb; he was rarely in his office, or was too busy, or in a meeting.

Caleb looked at the list on his desk and ticked off those who were on his side. Anna Lynn Page, of course; the Reverend Benson; probably Chauncey Roper; and most likely Foster Armuth. That left Leroy Williams and Henry Brighton. So, Caleb figured, even if Henry voted against the proposal, it should get through handily.

The phone rang on his desk, startling him. Mr. Gordon, the man whose aneurysm had ruptured on the table, had developed a bad pneumonia and wasn't doing very well; the residents were considering putting him on a respirator. It wasn't really urgent; the head nurse in the ICU just wanted him to know.

Now, if only he were a woman, he thought sarcastically, thinking about Maureen, he could simply guess what was going on up there in the ICU, and his intuition would surely tell him what treatment to recommend. Caleb headed toward the ICU, slamming the door behind him.

Porky was at the door of the ICU, holding two X-rays in his hand.

"Am I glad to see you, Dr. Winter!" said Porky with such a look of heartfelt relief that Caleb smiled.

"What's up, Porky?"

"It's Mr. Gordon, in bed five, the one we did the aneurysm on."

"He seemed all right this morning," said Caleb.

"Yes, he was, but about an hour ago he started to get really breathless. He was sweating, and of course Don thought he might have had an MI." Porky was hesitating, but Caleb said nothing. He wanted to see how Porky would phrase what he had to say without implicating his chief resident.

"His EKG didn't show much change, and his pressure went up just a bit. We drew some enzymes, 'lytes, a CBC, the usual stuff."

"Did you get a portable chest X-ray?"

"Yes, I just got them back," said Porky, brightening. He held the films up. "Do you have a minute to look at them?"

Caleb opened the door and they went into the Unit. The bank of six viewing boxes was just inside, and as Caleb flipped the switch they flickered and lit up, illuminating the doctors' faces with an unearthly white glow.

Porky put the two films up on the screens, and both men stared at them for a moment. Caleb noted that the left side of the chest film was lighter than the other.

"What do you see, Porky?"

Porky hesitated. "I don't see any lung markings on the left, Dr. Winter. I was thinking of maybe a pneumothorax."

"What does his chest sound like?"

"Well, that's why I got the films," replied Porky. "He didn't have any breath sounds at all on the left. Ed and I thought he'd got a pneumonia."

Caleb was already striding toward bed five. He opened the glass door of the cubicle and walked in. Mr. Gordon certainly did not look well. A nurse was wiping his forehead with a wet sponge, and he was breathing with difficulty although he was wearing an oxygen mask. He looked up and seemed relieved to see Caleb.

Caleb grinned reassuringly at him and gave him a quick once-over. It told him that the patient was breathing approximately three times faster than normal, he was using his accessory neck muscles to draw air into his chest, and the veins in his neck were dilated, which suggested that the blood was having difficulty getting back into his chest from his head and neck. In addition, his lips were bluish from lack of oxygen even though he was getting additional oxygen through the mask. So far it was a clear clinical picture, confirmed by the X-rays.

Caleb took the nurse's stethoscope from around her neck and pulled back the top sheet.

"Just taking a look, Mr. Gordon."

Porky noted how the very tone of Dr. Winter's voice reassured Mr. Gordon, and he filed that information away in his memory. No question about it, there was more to surgery than just cutting.

A quick glance under the dressing told Caleb that the long abdominal incision was intact, and he turned quickly to the chest. There was indeed no air coming into the left lung.

Marcie Cole, the head nurse, materialized soundlessly at Caleb's side. Young for such a position of responsibility, she was competent, pretty, and idolized Caleb.

"Thanks for coming," she murmured as Caleb straightened up.

"You have some air on the outside of your left lung," Caleb told the patient. "We need to get it out, because it's preventing air from getting *inside* where it needs to be. You'll feel a lot better after Dr. Rosen's removed it."

Porky's eyes widened, and a feeling of panic swept over him. Dr. Winter wanted him to do the thoracentesis? He knew more or less how to do it, of course, but neither Ed nor Don would have dreamed of allowing him to do one by himself.

"Do you have the tray ready?" Caleb asked Marcie.

"Right here." The tray was already on an instrument table, wrapped in a transparent plastic covering.

"Then I don't need to ask if the suction apparatus is ready."

Marcie smiled and pointed to a flat transparent plastic box about half the size of a briefcase. It was already attached to the wall suction and contained the blue fluid that would catch and trap the air and liquid that would come rushing out of Mr. Gordon's chest.

"Okay, Porky," said Caleb, "go to it."

But he must have seen the light of panic in Porky's eye, so without saying anything more he took off his white coat and rolled up his sleeves. "I'll give you a hand, if you like."

Porky flashed him a quick look of gratitude, and the two of

them did a brief scrub and put on gloves. Porky eyed the instruments on the table. They were shiny, sterile, and somehow threatening, as if they were telling him he had no right to touch them. He took a deep breath and looked around. Marcie and the other nurse were standing there looking at him, and Caleb was watching him too. They were all waiting for *him!* Suddenly a feeling came over Porky that he would remember for the rest of his life. He knew what needed to be done, and he also knew how to do it. A great wave of confidence swept over him, and it was pure bliss.

Marcie and the other nurse had taken Mr. Gordon's pajama top off, propped him up, and turned him on his side. Now Marcie was scrubbing a round area of his chest with iodoform.

"That'll do it," said Porky, and she stopped, surprised by the decisiveness of his tone. Porky quickly placed four sterile drapes around the cleansed area, and Caleb fastened them together at the corners with towel clips.

"Xylocaine, 1%, with adrenalin," said Porky calmly to the other nurse, who approached, holding out a red-topped vial with the rubber stopper toward him. His hand was as steady as a rock, and she sensed the change in Porky's manner. Even though she didn't know him well, she did know that Porky was often the butt of jokes that nurses and the other doctors made when he wasn't around.

With his gloved finger Porky felt for a space between the third and fourth ribs. When he found it, he couldn't help glancing at Caleb, who nodded encouragingly.

"You're going to feel a little stick, Mr. Gordon," said Porky, a shade loudly. "It's a local anesthetic, so you won't feel us poking around."

He pushed the slender needle into the skin and pressed gently on the plunger. A small white wheal rose up on the skin. Then he pushed the needle deeper to reach the muscles and membranes of the chest wall.

Caleb watched him with a pleased surprise. For the first time he could remember, Porky was acting like a real surgeon.

The big syringe was hidden under a green towel; normally Porky would have been so flustered looking for it that he would have upended the whole tray, but today he stayed admirably cool. He fitted the big needle with its plastic sheath on to the syringe, gritted his teeth, and pushed it firmly into Mr. Gordon's numbed chest. Then he slipped the needle out, leaving the stiff plastic tube in position, and attached the end to the suction tube. He nodded to Marcie, who turned the suction on, and immediately a gush of air and bubbles of reddish fluid came pouring out of his chest and into the plastic container, which bubbled and shook like a witch's cauldron. Porky quickly checked the tubing and the suction pressure; Mr. Gordon's color improved immediately, and his breathing slowed and became deeper. Porky quickly put a retaining stitch through the skin to keep the plastic sheath from falling out of the patient's chest, and applied an airtight dressing. It was all over in a few minutes, and as he took off his gloves he felt a thrill of achievement the like of which he had never known.

"Good for you, Porky!" said Caleb. "I knew you could do it."

Before leaving, Porky listened to Mr. Gordon's chest and had the satisfaction of hearing a normal flow of air in and out of both lungs. It was only after he got outside the patient's cubicle that he suddenly felt faint and had to sit down for a few minutes at the nurses' desk to get his own breathing back to normal.

Ten minutes later, when Porky was leaving the ICU in a cloud of pleasure at his own competent handling of the operation, he heard his name being paged over the loudspeaker system, summoning him to Dr. Brighton's office. He ran downstairs and arrived panting.

Dr. Brighton was standing behind his operations board, with some pieces of colored paper and a pair of scissors in his hand. He beamed at Porky out of his round, boyish pink face.

"Yes, Dr. Rosen. I managed to find a replacement for you, so you're fired, as of next Friday."

He turned his back on Porky, climbed up on the small step ladder, and started to rearrange the markers on the board.

· · · · · PART THREE · · ·

"Well, Dr. Winter, we don't see you down here too often," said Morrie Stein, the head of the department of radiology. His eyes moved from Celine back to Caleb, who had accompanied her down from the surgical floor, walking alongside her wheelchair.

"My team's usually in your department long after you've gone." Caleb smiled back, but he felt a little uncomfortable. It *was* unusual for an attending surgeon to come down to the X-ray department with one of his patients.

"I asked him to come," said Celine, smiling up at both of them. "In fact I told him I wouldn't have it done unless he was there."

"Of course," said Morrie quickly. He'd heard the rumors too, but had discounted them. "Yes, of course. We should be ready in just a few minutes."

Morrie went down the corridor to the special procedures room reserved for arteriograms and other tests that required the use of sterile equipment. Two techs, Selma Spratt, the department's black chief tech, and a new assistant were setting the room up.

"How long will you be?" inquired Morrie.

"We're almost ready," answered Selma, holding up a large, unusually heavy syringe in her hand. "I'm just loading up the injector."

Morrie watched her slide the barrel of the syringe into a machine standing by the table. It resembled a harpoon gun and was used for fast injection of contrast material into the arteries. The contrast fluid showed up on the X-rays, lighting up the blood vessels, which would otherwise be invisible.

"We'll need an extra lead apron," said Morrie. "Dr. Winter's going to be coming in with us."

Selma looked up in surprise. "Oh yeah?" she said. "Sure, no problem."

When Celine was wheeled into the room a few minutes later, Caleb went into the darkened control room, from where he could watch everything that went on. They were a really efficient team, Caleb saw that immediately. Everything was in position, nobody rushed around, each person there seemed to know exactly what he or she was doing. And there was no question that in that department, Selma was the unobtrusive guiding light. She was not attractive: heavy, slow-moving, with black braided hair pushed under a paper cap, and a flat, stubborn-looking face. Caleb knew Selma had started work in the X-ray department as a low-level filing clerk, had gone to training school, passed her exams, and was now the head technician in this large and prestigious unit. Good for her, thought Caleb. He watched the methodical way she positioned Celine, all the while explaining what she was doing.

Morrie appeared behind Caleb, his face illuminated by the red glow from the console lights which gave him an odd, Mephistophelean look. "What exactly are we looking for?" he asked.

"The CAT scan showed the tumor," replied Caleb. "I need to see its blood supply, the arteries going into it, the veins coming out. It'll help me decide whether it's operable or not."

Caleb was simplifying the problem; he knew that no arteriogram could give him more than an indication of the overall situation. The only way to know for sure was to have the patient open in front of him. Until then it was largely guesswork, although the studies certainly helped him to plan the operation.

Selma had bared Celine's right leg and groin, which had been shaved up in her room by Mrs. Koslowski; Caleb could see the scratches and angry red skin in the area. Sometimes that was unavoidable. Caleb became aware of Morrie Stein's beady-eyed interest as Celine's exquisite leg became visible in its entirety, and his lips tightened. Morrie was abusing his privileged position, not by what he was doing, but by what he was so obviously thinking.

Morrie caught Caleb's eye, and misread his thoughts.

"Nice anatomy, huh?" he said, then went back into the special procedures room, closing the heavy lead-lined door behind him. Caleb, seeing him speaking to Celine, turned up the volume on the intercom.

"We'll be passing this little tube all the way up inside the leg artery," Morrie was saying, "up to the arteries that go into the pancreas."

Caleb saw Celine's eyes widen. The stiff black catheter he was showing her was about the thickness of a wooden match, but it was several feet long.

"How do you know when it's in the right place?" she asked, trying to keep the fear out of her voice. In spite of all the assurances she'd received, she knew that this was a delicate procedure, and things could go wrong. Morrie had conscientiously spent a long time telling her about hematomas, different kinds of allergic reactions to the dye, blood clots, and a host of other dire possibilities.

Celine was astonished at herself; she was the one who'd wanted to be told everything, yet when Morrie Stein went on in such excruciating detail, she couldn't really understand what he was talking about, and it scared her enough that she didn't want to hear any more.

It itched and hurt like a burn where the Koslowski creature had shaved her. "Oops, sorry!" she had said a couple of times, smiling. It was obvious she really enjoyed her work.

In spite of having her entire leg, thigh, and groin exposed in full view of all those strangers, for some reason Celine didn't feel in the least embarrassed. The people now putting on green gowns and masks were, in a strange way, not human, but more like the high priests of a scientific religion. She felt numbed, almost hypnotized by this surgical ritual and the silent, methodical, and stylized actions of its acolytes. It made her think of Aztec prisoners being prepared for sacrifice to the sun god Tetualtehec.

Dr. Stein had a small syringe in his hand; the needle was tiny, only about half an inch long.

"Just a pinprick to numb the area," he murmured. Celine noticed that he didn't look her in the eye.

Lying on the hard table, trying to keep the bright overhead lights out of her eyes, Celine tensed herself for the needle prick. She felt a slight gust of wind from the opening door, then a sudden warmth on her forehead, and knew that some- body was standing directly behind her. With a sudden rush of gratitude she realized who it was. And she'd thought he'd left once he'd got her down to the X-ray department. She didn't move, nor could she see him, but the feeling of his closeness increased.

When Morrie said he was starting to pass the catheter, Ce- line came abruptly back to reality, and fear clawed at her again. She could feel her muscles tense, every tendon quiv- ering in anticipation of the pain she knew must come.

The behavior of the people in the special procedures room had also changed subtly; Celine sensed that Dr. Stein was uncomfortably aware of Caleb's presence, and the technician, Selma, occasionally glanced over Celine's head at him, in some way acknowledging that Caleb was the bestower of ap- proval, although it was of course Morrie Stein's procedure and officially Caleb had nothing to do with it.

"It's in."

Hearing the satisfaction in Morrie Stein's voice, Celine had an instantaneous feeling of relief. She'd barely noticed the catheter going in. From the strained tone of Stein's voice, she had got the distinct impression that it didn't always go in easily. She felt rather than heard Caleb move slightly to see the greenish screen of the monitor. Some of the shadows moved, and Celine could see what looked like a dark thread passing upward as Morrie expertly slid the catheter up the femoral artery into the aorta, the main artery of the body. The catheter had a little bend at the tip, which allowed Mor- rie to manipulate it with his instruments to guide it into the small arteries toward which he was slowly heading.

"You all right?" The lights were all out, and because of the masks Celine couldn't tell who had spoken.

"Fine," she answered. "How is it at your end?" Celine heard Selma's deep laugh, quickly suppressed.

"We're going up nicely. Dr. Winter, can you see all right? You can stand over on this side if you want to."

"I'm just fine right here, thanks." Caleb's voice was so close to Celine that she jumped, and Morrie's voice came at her sharply. "Don't move!" Then he gave a short laugh to dispel the sudden urgency in his voice. He doesn't feel too confident, Celine thought. Maybe he doesn't do these very often.

And then Celine felt a large hand come under the green drapes and gently grip her left shoulder. Her heart accelerated, and she felt breathless at his touch. Would this near-panic, the feeling that all her sensory systems were on overload, show up on the heart monitor? Her heartbeat remained right there, a steady series of green spikes traveling across the screen. Caleb's other hand came over her right shoulder and stayed there.

Morrie had warned her that when they injected the dye into the catheter it might feel hot, and it did. Everybody stood back. "Now hold it, don't move!" cried Selma in her deep voice. Celine heard the high whine of the injector, the clatter of the cassette changer under the table, and a blinding, searing heat exploded in her insides like a grenade. She almost screamed, and then it was all over. She felt as if she'd been run over: breathless, sweaty, and with a terrible feeling of weakness invading her entire body.

Caleb had stood back during the injection, but his hands gripped her shoulders again almost before the clattering of the cassette changer stopped. This time she could tell more about the size and feel of his hands, the sinews and the bones. They transmitted a capable, caring strength that she knew instinctively she could lean on totally.

"That's it, Celine, we're done." Morrie Stein's tired voice came in from a distance, an unwelcome interruption. The lights came on, and she blinked in their harsh fluorescence. Caleb's hands withdrew, leaving a coldness where they had been. Celine fancied they left her more slowly than they might have.

Back in the control room, Caleb watched over Morrie

Stein's shoulder as the films flipped up on the viewing screen. The network of white arteries showed up well; the tumor in Celine's pancreas appeared as a round blush the size of a tangerine in the center of the X-rays. There was no distortion of the venous pattern to suggest invasion or blockage.

"Nice study," murmured Caleb, his eyes moving from one film to the next, following the white threads of the blood vessels as they wound in and around the tumor.

Morrie looked at him expectantly, waiting for Caleb to say whether the tumor was going to be operable or not.

But after he finished his inspection, Caleb turned and left the control room without a word. He walked down the corridor at his usual pace, trying to sort out the various powerful emotions that had surfaced again in the darkened special procedures room. He'd almost rationalized the earlier encounter with Celine by telling himself that she was scared and needed comforting, and that what he'd done wasn't much more than the ordinary reassurance he might give any patient. But now, he knew it wasn't going to be as easy as that, because he'd never felt this way about a patient. It was surprising, exciting, and against all the tenets of medical ethics. A cautionary inner voice spoke to him. *If you have to get involved, at least wait until her operation's over,* it said. *For her sake, you can't jeopardize your good judgment at this time.* Okay, he replied, that's a deal. His step lightened, and he started to hum tunelessly to himself as he stepped into the elevator. But on the way up, he wondered how much of his feeling for Celine was a passionate desire for Celine's operation to succeed. But he knew the answer to that without asking. He'd had lots of other patients with problems as technically complex as Celine's, but once the routine politeness and interest he accorded any patient had been stripped away, that's all they had been to him, technically complex problems. But Celine de La Roche....
To Caleb, she was more than different. She was unique.

"Milo?"

The sound of the slightly hesitant voice made Milo almost drop the telephone. For one appalled moment he considered hanging up, or saying it was a wrong number, but he didn't have the strength of will to do it.

"Milo, this is Collie. Let's make it Friday, huh? It's going to be a very special occasion, you know that, don't you? I'm going to make us a marvelous feast that you'll never forget. This Friday, at my apartment, about seven, okay?"

Dry-mouthed, Milo barely managed to croak "Okay, Collie, see you Friday." Then he banged his head with the heel of his hand and started to curse in his native tongue until he ran out of words. The mere sound, the mere thought of Collie's name sent shivers up his back. Milo was working under a great deal of strain that came from several directions. He was so involved in his new project that he considered time taken from the task as theft, and that included extras such as eating and sleeping.

But his worst problem was undoubtedly Collie Zintel. Milo was both frightened and fascinated by her sexuality and the power she exerted over him. It wasn't the sort of power he was used to; he had plenty of that kind himself. It was much more subtle, like a snake charmer's, a pervasive, inescapable force. And he could feel the responding force in himself spreading like a hot, urgent glow throughout his body until it overtook his mind, his willpower, even his sense of self-preservation. The more Milo thought about it, the more he realized he had to do something to destroy that lethal urge before it destroyed him.

He could allow nothing to get in the way of his work, his new project, which he was convinced would take him in glory to the Nobel podium in Stockholm. So far they had encountered no major hitches, although Milo knew there would be problems along the way. That's what the best science consisted of; a brief illuminating vision, followed by months and years of hard work to turn the vision into reality.

Wasn't it strange that Collie had invited him to come that Friday, the very day he'd decided to do his own operation?

Milo worked in the lab until almost seven o'clock, long after everybody else had gone home. For the next half hour, Milo went around the lab collecting the equipment and instruments he would need, plus the supplies like gauze, the rubber-sealed vial of 1% Xylocaine he would use as the local anesthetic, Betadine to sterilize the skin. All he still needed was some 000 and 0000 gauge silk, and a small self-retaining tissue retractor. He wrapped the instruments in a gray towel and sealed the package with special tape that changed color when enough heat had been applied to sterilize the contents. The steam sterilizer was in a separate small room off the lab; Milo placed the package inside the shiny stainless-steel cylinder, closed and locked the heavy door, and set the timer. Doing all these little mechanical things soothed him, and by the time the sterile equipment was ready and packed into his briefcase he felt less tense. But he still had a vision of Ed's contorted face an inch from his, and he knew what Ed would do to him if Collie got hurt again.

Locking the lab door behind him, Milo started down along the darkened corridor toward the parking lot, firmly gripping his brief case. It was maybe just as well that Milo didn't have the knowledge to wonder whether his gruesome plan might be another manifestation of the mental condition known as *folie à deux,* in which he was already so profoundly emmeshed with Collie Zintel.

Back in her bed, Celine saw that more flowers had arrived, and the room was beginning to look like a branch of her local florist. Oncle Didi had sent a big gardenia plant in full bloom, and from Trevor and Catherine had come a hyacinth whose penetrating scent competed with the more refined perfume of the gardenia. A new bouquet of exotic-looking orchids in a transparent wrapping had just arrived, and Celine was just reading the card when Mrs. Koslowski came in. She wrinkled her nose at the varied fragrances.

"Did they tell you to keep still and not move your leg?"

"Yes, they did," replied Celine softly. "For two hours, and not to get out of bed for four."

"Good. We had a woman who almost bled to death from one of those arteriograms, not so long ago." Mrs. Koslowski looked around at all the flowers, and left. Learning back on her pillows, Celine felt a strange tingling, a tightness in her chest, and she knew that it was fear of another human being. It was an almost unknown sensation for her.

And her groin was hurting, not so much from the needle Dr. Stein had stuck in it, but from the rough shave that Mrs. Koslowski had performed. What was it with that woman? It was surely more than just resentment at being caught out by Celine in the matter of the milk of magnesia. Whatever caused it, the hatred was palpably there, and Celine knew that nothing she could do would make it go away.

For a second, she considered giving her presents, *buying* her care, but she knew Mrs. K would accept the gifts and wouldn't change her behavior; she'd probably just be more contemptuous. Complaints hadn't worked too well either. She thought briefly of getting a private nurse, but her pride didn't let her. She'd manage, in spite of Mrs. Koslowski.

Maybe she should tell Caleb; he'd know what to do. He always knew what to do. Caleb, Caleb, Caleb. She rolled the name around her mouth like a candy until it lost its shape and its meaning.

The feeling of his hands on her shoulders. Even now the thought of it gave her palpitations. She wanted that man, it was as simple as that. She twisted and turned in the bed, forgetting her instructions to keep still, thinking about it, wanting his body there, touching her . . .

The door opened and Caleb came in. She looked up at him,

flushed, and certain that he was able to see what was going through her mind. But if he did, Caleb showed no sign.

He glanced at the flowers and sat down in the chair facing her. A tuft of hair was sticking out over the top of his scrub shirt.

"Your arteriogram," he said, without preamble. "The good news is that so far your tumor looks operable." He paused. "The bad news—"

"I don't want to hear it," interrupted Celine. "That's something *you'll* have to deal with. When are you going to do the operation?"

"I have it scheduled for next Tuesday," he replied, "I'm planning on putting in the graft, so you won't need to worry about that Whipple. I'd like to talk to both you and Charles first, though, and explain the surgery in some more detail."

"You need to talk to Charles for *my* operation?"

"Yes. It's the law, for one thing, and simple courtesy for another." Caleb seemed ill at ease, as if he wanted to stay but couldn't find a legitimate reason, and left soon after.

Celine lay against her pillows, happy that her old life was dead, and that the new one was just beginning.

HORS D'OEUVRE MUSCOVITE
TORTUE CLAIR
GERMINY
TRUITE AU CHAMBERTIN
MIGNONETTES DE SOLE
WHITEBAIT DIABLES
CAILLES À LA TURQUE
BARON D'AGNEAU DE LAIT SOUBISE
PETITS POIS À L'ANGLAISE
POMMES BYRON
SUPREME DE VOLAILLE JEANETTE
NAGEOIRES DE TORTUE À LA MARYLAND

Collie had about a dozen cookbooks, which she stored tidily between two soapstone hamadryads on the top of her refrigerator, and at the moment she was leafing voluptuously through *Escoffier*; the menus were awe-inspiring, but if she gave Milo a feast like that, he would probably fall asleep over the *Fraises Chantilly,* and certainly wouldn't have the energy for the main course—which of course was to be herself.

In her mind, Collie had prepared a feast of Lucullan dimensions, with special music, soft lights, and fine wines, after which she would lead Milo unresistingly to her red velvet-canopied bed for the slow, love-drenched consummation of the final act. But she knew the meal would have to make concessions to the world of reality; even at this time, when the basic fabric of her mind was unbalanced and shifting, Collie retained a strong practical streak; the plan might be born of insanity, but her methods would be well thought out and effective.

Something came into her memory; oysters—wasn't that said to be an aphrodisiac food? And there were others—fish, salmon roe, or was it caviar? She turned to Frank Davis's *Seafood Notebook,* put a marker at the recipe for Oysters Rudolph, which looked delicious, then wondered if she should try a Yugoslav recipe—something to make Milo feel at home? The trouble was, she didn't know a single Yugoslav dish except for goulash, or was that Hungarian? She put the books back on top of the refrigerator thinking that she'd stop in at the public library the next day. There they had a whole section on international cookery.

Collie could feel the excitement rising as she looked around her small apartment. She could see Milo as clearly as if he were actually there, smiling at her from beside the window. When she looked at the bed he was there, lying beautiful and naked, his dark muscular arm urgently beckoning her to come. And when she thought of him, Collie could feel herself getting wet, swelling, tightening, relaxing, as if that part of her anatomy had a life of its own, responding only to Milo.

And for so long it had been Ed, and it hadn't been bad with him, far from it. Sexually, Ed had seemed competent enough until Milo grabbed her and swung her mind and body up to the dizzying, jagged peaks of total ecstasy. Milo had liberated something she knew had been crouching there in her subconscious mind all her life. There was no coming back down after that. Collie had often thought about death ever since she was a little girl, never with fear, and sometimes with longing. Once she'd seen a cat hit by a truck, and it lay twitching in the gutter for a while before it stopped moving and its soul went up to heaven. That evening Collie swore to her parents that she'd seen it, a thin, transparent white cloud soaring straight up into the sky. After it died, the cat looked so peaceful, as if it had done what it had to do and was now free. As a nurse, Collie had seen many people die badly, and she never wanted that to happen to her. She had chosen the most wonderful way to die, Collie was quite certain of that. It would be at the time she had selected, and in the way she desired above anything. Collie sat on the stool in her kitchen, and stared into the distance, dazzled by the prospect. She was going to explode the bonds of her life at the very peak of passion, and Collie felt herself start to tremble all over. She couldn't wait.

Caleb's students were waiting for him in the outpatient clinic, looking unhappy and concerned.

"Dr. Winter, do you remember that woman Bridget Coughlan?" asked Phil.

"I certainly do," he replied. "Have you been following her?"

"Yes," said Miss Fraser, looking anxious. "She's still in the hospital. We think she's still having emboli into her lungs in spite of the heparin."

"She's really breathless," said Phil. He swallowed. "We're worried that . . . that . . . ."

"That she might die," said Miss Fraser.

"We'll go see her as soon as we're finished here, okay?"

The students exchanged looks and Caleb could see they were relieved. A thought struck him.

"Whose service is she on?"

"Dr. Brighton's team, Dr. Winter," replied Miss Fraser. She hesitated as if about to add something, but changed her mind.

Phil broke in. "The first time we talked about Bridget, Dr. Winter, you said one thing we weren't able to figure out." He had lost some of his arrogance in the intervening time, Caleb noticed. "You said it had been about ten days since she had her child, and actually it was eleven, but we wondered how you knew."

All the students were watching him now, and Caleb could see they thought he'd been putting them on.

He sat down on the edge of the examining table. "What do you know about the effect of trauma, operations, and other injuries on the blood-clotting mechanism?"

The students looked at each other. Phil muttered something about fibrinolysins, but his line of thought petered out quickly.

"Okay, let me put it another way," said Caleb, hiding his impatience at their ignorance. "When is the blood most coagulable after injury or pregnancy?"

Miss Fraser, with her eyes on the floor, put two and two together and suggested ten days.

"Right. Good. So ten days after her delivery was when she was most likely to develop a clot, and that clot then travelled up into her lungs as an embolus, right? *Quod erat demonstrandum.*"

"Quod what?" asked Miss Fraser, so quietly Caleb barely heard her.

"It doesn't matter," said Caleb. "Let's go and see her."

That morning, when Charles came back into the house after seeing Jeremy and Corinthian off in a vast horsebox, he stopped to pick up the mail off the hall table. He leafed quickly through the *Times* and was about to put it down when he recognized a face in a society photo taken at a charity function the night before. "Socialite real estate developer Anwar Al-Khayib and new wife Vaughanna fight the good fight against cancer," read the caption. The picture showed a handsome middle-aged man sitting with his arm around a shapely blonde at a table at the Pierre, a bottle of champagne in front of them. Of course Charles knew about Celine's run-in with Al-Khayib, but he had never seen him. And it hadn't been Anwar who had first caught his eye but a slightly out-of-focus figure sitting next to them at the table, smiling benignly, with only just enough of him in the picture to be recognized. It was none other than the rotund and jovial Didier Franchet.

Charles studied the photo for a full minute to be sure, then walked slowly into his study, still holding the paper. Charles didn't believe in coincidences. He looked at his watch, picked up the phone, and made two calls, one to the banker C. Gottlieb Ludman, who said he'd have to call him back with the information he needed, the next to Dan Carfield, with whom he had a long talk. Ludman called back an hour later.

"Well, Charles, I may have found something." Gottlieb's voice was low and precise, and Charles could visualize him in an immaculately tailored suit, short, bald, with careful, intelligent eyes looking out of a dark-skinned, almost Levantine face. "My brokers tell me somebody else is out there quietly mopping up Fortman and Canfield shares." He paused. "Apparently it's somebody working on behalf of an offshore corporation called Redi-Tech, but that's all I can tell you right now. Now, is there anything else you can tell me?"

"I think the person behind it could be a guy called Didier Franchet," said Charles, "possibly with Anwar Al-Khayib, the real-estate developer."

"It helps a lot to have names," said Gottlieb. "I can find out if they're principals in Redi-Tech."

"Would you like to call me back?"

"If you can just hold on for a minute, I can probably find out for you right now," said Ludman, and for a couple of minutes Charles listened to on-hold music. "Here we are," said Ludman, back on the line. "Redi-Tech, trading corporation registered in Hamilton, Bermuda, 1986. Nominal capital is one dollar. Let's see. . . . Chairman is Didier Auguste Franchet. Yes, Anwar Al-Khayib is down here as a board member. Anything else you want to know?"

"That's great, thanks, Gottlieb. I have a couple of other things I need to check on, and I'll call you back within the next couple of days. I'm going to need your help on this one, old buddy."

Since his interview with Dr. Brighton, Porky had been doing his work as best he could. Don McAuliffe was sympathetic but kept his distance, and of course Ed Van Stamm had problems of his own to worry about.

What concerned Porky the most was what he was going to say to his family. There was a lot of surgical tradition there; his father, a well-known orthopedic surgeon, had been enthusiastic in his support of his son, and Porky's older brother was finishing his surgical residency in Boston in style, having published several papers and been offered a job in a major university center in Chicago. The thought of going home and confessing that he'd been fired sent shivers up Porky's spine.

Porky was covering for the day on one of the other surgical services, much to the annoyance of Don and Ed, but as it was

Dr. Brighton's service, there wasn't much they could say about it. The other members of Dr. Brighton's team had ignored him on rounds since they knew he'd been fired and would be gone in a few days. Porky could see immediately that the services wasn't run nearly as efficiently as Dr. Winter's. There were undiagnosed patients who'd been in hospital undergoing tests for far longer than Caleb Winter would have tolerated. The most serious problem though, was a young woman by the name of Bridget Coughlan, who was having what sounded like recurring pulmonary emboli and wasn't responding to the heparin she was getting to prevent her blood from forming more clots. In theory, that medication should have stopped the process, but she kept on having sudden episodes of chest pain and spitting up blood. Now she was breathless just lying in bed.

Dr. Brighton had been round with the team earlier, in his usual hurry, and they'd stopped at the foot of Bridget's bed. The senior resident had glossed over the case because they had a patient waiting in the operating room, and he didn't want to get into a long discussion with Dr. Brighton. And Dr. Brighton hadn't noticed how ill Bridget looked, how breathless she was when she answered his greeting, and in the poor light he had missed the bluish color of her lips.

But Porky had noticed all those things and ordered a lung scan for her without consulting the others. He felt sure she was having more emboli, and the scan would show them. If he was wrong, they would go after him unmercifully, but Porky didn't care. He had nothing more to lose.

A small group of students was standing around Bridget's bed when he came in, and to his surprise Dr. Winter was with them. Usually on student rounds the attending surgeons would only visit and discuss their own cases.

Dr. Winter looked up and said, loudly enough for him to hear, "Maybe Dr. Rosen can tell us what's been going on here." Porky suddenly felt very relieved to see him; just telling him about Bridget's condition lifted some of the burden of responsibility off him.

Caleb's brows came thunderously together as Porky's story unfolded, and at the end he stood up, smiled at Bridget, borrowed a stethoscope from one of the students, and listened to her chest. He looked around for the cardiac monitor, but she wasn't hooked up to one. He called to the ward clerk, who hurried over.

"See if you can reach Dr. Brighton for me, please." His calm voice suggested that he merely wanted to discuss some minor clinical problem, but Porky, who had worked for him and knew the signs, could see that Caleb was furious.

While they were waiting, Porky hurried off to see if the scan was ready, and after several minutes he came back triumphantly holding a batch of small films. He handed them to Caleb, who held them up against the light.

"The admission scan's at the back," said Porky, who knew Caleb would want to compare them. Porky and the students followed him into the doctors' room, where Caleb put all the films up on the X-ray viewing box.

Methodically he pointed out the changes that were seen only on the new scan. Most of the right lung was blacked out, and a good part of the left upper lobe was also not functioning. Taken with the blood oxygenation tests Porky had also ordered, it looked as if Bridget was running on about twenty percent of her normal lung function—barely enough to keep her alive.

The door of the ward flung open, and Dr. Brighton came marching up to the secretary's desk, glancing up just long enough to see Caleb and his students. He ignored them, and with a crash yanked a chart out of the rack; Porky assumed it was Bridget's. Meanwhile Caleb calmly went on discussing the diagnosis and treatment of pulmonary emboli with the students, who were nervously keeping one eye on the chairman. Finally Dr. Brighton put back the folder and squared his shoulders before coming down toward the group.

"An interesting case, Ms. Coughlan," he said. "I hope Dr. Winter agrees with our present plan of treatment." He looked challengingly at Caleb.

"Certainly," said Caleb, cool as a gust of arctic air, "as long as that includes immediate transfer to the Intensive Care Unit, oxygen, and putting in an inferior vena cava filter to stop the emboli."

Brighton's eyes flickered over the group, resting for a moment on Porky, then coming back to Caleb. "That's precisely what I had in mind," he said suavely. His eyes hardened. "Dr. Rosen, I don't know why it's taking you so long, but I'd be grateful if you'd get her over to the ICU as soon as possible, and get the oxygen and other things under way."

He must think I called Dr. Winter in, thought Porky. What the hell, it didn't matter now. The important thing was that Bridget wasn't going to die there from lack of treatment.

Noticing Porky's expression, Caleb rose from his chair, and the students stepped back to make room for him. "Porky, come and see me in my lab when you're finished, okay?"

Porky looked surprised. "Yes, sir," he said.

Caleb nodded coolly at Henry and led his students off to see another patient, this time one of his own.

In the operating room, Don McAuliffe was helping Ed van Stamm do a cholecystectomy. It was Ed's first gallbladder; and although he'd been looking forward to performing the operation for months, he felt shaky and ill at ease now that he was actually doing it, especially with Collie standing there right beside him. The fact that he'd half-killed Milo hadn't helped; there she was, serene and content with her black eye and God knows what other bruises. Worst of all were those purple marks on her neck. Collie was barely able to croak when she tried to speak.

At this point Ed understood that he had totally misread Collie, and that unsuspected, dangerous passions lived inside her head. He couldn't reconcile the Collie he had known with what must have been going on between her and Milo Zagros. Then he remembered the way Collie made love, the way she talked gibberish to herself, the lack of fulfillment he always sensed in her. For the first time, it occurred to Ed that Collie might be insane.

"See if you can get a right-angle around the cystic duct," Don was saying. He was making it very easy for Ed, identifying the structures, lifting them so he could separate them easily from the surrounding tissues. Ed tried to concentrate on what he was doing. A cholecystectomy was a landmark operation for a surgeon in training, and no surgeon ever forgot the first one he did, or who helped him, or what the patient's name was.

"Two-oh silk tie, please, on a right-angle." He forced his voice to sound normal when talking to Collie, but it wasn't easy. The clamp with the black silk tie firmly in its jaws appeared instantly in his hand, and he slid it around the cystic duct close to where it joined the common bile duct.

"How d'you know your tie isn't around the common bile duct?" asked Don. Accidentally tying off the common bile duct was a major catastrophe, but it did happen from time to time. Then the bile would back up, the patient became jaundiced, and only prompt reoperation could save the patient's life.

"I make sure I can clearly see where the cystic duct enters it," replied Ed automatically. He'd assisted at so many gallbladders that it was familiar territory.

"Right. Now put a bit more tension on the tie," Don said. He was itching to make the moves that Ed, from inexperience, hesitated to make. But he forced himself to tolerate Ed's slow progress, remembering his own first cholecystectomy. Dr. Winter had assisted on that momentous occasion, and Don had felt privileged that he'd taken the trouble. The case had gone well, Dr. Winter had complimented him, and afterward Don had felt like the king of creation.

"Now you can see the cystic artery, right there." Don pointed to it with his forceps. Luckily for Ed, the patient was thin and the structures were easy to identify. The cystic artery had to be clipped and cut before proceeding, otherwise the bleeding could be troublesome.

Collie had the clips ready for him before he asked for them, and a fresh wave of anger welled up in him. She was so infuriatingly calm. Damn the woman, he thought, she seemed to be reveling in this sordid and dangerous brutality.

Ed missed with the first clip, and Don retrieved it from the depths without comment. Again Collie was ready with the replacement, and his rage at her coolness made his hand tremble.

"Take it easy, Ed," murmured Don, assuming that Ed

was nervous because this was his first major operation. "Everything's going nicely."

The gallbladder looked like a flaccid toy balloon, Ed thought. Except that this one was full of little stones about the size of lentils, as far as he could tell by feeling them through the thin, greenish wall of the gallbladder.

Did Collie realize what was going on? Did she know that that kind of game could result in serious injury? Ed couldn't prevent himself from looking around at her, and when he moved, he dislodged the clip from the cut end of the artery. The bleeding was brisk, and it took Don a couple of minutes to get things under control again.

"Ed, you're going to have to pay attention," said Don brusquely. "I don't want to take away your first gallbladder, but one more problem like this and I will." And he meant it. Teaching somebody how to operate was one thing, but if the pupil hadn't reached the proper level of proficiency or wasn't concentrating, the patient was at risk. And that should never be allowed to happen. It was one of Dr. Winter's firmest rules, and Don had adopted it as his own.

For the remainder of the case, Ed pulled himself together and shut Collie out of his mind until the gallbladder was tucked away in the specimen jar. While they were closing, though, Collie's presence next to him was a torture. He oscillated between wanting to shout and curse at her for her unfaithfulness and aching to take her in his arms and hold her the way he'd done many times before.

After the case was over and the patient had been trundled into recovery, Don and Ed went to the changing room.

"What happened yesterday, down in the lab?" asked Don. "Did you talk to Milo?"

"I sure did," said Ed grimly. "But I don't know if it did any good. I'm just scared that something really bad's going to happen to Collie."

"Well," said Don, in his usual chilly way, "I guess it's not your problem anymore. Forget Collie, go find a girl who appreciates you better." Don threw his scrub shirt into the laundry hamper. His body was pale and he was thinner, more muscular and wiry than he looked with his clothes on.

"Have you mentioned it to Dr. Winter?"

"No, of course not. Why?"

"Well, Milo Zagros works for him, and whatever Zagros does ultimately reflects back on Winter and his unit."

Don pulled his pants on and took the loose change from his locker and put it in his pocket. "Dr. Winter wouldn't want any of his people getting themselves into trouble, especially that kind. You know what he's like. And that's exactly what Zagros is doing."

Don looked at Ed's face and was shocked by the expression of sheer misery in it. "You're going to have to do something," he said. "Otherwise it's going to drive you nuts. What's more," he went on, "it's interfering with your work."

Ed stayed in the shower for almost ten minutes, during which he went over and over everything he knew about Collie. As he did so, the question of her sanity loomed larger and larger until he was certain. The problem was what to do about it.

Caleb reached for the interphone on his desk that communicated directly with the special care units. By now they should have got Bridget Coughlan into the ICU, but there was no harm checking. The phone rang before he picked it up. It was Porky, wondering if Dr. Winter had time to see him. He arrived at the lab a few minutes later, breathless, having run all the way over. Maureen opened the door for him, and Porky, who liked Maureen a lot, talked to her briefly while he caught his breath.

"I did my thesis was on the immunological control of rejection," he told her when Maureen asked if he was interested in what they were doing in the research lab. He looked around curiously. "I really miss working in the lab."

"Then come back and talk to Milo Zagros when you're through with Dr. Winter," she suggested, smiling at his enthusiasm. "I'm sure he'd be happy to show you what we're doing here."

Caleb came up at that moment. "How's Bridget?" he asked Porky.

"Okay. There wasn't anybody at transportation, so I grabbed a couple of students and we took her over ourselves."

Caleb nodded. It was what he would have done.

Porky was hesitating.

"They're going to put in an inferior vena cava filter," he said, an odd inflection in his voice.

"Good. That's what she needs."

"Yes, right, but Dr. Brighton's decided to do it himself, with his senior resident." Porky took a deep breath, then burst out, "I'm really worried, Dr. Winter. He was reading the in-structions on the outside of the filter pack, and I heard him tell the head nurse he'd never used one like that before."

"Porky, don't you worry about that. Dr. Brighton knows what he's doing." Caleb laughed a little incredulously. A first-year resident worrying about the technical competence of the chairman of the department! "Porky, what I wanted to see you about was your own situation. I understand that you've been fired?"

Porky's shoulders collapsed. "Yes," he said, looking at the floor. "I knew he was going to—he was just waiting to find somebody to replace me."

"Well, I think that's a pity," said Caleb. "I must say until quite recently I thought you were a lousy resident, too, and if I'd been asked if you should go, I'd have to have said yes."

"I know it, Dr. Winter. But I thought I was really getting the hang of things now, and he might give me another chance."

Caleb picked up the phone without taking his eyes off Porky. "Page Dr. McAuliffe for me please," he said. Don called back almost instantly.

"Don, how's Porky been doing? I mean recently?" Caleb watched Porky while he talked, and Porky flinched under his scrutiny. "Good. That was my impression too. No other prob-lems?" Caleb listened for another few moments then hung up.

He sat back in his chair and put his hands flat on the desk. "Well, Porky, you seem to have been doing all right on the service. Don didn't have any complaints about you, and that's a change." He stood up. "Let me see what I can do. No guar-antees, you understand?"

A glow of pure relief spread over Porky's face. He couldn't have hoped for more. The mere fact that Dr. Winter was going to take up the cudgels for him was wonderful.

"Gee, thanks, Dr. Winter. I . . ."

"Don't thank me," replied Caleb. "And don't even think I'm doing it for you. It's the principle of the thing. Now you go back," his grin had just a trace of malice, "and make sure Dr. Brighton puts that caval filter in the right place."

On the way out, Porky stopped to talk with Milo Zagros,

as much out of curiosity as anything. But by the time he left, he was so impressed with the level of work being done in the lab that he asked if he could come back and visit when he had more time.

About the same time next day, Porky walked toward the intensive care unit. He was in a position familiar to many interns; he knew that something was wrong, but wasn't sure exactly what it was, and therefore he didn't know what to do about it. Bridget Coughlan hadn't really improved since Dr. Brighton had put the little umbrella-shaped device into the inferior vena cava in an effort to prevent clots from coming up through it and into her lungs.

That had been the worst procedure Porky had ever been involved in. Dr. Brighton hadn't been familiar with the device and had only put it in because Caleb had forced him to. Henry had lost his cool, shouted at everybody, and there was blood everywhere from the incision in the neck vein he'd used to pass the closed umbrella down into position before opening it.

Even after that, Bridget's breathing hadn't improved, although Dr. Brighton kept saying how much better she looked. So that morning Porky had ordered another X-ray, just to be sure the umbrella was still in the proper position, and now he was on his way to see the films in the ICU.

He stopped at Bridget's bed. The white X-ray envelope was in the pocket at the foot of the bed. It had a blue strip across the top to indicate that the patient was in the ICU. Bridget was sitting up, wearing an oxygen mask, but her breathing was still labored. She smiled wanly at Porky. He was the only doctor she recognized, not only because of his size, but by the fact that he was kind and spent more time with her than the others.

Porky smiled encouragingly at Bridget, but didn't say anything. He found it hard to talk to somebody who was having difficulty breathing. He picked up the envelope, took it back to the bank of viewing boxes behind the nurses' station, and flipped up the new films.

"Oh shit!" he breathed, then quickly pulled one of the old

films out of the envelope for comparison. The little umbrella showed up very well on the X-rays because it was partly metallic. It was supposed to be horizontal, with the spokes of the umbrella pressed evenly around the inside wall of the big vein. But now it had slipped out of position and was leaning drunkenly to one side. No wonder poor Bridget wasn't doing well. The clots were still sliding past the umbrella and getting up into her lungs.

Porky stared at the films, wondering what to do. If he told Dr. Brighton, he knew that somehow he'd get blamed for it. Maybe he should call the residents, but they were both in the operating room.

"You've got a problem there, Porky," said a voice over his shoulder. It was Dr. Winter. "Didn't I tell you to make sure he put it in right?"

"It *was* in right, Dr. Winter," replied Porky earnestly. "It's moved."

"So what are you going to do now?"

"I was just wondering about that," said Porky. "Honestly, I don't know."

"What'll happen if you do nothing?"

"I'd be worried the umbrella might move more, get dislodged. It's not stable the way it is."

"Right. Then what would happen?"

"It could block the veins from the kidney, or even . . ." Porky gulped, "it could travel right up into the heart, I suppose."

"With what result?" asked Caleb remorselessly.

"Sudden death." Porky's voice was almost inaudible.

There was a pause while Caleb let the significance of that sink in.

"Has Dr. Brighton seen those films yet?"

"Dr. Winter, I just got them back this minute."

"You'd better tell him right now," said Caleb. He saw Porky hesitate for a second, and knew why. Caleb went to the phone himself and paged Dr. Brighton for the ICU. That was a summons no doctor could ignore. A moment later Brighton answered, and sounded shocked to hear Caleb's voice. Yes, he said, he'd be right up.

"Beat it," Caleb said to Porky as soon as he put the phone down. "Come back in ten minutes."

When Henry Brighton arrived a few minutes later, his little eyes showed that he was expecting an onslaught from Caleb.

"What's on your mind, Cal?"

Caleb pointed to the X-rays. Henry put on his reading glasses to examine them, and Caleb watched his expression change when he saw the tilted umbrella. Henry was in double trouble, because he knew that the only way of dealing with this was to remove the umbrella surgically, and that wasn't the kind of surgery he'd been trained for, or even kept up with.

"Maybe it'll just stay there and not move," he said, but there was a slight shake in his voice. "Actually it must be pretty securely fixed by now."

Caleb's face turned stony. If there was one thing he could not abide, it was a surgeon who wasn't honest about the job he was doing, who tried to cover up problems instead of facing them.

"When are you going to take it out?" he asked quietly, ignoring Henry's suggestion. "You know as well as I do that she could die any second, with this thing hanging by a thread in her circulation."

Henry started to bluster, but Caleb didn't give him a chance. "I'll call the operating room right now," he said. "If you schedule it as an emergency, and it sure as hell is one, we should get a room within an hour. That'll give you time to check her blood gases, electrolytes, and have the anesthesiology people see her."

He looked at Henry's helpless expression, and suppressed the contempt he felt. "I'll call your team, if you like, so they can get up here and get things moving."

Henry's voice was very different from his aggressive tone of a few moments ago. "Cal," he said, "this . . . this isn't a surgical area I'm really comfortable in." His hands fluttered.

Caleb looked at him for a second, unwilling to believe what he was hearing. Henry Brighton, chairman of a major department of surgery, admitting he'd got into a surgical situation he couldn't get himself out of. It was outrageous, and so utterly humiliating. A sudden gleam came into Caleb's eyes.

"Would you like me to take care of it?" he asked, looking at his watch. "I have office hours, but I can cancel them."

Henry looked at him with an expression of craven gratitude. "I'd really appreciate it, Cal. I actually have a very busy afternoon ahead, so if you could . . ."

"I'll make a deal with you, Henry," said Caleb. Henry's eyes narrowed. He could guess what was coming. Cal would do the Coughlan woman's operation in exchange for his support on the transplant project at Monday's committee meeting. Henry braced himself. He was really on the spot now.

"What kind of deal," he inquired, his palms suddenly wet.

"I take care of this patient, you give Porky back his job."

Henry's mouth opened slowly, then he caught himself. "I think we can find him a slot, yes," he said, his words falling over themselves in his haste. "As a matter of fact I was intending—"

"Good. That's a deal," said Caleb brusquely, trying to keep what he felt out of his voice. He picked up the phone and called the operating room. A case was finishing in five minutes and the room would be ready in half an hour.

Henry went off with pure joy in his heart. It had been clever of him to agree so quickly and not give that damned Caleb Winter time to ask for any more concessions. But then Henry Brighton had been at this game for a long time, and had a pretty good idea how to get the most mileage out of a situation. After all, that was what running a major clinical department was all about. At the door, he almost bumped into Porky, and to Porky's utter astonishment and instant terror, he stopped him.

"I need to talk to you, Porky. In my office. Yes, now."

Numb, Porky followed Henry in silence down to his office. He didn't even feel too apprehensive, as there was little Henry could do to him that he hadn't done already.

"Porky, I've decided to give you another chance . . ."

Porky sat very still, hardly able to believe his good fortune. He'd figured that his involvement with Bridget Coughlan would nail down the lid on his career as a resident.

Henry hid his expansive mood with a contemptuous smile. "I think that one of the things you've been lacking is guidance, Dr. Rosen. I propose to correct that deficiency."

Porky blushed and moved his feet. Didn't Dr. Brighton know he'd been on Caleb Winter's service, known to be the most efficient in the hospital? He mumbled something unintelligible, and Henry's lip curled again in disdain.

"I've decided to put you on *my* service for the next three months," he said. "Then I'm going to schedule you to spend six months in the lab, doing research. Possibly you will find some kind of aptitude there."

Porky raised his eyes. Six months in the lab! That meant working with Dr. Winter. Wow! Porky couldn't believe his good fortune. Much more senior men than he lived in hopes of being invited to spend time in Caleb Winter's lab, knowing that if they made a success of it, they would go straight into the fast lane of surgical research.

"Gee, thanks, Dr. Brighton." Then a thought struck him. "Does Dr. Winter know . . . ?" His voice faded when he saw Dr. Brighton's expression.

"Dr. Winter has nothing whatever to do with this," he said stiffly. "You will be working directly for me. Now, you get back to your duties. I have a great deal of work to do."

Porky headed for the door, his head in a whirl. What did he mean, working directly for him? Porky had never heard of any research Dr. Brighton was doing—he didn't even have a lab. His thoughts were interrupted by Dr. Brighton's nasal voice.

"One other thing, Porky. Get a clean coat, for God's sake, and I really insist that you start losing some more weight. I find your obesity personally offensive to me."

"I've never seen a patient cause as much of a stir as you," said Porky, smiling. He had gone straight up to Celine's room to tell her about his next-to-miraculous reinstatement, but the gossiping he'd heard at the nurses' station had caught his attention. The whole hospital was buzzing about a new, epoch-making surgical procedure that was about to be performed by Dr. Winter. They were also saying that he was having an affair with the patient he'd be operating on.

"I'm not doing anything," replied Celine, smiling. She had a pile of manuscripts and papers spread out on the table and spilling over on to the bed. "I'm just sitting here minding my own business, trying to get my head ready for next Tuesday." She shivered.

"They're saying that you and Dr. Winter . . ." Porky hesitated. Celine laughed, and pulled the bedcovers closer around her.

"Isn't every woman supposed to fall in love with her surgeon?" she asked, smiling, making a joke of it, but she watched Porky very carefully. "But surely by now he's immune to that kind of thing?"

"Not from what everybody's saying," replied Porky. He was smiling too, but a concerned seriousness lurked there; doctors weren't supposed to develop that kind of relationship with their patients, and he felt sure Caleb Winter would never do anything that wasn't completely ethical.

But Porky's words sent an excited warmth through Celine's entire body.

"You mean he's really human after all?" Celine felt she had to keep this conversation going.

"Oh, he's human all right," said Porky, as he headed for the door. He fingered the stack of dog-eared cards in his hands. "We always thought he had something going with Maureen Spark, a really nice woman who works for him."

Celine didn't want to hear any more, but resolved to find out more about Maureen Spark later. She'd ask Caleb about her; that way she'd know immediately if there was something to worry about.

Soon after Porky left, Celine heard Caleb's step coming down the corridor outside her room. He knocked with one hand and pushed the door open with the other.

"Come on in," said Celine when he was well inside the room. If she meant it as a rebuke he didn't notice.

He sat in the chair by the window.

"Celine, I've been thinking about what's going on. I mean, personally, between you and me."

"So have I," replied Celine, relieved but nervous that he'd brought the subject up. "Quite honestly, I've been thinking about little else."

Caleb shifted uncomfortably on his chair.

"It has to stop."

Celine's eyes opened a little wider. "There hasn't really been much to stop, has there? What do you mean?"

"You know damn well what I mean," said Caleb. He wasn't entirely sure if Celine was teasing him. "I have to explain something to you . . ."

"Don't bother," said Celine, suddenly feeling chilled. "You're going to tell me that you can't develop an emotional attachment with somebody you're going to be operating on, right?"

Caleb's mouth opened slightly, but he didn't say anything.

"And that it's against the Hippocratic Oath, or something like that, too?" Celine smiled, although it hurt.

"Something like that," Caleb admitted. "But I have a suggestion."

Celine sat very still, waiting.

"Right now, we shall remain doctor and patient," said Caleb firmly. "But after the operation's over . . ." He let the words hang in the air.

Celine smiled, hoping her relief didn't show. "Caleb Winter," she said, with equal firmness, "that's fine for you, but I reserve the right to feel what *I* want to feel, and when *I* want to feel it." She got out of bed, and advanced purposefully toward Caleb. "You can keep to whatever schedule you want, but I'm going to keep to mine."

It was Friday evening.

Milo unpacked the sterile instruments, syringes, the packet of gauze pads, the vial of Xylocaine, and all the other surgical paraphernalia from his briefcase on to a small coffee table in his bedroom. There wasn't room on the table for the big *Illustrated Atlas of Urologic Procedures* he'd borrowed from the library, so he set it on a chair within easy reach. Milo had thought about doing the operation while sitting in a chair, then realized that he might faint; so he decided to do it lying on his bed, which was just a box spring and a mattress set on the floor. He stacked a few pillows at the head of the bed, shivering slightly now. His hands felt cold, almost numb. It had seemed like a straightforward procedure when he was reading about it, but he was beginning to have second thoughts.

He stopped for a moment and surveyed the instruments laid out on the table. He had brought only one pack of sterile latex gloves, which might not be enough. If he got them contaminated in any way, he didn't have a backup pair.

The first thing he needed to do was to shave his pubic area, so he went into the bathroom, soaped up the hair, and went to work with his twin-bladed razor, watching himself in the mirror. The hairs pulled, and then got stuck between the blades. It took Milo the better part of half an hour to get a reasonably good shave. Each hair felt as if it were being individually yanked out. By the time he'd finished, the skin was pink and raw-looking and very tender indeed.

Milo put the book on the floor, and opened it at the appropriate page, which was headed "ORCHIDECTOMY." A strange name, thought Milo, it sounded more like something out of a gardening book.

First, the antiseptic. He opened the foil container for the Betadine stick, which had a blob of antiseptic-soaked cotton wool at one end, and smeared the solution around his groin; it started to burn quite painfully in the raw parts. This was as far as he could get without directions. Milo scanned the page and found the section he was looking for. "*Although it is possible to do this operation under local anesthetic,*" he read, "*general anesthesia is preferable.*" Milo didn't remember having read that before.

He cleaned the end of the Xylocaine vial with an alcohol swab. This part was easy—he must have used Xylocaine or similar stuff on hundreds and hundreds of mice and other animals in the course of his experiments. He drew up about fifteen milliliters; that should be more than enough for both sides.

Now the injection. Milo glanced at the diagram in the book. It showed the incision, parallel to the groin crease at the top of his leg, and just above it, going perilously close to the root of his penis. He'd have to be careful about the main artery and vein going to the leg; they were frighteningly close by. He didn't have to worry about putting his sterile gloves on yet: that would come after he'd put in the Xylocaine. All kinds of questions were now surfacing that he hadn't thought of. Should he put the local anesthetic into both groins now, or do one side first, then the other? He decided to do one side at a time. Putting in the injection would hurt, and too much pain at one time might make his hands too shaky to function properly.

Milo sat down on the bed, pulled his shirt up under his armpits and looked at his groins. They seemed a little swollen, and red scratches had appeared where the razor hadn't turned the corner at quite the same angle as his skin. He aimed the syringe carefully, took a deep breath, and repeated the phrase of his boyhood, learned in school—"*Onward and upward with Tito!*" then stuck the long needle into the skin over the left groin. It burned where he injected the Xylocaine and was agonizingly painful at the top of his scrotum. Sweat broke out on his forehead, and he waited for a few moments, his chest heaving. He had injected a little less than half of the syringeful. It took a couple of minutes for the area to get satisfactorily numb. He pulled out the needle and gingerly pricked his skin with it. There was no sensation at all, not even a feeling of pressure. Great, he thought, we're ready to go. He had stopped breathing without knowing it, and now took in a huge lungful of air.

He put the syringe on the table, away from the sterile instruments, then picked up the flat paper envelope containing the gloves and opened it. He knew how to take them out. . . . Damn! he thought. He'd forgotten to wash his hands. Well, it was too late now, the glove pack was open. He reached in, pulled out the gloves and put one on, holding it by the cuff so as not to contaminate it. With his gloved hand, he picked up the other glove, slipping a finger under the cuff, and pulled it on to his other hand. Now he had to be careful not to touch anything not on the sterile tray. Suddenly his heart thumped; how would he turn the pages of the book? He needed to see the diagrams for reference, and they covered several pages of the *Atlas.* Finally he figured out a way of doing it with his elbow, but the episode jolted him, and he began to wish he'd never started this whole procedure.

The first illustration in the book showed a knife opening the tissues under the skin. The next one showed the spermatic cord, a bundle of nerves and blood vessels which formed the lifeline of the testicle, curving down into the scrotum. Milo picked up the scalpel, and with great care cut into his own skin, exactly matching the cut in the diagram. A little blood welled up but not too much, and Milo sponged it up carefully with a piece of gauze. He felt no pain, the Xylocaine had worked as advertised. Inside the cut, Milo saw a sizable vein. He started to sweat; if he had severed that vein with his first cut he'd suddenly be in the deepest kind of trouble. But he knew how to handle it: he passed a curved forceps underneath the vein, freed it up, passed a silk tie underneath it and tied it off neatly twice. Then he cut the vein between the two ties. Suddenly, Milo's confidence returned. Caleb would be proud of him, he thought—just before it occurred to him that Caleb would think he was totally insane.

He worked rather breathlessly, but very carefully for about half an hour, until all the tissues around the spermatic cord were cleared and separated. He would have to clamp the cord, then cut it, before starting to pull the disconnected testicle out of its scrotal sac. Gently, very gently, he eased the cord up so he could get one of the big Kelly clamps across it.

All seemed to be ready now, and Milo took a deep breath. This was the moment of truth. He picked the Kelly clamp off the tray, opened it, and with a determined movement, closed the clamp across the spermatic cord. Instantly an agonizing, horrifying pain exploded inside his groin, seared upward in a blinding flash, and burst inside his head. Milo screamed with the dreadful agony, and tried to get the clamp off, but it was firmly set. He couldn't stop screaming; he felt that his mind was going to shatter into splinters with the pain, which shot from his groin to his head as if he were attached to a high-voltage cable and couldn't let go. Tearing and twisting, he finally got the clamp off, and then, drenched in sweat, sobbing with terror and pain, he fainted.

He was unconscious for not more than a couple of minutes, and when he came to, he saw that only a little blood had trickled down from his incision. He lay still, panting, terrified that the pain might come back in its full force if he moved. As it was, there was a dull, grinding ache in his groin, but he could bear that. After resting for several minutes, some of his strength came back, and he considered the situation. He couldn't go on without clamping the spermatic cord, and *nothing* was going to make him touch it again. His right hand was trembling so badly that he had to support it with the left, but he managed to put in a few stitches to close the incision. Then he covered it with a dressing and got up, his legs so weak that he barely made it into the kitchen. Leaning against the sink, he reached up to the closet where he kept a small store of liquor, and with trembling hands he poured himself a tumblerful of vodka. He swigged it all down in one gulp, spilling a little on his shirt.

He refilled the tumbler. This time all of it went down his throat, and he felt as if he were coming back to life. He looked around the kitchen, dazed, slowly realizing what had happened. He still had his testicles, although he had almost died trying to get rid of them.

And then, an incredible thing happened. He looked at the clock and remembered that he had a dinner date. Still barely able to keep his balance, he went into the bedroom, somehow fumbled into his clothes, and headed unsteadily for the door, leaving the mess of instruments, towels, and bloody gauze where it lay.

Now nothing much seemed to matter to him, except the memory of the alluring body and beckoning hand of Collie Zintel.

Collie fell asleep almost as soon as she lay down on the sofa. The strain of the last few days had taken its toll of her energies. When she wakened it was dark. She put her clothes on as if in a dream, first the lacy underwear, then the new pantyhose, then the tight-fitting dress that showed her cleavage so nicely. She glanced at the clock: Milo was late, very late, but somehow she had known that would happen. Putting the finishing touches to the dinner, telling herself that he would be here shortly, she worked with a sense of unreality, as if time had stopped, then started to retreat instead of advancing. She checked the clock. Sure enough the second hand was traveling around, but it was really telling yesterday's time, or perhaps tomorrow's . . .

There must have been a sound, because Collie raised her head, then went to the door. This was exactly the time she knew Milo would come. And there he was, smiling, a little pale perhaps, looking just the way she expected him to look, and carrying a bunch of red roses, which he held out to her.

Next morning, the whole hospital was again alive with rumors. At this stage, only certain things were known to be true.

For instance, the E.R. log showed that one Milo Zagros had been brought in under police escort. The story that received most credence was that Milo had been picked up by a patrolling police car, incoherent, walking around the streets some distance from his home. At the station, they saw blood trickling down his leg, so they rushed him to the hospital. The record showed again that Dr. Ambrose Rosen, on duty for the surgical service, was asked to see him by the E.R. physician, Dr. Robert Aminoke. Porky found that there was no life-threatening problem, just some bleeding from what looked like a self-inflicted wound in the left groin. The strange thing was that it had been sutured, and quite carefully. Milo was clearly disoriented and would say nothing except what sounded like curse words in some foreign language. Porky wisely called Caleb, who came in immediately and took charge of the case hinself. Milo calmed down a bit when he saw Caleb, and they talked for a while behind the curtains in the emergency room booth. When Caleb came out, he looked very grim, and said Milo should be moved immediately to a private psychiatric hospital for evaluation and treatment, and that he was not to be interviewed at this time by the police or anyone else. He agreed with Porky that the physical injuries were not serious, and just needed some antiseptic cleansing and an antibiotic coverage. Caleb left soon after, his face as grim as anyone there had ever seen it.

Collie wasn't found until later that morning. The operating room supervisor phoned her apartment when Collie, always meticulously prompt, hadn't come in by nine. There was no answer. A specific order in the procedures book stated that in such cases, where there was no reason to believe that the individual might be away from home, the police must be called. The supervisor did so, and within ten minutes two officers were at Collie's apartment. They found Collie's naked body on the bed, with a nightie on the floor nearby. There were some old bruise marks on her neck, breasts, and arms, but no sign of any struggle, and no recent injuries that they could detect. The apartment was extraordinarily neat and tidy; nothing appeared to have been disturbed.

The first thing that puzzled the two officers was the discovery of an untouched glass filled with wine on the coffee table, as if it had been set down there for a guest who hadn't arrived. In the dining room, two places had been set with food and drink, but the food had been eaten and the wine drunk from only one of them. On the other blue place-mat was a perfectly centered plate with a pear half containing shrimp. On another plate, to one side of the first, were finely sliced pieces of meat with vegetables, and next to that was a bowl with cherries in a red sauce. It was like a scene from *Sleeping Beauty*, except that here the beauty was dead.

"This is weird," muttered one of the cops, "real weird."

"Yeah," said the younger one, feeling his neck hairs standing on end. "It looks like she had a ghost in to supper."

"Maybe they'll find fingerprints on the glasses, or maybe the plates," said the older cop, but both knew that the only fingerprints they would find were those of Collie Zintel herself.

The police surgeon later found an empty Seconal bottle by the sink in the bathroom, next to an almost empty bottle of gin.

He came through into the bedroom and put his nose near Collie's mouth and sniffed.

"Yeah," was all he said.

Cal sat down heavily at the desk in what had been Maureen's office, and he needed several minutes to prepare himself for one of the more difficult tasks he'd ever had to do. Finally he picked up the phone and dialed a number. It rang several times, and his grip tightened with apprehension. Finally the receiver was lifted, and Caleb sighed with relief.

"Maureen?"

The silence at the other end was palpable.

"Maureen, there's been a tragedy. In fact two tragedies." Caleb told her what had happened. "No, Milo didn't do it," he said in response to a question. "The police have cleared him. Collie's death was a suicide, but a really strange one."

Maureen, who had already heard the highlights of the case on the radio, waited for Caleb to come to the point. She knew what he was going to say, but was curious to know how he would go about it.

"You know our first transplant is scheduled for Tuesday of next week, don't you?" he started, trying to keep his voice as matter-of-fact as possible.

Maureen's silence was beginning to get on his nerves. "Maureen, are you still there?"

"Yes," replied Maureen in such a harsh voice that Caleb's grip tightened again.

"With Milo out of circulation—and I have no idea when he'll be able to come back—and with you having left the team, I don't see how we can possibly do the graft. There's no antirejection protocol, and I can't prepare the graft and do the operation at the same time."

Maureen still didn't say anything, and Caleb felt his anger and frustration building up to bursting point. He took a deep breath.

"Maureen, if I can't put in the graft, I'm going to be forced to do a Whipple on this young woman. I am asking you, for the sake of the patient, to come back to the lab long enough to see us through this case. After that . . ." Caleb paused. "After that, of course, you would be free to do whatever . . ." His voice died out.

Again there was a long silence from the other end, and for a moment Caleb thought Maureen was just going to hang up. But finally she did speak.

"I'm sorry, Caleb," she said, her voice flat and impersonal. "But I can't help you."

Furious and completely taken aback, Caleb slammed the phone down, and sat with his head in his hands for a while. Somehow he had to get things ready for the operation. The thought of performing a Whipple procedure on Celine made him go weak inside.

He got up. Okay, he thought, where shall I start? The obvious place was the antirejection protocol, and Cal went along the corridor to Milo's lab. The computer was there, with its box of labeled floppy disks. Caleb turned the machine on, and the clicks and beeps of the startup, plus the faint whirring of the cooling fan, reassured him. That was as far as he got. He couldn't get into the master program because he didn't know the keyword, and there didn't seem to be any way he could find it. He tried dozens of words, went through every disk in the box, but every time the screen came up monotonously with the same words "incorrect command." It occurred to Caleb to get around the problem by using one of the standard kidney transplant protocols, but he rejected that idea almost immediately. The problems to be faced were too different to take that risk.

Three hours later, when Caleb had switched the computer off in total frustration and was getting ready to go home, there was a knock on the door of the lab. Expecting the cleaners to be coming in with their mops and pails, Caleb opened the door. Maureen stood there in the doorway.

"I couldn't let your patient suffer through a Whipple," she said calmly. "I'm coming back for her, not for you."

She slipped quickly around Caleb, went into the office, and pulled on one of Milo's white coats. "I can take care of harvesting the graft," she said. "But I can't help you with the antirejection protocol. Milo's the only one who knows it." An idea came to her. "Did you know Porky did his thesis on immunology? Last time he was here, Milo talked to him and showed him what he was doing."

Before she'd finished speaking, Caleb was on the phone. When Porky came down a few minutes later, Caleb explained the problem to him.

"I honestly don't know," said Porky, very flustered. "I only spent twenty minutes talking to Dr. Zagros."

The three of them spent almost the entire weekend in the lab. Porky had to leave from time to time to take care of his clinical responsibilities, and Caleb and Maureen worked on the time-consuming preparations to harvest the pancreas graft; Porky noticed a chilliness between the two of them, chiefly emanating from Maureen, but when she came over to help him decipher what was on the computer program, she couldn't have been nicer or more helpful. When she leaned occasionally over his shoulder to look at the screen, Porky felt

tingly and happy. He'd never felt so part of a team before, and he was determined not to let them down.

Late on Sunday evening, Porky, to everyone's amazement,
managed to extract a complete printout of the protocol, and
all was ready for Maureen's harvesting of the graft in the early
hours on Tuesday. Celine's operation was scheduled for later
that morning, the day after the committee meeting.

The meeting of the Ethics and Public Welfare Committee took place at nine o'clock the next morning. A little over an hour later, Anna Lynn Page called Caleb from the phone outside the boardroom. He didn't hear his name being paged; he was in the changing room, having successfully removed the misplaced umbrella from Bridget Coughlan's inferior vena cava. All his students had wanted to be there, and had stood watching on a long footstool behind him while he operated. Caleb was not at all happy about the case or the eventual outcome; the traveling blood clots had already done substantial and permanent damage to Bridget Coughlan's lungs.

"Phone, Dr. Winter!" the O.R. secretary called to him through the intercom as he was getting out of his scrub clothes. Wearing only his shirt, he picked up the wall phone.

Anna May was so furious that it took her a few moments to compose her words. The committee, she finally informed him, had turned down Caleb's application.

The meeting had started off very pro-Winter, and she herself had said how great it was to be able to help a project that had such potential for humanity, and Dr. Armuth had sat there, nodding in agreement. Henry Brighton had then got up and said it was essential that work of such importance be done at the proper time, and that they must make quite sure that all that splendid effort wasn't lost by prematurely attempting to apply it to humans. His main concern, he said, was for the reputation of the hospital and the medical school, but even more to preserve Caleb Winter's own reputation as a first-class research surgeon. The techniques were not per-fected enough, he declared, and in this time of multimillion-dollar malpractice suits, to allow him to go ahead might mean bankruptcy for both the hospital and the medical school, since the insurance carriers would consider this to be experimental surgery, which was not covered by their policies.

Recounting all this to Caleb, Anna Lynn was stammering with rage. The others, she said, had been strongly swayed by Brighton's forceful comments. As Leroy Williams had said, Henry Brighton was the head of the department and knew more about that kind of thing than any of them, so they were pretty well bound to go along with his recommendations. L. Graham Benson, the chaplain, had hemmed and hawed, but had finally voted with Anna Lynn. Chauncey Milford Roper, the pharmaceutical manufacturer, had said nothing but had voted with Henry Brighton. Old Dr. Armuth, the chairman, had obviously been in two minds; he had felt that Dr. Winter's application was a strong one, that he had the confidence of the NIH to the tune of two and a half million dollars, and that the results of preliminary animal studies were excellent.

"I'm concerned about the effect of a turndown by this com-mittee on his overall research effort," he'd said, but Dr. Brigh-ton had reassured him on that score. He'd announced that he himself had recently been awarded a very large grant, and promised that enough money would be diverted to continue Dr. Winter's projects, even if at a reduced level. And of course, he would be closely supervising Winter's research.

Accordingly, Dr. Armuth had voted against the application. And that was that.

"Thanks for letting me know, Anna May," said Caleb. He knew that the shock would be delayed—at the moment all he could feel was surprise.

A few moments later, Caleb was called to the phone again to speak to Leroy Williams, who came straight to the point. "I voted against you," he said, "just like I said I would. But I thought I'd be the only one against. You got yo'self fucked over at that meetin', my man. Your Henry Brighton, he wanted to save your reputation so bad he shit all over it."

Caleb put the phone down, his rage starting to swell. Celine's transplant operation was already scheduled for the very next day, and everything was ready. It looked as if Don McAuliffe might get to do his Whipple after all.

Caleb went down to the lab, where Maureen was making up infusion solutions, preparing the instruments and getting everything in readiness. For her and her two technicians, the next day would start at five. By eight, said Maureen, the graft would be ready. It would be viable for five hours on the infusion pump, she said, which should give him plenty of time.

Caleb felt sick at heart. All that successful work at the weekend had made Maureen happy to be back, and she was so full of enthusiasm for the big breakthrough that he didn't have the courage to tell her it was all off. But he'd have to tell her soon, before she wasted much more time on it.

He went along the corridor to the immunology lab. Milo's chief tech was working rather aimlessly on a large plastic model of cellular antigen receptors; it looked like a giant orange studded with octopus suckers. Caleb couldn't think of anything to say to him, nodded, and went back to the ICU to check on Bridget Coughlan.

Red Felton kept his ear close to the ground, and soon heard the news. He cursed quietly to himself. Caleb Winter had been his bulwark, and Red had trusted in his proven ability to get the better of people he had to tangle with. But it certainly looked as if this time Caleb had lost not only the battle, but the entire war.

And now, thought Red, the outlook was as sunny as twelve inches up a rattlesnake's ass. Henry would bear down on him to work at his research project; he'd expect him to do research reports, give talks and lectures at national meetings. Red's lanky frame quivered at the thought. The worst thing would be the sniggers from his colleagues at these meetings. Red knew only too well what academic surgeons around the country thought of Henry Brighton.

He reached for the tin of Red Man. Maybe he should give it all up and go into private practice. But that would only be falling from the fry-pan into the campfire. He'd have to work a lot harder even than for Henry Brighton, and on top of that he'd have to pay his own malpractice insurance. This last thought was enough. He'd simply have to do what he could do to restore good ol' Caleb Winter to his rightful place at the head of the department research effort.

The problem was that his influence was limited, except of course with the students and the residents. Red opened the tin, pulled out a chaw of Herculean dimensions, and thought some more.

Caleb appeared, grim-faced, in Celine's room, soon after learning the news of his defeat at the hands of the Ethics and Public Welfare Committee. He sat down heavily in the chair by the window.

"We have a problem," he said, trying to cover the anger in his voice.

Celine sat up in bed and put her hand to her mouth. She had never seen Caleb upset. "What's happened?"

He told her about the committee's decision.

"Can't you appeal it?"

"It would take months. And with the problem you have, we don't have that kind of time."

"So what are our options now?"

Caleb put his head between his hands. Celine slipped out of bed and went to him. She stroked his head, comforting him. Caleb stood up, and Celine took a small step closer. Almost unwillingly, he opened his arms out to her, and held her close.

"Options?" Caleb spoke over her shoulder, scarcely feeling her body against his. He sounded numb. "We don't have any, now."

Don McAuliffe and Ed van Stamm were at the nurses' station when Caleb came out of Celine's room, and he had the distinct impression that they were waiting for him. Certainly Don was, from the steely glow in his eye.

He stepped forward. "I see you've got Mrs. Roach scheduled for tomorrow," he said, tapping the operating list in his hand. "If you're planning for her to have a Whipple, I was wondering if you would help me do it. I've only four months to go in my residency, and I haven't done one yet." He stood in front of Caleb, a strange mixture of truculence and deference.

Caleb stared coolly at him, and Don's gaze dropped to the floor. He knew that he had just committed an astounding breach of protocol; Celine was a private patient, and it was entirely Caleb's decision who would do the surgery. But Don was on the home stretch, punch-drunk from four years of a tough surgical training program and chronic lack of sleep. At this point, all he wanted was to do the Whipple procedure that the system owed him, and after that they could all go and disappear up their own asses.

"Actually, Don, I haven't quite decided what the best operation is for her," said Caleb politely. Ed, who was listening from the other side of the nurses' desk glanced quickly at them. He knew that Don's chances of doing a Whipple in the morning had shrunk to zero.

At this moment the idea of Don McAuliffe even touching Celine angered Caleb, and he couldn't imagine himself allowing any other surgeon to take a knife to her.

Caleb walked past them and headed toward the operating suite. "Hi, Barb," he said to the clerk. "Have you printed up tomorrow's operating schedule yet?"

Barbara indicated a sheaf of papers on the right of her desk. "I'm just about to send the list down," she said.

"I need to make a change," said Caleb. Barbara pulled one sheet from the sheaf, and he scanned it. There it was, his first and only case for the day, scheduled for seven-thirty; he took a pen out of the pocket of his white coat, crossed out what was already in the "procedure" column, and in his firm, meticulous script wrote the words; Celine de La Roche: Whipple Procedure.

When Caleb came in that evening, Charles had just arrived, and the tension in the room was palpable.

"Good," said Caleb briskly, addressing Charles. "I'm glad you're here." He got down to business immediately. "I've already told Celine the committee turned down our application." He then described the operation that he would be performing on Celine, and tried to accent the positive aspects. "It's the standard procedure for this kind of tumor," he told them. "A Whipple is what they would do in any major center in this country."

"I don't understand," said Charles. "You're the surgeon, and we have complete confidence in your judgment. How can a committee tell you what you can or can't do?"

Caleb explained. "It's not like the old days," he said, trying to hide his own anger and frustration. "Nowadays we all have to take orders, and not always from the people who know best."

Charles glanced at Celine before addressing Caleb. "Now if there's any thought in your mind about a malpractice suit, or anything like that . . ."

"Charles!" said Celine, sitting bolt upright, her eyes flashing. "Of course there's no question of such a thing."

Caleb ignored the interruption.

"I'm sure that you are aware," he said, "that our whole lab was geared up to do the transplantation." He smacked a fist into his open palm, and thought bitterly about all the years of work that had gone into the transplant project, and all for nothing.

"If Celine agrees, I think you should go ahead with it," said Charles, getting up. "And we'll both back you to the limit if there are any problems."

"I appreciate your support," replied Caleb, sounding defeated. "But you can see that I can't disobey the most specific instructions from the hospital. In the long run, it would do more harm than good."

Caleb then told Celine that she'd be in intensive care for a day or two afterward, that she might have a tube in her throat for a few hours to help her breathe, that she would have tubes in her stomach, IVs and arterial monitoring lines, and would most likely need a blood transfusion. While he explained, Celine listened with a curiously blank expression, and Charles paced up and down the room, unable to listen to the details of this ghastly procedure.

* * *

With a swift, precise movement, the knife swept in a dome-shaped curve from one side of the abdomen to the other. A wake of blood welled up behind it. The suction hissed, the coagulator crackled, and the hemostats clicked, fast and efficient. The scalpel went deeper, the muscles were cut, the large blood vessels tied off.

"Pick up on your side," said Caleb to Don, lifting the thin, membranous veil of peritoneum with his forceps.

"Metz," he said to the new scrub nurse, Fran Dixon, who instantly put the Metzenbaum scissors in his hand. She was doing well so far and felt a kind of tremulous confidence. Up to now, she'd been able to predict everything he'd needed.

Caleb opened the membrane, revealing the wet, glistening abdominal cavity. He put his gloved hand in, expertly evaluating, feeling the texture and consistency of the tissues and organs, the soft, rubbery liver. It had a nice sharp edge, a young liver. He swept his hand over its dome, then underneath, where the soft gallbladder felt like a silken pouch. No metastases, no sign of spread. Over on the right, he felt the firm fist-sized spleen tucked out of the way under the ribs, then the colon, the stomach, and finally the pancreas. He knew pretty well what to expect from the arteriogram, the CAT scans, and the ultrasound. They had confirmed what his fingers had told him when he first examined her in his office. God, how long ago was that? Less than two weeks, he reminded himself. Winter's hand slid around the smooth lump. It was growing forward out of the pancreas, pushing on the stomach and other structures. He evaluated the texture, the feel. It was firm, almost hard. With his fingertips he gently explored the mass, trying by some kind of digital magic to decide whether it was solid or fluid-filled, maybe even cystic. Was it a cancer? Fingertips consulted memory banks, intuition, and experience. The answer came back. Yes. Probably.

"Don, put your hand in there, gently. Tell me what you feel."

Caleb turned away from the table to a basin and washed the blood off his gloves. He could feel his heart pounding. Maybe it was benign. He angrily pushed the thought out of his mind: It was malignant and he knew it. He still had to take a biopsy, so there was maybe half an hour before the pathologist came back with the positive answer.

In his mind he went over the various steps of the Whipple procedure. The first thing was to make sure the tumor could be removed completely. Unless he could be certain of that, there was no point going on, and he would then close up. Celine would get chemotherapy, like that unfortunate young woman he'd seen in the outpatient clinic the same day Celine had first come to see him. He pushed away the memory of that patient's sunken, ravaged face and hairless, skeletal body. If there was no sign of spread, and the blood vessels were clear, he would remove Celine's pancreas, part of the stomach, the spleen, part of the intestine, the gallbladder. Although he had performed this operation several times, Caleb was still revolted by the degree of destruction it entailed.

Using a long knife with a small blade, Caleb removed a small piece of the tumor and placed it in Fran's outstretched Petri dish. The pathologist was waiting outside for the specimen, and the circulator hurried out with it.

While they waited for the pathologist's report, Caleb showed Don how to separate the tumor from the surrounding structures, and how to expose the important blood vessels that passed so dangerously close to the tumor.

"Don, I've freed up the tumor on your side. Slip your hand in. There, can you feel the superior mesenteric vessels?" Don put his hand in and looked over Caleb's shoulder at the wall.

"Yeah, I can feel them." But from the tone of his voice, Caleb wasn't so sure.

"Porky, pull a little harder," he said, and Porky leaned back on the wide metal retractors that were already cutting into his hands. "Look, Don." With a long forceps Caleb gently pushed the tumor away from the vessels. "You see, they're free from the tumor. Now let's check the inferior vena cava."

It took Caleb forty-five minutes of fast and accurate operating just to prove that the tumor was operable.

The intercom hissed for a second, then the head nurse's voice came over. "We have the report, Dr. Winter. Shall I read it?"

"Send the pathologist in with it, please," said Caleb. Don

was watching him with an odd expression, although only his eyes were showing between his mask and the hood. He was waiting, still hoping that Caleb would say "Don, why don't you go take it from here, and I'll help you through the difficult parts."

Dr. Ben Harris, the attending pathologist assigned to do frozen sections that week, came in, his senior resident following behind him, holding four slides in his hand.

"It's malignant, Dr. Winter," said Ben.

"That doesn't come as a total surprise," said Caleb, his voice snappier than he wanted to sound. "What's the cell type?"

"Adenocarcinoma," replied Ben. "But it looks slow-growing, very few mitotic figures, and there's a fair amount of fibrous reaction."

"How about the lymph nodes?"

"We didn't see any tumor cells, but of course we'll need serial sections to be certain."

Caleb nodded. Now everything pointed to the possibility of a complete cure, and that all the cancerous tissue could be removed. The message hadn't been lost on Don either, and his restless eyes searched Caleb's.

When the two pathologists had left the operating room, Caleb took his habitual little step back from the table. Don stared hard at Caleb, willing him to give him the case.

Caleb took a deep breath. "Call my lab," he said to the circulator. "Tell them we're going to put in the graft."

Caleb could feel Don's shock and anger; everybody in the hospital knew that Caleb had been refused permission to perform this operation. For a second Caleb thought that Don was going to walk out on him. In his silent fury, Don briefly considered that option, but he knew that even in the final months of his residency, he would be fired for such an outrageous action.

It took Caleb another two hours to remove the tumor and the pancreas with it and place metal strips where the tumor had been.

"Dr. Winter, would you explain why you're doing that?" asked Porky. The operation had been conducted in near silence, and his voice sounded unnaturally loud.

"If you heat living cells beyond a certain temperature," replied Caleb, "they die. Cancer cells are more susceptible to heat than normal cells. Those strips are to capture and reflect microwave radiation she'll get postoperatively, and convert it to heat."

He looked at Porky to see if he understood, and was surprised by the young man's expression. He was looking sorry for him. Caleb grinned, touched by his concern. "It's okay, Porky," he said. "It is a new protocol, but it belongs to the oncology department, and that one *has* been approved." Porky flushed and smiled sheepishly, but Don's lips just tightened visibly under his mask.

As the operation proceeded, Caleb became aware of a certain amount of activity outside the operating room. Twice

Henry Brighton came to the window and looked in, just for a second. Then Marshall Prince, the hospital administrator, appeared, looking uncomfortable in operating room greens; even he wasn't allowed in the operating suite without them. He caught Caleb's eye for a second, and then he was gone. Caleb smiled grimly to himself and continued in his careful way.

Don, amazed by Caleb's phenomenal dexterity and expertise, was thawing. For the first time it dawned on him that he was working with a surgical genius on a quite extraordinary case, a privilege he might never have again. He took a deep breath, decided that this was even more important than doing a Whipple, and started to assist with a new vigor and enthusiasm.

Caleb noticed the change, and grinned at him briefly. "You've just joined the fellowship of surgeons," he told Don quietly, but of all the people around the table only Don knew what he meant.

Once the graft was in, the ducts had been joined and the feeding arteries and veins attached, the atmosphere changed. Normally it would have been a time for a modest feeling of celebration; a new surgical frontier had been breached. But instead there was a solemnity, a fear of what was going to be unleashed as soon as the case was over.

It's a hostile world out there, thought Porky, looking at the window. He was surprised at himself; normally he would have been feeling exhausted and numb after holding retractors for all this time. His hands hurt, certainly, but he was alert, reviewing the postoperative orders he would be writing. Maybe he too would be allowed to join the fellowship of surgeons some day.

As they were closing, Caleb went over every detail of Celine's postoperative care with Don and Ed, who listened carefully. He knew that, depending on what actions were taken against him by the hospital authorities, he might not have much say in her treatment once Celine left the operating room. And whatever happened, she had to make it.

* * *

The word went out instantly from the operating room that Caleb Winter was placing a pancreatic graft in a patient in open defiance of the hospital's ruling, and within an hour, a hurried emergency meeting was convened in Marshall Prince's office. The dean of the faculty of medicine was there, together with the hospital's chief of staff, and of course, Henry Brighton in his capacity as chairman of the department of surgery.

"Don't you think we should get Dr. Winter down here?" asked Marshall Prince. "There may be a perfectly sound reason for him to have gone ahead with that transplant."

"He's still in the operating room," said Henry. "I'd guess he'll be there for another couple of hours." He spoke with authority, as if he himself did transplantations every day.

The chief of staff looked exasperated. "In that case, aren't we jumping the gun? Wouldn't it be better to wait until he's able to talk to us?"

Henry shrugged. "As we're here, we might as well do what we have to do."

Half an hour later, they had decided that if the facts were as they seemed to be and Caleb Winter had carried out a pancreatic transplant in the face of official prohibition, the hospital administrator would suspend Caleb's hospital privileges on an emergency basis, with one exception. He would be permitted to take care of Ms. Celine de La Roche, the transplant patient, and only her. And that was only because there was nobody else in the hospital with enough knowledge and experience to undertake that responsibility. Even Henry, who would take on just about anything, hesitated. "I'd do it," he told Prince and the others around the table, "but really I can't spare the time. I can't allow my own patients to suffer."

Didier Franchet had some fairly urgent business to attend to back in France, but since Celine's situation was unresolved, and he still needed a small block of Fortman and Carfield shares for his takeover, he was forced to stay in the U.S., although he didn't like the language, the climate, or the people. The best thing about the United States, he had decided some years before, was that it was the easiest place in the world to raise capital. In most countries, he found, and particularly in France, bankers lent money with marked reluctance, as if it were coming out of their own pockets. They also required tiresome details about how the money was to be used, and checked carefully at frequent intervals to make sure it was being spent as planned. After a few painful experiences with the Crédit Lyonnais and the Banque de France, Didier had turned to the U.S. American lending institutions were federally guaranteed, and bad debts could be written off. Didier's own best experience, and one he liked to tell his friends, had been with a certain savings and loan association in Kansas City. He had borrowed a substantial amount for a real estate conversion deal that had gone sour, to the bank's considerable loss. But such was Didier's confident manner that he was able to get another loan for a second project from the same institution *the very same day.*

He looked at his watch and reached for the phone. He had found that a small but critical percentage of the outstanding shares were presently in the hands of an elderly couple who lived in Peekskill, New York. Didier was going to take the unusual step of personally making a direct offer to them, one they couldn't refuse.

Charles sat in the waiting room outside the operating suite, feeling like a prisoner waiting for the jury's decision. Celine's illness had upset him more than even he realized, particularly now that he understood the full gravity of her situation. Looking around the waiting room for something to occupy his mind, Charles noticed a Hispanic family waiting at the other end. A nurse came and stood in the doorway.

"Mr. Gonzales?" she looked at him, and Charles smiled briefly and shook his head. The man with the two children got up. "Phone," said the nurse, and she escorted him into the corridor. His two children, a boy who looked about four years old, and his sister, about two years younger, were sitting on the floor, playing with some large glass marbles. As Charles watched, the little girl picked a marble up and put it into her mouth. In a second, without even thinking, Charles bounded across the room, picked up the little girl, and suspended her by her ankles, her head a foot from the ground, while the little boy watched, his mouth open in astonishment. The child screamed with the shock of being so unceremoniously upended, and the marble fell out of her mouth and rolled over toward the door, which opened at the same moment, as the child's father came back into the waiting room. The father stood at the door, amazed, while the child's howling drowned out Charles' attempts to speak. The father went red in the face and bunched his fists, and it could have developed into an ugly scene. Charles did his best to explain in his awful Spanish, but luckily the nurse came back in, picked up the marble, and told Mr. Gonzales that Charles had probably saved his daughter's life.

Charles turned the child the right way up, handed her back to her father, and returned to his seat, amused for a moment, but his heart sank again as soon as the excitement was over. A few moments later, another nurse came in, wearing a green scrub dress, with a message for him from Dr. Winter. Everything looked good so far, she said, smiling. Charles was reassured, more by her expression and the way she looked directly at him than by what she said. Celine would be going directly to the intensive care unit, and he would probably be able to see her in an hour or so, maybe a little longer.

Feeling immensely relieved, Charles sat down again. The Hispanic family had left, and Charles thought about the father's expression when he saw his daughter suspended upside down and howling to beat the band. A slow smile spread across his face, and simultaneously he felt a sudden upsurge of confidence. Celine was going to be all right; her illness would be an opportunity for them to rethink their marriage while she was convalescing at home, away from the strains of managing her business, and away from Dr. Winter. Charles hadn't missed a beat of what was happening there. They would do some traveling, get more involved in things together. Everything was going to be all right. He picked up his copy of *Horse and Rider* and settled in for a long wait.

Since his nonstop working weekend, Porky had come down to the lab every day, and when he heard about Caleb's suspension, he hurried down to talk to Maureen about it. Maureen, who had become fond of Porky in the brief space of time they'd worked together, shook her head when he brought up the topic. She understood how the system worked.

"There are ways of breaking rules," she told Porky, still wondering at Caleb's rash action, "but one of the things you don't do is crash straight into them. Unless you're in a fireproof position," she added. She smiled at Porky, who was hanging on to her every word. "Don't underestimate Caleb," she went on, mostly to bolster up her own feelings of insecurity, "he's been around the block a couple of times, and he's a lot smarter than most of those people who're trying to get him."

The shock waves were felt throughout the hospital. It was the only topic in the corridor conferences and unplanned cafeteria meetings that formed the hospital information network. Opinion was sharply polarized: most of the academic surgeons were on the side of what they called law and order. Winter had blatantly broken the rules and should not be allowed to get away with it. Many of the town doctors, on the other hand, felt that this was yet another encroachment of ignorant bureaucracy on medical freedom. Winter was an authority of worldwide renown, and it was intolerable that his expert judgment should be overruled by a committee composed of pimps, clerics, and housewives.

The only person who seemed to take it all calmly was Caleb himself. As soon as Celine's operation was over, he went down to Marshall Prince's office and told him what he had done. Marshall was coldly angry with him.

"To me, Caleb," he said, "that was an extraordinarily arrogant and unwise thing to do, the *day* after you had been specifically forbidden . . ." He reached automatically for his pack of cigarettes, wishing he could smoke two simultaneously. "Not only that, but you're rocking the boat at a bad time," he said. "We have contracts coming up with the clerical and nursing unions, and if this story gets into the media it'll add fuel to the flames and weaken the management position."

"I guess we each have our own point of view," replied Caleb calmly. "My primary concern was to make the best medical decision for my patient, and that's what I did."

Marshall looked at him with a puzzled expression. "But surely, man," he said, allowing his anger to flare for an instant, "surely you understand that taking the best care of this one patient may prevent you from taking care of others? Not only that, but I'm sure you're well aware that certain people in this institution are only too happy to get an opportunity to clip your wings. They'll try to do it permanently, don't you see that?"

"Marshall, I have to make the best decisions I can for each individual patient," replied Caleb, not looking concerned. "That's the main responsibility of any physician."

Marshall took a deep breath, stood up, and looked Caleb straight in the eye.

"Dr. Winter," he said formally, "I have to inform you that your admitting and operating privileges at this hospital are rescinded as of now." He looked at the clock and made a notation of the time on a piece of paper in front of him. "There will be one single exception, and that is for your transplant patient. You retain full authority to prescribe and supervise any treatment for Ms. de La Roche." Marshall paused and leaned over the desk. "Until the matter has been fully reviewed by the supervisory committees and the hospital board, you cannot admit patients or do any surgical operations whatever. Is that clear?"

Caleb nodded.

"I'm sorry, Caleb," said Marshall in a gentler tone now his duty was done. "but you gave me no choice. One more thing," he went on, "I'd appreciate it if you wouldn't discuss this situation with anyone at this time, including the media."

"Don't worry," replied Caleb. "Of course I won't. And I hope that this whole business can be resolved as quickly as possible."

Marshall stared at him. "It will be," he said, "but don't expect it to be resolved in your favor."

After Caleb left his office, Marshall smashed his fist on the desk. Why had he gone into medical administration? he asked himself. Why had he taken one of the few administrative jobs in the entire world where he had to deal with people who thought they were God?

Porky went back to work, still feeling shattered. "I can't believe they actually pulled his privileges!" he said sadly to Don and Ed later that day when were grabbing a bite in the deserted cafeteria. Both Don and Ed, who had problems of their own, ignored him. But Porky felt as if he'd been hit over the head. In his father's day, he knew, nothing like this could have happened; he'd heard enough stories about how the senior hospital doctors used to walk the wards, totally in command of the patients, the nurses, the labs, everything. Nobody told *them* what to do; if they wanted to try a new kind of treatment, they did it, often without even telling the patients concerned.

Porky wanted to let Dr. Winter know that he was totally on his side. He straightened out his fingers, still stiff from pulling on retractors. But what could he do? His hold on his own job was precarious enough.

Don McAuliffe looked up from his patient cards for a second. "Porky, go down to Red Felton's office and pick up next month's lecture schedule," he said. Porky got up, with the distinct impression that he and Ed wanted to talk without him around.

Red Felton was in his office, as usual with his boots up on the table. The Stetson was hanging from a hook on the back of the door, but Red wasn't wearing his usual relaxed expression, and he was chomping on his Red Man chaw at twice the usual speed.

"Hi there, Porks," said Red, looking over the top of his paper. When he saw that Porky wanted to talk to him, Red pointed a long finger at a chair in the corner. "Pull up a loose stool, boy. Tell me what's exercising them brain cells of yours."

Porky asked him if was true that Dr. Winter's hospital privileges had been withdrawn.

"Sure sounds like it, boy." Red didn't know much more than Porky did, but he was able to tell him that Dr. Winter would still be taking care of the lady he'd operated on, the one all the fuss was about.

"What can we do?" asked Porky. "We can't just let—" Porky's hands flapped ineffectively, and recognizing that, he sat on them.

"I was just wondering the same question, Porks," said Red thoughtfully. "Only I ain't come up with nothin' just yet."

A silence ensued, while Red pushed the plastic-lined can out from under the desk with his boot and spat a long, contemplative jet of brown tobacco juice into it.

"Maybe we should do a job action," suggested Porky breathlessly. "Maybe if all the residents and the other doctors went on strike . . ."

"We'd never get them to do that," interrupted Red, a gleam suddenly lighting his eye, "The residents maybe, but not the staff docs." He swung his boots off the desk. "You came for the schedule, right?" He pushed a piece of paper across the desk. "Thanks for stopping by, Porks. I think maybe you gave me an idea."

Red took out the phone book and opened it near the back. "Wilks . . . Wilkins . . . Here we are—Williams." He kept his long finger on the name while he dialed the number.

Celine woke up slowly; she was choking, coming out of a dark tunnel . . . something was in her throat and she couldn't breathe or scream, and she couldn't move. She tried to open her eyes, and the brightness was like glass shards being pushed into them. She closed them again, but something pulled them open and she saw a nose, a frighteningly distorted upside-down face. . . .

"She's reacting." The words came from far away, like a record being played at the wrong speed, then there was a painful, deafening crash of something falling on the floor. The thing in her throat made her gag, and she tried to sit up but a sudden horrific pain in her belly made her scream soundlessly. Soon after, she felt the trundling of the stretcher, was conscious of lights passing by, the noise of voices coming and going, then somebody said "One, two, three ... *now!*" and she was lifted onto another bed. She felt hands around her face then one hard puff of cold air after another, as if somebody was blowing into her lungs when she was trying to breathe out. She tried to resist it, and felt the panic rising; she was sure she was going to die, choking, unable to breathe.

"Just breathe with the machine, Celine." Caleb's voice came through the darkness to her, and its strength and encouragement brought her to a different level of consciousness. She felt his hand take hers. She tried to say something, but the puff of air hit her again and distended her lungs.

"You have to breathe *with* it," said Caleb, his mouth close to her ear. "When I tell you, breathe OUT ... now let the machine help you breathe in ... right, that's it ... here, I'll slow it down a bit, more like your own speed ..." Celine shut out everything except the life-saving sound of his voice.

"Remember what I told you," he said. "You won't be able to say anything with that tube in your throat. Just answer questions by squeezing my hand, once for yes, twice for no. Do you understand?" Celine tried to nod, then remembered what he had just told her. "Are you having pain?" There was a pause before she gave one squeeze, just strong enough to let Caleb know it hurt, but she could bear it. Caleb stayed with her until the panic had passed and her breathing was regular.

"I'm going into the waiting room now to talk to Charles," he said quietly, his mouth again close to her ear because of the hissing noise from the respirator. "I'll be back in a few minutes."

For the next several hours, Celine's existence was merely an alternation of light and dark; light when Caleb was there, holding her hand and talking gently to her; dark during the horrible times in between. Strange voices asked her if she wanted anything for pain. When she found the medication made her sleepy, she tried to hold off if she thought Caleb was due soon, because she didn't want to be asleep when he came. The anesthesiologist, Dr. Pinero, fussed in and out, asking questions she couldn't answer. After a while, Celine became aware that she couldn't move either of her arms; they seemed to be tied down. From time to time, somebody would come and do something, and her arms hurt.

After a while, Celine was able to focus enough to see what was happening. Plastic tubes were running into her arms, attached to a cluster of bottles and plastic bags above her head. From time to time, a girl in a white coat came with a wooden basket full of syringes and needles to draw blood out of the tubing.

"Blood gases are pretty good," she heard Dr. Pinero say. "I think we can extubate her." He detached the tape from one of the two tubes going into her nose, and it hurt, as if someone had pushed a thick finger up her nostril. And then he pulled the tube out, and it felt as if he was pulling her lungs out with it. It brought tears to her eyes; a dreadful taste filled her mouth and nose, and she coughed. The pain hit her in the belly like an ax, and she tried to think only of Caleb, his hand, his presence, a talisman to protect her from all the dreadful things that were happening.

And suddenly she could breathe normally again. The air felt like sandpaper going into her lungs, but at least *she* was deciding when it went in, not the machine. She opened her eyes, and Caleb was smiling down at her. He took a paper tissue and wiped her face and nose—she felt like a child again, with her father blowing her nose for her when she came in from playing outside in the cold garden.

Charles was allowed in after she'd been extubated. They made him put on a gown and mask; he could only stay for a minute, they said. He stood there watching her, silent. For one moment, he touched her fingers, the only accessible part of her hand, which was immobilized on an I.V. board and kept in position by a large gauze bandage.

Caleb came up while Charles was there. "She's doing nicely," he said, glancing at a computer readout in his hand.

He smiled, and put a hand gently on Celine's shoulder, and she turned her head to look at him.

"Maybe we can get her out of here by tomorrow morning," said Caleb.

"That would be wonderful," said Charles. He must have seen something very disturbing pass between Celine and Caleb, because all his thoughts about rethinking his marriage and traveling with Celine went straight out the window.

He looked Caleb straight in the eye. "As she is in such competent and *loving* hands, I assume you'll be able to do without me for a while."

Celine's eyes grew larger as she listened to him, and when Charles turned to face her there was a coldness and finality about his voice that shocked her. "Celine," he said clearly, "I'm assuming you can hear me. I'm going to Atlanta tomorrow and won't be back until some time next week." He went quickly toward the door. "Good luck," he said. "Both of you."

Even in her pain, Celine felt a jolt of anger and betrayal. Go, she thought, I don't ever want to see you again.

Caleb Winter could not truthfully have said that he hadn't expected it, but the shock of having his hospital and operating privileges taken away had nevertheless shaken him. As he passed through the doctors' lounge the next day on his way to the ICU, the buzz of conversation stopped.

Gabe Pinero got up hurriedly and came over. "You did the right thing, Cal," he said loudly. "Everybody's on your side."

Caleb thanked him, but he noticed that several of the other doctors in the room studiously avoided his gaze. The news had traveled like a sonic boom around the hospital, and now, twenty-four hours later, there wasn't an employee or physician who hadn't taken sides. The administration, in an unprecedented effort to keep the news out of the media, had forbidden all employees from discussing the case outside the hospital, under pain of dismissal. Marshall Prince instructed Armon Willis, the head of public relations, to prepare a statement for the media if the news did leak out. The statement was passed through the legal department, then passed back to Prince, who turned it back into dry, administrative but comprehensible English, amputated of the heretofores and herinafters inserted by the hospital's legal fraternity. Prince shook his head as he signed the statement. Those lawyers seemed to multiply like rabbits every year; the legal department now occupied the entire fourth floor of the administrative building and threatened to spread to the floor above. Looking at his legal expenses in the hospital's annual budget, he was reminded of the pigs in *Animal Farm*.

Relieved of all clinical and administrative duties in the hospital, Caleb found an unexpected freedom. He didn't have to operate, help the residents, teach students, or attend rounds or committee meetings, and that gave him time to work in the lab and catch up with his research reading. Just keeping up with everything in his own narrow specialty required, Caleb figured, at least three hours' concentrated reading every day. And he watched over Celine like a mother hawk over its chick, anticipating and averting problems before they had time to develop.

"He's doing my job," said Porky to Celine, amazed, having just met Caleb coming out of her room carrying a dressing set and green towels after changing her abdominal dressing. "Next he'll be drawing blood from you!"

"He did," whispered Celine through dry lips. "A little while ago. Isn't he supposed to?"

"Dr. Winter can do anything he wants, as far as I'm concerned," said Porky stoutly. "I'm just happy they let him keep on taking care of you."

"So am I, Porky." Celine was so weak that her voice faded at the end of the sentence.

In spite of the pain in her belly, the fearsome agony of coughing, the immobilization of her arms, and the unremitting discomfort of the remaining tube which passed through her nostril down into her stomach, there was a new glow about Celine, and Porky wondered about it.

An hour or so later, Caleb crept quietly into her room, thinking she might be asleep. Her eyes were closed, and she looked drawn and white. Gently he touched her fingers.

"Hi, Caleb," she said, without opening her eyes.

"Either you have second sight, or you were taking quite a risk there," he said, smiling.

She flexed her fingers, trying to hold onto his hand. "I feel like hell," she said.

"Good. That shows you're making progress," he said, and sat down, still holding her fingertips.

They sat like that, without speaking, and Celine drew strength from him, like water from a well.

* * *

Caleb's colleagues watched and talked with consuming interest about what was now being called the Winter case. Henry Brighton, who was spending a fair amount of time with Red Felton to bolster his commitment to the ulcerative colitis research project, kept pretty quiet about Caleb, but was no match for Red's adroit questioning.

Red was on his best behavior these days. He stopped chewing tobacco in Henry's presence, took his boots off the desk when the chairman came in, and generally treated him with a friendliness and deference that would have made anyone else deeply suspicious. But Henry felt that he had finally brought Red into line, and responded with an effusive affability that privately nauseated Red.

The morning after Celine's operation, Henry Brighton came striding into Red's office, pink with pleasure, and waving a closely typed piece of thin airmail paper.

"Here it is!" he said, slapping it down on Red's desk. "The official word!"

The letter was from a Swiss bank, in English, and the first paragraph stated that it was representing the Helvetia Consortium, comprising several pharmaceutical companies, which, as Red noted, were not named. A grant in the amount of $560,000 had been awarded to Herr Professor Doctor Henry Brighton, in recognition of his major contributions to surgical research. The money would be paid into a separate research account to be audited by the university, the results of said audit to be forwarded to the bank within one month of its completion. The money would be made available in accordance with previously agreed criteria, not sooner than October twenty-second of the current year.

"Well, congrats and all that kind of horse manure, old buddy," drawled Red. "That shore is a remarkable piece of timing."

"What do you mean?" asked Henry, still grinning ear to ear.

"Cal's NIH grant expires that very same day," replied Red, "but I don't expect you knowed that. How're y'all gonna do the switch? At midnight on the twenty-first? All yore stuff going in one door, and his going out the other?"

"No problem," said Henry. "I'm sure Cal and I can work out an amicable solution. Anyway, that's not the point. It's real—it's really happening." He picked up the letter and waved it. "This is as good as money in the bank. Can you believe it—over half a million bucks!" He looked at the letter again as if the words might suddenly disappear before his eyes.

"What was that bit about previously agreed criteria?" Red sat back in his chair and reached for the tin of Red Man, but remembered just in time. "What d'you have to do for them? I mean the drug people who're financing this. TV spots for them in fancy dress? Paint aspirin ads on the hospital walls?" Red's smile was friendly, but his eyes didn't leave Henry's face for a second.

Henry's gaze flickered. "Of course not. You really are crass, Red. It's just a kind of formality, something we all agreed on. Not any problem." Henry took a deep breath, and his high spirits returned. He leaned confidentially across the desk, his round pink face glowing with friendliness, and Red repressed a humanitarian desire to smash his fist into it.

"Red, I want to show you it's worth your while being on my team. What I'm going to tell you could make you a rich man." Henry paused to let his words sink in.

Red sat very still.

"Okay," Henry went on, "this is a kind of tip. I have some very powerful friends in the drug industry ..." he grinned and waved the letter again, "as you may have guessed. Now, for various reasons, the price of the stock in this particular consortium is set to *triple* in just a couple of weeks." Henry pulled out his diary; Red noticed that it was the kind the drug reps handed out around Christmas every year. "On the twenty-ninth of September, to be exact." He flicked the diary shut, and told Red the name of the corporation. "It's traded over the counter in the U.S., so there isn't the kind of scrutiny ... Anyway, to show you how serious I am about this, I personally have spent every penny the Squeaker and I possess and more to buy stock and call options."

"What's that?" asked Red. "Call options? Is that a list of good-time gals you can choose from?"

"No, no, no," said Henry, sounding very superior. "A call option's a contract to buy stock at a specified price at a specific time in the future. When the price goes up in the interim, that's when you make your profit."

"Sounds good to me, just as long as it goes up, like you said."

"You take my advice, Red. But do it now; the price is already creeping up a bit. Some other people must have an idea there's something good brewing."

"Well, thanks a bunch, old buddy. Really. I'll just mosey on along home and see if mah honey's left any money in our ol' piggy bank. Sounds like a good tip. You going to retire? I mean after you make all this money?"

"To tell you the truth, Red, according to my calculations, I could, and handsomely. But there's too much to do here, and quite honestly, there's nobody else who could accept the level of responsibility I have to deal with. No I'll be staying in harness, I guess."

After explaining the need for absolute secrecy about the stock deals, Henry went down the corridor, rejoicing. Everything was going his way, and he whistled the appropriate song from *Oklahoma* as he walked jauntily back to his office.

Red sat back in his chair, and reached for the tin of Red Man. He wasn't averse to getting rich quickly any more than the next guy, but the idea of getting rich on a tip from Henry Brighton stuck in his craw. What really interested him was Henry's mysterious grant and his excited tip about the Consortium's share prices going up. Maybe Caleb would understand what it all meant.

"But when will I be able to speak to her?" Tom Pfeiffer's voice, muffled by the sound of traffic, sounded on the verge of tears. "The most dreadful things . . ." Tom caught himself. Celine had told him long ago not to involve Charles in matters that had to do with the company.

"What's happening, Tom?" asked Charles quietly, looking at the clock. He had to be on his way to La Guardia in a few minutes. Tom paused, thinking that after all Charles might be able to help. He wasn't one to panic or give advice he hadn't carefully considered. And anyway, what more was there to lose, at this stage?

"Everything was going so nicely," said Tom, shouting to hear himself. "We made the move to the new offices in one day with no problem. Everything's in, the terminals, the office equipment, the copiers, the furniture. The only thing that got broken was my mug with a three-dollar bill with Richard Nixon's face on it . . ." For a few moments the sound of traffic drowned out the sound of his voice. "Here's the problem," shouted Tom. "The utilities and the telephone companies won't connect us, so we're completely paralyzed. The office is like an oven, and we can't get in touch with our reps, suppliers, or anybody." There was a pause, and Charles could hear the sound of muffled voices. "Somebody trying to get into the booth," explained Tom. "I did the best I could," he went on, "but apparently the building's in violation of the city fire code, and by law they're not allowed to install services until the violations have been corrected."

"Did you call Mr. Al-Khayib?" asked Charles. He sounded so relaxed and confident that Tom felt his pulse coming down to below a hundred for the first time in days.

"I couldn't reach him," he replied wearily. "And nobody else knows anything. I'm getting the runaround, the New York City runaround, Mr. Forester!"

"Where are you now, Tom?"

"In a phone booth down in the lobby. I've been here all day, and I daren't leave, even to go to the men's room, because I'm waiting for some calls. Mr. Forester, at this point I really don't know what to do."

"Okay, Tom," said Charles after the briefest of pauses. "Here's what you do. Call the nearest cellular phone company and order all the phones you need. With an order like that they'll be on your doorstep in fifteen minutes." As he spoke, Charles opened the big Manhattan Yellow Pages and flipped through them. "As soon as you've done that, call the Antarctica Portable Air Conditioning Company, and tell them you need emergency assistance. You can reach them at . . ."

After Charles had given him the number, Tom said "That's a fine idea, but it'll cost us a fortune. We can't afford it."

"Mr. Al-Khayib's paying for it. Under the New York City Statutes, I don't remember which one, 'If a landlord, by his neglect or default causes interruption of essential services in the leased premises, he is responsible for restoring same and for emergency services until such essential services are restored.' Tom, don't worry. I'll make sure Mr. Al-Khayib hears about it, and I'll guarantee he'll take care of the problem in a day or two."

Charles hung up, then sat looking at the phone for a few moments, again feeling annoyed that Celine had always excluded him so totally from her business.

Tom put the phone back on its cradle, then fainted, right there in the booth. He woke up a second or two later, unhurt, and in a sitting position. It was the heat, he told the black man who stopped to help him up. Just the heat.

Porky, now an honorary member of the lab, was spending as much time as he could there; even after Milo had gone, the atmosphere was like balm to Porky. And Maureen, who had not left after the transplant as everybody had expected, was very taken by Porky. She discovered that he had a gentle but penetrating sense of humor when he wasn't too tired to see straight.

Maureen took one look at him when he appeared at the door on the second day after Celine's transplant, and said, "You'd better come in for a cup of coffee. You look as if you could use one."

Porky smiled gratefully, opened the door for Maureen, and followed her in. The coffee seemed to bring him back to life. He listened while Maureen told him about the future plans for the lab, and he became so excited he could hardly speak.

"You're good at this stuff," said Maureen, remembering Porky's sterling efforts over the weekend. "Why don't you talk to Caleb about doing an elective with us?"

Porky hesitated, and Maureen went on, "You might even like this better than surgery."

Porky's head came up. "Oh no. You see, we have a kind of surgical tradition in my family. My father's a surgeon," he told Maureen, "and so is my brother. It seems to run in the family, like Huntingdon's chorea."

Maureen laughed, a musical, soft laugh, and Porky felt enormously attracted to this young woman, and not just because she didn't treat him like an incompetent fool. Porky had forgotten what it was like to discuss things openly on an equal basis, rather than to have his thoughts dismissed because of his lack of seniority.

Caleb came in to talk to Maureen, and joined the discussion. They seemed to be getting on better, Porky thought, as if some point of contention had been settled. They talked about Celine's immunosuppressants; the protocol seemed to be working nicely, although of course it was too early to come to any firm conclusions.

"You know, Porky," said Caleb after a while, "maybe you should spend some time working here in the lab."

Porky smiled quickly at Maureen, then hesitated. "I'd love to, Dr. Winter, I truly would, but . . ." His eyes flickered up briefly to meet Caleb's. "But Dr. Brighton told me I'll be working in *his* lab in a few weeks, and . . ." Here Porky drew a deep breath before going on. "I've heard that your lab's going to be closing."

"Now, Porky," said Caleb, "you know I wouldn't offer you a job that didn't exist. I have no plans for shutting down this lab." He cracked a lopsided grin, "Although I'm well aware that some others are working at it." He got up. "Give it some thought, Porky. I believe you'd be a lot happier working here than on the surgical service; you might even consider a research career. Or you could be like me, and do both. Anyway, talk to Maureen. She'll fill you in on what we're doing here."

"Wow!" said Porky, awed, after Caleb had gone. "I sure hope he's right. I mean about the lab staying open."

Maureen was hoping precisely the same thing.

During Celine's brief stay in the ICU, she was only dimly aware of the activity around her. She certainly hadn't noticed the comings and goings in room 10, the one nearest the door. In most of the rooms the bright lights were put out at night to let the patient get some sleep, but in room 10 the lights were on all the time, turning it into a kind of lighthouse in the darkened unit, a place of grim, frantic activity.

Inside the room, the respirator, attached to the patient by flexible tubes, sighed mechanically, mindlessly pumping in exactly 480 milliliters of air containing 40% oxygen per breath, fourteen times per minute, accurate to the nearest two seconds. The levels of carbon dioxide, oxygen, potassium, sodium, and chloride were being measured regularly, and, a little less often, the patient's blood urea nitrogen and blood coagulation factors. Judging from the results of the tests, which came back neatly printed out on perforated computer paper, the patient was doing quite well. By any other criteria, Bridget Coughlan was dying.

Her mother, Mary Coughlan, was allowed into the ICU to see her for five minutes every hour, and that time limit was strictly enforced. Five minutes was really enough, anyway, because Bridget was in a coma, and Mary didn't think she knew her or anybody else. Bridget lay there, sweating a lot, breasts mostly uncovered, eyes half-open, with only the whites showing. The tubing from the respirator went into a tracheostomy tube in her throat. It helped her to breathe more easily, the doctor had said.

Mary followed exactly the same routine every time she came in. She glanced at Bridget's puffy face, then covered her chest with the sheet. Then she gently picked up Bridget's flaccid hand in hers, and sat down in the chair beside her.

"How you feeling?" she asked softly. "The nurses say you're doing good." She pressed her daughter's hand encouragingly, hoping each time to get an answering pressure. "The baby's fine," she went on, "took his dinner like a real champeen tonight, but he ate too fast, and a bit came back up. You were like that as a baby, you know. You'd eat so fast there was no keeping up with you, and then back up it came. Not that it bothered you, you smiled through it all."

Then Mary would pause, watching for some sign of life from her daughter. If that machine stopped hissing air into her, she wondered, would Bridget be dead? Her hands were warm, and that was a good sign. Her own mother had always told her that warm hands were a good sign when somebody was really ill; it meant they would get better.

After a moment or two, Mary took a large cotton stick with glycerine on it, and moistened Bridget's cracked lips. At first she hadn't dared to touch her, but now she turned her lips out, the top one first and then the lower one, to moisten them properly. Sometimes Bridget's tongue came out a bit, dry, meaty-looking, and Mary hoped then that she was wetting her lips and getting ready to say something, but that never happened.

"Okay, Mary, time's up," the nurse would call in quietly through the door, and Mary would get up instantly. She didn't want to bother anybody or cause any trouble. The nurses were really nice to her, remembered her name, told her what was happening, and tried to keep her spirits up. Mary usually brought something in with her for the nurses, sometimes candy, occasionally fruit. Everybody was so kind—the doctor they called Porky was especially nice, and once he'd even taken her down to the hospital cafeteria for a cup of coffee. She'd been so embarrassed, with all those busy and important hospital people around, she couldn't think of anything to say to him, but it didn't seem to matter because he chattered on. He asked her about the baby, little Kevin, whom Mary had brought with her a couple of times, and inquired if there was a father around. Mary shrugged and said nothing.

"Will you be able to take care of him?" Porky asked her gently. Mary shrugged again. She knew that people like her had to be fatalists, because they had no means to change the future, even in little things.

"I'll have to, won't I?" she said, and there it was. Mary knew what Porky was telling her, but she knew already. Porky got upset and seemed to be blaming himself for what had happened to Bridget, so Mary finally took his hand and explained to him.

"Our family's always been good Catholics," she said. "I believe, and so does Bridget, that God decides when our time has come, young or old, ready or not. It's out of our hands, you see, and I don't mean any disrespect for you and Dr. Brighton, I know you've all done your best, but it's God's will, that's all."

Because there didn't seem to be much hope for Bridget's recovery, she was transferred out of the intensive care unit to the only room available on the surgical service, the one across the corridor from Celine.

Celine wakened intermittently through a drug-induced

haze. The pain medication made her feel woozy and nauseated, and once when she tried to turn on her side, the pain hit her, but she didn't have the strength or the breath to scream. When she woke, it was to the continuous discomfort of the tubes in her nose, the IVs in both arms, the constraints of the EKG wires on her chest; she felt like Gulliver, tied down by countless tiny bonds, barely able to move. Her mouth was dry, and no amount of mouthwashing or wet gauze pads helped. And when Mrs. Koslowski was on, everything seemed to be worse, but she didn't understand why until the time she glimpsed the empty syringe before the needle was stuck into her. Had Caleb been in? Of course, early, even before the nurses started to bustle about with their morning medicines. Caleb had come in with the first rays of sunlight.

"Did you come in while I was asleep?" she said. Her voice was halfway between a croak and a whisper.

"Several times. Everything's going well, your tests are looking good."

Celine hung on to his hand like a life raft.

"Cal, I don't want you ever to leave me."

Caleb returned her pressure. "Baby," he whispered back, "you're the one who's going to be leaving." His voice sounded light, but his lips were dry when he got up a few moments later. Plenty of patients had fallen in love with him during his career, but this was the first time it had happened to him. It was a wonderful feeling, but behind the glow of pleasure and excitement he felt a frightening sense of insecurity. Caleb wasn't used to situations where his happiness depended on someone else, and that was made worse by the fact that he hardly knew Celine in the conventional way. In other ways, of course, he felt he knew her better than anyone—as a surgeon he saw people under unique circumstances, with all pretense stripped away. He'd seen Celine at her worst, at her most vulnerable. Maybe he was attracted by the vulnerability behind Celine's well-fitting mask of a competent and assured businesswoman.

Caleb Winter, he said to himself as he walked toward the operating room, maybe you're just too used to being in control of everything, and being the one who calls every shot.

And now, for the first time, you're in a position to be the one who gets hurt.

Maureen had backed down almost completely on her resignation from Caleb's lab, but as a token gesture of protest, she didn't come in on Wednesdays. She was an integral part of the transplantation team, a scientific family she could not really leave. And it was also time to circle the wagons; Maureen knew the entire research effort was in mortal danger, although Caleb seemed to be unconcerned about the situation.

Caleb was in the lab, looking relaxed and reading a research journal when Maureen came in, and his nonchalance got to her.

"Damn it, Cal," she said, and Caleb raised his eyebrows at her in surprise. "What's going to happen to us all? Not just you, although you're in the deepest trouble of any of us, but what about the lab? If we fold, if the NIH grant folds, what are you going to do about jobs for people like our technicians? Don't worry about me, I can go back to New York."

Caleb just grinned sardonically at her, and Maureen responded by raising her voice. "You just go along like a fool," she said angrily, "as if nothing's happening, as if Henry Brighton isn't busy trying to destroy you, your reputation, and your lab."

Caleb slowly put this journal down, and Maureen, seeing the change in his expression, realized that he wasn't taking it lightly at all.

"Don't you worry your pretty little head about such things, Maureen," he said, his voice icy. He didn't like being called a fool by Maureen or anybody else. "As long as your paycheck comes in every week, what do you care?" He raised his journal again. "Just you leave the worrying to the grown-ups," he said, "and concentrate on things you can understand, like keeping the grant applications in alphabetical order."

Maureen could strike like a cobra, but Caleb caught her wrist in time, and held it hard for a moment, just hard enough to hurt. Then he smiled, got up, and left the lab, looking as unconcerned as ever.

Maureen watched him leave. For a moment she thought his outburst was because of all the strain he was under, but she knew that he normally reacted by becoming quieter and less communicative. No, that wasn't it. Maureen rubbed her wrist where Caleb had grabbed it. Then she gave a little, sad laugh. "Caleb Winter," she said softly, "being in love doesn't agree with you."

Caleb, feeling irritated and unsettled, went down the corridor to talk to Art, Milo's technician, where the work of growing embryonic pancreatic tissue from a tiny blob of precursor cells was progressing. Caleb sat down opposite him and looked into the second eyepiece of the microscope, through which he could see exactly the same field as Art.

"Can you differentiate the cell types yet?" Caleb asked. Although Caleb was an expert, the cells all looked the same to him, round, with big nuclei and without much to tell them apart.

"Not on this particular one, not yet," replied Art. He was an experienced but slow-sounding Maine boy who'd picked up a lot in the two years he'd worked with Milo. "But I've got one where you can see the ducts developing."

"Any signs of beta cells?" asked Caleb.

Art hesitated. "Hard to tell, at this stage. I think so, but I wouldn't swear to it. Maybe Milo would have been more positive."

"Let's take a look."

When Art put the tissue culture slide on the microscope stage, Caleb was pretty sure he could detect some clumping of cells that showed early duct development; between the clumps he could just detect a few cells with a slightly different coloring. These might well be the insulin-producing beta cells, and Caleb decided, for reasons that had nothing to do with science, to assume that they were, until he was proved wrong. That assumption fitted in nicely with the larger aspects of his plan. Caleb glanced up at the *Playboy* calendar at the side of Milo's desk. Very nicely indeed. Caleb pushed back his chair and stood up. "Great work, Art." He smiled. "I'll be seeing Milo and you in Stockholm."

Walking back along the corridor, Caleb pondered what
might be the biggest question of all. Was Celine's graft going
to take? They wouldn't know until the fourth postoperative
day, and until then he would just have to grit his teeth, never
relax his vigilance, trust in the antirejection drugs, and keep
on looking unconcerned. The tension would have been bad
enough if it had been just another patient, but when it was
Celine's life and health in the balance, it was almost too much
for him to bear.

The first few days after Celine's operation blended into a
blurry period of pain, nausea, and an overwhelming thirst.
God, that thirst! She was allowed only one ounce of water an
hour, one precious ounce, brimming in a little plastic cup.
And of course, as often as not, Mrs. Koslowki deliberately
poured the water on the floor by the bed. "Never mind, hon,
you'll get some more in an hour." Almost as bad were the
pain shots that didn't work. Celine was too weak to fight, too
exhausted to complain. Caleb came in and out all the time,
occasionally ordering medication for her and watching it being given. It was as if he lived in the room with her, only
leaving occasionally when he had to. And it was during one
of those moments when Caleb wasn't there that Celine
woke up and felt such a sense of loss, of emptiness, of pain
and need, that she realized how much in love she was with
Caleb.

Henry Brighton was so busy that for the first time anybody
could remember, his wall board, with all the movements of
the surgical residents so meticulously marked out in colored
squares, had been left untended, and his secretary had had to
make some emergency decisions about where the residents
were to go.

Henry was orchestrating Caleb Winter's dismissal from the
hospital staff, to be followed immediately by his forced resignation from the faculty, and the task was turning out to be
harder than he'd expected. He had anticipated an uproar from
Caleb's colleagues, but they were surprisingly apathetic, pre-
ferring to wait and see what happened before getting involved. They all had their own problems, and were reluctant

to get into a fight with the chairman of the department until they knew which way the wind was blowing.

The two groups giving Henry the most trouble were the hospital board and the students and residents. Anna Lynn Page had phoned to attack him in what Henry considered a personal and totally inappropriate way, and the students and residents had sent a delegation to fight for Caleb's reinstatement. Well drilled by Red Felton, they marched into Henry's office, saying that they supported Caleb Winter and were prepared to consider further action if Dr. Winter didn't get his hospital privileges restored immediately.

Henry was furious, and noted the spokesmen for future retribution, but he stayed cool. At this stage, he told them, not even an armed revolt by the residents and the entire student body would have any effect on the course of events, and they were ill-advised to resist the forces of discipline and good order. Winter had blatantly transgressed the rules, he told them, and was paying the penalty just like anybody else. Henry didn't tell them that for the same reasons, the Quality Assurance Committee, the Executive Committee, and the board, Anna Lynn Page notwithstanding, would be forced to go along with him. Caleb Winter's actions hadn't given his supporters any leeway to work in.

From Atlanta, Charles kept in close touch with Tom Pfeiffer about his problems.

"It's all going nicely," said Tom, whose confidence had returned completely. "We got the emergency power and air-conditioning running, and nobody's died of heat stroke yet." Tom was in his shirtsleeves reviewing a jacket cover when Charles called; he'd just finished talking to the chief buyer at B. Dalton.

"Did you know those B. Dalton guys have a *policy* of not selling new hardcover authors?" he asked Charles indignantly. "But I think I maybe got around it." He grinned. "This is like a madhouse right now, but everybody's working like their job depends on it. How's Celine doing?"

"She had her operation, and so far she's doing well," he replied. "She'll be glad you've got everything under control here. Did you manage to reach Anwar Al-Khayib?"

"He doesn't return calls," replied Tom, "but I talked to Ira yesterday, and he's going ahead with an injunction."

Charles grinned; Tom seemed to be rising very nicely to the occasion. But as he put the phone down, Charles reminded himself that the real battle for the survival of Celine's company was not going to be taking place in her offices.

Everybody in the hospital seemed to know that the success or failure of the graft would be learned on the fourth day after Celine's operation, and curious looks followed Caleb that morning as he walked back from Celine's room toward his lab.

For once Don and Ed were listening to Porky. "They can measure the level of nonhuman insulin in her bloodstream," he explained rather self-consciously. "If they find even the smallest trace, that would prove it came from the graft." They were in the O.R. lounge, waiting for their next patient to come up.

"Not in the hospital lab they can't," said Ed, who had worked there at nights as a medical student. Ed was pale and had dark rings around his eyes. He looked ten years older than he had a few days before.

"They'll do the test in Dr. Winter's lab," said Porky. "Apparently it's quite a procedure. First they have to separate the plasma—"

"Big deal," interrupted Don. "I just want to know if the graft took. I didn't ask you for a course in biochemistry."

"When are they going to do the test?" asked Ed. Don and Ed looked expectantly at Porky. They knew how important the result would be, and not only to Celine de La Roche.

Porky looked up at the clock. "They should be starting it about now," he said.

In Caleb's lab, the tension was mounting. Red Felton had come in, ostensibly for a cup of coffee, but he was as anxious as any of them. When the technician came in with the blood sample she was carefully ignored, and everybody found something to do while they surreptitiously watched her put the tube into the centrifuge, the initial step of the test.

"How long is this going to take?" Red grumbled quietly to Maureen. "Can't you tell by just holdin' it up to the light?"

"Have some more coffee," said Maureen, "and don't hold your breath."

Caleb came in after a while and sat down with them in the small conference area. Red put his feet up on the table, trying to look relaxed. "It should happen about now," he drawled.

"What?" asked Maureen.

"The tech drops the tube and has to start all over again."

"Not this tech," said Maureen.

About fifteen minutes later, a buzzing noise emanated from the printer, then a clattering as the paper spilled out. Red and Maureen jumped up, and everybody in the lab quietly left their places and came over to join them in the conference area. Only Caleb remained apparently unconcerned; when the tech approached with the readout, he had his notebook on the table and was checking his appointments for the next day.

The tech handed him the paper and stood back, waiting and watching him with the others. She didn't know the result; only Caleb could interpret the data.

For a long minute Caleb examined the columns of numbers. "The graft is functioning," he said finally. "Thank you all." He looked around his group and smiled. "We'll celebrate this in the usual way at five."

He got up very deliberately, but Maureen saw the look in his eye and knew where he was going. She went to the phone and paged Porky. He certainly had a right to be one of the first to know, and anyway, she wanted to talk to him.

Caleb kept his joy under tight control as he went up the Harkness elevators. Gabe Pinero, who had turned out to be one of his staunchest supporters, got on at the fifth floor. "I hear everything's going well." Gabe spoke cautiously, not wanting to give the impression that he was snooping.

Caleb couldn't prevent a wide grin from appearing on his face. "The graft's working," he said, trying to keep the triumph out of his voice. The doors opened, and Gabe watched him hurry down the corridor toward Celine's room, his white coat fluttering behind him, until the doors closed again.

Celine was sitting up in bed, her IV hanging from a pole beside her, and writing in the margin of a manuscript when Caleb came in. She was looking drawn and pale, but all the fire was still there.

Caleb pulled up a chair and sat down, close to her. "I have some news for you," he said.

Celine's eyes widened slightly, but she said nothing. She held his arm tightly, searching his eyes.

After her told her the results and they discussed it, he sat with her for a while. It seemed like a good time to start tentatively discussing their future together, but Caleb held back. In spite of everything, she was still his patient, and it didn't seem right for him to open that discussion just yet. Even the thought of talking about it made him feel uncomfortable.

"What's the book?" he asked, to change the subject. He looked at the manuscript.

"It's a novel," she replied. "Terrific stuff, about horse-racing in the old days." As usual, Celine's enthusiasm came easily to the surface. She reached for Caleb's hand. "Did you know that most thoroughbreds can be traced back to an English horse called Messenger? It came over to Philadelphia in 1788, and—"

Caleb's smile interrupted her. "No, I didn't know. As you can imagine, that's not the kind of thing I would read about."

"Oh." Celine was taken aback for a moment. "What *do* you like to read?"

Caleb hesitated. "Mostly medical journals, I suppose. You can't imagine how much stuff gets published nowadays. I could read all day and not keep up with everything that's happening in medicine."

"But what do you read for fun, Cal?" persisted Celine. She was going to add, "and to understand what other people think and care about," but she decided not to. She could see Caleb was already on the defensive.

"Oh, I occasionally pick up something at the newsstand," he said quickly, then got up. "Well, I'd better get back to the lab." He smiled, trying to recapture the mood of euphoria he'd had when he came in, but it was gone, he didn't know where or why. He planted a quick kiss on the top of her head and left.

The news of the graft's success got out rapidly, and there was both joy and recrimination in the hospital. Red went to fetch a six-pack of Dos Equis up to Caleb's lab, and at five o'clock, the traditional time, they all gathered for a restrained but heartfelt celebration. Everyone knew how crucial that test result had been.

"You gonna tell the press, Caleb? An' the Teevee? It sure wouldn't do yore case no harm." Red's eyes showed his concern: he knew that Caleb would need every scrap of help he could get, because Henry Brighton was like a pit bull terrier; once he had his teeth in a victim, he wouldn't let go until one of them was dead.

"All in due course, Red," said Caleb.

Maureen had made a punch using lemonade, fruit juice, and absolute alcohol from the lab. It tasted inoffensive, but packed a wallop that loosened tongues and lightened the spirits of the exhausted team.

Maureen had invited Porky to come by for the celebration if he could spare the time, and as luck would have it, he arrived at the door of the lab just as Henry Brighton was passing. Porky blushed and slunk in, feeling like a criminal, and Henry, hearing the sound of laughter and knowing its cause, scowled grimly as he strode past, ignoring Porky.

Inside, Porky was quickly caught up in the emotional high that occasionally punctuates the months and years of hard work, the insecurity and the inevitable failures of a research lab, and he desperately wanted to be a real part of this scientific team. Porky also loved dealing with patients, and now that he had been reprieved, was also grimly determined to finish his residency. That was one of the wonderful things about a career in surgery, as Caleb had told him. If things worked out right, he would be able to take care of patients and also do research.

"Hey, Porky!" said Red, coming over and putting a plastic beaker full of pink liquid into his hand, "You know anything about this here immunology stuff? Would you reckernize an antibody receptor site if it jumped up and bit you on the leg?" Firmly under the influence of Maureen's fruity concoction, Red was feeling no pain. He looked around like a stage conspirator. "Porky, you lissen ta me." He put a friendly arm around Porky's shoulder. "I don't know diddly-squat from immunology, but I can tell you one thang. This here lab is doomed. Don't you get involved, ya hear? Two months down the road, this here will be under Noo Management." Red stared into his empty glass. "God help America," he said, and went off unsteadily toward the makeshift bar and the Dos Equis.

Celine woke up to find an unfamiliar nurse standing in the doorway. "I'm Cathie Allen," the girl said, rather hesitantly. "I don't know if you remember me," she said, "You gave me a silk scarf . . ."

Celine had quite forgotten the episode, but she remembered the face. Cathie seemed nervous, even apprehensive, as if Celine might start shouting at her.

"Come in," said Celine. Her voice was still unrecognizable, but Dr. Winter had said the last remaining tube in her stomach might be coming out the next day. Cathie came in and stood by the bed.

"How did you know I was here?" Celine could barely get all the words out.

"Everybody knows about you," replied Cathie with a grin. "You're famous. You're in all the papers. D'you mind if I sit down?"

Cathie had two small children, and the photos came out within a couple of minutes.

"And of course you have the hospital dreamboat as your surgeon," said Cathie, glancing shrewdly at Celine, who gave a little shrug and looked away. Cathie smiled. "Yeah, I'd feel the same way, I guess. Half the hospital's in love with him—I mean the female half."

Mrs. Koslowski came clumping in with Celine's water ration. Her little eyes flickered over to Cathie, whom she recognized, and she frowned. "Whatcha doin' here?"

"Just visiting," replied Cathie coolly. Mrs. Koslowski's eyes moved over to Celine. She hesitated for a second, then put the tiny plastic water container on the bedside table. "Drink it up, Mrs. Roach," she said. "You know I have to see you drink it."

"What's her problem?" asked Cathie when the door had closed behind Mrs. Koslowski.

Celine turned on her side with a grimace of pain. "That goddammed bitch," she said with a flash of her old fire. "Usually she spills my water on the floor."

Cathie took a wet facecloth and gently wiped Celine's forehead.

"And she gives me pain shots with an empty syringe." Celine ran out of steam and lay back, closing her eyes.

"I've heard about that woman," said Cathie. "Did you report her to anybody?"

Celine told her about the episode with the milk of magnesia. "It doesn't matter now," she said. "I won't be needing the medicine so much. I'll be out of bed soon, then I can get my own damn water."

Cathie laughed, but her eyes were thoughtful. "An empty syringe, huh. Are you sure?"

"Yes, of course. And I think I need a pain shot now," said Celine. "Would you mind staying until I've had it? If you're here, I'm sure she'll give it the way she's supposed to."

"I think I have an idea," said Cathie. "Let's you and I put our heads together and fix that bitch. Can you do without that shot for a while?"

"As long as it takes," said Celine stoutly, the light of battle in her eye. "Right now I'd walk a mile on broken glass just for a chance to get even with her."

Mrs. Koslowski was not having the best of afternoons. One of the aides was off sick, and the other one was new, so a lot of the work didn't get done in time, but one thing Mrs. Koslowski never did was stay one minute after her shift was over. Once you started doing that, she knew, they'd take full advantage; they'd have you working your butt off forever if you let them.

At five minutes before five, she paid a last visit to the Roach woman. There had been visitors in the room most of the afternoon, and of course her boyfriend Dr. Winter had been in and out—he just couldn't stay away from her. But Mrs. Koslowski wouldn't want to be in that woman's shoes, even with all her money and all the clothes she had.

"Report's dictated on the machine," she shouted to the nurses coming on. "There's nothing much happening."

It was exactly five o'clock, and she was on her way. She could hear her feet slapping along the corridor. They hurt, not surprising with her being on them all day. She decided to stop by the store for some new arch supports. There was only one other nurse in the locker room, a thin, older woman she knew by sight. She was sitting on the long central bench, very breathless, and was holding onto the bench with both hands.

Mrs. Koslowski pushed past to get to her locker. There wasn't much room, and she almost knocked the woman off the bench.

"Sorry," she muttered, opening her locker. She pulled her outdoor shoes from the top of the locker and sat down on the bench. The woman was saying something, and Mrs. Koslowski scowled over at her.

". . . My heart medicine," she was saying. "It's up in my locker . . . I can't reach it . . ."

"Jesus," thought Mrs. Koslowski. "They shouldn't have sick people working here. I'd better get out before she keels over." What she said was, "Sorry, lady, I'm in a hurry. Somebody'll be coming in soon."

It took her a few minutes to change, and she kept looking apprehensively over at the older nurse, then Mrs. Koslowski grabbed her purse, slammed her locker shut, and hurried past the woman again, sighing with relief when the changing room door closed behind her.

Mrs. Koslowski was proud of the fact that she was usually

first out from her shift, and today was no exception. The corridor was almost deserted, except for the two guards at the door, one of whom politely opened the door for her. The other one was standing in her way, and she tried to push past, but he didn't let her.

"Whassamatter with you?" she asked, looking up at him. Suddenly both the guards were in front of her, blocking her passage.

"Could we see your I.D., please, ma'am?" said the older one.

"I come out this entrance every day and nobody ever wanted to see my I.D. before," she grumbled, raking about in her purse.

The guard looked at the photo, then at her. "Your name is Marsha Koslowski?"

"That's what it says, right?" Mrs. Koslowski put her hand out for it.

"We need to examine the contents of your purse, ma'am," The short one had a small mustache and looked tough. Furious, Mrs. Koslowski grabbed her purse and tried to push the older guard out of the way, but he was ready for her. Mrs. Koslowski was strong, and a scuffle developed. She didn't see the police car make a U-turn from where it had been parked on the other side of the street. It drew up at the curb next to them. Two officers got out, and the men bundled her into the back, now kicking and biting, but not before she'd tried to empty her purse out on the sidewalk. At the station, they found three 100mg ampoules of Demerol in her possession, and when they checked her locker at the hospital they found a sizable cache of amphetamines, Valium, and sleeping pills. She was therefore charged with a variety of offenses, including theft, possession of drugs with intent to sell, resisting arrest, and assault of a police officer.

Celine didn't hear about it until next morning, but the success of Cathie's hunch greatly brightened her day.

Caleb took the last stomach tube out about eleven, and then he helped her to get out of bed for the first time. It felt dreadful; the pain in her belly cut like a knife when she sat up, and again when she walked. He just wanted her to take a couple of steps and get back into bed, but Celine insisted on walking out the door and into the corridor. There was a sad-looking woman waiting outside the room opposite, and Celine asked Caleb about her. He told her briefly about Bridget Coughlan, her baby, the problem with her lungs, the treatments that hadn't worked.

"Is there anything at all I could do for them?" asked Celine.

Caleb, supporting Celine with one strong arm and pushing Celine's IV pole with the other, shook his head. "I don't think so. You've walked far enough, let's get you back into bed."

"No, I think I'll sit by the window for a while, if that's all right." Celine felt old, bent, exhausted, dirty, dry, smelly, and thoroughly disgusting, but she wasn't going to let that stop her.

Caleb stood by her chair, his hand on her shoulder. Celine put her hand up over his, and they both stared silently out the window. Aside from matters that directly involved Celine's operation or her convalescence, there didn't seem to be much to discuss. It worried Caleb that he couldn't think of anything to say to her outside the medical context, and Celine wondered if he just felt uncomfortable talking about things he wasn't an authority on. After a couple of minutes, Caleb bent down and brushed the top of her head ever so lightly with his lips, then left.

Celine stood up, retied her gown, and went slowly toward the door, pushing her IV pole in front of her. Mrs. Coughlan looked up from her chair.

"How's your daughter doing?" asked Celine.

"Not much change, really," she replied. "Everybody's doing their best for her."

Celine sat down stiffly in the chair beside her.

"Oh, you don't look as if you should be out of bed," said Mary, concerned. "Shall I get the nurse?"

"I'm fine. How are *you* managing?" Celine's voice was weak but so full of concern and sympathy that Mary was touched.

"It's not easy," she replied. "The baby . . ." Mary shook her head. "I can't carry him all the way here, and I don't like to leave him with neighbors all the time."

"How far do you have to walk?"

"I live over by Warren Street. It's a bit over two miles. I'm all right, really," went on Mary, embarrassed, sensing that Celine wanted to help her. "I can manage." She smiled. "You don't have to worry about me."

Celine looked at her; according to Caleb, Mary's only daughter was dying, she had a tiny grandchild to support, and there she was, as calm and accepting as she, Celine, had been hostile and difficult. A nurse came out of Bridget's room and talked for a few moments to Mary. Then Celine asked Mary about Bridget and the baby, and they talked until Celine got so weary she had to go back to her bed. And then she lay back and thought about the Coughlan family, and how very different their approach to life was from hers. After a while she picked up her bedside phone and called the hospital's social service department. The woman who answered was surprised at Celine's request, but promised to arrange transportation for Mrs. Coughlan to and from the hospital.

· · · · · · · · · · · 37 · · · ·

It started as a rumor, but as rumors will, it flickered around the hospital like summer lightning, glowing, dying, reappearing in unexpected places. One of the things that lent the story instant credence was the fact that Henry Brighton had been seen that morning almost running into his office, his face full of thunder, and various important doctors and other people from the hospital and medical school had started to meet in hastily summoned conferences, held in last-minute places like the nursing conference room and the small lecture hall next to the library. Red Felton, his blue eyes big with innocence, asked Caleb if it was true, but Caleb just shook his head. Either he didn't know, or wasn't talking, or both.

The first confirmation of what was happening was an article published in that afternoon's *New Coventry Register*, obviously planted there by someone in the know.

"RAW DEAL AT NEW COVENTRY UNIVERSITY HOSPITAL," ran the headline, and the article went on to say that famed transplanter Dr. Caleb Winter had lost his hospital privileges and was in the process of being expelled from both the hospital and the university.

"Totally unfair and illegal," said local activist and hospital committee member Leroy Williams. Committee results were rigged, according to Williams, 42, in order to prevent Winter from carrying out vitally needed transplant operations. Williams is fighting to have the committee reconvened, and soon. "We won't let that happen again," vowed Williams. "Winter is a noted leader in the field of transplantation, and we should be helping rather than hindering his efforts." Williams, who has a long record of activity in social issues affecting New Coventry, hinted that if Winter wasn't immediately reinstated and the committee reconvened, the black community might be forced to become seriously involved, together with the medical students and residents, who, Williams stated, were on the edge of revolt. An unnamed hospital spokeswoman was reached by phone and said, "We are actively and carefully studying the issue, but we have no further comment at this time."

Caleb was summoned to an emergency meeting in Marshall Prince's office, but denied any knowledge of the matter. He seemed genuinely surprised, and such was his reputation for straightforwardness that only Henry Brighton questioned his truthfulness.

"Then where else and why would such a story originate?" Brighton asked with a barely disguised sneer. "You're the only person it could possibly help."

Caleb shrugged. "I don't know anything whatever about this," he repeated. "Why don't you ask Leroy Williams?"

The local newscast that night ran a television interview with Leroy, surrounded by a mob of noisy people, many of them black, but with a sizable contingent wearing white hospital jackets. "We're here to see justice done," shouted Leroy over the din. "There are racist overtones here which we cannot and will not tolerate. Tomorrow, Dr. Winter gets reinstated or we march. Right, brothers and sisters?"

The answering yell left no doubt as to the feelings of the crowd, and Marshall Prince, watching the news at home, gripped his fists tightly in apprehension. At eight o'clock the next morning, the hospital spokesperson announced that Dr. Winter would have his full hospital privileges restored pending a complete investigation of the circumstances. "It is not our purpose," said the spokesperson, "to punish Dr. Winter or any other physician before a full review is made of the relevant facts."

However, just to ram home his point, Leroy and a hundred of his followers stood outside the main entrance of the hospital for an hour that morning with banners and much noise, and for a while they were joined by a large group of medical students and junior hospital doctors. Leroy and his troops then returned peacefully to Washington Avenue, where free beer was served on trestle tables set up in the street.

"Why?" shouted Henry Brighton at the television screen. He was both furious and mystified. "Why is this goddamn nigger getting himself involved in our business? How did he get the students and residents into this? What in Christ's name is in it for him?"

That question, although generally worded in more temperate terms, was being asked by people well beyond the confines of both the hospital and the university. And for a while, absolutely no answers were forthcoming.

Caleb's colleagues stopped him in the corridors to congratulate him on his victory; his back was slapped at least twice in the cafeteria, and his students cheered him proudly the next time he met with them. They knew that he'd got his privileges back at least in part because of their demonstration. Caleb just went on his way, apparently unmoved by all the fuss around him.

"Ol' Henry's spitting tacks," Red told him, "but he figures that he'll get rid of you in the long run. This whole thing with Leroy Williams, he said, was cooked up by you and Anna Lynn Page, an' y'all must have bribed him big."

Caleb smiled grimly but said nothing. Red went on. "He said that Ethics and Public Welfare Committee ain't gonna reconvene, or if it does, it'll be over his dead body."

"Maybe we could arrange that," said Caleb in such a chilling tone that Red stared at him for a second.

He went on hurriedly, watching Caleb as he spoke, "Henry said the committee was legally convened the first time, an' just 'cos some Nigra fella wants it, that ain't sufficient reason to start all over again."

"We'll just have to wait and see," replied Caleb calmly. "Meanwhile, how's your studying coming along? Henry's going to want some real work and real results out of you when his lab opens—more than just talk and tobacco juice."

"Do you think Henry's lab's really going to open?" asked Red, a scratch of nervousness appearing in his voice. "I just cannot imagine that."

"Red, you've got to trust Henry. Remember, he's our chairman, and now also your mentor." Caleb grinned again, gave Red a light punch on the arm, and was gone.

"Exactly what are his allegations?" Henry Brighton asked. Dr. Karl Liebowitz, dean of the medical school, a bearded, usually voluble psychiatrist, glanced at Marshall Prince opposite him before answering.

"According to Leroy Williams's letter," he said, indicating the piece of paper in front of him, "the committee was grossly misled about the actual level of progress of Dr. Winter's transplant project."

"The actual level of progress was outlined in Dr. Winter's own application," replied Henry sharply, "and in some detail. I can't help it if—"

"No, no," said Liebowitz, looking at Henry over his half-glasses. "He was referring to comments made by . . ." He looked at the paper and pretended to read it again. "Actually by you."

Henry's eyes narrowed, and his lips compressed into a straight line. "As the only surgeon there, and therefore as the one who knew most about this kind of thing, I was asked to give my opinion, which I did, and as honestly as I could."

"Yes, of course," said the dean in the soothing voice he used with his more difficult patients. "You must excuse me. I didn't realize that you were an expert in transplantation and immunology." The silkiness of his tone warned Henry.

"I never claimed to be any such thing," he replied indignantly, "but as Dr. Winter is a member of my department, I felt that the responsibility—"

"Not being an expert, then," said Prince, his deep voice sonorous in the high-ceilinged office, "you must have spent a great deal of time with Dr. Winter and his staff, going over his data, before you could feel comfortable giving the committee a considered opinion on this matter."

The words were not set in the form of a question, but still they cried out for an answer. The silence deepened. Both men looked expressionlessly at Henry, waiting.

"Of course I keep up with the work in other parts of my department," Henry started to bluster. "So I'm in a very good position to give a, well, an arm's length evaluation."

This time the silence was so thick a spoon would have stood up in it.

"Mr. Williams says here that you gave them a totally incorrect evaluation," said Marshall, looking at the letter. His voice was that of a perfect administrator, devoid of anger, criticism, anything.

"Damn it," exploded Henry. "How does some whoremaster think he knows more about transplantation than I do? Why don't you talk to Dr. Armuth, who was chairman of that committee? He's a physician, and he'll tell you how it was."

"We did," said Liebowitz in a voice filled with regret, "and, I'm embarrassed to say, he agrees in every detail with Mr. Williams."

Henry slammed the flat of his hand on the table. "But my evaluation was correct," he shouted. "The whole concept of transplanting pancreases into humans *is* premature, dangerous, and really not likely to succeed, in my opinion."

Henry sat back, feeling that he had control of the situation again. There wouldn't be too much they could say to contradict that.

"But he did it," said Marshall softly, "and the graft is functioning, according to this morning's lab results. That proves that he was ready, doesn't it?"

Henry was so taken aback by Marshall's words that he couldn't think of anything to say. He sat there, dumb, his mouth opening slowly.

"In the circumstances," said the dean heavily, "I have decided to reconvene the Ethics and Public Welfare Committee."

Henry nodded. There was not much else he could do. Sure, he was beaten, for now. But once the committee met again, he could get them to confirm its previous decision. After all, he would still be the principal authority among them. But Dr. Liebowitz was saying in his fruity psychiatric voice that

in view of Henry's other important commitments and responsibilities, he would no longer be required to serve on the
Ethics and Public Welfare Committee, and would be replaced
by another member from the surgery department, Dr. Red
Felton.

Henry left the meeting white with fury. His grant from the
consortium now hung in the balance. The deal had been ex-
plicitly stated by Herr Ortweiler—the money would be paid
only after receiving proof that Caleb Winter's transplantation
program had been crushed. Henry had already written to Herr
Ortweiler to report the committee's first decision, and had
included a Xerox copy of its official letter to Dr. Winter. On
reflection, however, Henry felt there was no need at this time
to tell Ortweiler that the situation had changed; that could
only undermine the consortium's confidence in him and
would serve no useful purpose. In any case, the appointment
of Red Felton to the committee maybe wasn't so bad; he was
Red's boss and could apply a fair amount of pressure on him.
It would take a long, serious chat with Red, and he would
soon see things his way. And if it came down to that, he could
bribe him; Henry's advance knowledge about the consortium's oral insulin preparation would very soon make him rich
enough to make a small secondary research grant to Red,
enough to give him some degree of professional indepen-
dence. And of course, any such gift would be wholly tax-
deductible.

Maureen, who had been hearing more and more about the relationship between Celine and Caleb, finally couldn't restrain her curiosity any more and made her way up to the Harkness Wing. Celine was still far from recovered; she had IV lines in both arms but was out of bed, working with a pile of manuscripts and correspondence on the table by her chair. Even without makeup, and with her hair a mess, Celine still managed to look regal. Her lips pursed when Maureen came in. Celine knew immediately who she was; Porky had mentioned Maureen on several occasions.

Maureen, obviously tense, hesitated by the door before entering. She had beautiful legs, Celine noticed, not long, but perfectly proportioned.

"I'm Maureen Spark," said Maureen softly. "I work with Caleb Winter. . . ." Celine, ready to dislike her on sight, intuitively felt that Maureen had problems of her own, and felt her antagonism waver.

"I was involved in your operation, so I came by to see how you were doing." Maureen smiled as Celine's eyebrows went up, and she told Celine about how she'd come back to help out when everything was collapsing in the lab. "I just couldn't bear the idea of you having a Whipple," she said, rather lamely.

"I appreciate that, but you didn't know me, or anything about me," said Celine, surprised.

"Oh but I did." Maureen smiled. "You're like Caleb. You

both attract rumors, and I found out everything I could about you."

There was a pause.

"What do you want?" said Celine, not unkindly.

"I'd like to talk to you about Caleb," replied Maureen quietly. "Woman to woman."

"Go ahead," Celine said in as strong a voice as she could manage, although it hurt to talk. "I'm listening."

"I've known and worked with Caleb Winter a long time," she said, not sounding too sure of herself. "It's taken me years to get to know who he is."

Listening to Maureen, Celine got a glimpse of her sadness. She's trying to hold on to Caleb the Comet, she thought, and she's burning her fingers.

"And now you're developing a relationship with him," went on Maureen. "I don't know how far it's gone ..." Her eyes searched Celine's but found nothing there to help her. "And you need to know something about him. I mean, more than just the fact that he's Dr. Winter, the famous surgeon."

Celine's incision was beginning to ache, but she wasn't about to interrupt this just to get a pain shot.

"I think I do know quite a bit about him," she replied. "I just see him from a different perspective."

"That's true," admitted Maureen, "but it's a most unrealistic one. Right now you're totally dependent on him, he's cured you of a bad disease—"

"Wrong," interrupted Celine, gathering strength with every moment. "I don't like being dependent on anyone, including him. There's much more to it than that."

Maureen flinched as Celine went on. "You see, you're involved with his work and I'm not. Caleb needs to get away from his work, have his horizons opened, smell the flowers, enjoy the rest of the world." She paused, out of breath. "That's what he's missing, and he knows that's what he can get from me."

Maureen just shook her head. "Caleb Winter's a different man outside the hospital," she said. "His whole existence is tied up in here. He isn't really interested in anything else.

Not only that, but you'd never get really close to him. Eventually he'd break your heart."

"From the sounds of it," said Celine curtly, "mine's a tougher organ than yours. I think I could handle him."

Maureen sat down on the end of the bed, facing Celine. "It's not a question of handling. You say you want to get him away from his work, but that's what he lives for. That's the very first thing you need to understand about him."

Celine felt the first germs of doubt taking hold; somewhere at the back of her mind that very same question had been lurking. Aside from Caleb's impressive professional accomplishments, what was he?

Maureen stood up and went to the window. Her voice was stronger now, and her confidence was coming back. "And another thing. You said you weren't involved in his work. Celine, you have to understand—right now you *are* his work. That'll be over soon, though, but his work'll go on. Do you understand what I'm saying?"

Celine's insides slowly started to turn to stone. Maureen was putting her own worst fears into words. But there was no point in letting Maureen know it. "You've always worked for him, Maureen. Face up to it, girl—*that's* your relationship with him; it's established. You're his assistant. How could you ever expect to get anywhere with a man like him?"

Maureen's eyes flashed. "I did," she said.

"But not the way you wanted to, right?" Maureen's gaze flickered, and Celine went on remorselessly, her pain making her want to share her hurt. "He's outgrown you; you're still a lab assistant, and now he's a famous surgeon."

Celine started to cough, painfully. She held on to her tummy; it felt as if it were going to split wide open. She took a few deep breaths. She *had* to avoid coughing again. "He's not for you," she wheezed quickly, "and you know it. Go find a guy who needs you."

"You may be right," replied Maureen steadily, "and maybe I already have." Then she smiled. "Now that we've settled each other's problems," Maureen went on in her soft voice, "how about if I go get us some coffee?"

After Maureen had finally gone, Celine sat very still on the window chair. At first she'd thought that Maureen's portrayal of Caleb was twisted and self-serving, but as they talked Celine began to realize that Maureen knew what she was talking about, and wasn't even trying to put her off Caleb. The conversation left her feeling cold and empty.

Didier Franchet was feeling very pleased with himself. He'd talked to the couple in Peekskill, and the old gentleman, a retired engineer, had agreed to sell their shares in Fortman and Carfield at the price he'd offered. Didier was now on his way to clinch the deal in person.

The phone rang in his suite; it was the front desk telling him that his car was waiting outside. Didier grabbed his briefcase and went out. Two men were standing in the corridor outside. Just before closing the door Didier remembered that he'd left the room key inside, and went back for it. The men were still there when he came out.

"Can I help you?" he asked them coldly.

"Sure you can, Mr. Franchet," said the shorter one, looking Didier in the eye. "My name's Bert Zeigler, and this is Alvin Smith. I'm an investigator from the Internal Revenue Service, and Alvin here is from the Securities and Exchange Commission." Bert opened his wallet, and Didier saw the silver flash of a badge.

Calmly Didier reopened the door and motioned them both in.

"Well, what can I do for you?" he asked rather brusquely. "I have a car waiting."

Bert put his briefcase on the table. It was an old one with curly leather straps. He opened it, very deliberately.

"Nice suite you have here, sir," said Alvin pleasantly, from the window. He was looking out over the park.

Bert pulled a sheaf of papers from his briefcase. "Why don't you sit down, sir," he said. Didier pulled out a chair and sat down at the table, wondering what all this was about.

"There are a couple of things," he said. "One is your income tax returns, or rather the lack of them, from 19 ..." Bert looked at his papers. "From 1949 to the present time, sir, covering a period of—let's see, just about forty years." He smiled brightly at Didier, as if he were wondering how such a matter could have slipped his mind for so long.

Alvin had come back silently from the window and materialized behind Didier's back. Unlike Bert's, Alvin's voice was harsh and accusing.

"You purchased a large block of shares in Fortman and Carfield, a registered corporation, five months ago," he said, and Didier started. "This transaction was not reported to us, nor was it recorded, in violation of SEC rules. In addition, attempts were made to conceal that fact, also a violation of the rules. I have to tell you, Mr. Franchet, that if you are tried and found guilty you will be liable to a substantial fine and imprisonment."

Didier smiled, not at all perturbed. "Gentlemen, thank you for this information." He turned to Bert. "I have to inform you that I didn't make income tax returns in Brazil, El Salvador, Tahiti, Australia, or the Easterly Islands. And that . . ." Didier suddenly pushed back his chair and stood up, angry at these stupid men, ". . . is because I don't live there any more than I live in the United States. I would remind you that as a visitor and citizen of the French Republic, I am not only entitled to the courtesy normally accorded to visiting foreigners, but also to freedom from harassment by the Economic Police, or whoever you are!"

Bert sighed, as if this affair was causing him much distress. He reached into his briefcase and pulled out a photostated copy of a document. "This is a copy of your certificate of citizenship of the United States of America," he said sadly. "It's dated June 13, 1949. And as a citizen you are required annually to make a sworn declaration concerning your income for the past fiscal year."

"Nonsense," said Didier. "I'm not a resident of the United States. Don't you think I have accountants? Do you take me for a fool?"

"We can discuss all that downtown, sir," said Alvin. "Meanwhile, maybe you want to cancel your car."

Soon after, as they all went down in the elevator, heading for the downtown offices of the IRS, Alvin told Didier confidentially that he was in deep shit, and, quite off the record, he'd heard they were going to throw the book at him.

In the IRS office, Didier refused to say anything until he could speak to his attorney, Gene Mescher. Mescher was apparently out of town, but within half an hour Greg de Vito, who'd signed all the correspondence and knew about Didier's transactions, appeared.

"I think they're probably wrong," said Greg after Didier had explained his predicament. "But it would have helped if you'd told us of your U.S. citizenship."

Didier shrugged. "My tax home is Andorra," he said.

"But you do business in the U.S." Greg opened his folder. "It's going to be very complicated." He stared at Didier with a frown. "You've been coming in and out of the U.S. on a foreign passport for years," he said, "and nobody ever paid any attention. What do you think drew their attention to you?"

"I have no idea," replied Didier, shrugging angrily. "Now what about the SEC problem?"

Greg shook his head. "I think they may have you there," he said, flipping the sheets in the folder. "We did remind you. I have copies of several requests from us to register your stock purchase as required by SEC regs."

Didier's lips tightened. He knew that Greg's first concern would be to keep himself and his firm out of trouble.

"I'm a bit puzzled," Greg went on. He looked around the cell-like cubicle the agents had given them for their consultation. "I work with those SEC and IRS guys all the time, and they don't usually act like this. I mean, like pulling you out of your hotel." He looked at Didier thoughtfully. "Maybe somebody put the finger on you. And if they have enough clout to do that, you could be in some trouble. No, I don't mean *real* trouble," he added, seeing Didier's expression, "unless there's other stuff you haven't told me about. What I mean is, just with this stuff," he patted the folder, "they could tie you up forever. The tax code concerning foreign and domestic earnings by nonresident citizens isn't that clear, and can be interpreted in different ways."

All the time, Didier was racking his brain to figure out how this could have happened, who could have blown the whistle on him. Finally it hit him like a hammer blow. Charles Forester! Of course! The *salaud!*

"It was a piece of cake, ol' buddy," said Red in a pleased, aw-shucks tone. He was feeling very expansive, and secretly proud to have been a member of the reconvened Ethics and Public Welfare Committee. Sitting in Caleb's office, he wondered if he could put his feet up on the corner of the desk. He decided against it. "There wasn't a word raised agin you, not from nobody. One hunner percent in favor, and I can tell you without a word of a lie that the cheerin' was led by yours truly."

"What did Leroy Williams have to say?" asked Caleb, his eyes fixed on Red. "I'd really like to know what made him change his mind so suddenly."

"Well he was a-rantin' and a-ravin' on about the last meeting, and the lies that our friend and leader Henry had told about your work. Then he started about how for years we'd bin denyin' the medical rights of the black community." Red yawned, then felt in his pocket for the round tin of Red Man. "Somebody said later there's some ol' Nigra woman down there in town who maybe needs your kind of surgery, and he used that as a bandwagon to climb onto. I don't know. I got tired of listenin' after about an hour, so he could have said just about any dam' thing an' I wouldn't have knowed."

Red flashed his famous lopsided grin, which was reputed to raise the pulses of his female students by about twenty beats per minute. "All I could think of was keepin' my eyes open, 'cos ol' Dr. Armuth, the chairman, he was watching everybody, an' he has eyes like a gimlet, that ol' boy does."

Red stopped talking long enough to pack his chaw, and

Caleb wondered again about Leroy's about-face. There had to be some reason that hadn't surfaced yet; what kind of favors would Leroy expect in return?

"Well, I hope all this won't affect your career as a researcher," said Caleb. "I guess Henry's going to have to find himself another lab to steal."

"Henry? Oh man, you shoulda seen his face," said Red, his jaw working rhythmically. "To say he was in-furiated just don't say the half of it. He was madder'n a snakebit coon, he was. 'What happened?' he said to me, snarling. 'How come that vote was u-nanimous?' An' he was starin' at me like he was flyin' right off his trolley."

"So what did you say?" Caleb was impressed with Red's courage; Henry in a fury was a daunting sight.

"Well, I had to think of somethin' . . . so I leaned up to him and whispered in his ear. 'You know that nigger on the committee?' I says to him. 'Yes, yes, of course, you must mean Mr. Williams,' he says back to me, kina irritated-soundin'. 'What about him?' So I had to think of somethin' real fast, so I said to him that Leroy had threatened to cut my balls off if I didn't vote along with him."

"Henry must have loved that," said Caleb.

"Yeah. You should have seen the look he gave me. I have a feeling Henry may try to fire me any second now, but if that happens I plan on appealin' the matter to the Ethics an' Public Welfare Committee. Anyway he flew off to Zurich or some such heathen place this morning, an' he can't do me much harm from there."

Caleb's head came up. "Zurich, huh? Isn't that where his consortium or whatever he calls it, is?"

"Yes siree bob, that's the place. But maybe after all this carryin' on, he's just takin' a well-deserved vacation."

At that moment, Henry Brighton was not feeling in a holiday mood at all. The ride on Swissair had been pleasant enough, the food adequate, and the stewardesses, with their soft Swiss English, efficient and unobtrusive. Henry, wrapped in his own concerns, noticed none of this. His only recollection of the flight was the bumpy descent over the Alps, culminating in a bone-shaking landing at Zurich-Kloten airport which left him breathless. Then the shuffling wait at customs seemed interminable. Henry felt edgy and angry enough to burst.

A recollection surfaced from the day before; Red Felton's long, insolent cowboy face telling him why he hadn't voted against Caleb's project. Well, he, Henry Brighton, would fix Red's wagon for that. If he once allowed his staff to get the better of him, there would be no end to it. And he'd been so good to Felton, damn him! Henry slid his bags forward a foot and bunched his fists. That disgusting, tobacco-chewing cowboy didn't have an ounce of loyalty in him, and that was something Henry could not forgive. Loyalty in a department was of paramount importance. He slammed his fist on his thigh, and the middle-aged Swiss businessman beside him gave him a strange look through his rimless glasses and edged away.

Henry caught sight of the large, brightly colored coat of arms hanging high over the customs hall, the Zurich city seal. Henry stared at it, startled. It showed three decapitated men standing together, holding their heads under their arms. Henry was not normally superstitious, but this was surely the worst possible omen.

The next bad sign was that Ortweiler's people hadn't sent a car to meet him. He searched among the waiting dark-uniformed chauffeurs, some with signs—"Mr. Bemelmans, IBM"—and one very tall, cadaverous driver holding one up that read "Cardinal Elphinstone" in fine Gothic script. There was no one for him. One of the chauffeurs, seeing him checking the signs, asked if he wasn't Maurice Kovacs from the State Department, and Henry snapped at him and hurried away. In German-speaking Switzerland, where they like titles almost as much as the Germans do, his sign would have read "Herr Professor Doktor Brighton." Henry would have liked that.

Finally he picked up his bags, went into town by public transportation, then took a taxi to his hotel, the Metropole. By the time he arrived there, he felt so hot, angry, and frustrated that he picked up a hand towel in the bathroom and ripped it into four pieces. He stood there, panting, looking at the pieces, feeling momentarily pleased. He hadn't realized he was so strong.

He drank a couple of glasses of ice water, then lay down on the bed to await his phone call. Five hours later he was still waiting.

Late that afternoon, Henry finally received a telephone call from Herr Ortweiler's secretary, asking him to be at their head office at seven o'clock that evening. There was a special reason for the late hour, she told him, and he should make every attempt to be there promptly. The offices were on the other side of the lake, about an hour's ride. No, she said, unfortunately no company cars would be available at that hour, but he could take a taxi. Or if he preferred, the public transportation system was very reliable.

Henry took a taxi. It was still warm outside when he left the hotel, despite a steady breeze coming off the lake.

The headquarters of the consortium were not visible from the road, and the driver had to negotiate a sharp turn into a driveway lined with pine and fir trees. The house appeared after a short drive. It had once been a luxurious villa, set back from the waters of Lake Zurich by a lawn so smooth it looked like green velvet. As they approached, Henry could see that the house was built along the late-Victorian lines once popular in Switzerland, with brick turrets and gables, three stories, a square stone portico, and a massive front door. He also noticed a forest of radio antennae on the roof, gleaming in the late sunlight. He smiled briefly to himself—these people weren't just a bunch of shirt-sleeved men anxious to get back to making pills. He was about to be admitted to the nerve center of a very sophisticated industry.

The Mercedes taxi pulled up under the portico. Henry got out, paid the driver, and walked up the steps to the front door. Henry had an impression of unobtrusive but tight security; there was at least one closed-circuit camera scanning the entrance, and another over the front door. He rang the doorbell, and a young man, neatly dressed in a morning coat, opened the door for him. Henry hadn't seen anybody wearing one of those since he was last in London and had cashed a check at Coutt's Bank.

The young man led Henry through the huge, ornate entrance hall, up one curving flight of softly carpeted stairs, past life-size portraits of men with grim mustaches and grim beards. They stopped outside a large oak door, which the young man opened with a key. The door had a fine antique brass doorknob, but that was evidently just for ornament.

Inside the high-ceilinged room was a long, polished table with twelve high-backed leather chairs set around it. At each place on the table was a leather blotter, a notepad surmounted by a neatly centered gold pen, and, mounted on the side wall where everyone could watch it, a large television projector screen. Three high windows looked out over the lake.

Henry didn't have time to admire the view. About half the seats were taken, and Herr Ortweiler, sitting at the far end of the table, stood up and welcomed him.

"I think you know Dr. Hans Saltzman, our research advisor, and Dr. Ivan Gross, from Basel . . ." Ortweiler rattled off a list of names, all of which Henry forgot instantly. They were apparently CEOs of several large pharmaceutical firms, located mainly in Switzerland and West Germany. Henry shook hands all around, and the beaming Herr Ortweiler indicated a chair for him. With a sinking heart Henry realized that Ortweiler was still under the impression that Caleb Winter's project had been terminated. Somewhere along the line he would have to tell them, but this wasn't the moment.

"We're sorry to bring you here so late, Professor Brighton, but I thought you might want to be here to see the results of our announcement on the New York Stock Exchange." Ortweiler looked at his watch. It was seven o'clock exactly. "We have been here all day," he went on, "coordinating the entire operation. The timing is very important, I'm sure you realize that, as we wish to avoid delay for any of the markets around the world."

Henry nodded briskly as if he understood what Ortweiler was talking about.

"It is now exactly two P.M. New York time, and the announcement was made in the Stock Exchange a short time ago." Ortweiler stopped talking suddenly and his eyebrows went up a fraction when the door opened again and the young man came in carrying a portable telephone. He whispered briefly in Ortweiler's ear, and Ortweiler's gaze flickered over to Henry for just a second. He picked up the phone and listened. As the men gathered around the table watched, they heard him draw a deep breath, and saw the hand holding the telephone start to shake, as if he were about to have an epileptic attack.

Putting the phone down, Ortweiler controlled himself with an effort. He waited until the young man had left the room, then put both hands flat on the table in front of him.

"Gentlemen, I have just heard ... There is a television news program from the United States which our studio upstairs started to tape a few moments ago. They will project it on this screen as soon as possible."

After that, Ortweiler sat as if in a trance, staring straight in front of him. The others watched him in a puzzled silence, wondering what could possibly have happened. Henry could feel his nerves on edge; had they canceled the planned announcement of the oral insulin preparation? Had they found it had dangerous side effects? His conjectures were interrupted when the screen became bright, then showed, with astonishing clarity, Caleb Winter standing on a podium in front of a battery of microphones. Henry gasped audibly. He recognized the setting, the main conference room of the New Coventry Medical Center.

The program had been hurriedly taped, and the interview

had been going on for a few moments before the recording had started.

"... will revolutionize the treatment of diabetes," Caleb was saying. "The implantation of embryonic pancreatic tissue into humans is now a practical possibility, which will mean the end of the need for those sufferers to take insulin." The screen went blank for about three seconds while Henry's nails bit into his palms. Then it flashed on again, and an excited announcer appeared, blond hair blowing and his eyes scrunched up as he faced the sun outside the New York Stock Exchange. "A surprise announcement concerning a new oral preparation of insulin, the life-saving medicine for diabetics, was made here with some fanfare a short time ago," the reporter said, "but this news has been swept away by the announcement from the New Coventry Medical Center in Connecticut that injected fetal pancreas cells will soon replace any need for insulin in these same patients. The market has responded by a dramatic fall in pharmaceuticals, and that trend is expected to continue, as the new procedure will eliminate the need for one of their major products. Now we return you to our reporter in New Coventry, who is standing by with fresh news on this dramatic medical breakthrough ..."

Henry didn't wait to hear any more. He got up, walked to the door, and let himself out. There was no one in the stairs or downstairs in the hall. Outside, walking down the driveway like a man in a trance, he started to make his way back to Zurich on foot. He had spent his last penny buying stock and futures in the consortium; not only had he lost all that, but he would have a margin call to face when he got back to New Coventry, and he had no money to pay for it. Henry walked on, not even certain whether he was going in the right direction.

As soon as the television lights were switched off, Caleb stepped down from the podium to meet a barrage of questions from reporters. A gray-haired man with thick horn-rimmed glasses, a veteran science reporter from *The*

New York Times, was near the front. "Wasn't this announcement a bit premature?" he asked Caleb. "I've been following your career, and I know you usually wait for more definitive results before making an announcement of this kind."

Caleb grinned at him. "I quite agree. But the results we have in this case are extremely promising. Tissue culture growths have been astonishingly successful, thanks to new techniques we've developed here." He paused. "There were other considerations, but I am not prepared to discuss them at this time."

"Dr. Winter, was there any connection between your announcement and the news we've just heard about a new oral insulin preparation?" This was from a young woman with an earnest, birdlike face and short hair.

Caleb turned to her and gave her a full dose of his charm. His eyes crinkled, and the corners of his mouth turned up just a little. "We only heard about that a few minutes ago," he said innocently. "You must remember that here in New Coventry, we're out in the boondocks, and news travels slowly." He looked at his watch. The press conference had taken longer than he'd expected, and he was late for his outpatient clinic. He excused himself and headed for the door. At the speed he went, nobody even thought of stopping him.

A half-dozen people were sitting in the waiting room—he was almost an hour late because of the hastily convened press conference. He mumbled an apology as he passed through. Nurse Allen, looking crisp and ready, had a stack of patient folders on the desk.

"Dr. Winter," she said. "There's a Mr. Leroy Williams in your office waiting to see you."

Caleb nodded slowly. He went down the short corridor to his office. Leroy was sitting on the bench, looking very relaxed. He stood up, his lanky body stretching almost lazily. "Hi, Doc," he said, his strong white teeth showing in a wide grin. "Good to see you. I'm real happy everything turned out okay for you in the committee."

Caleb waited.

Leroy turned and pointed to a small, wizened black woman sitting next to him, skinny legs apart, looking brightly up at Caleb through bottle-glass lenses. "I'd like you to meet my aunt Allie. The doc up in Willimantic where she lives, Doc Weinstein—he says she has a tumor on her pancreas, and you are the guy to take care of her."

Celine wakened with the realization that this was her last day
in the hospital. She sat on the edge of the bed, feeling stiff
and creaky, but wonderfully alive.

There was a knock at the door, and Etta Pringle, the head
nurse, came in, followed by her team. "Well, Celine, are you
all set?"

"Just about. I still have to pack."

"I mean for the reporters, the TV cameras, all that stuff."
She paused, and Celine saw that the other nurses were watching her with wide eyes. She had become a celebrity.

"They're coming in here?" Celine sat bolt upright.

"No, no. When you leave. They're setting up their cameras
and stuff outside the main entrance, and we'll all be coming
out with you." She hesitated. "Ms. de La Roche, I must tell
you, you turned out to be a great patient. We learned a lot
from you. It's been a pleasure." Etta put out her hand and
Celine took it. This must be their standard speech, she
thought, but Etta sounded sincere enough.

"Dr. Winter should be here soon," said Etta, shepherding
the nurses out. "After we come outside with you, I hope we
never see you again."

Celine's mouth opened for a second, then she understood.
It was the standard friendly farewell, a wish for her continu-
ing good health.

A few minutes later, Cathie poked her head around the
door. "I just wanted to say good-bye," she said, coming into
the room. "You look ready to take on the world all over again."

"Are you kidding? I'm barely able to stand up by myself."

"How d'you feel? Really?"

"Great. I've been thinking about all the things waiting to be done out there. I just finished reading a manuscript that's going to be a best-seller, our sales are up, and I can't wait to get back."

"It's going to be business as usual, huh?"

"No, actually it's going to be very different." Celine sounded very positive, but she didn't elaborate.

There was a pause. Without thinking, Cathie pulled out a pack of Marlboros, looked at it, then put it back in her purse.

"What time is Charles coming to pick you up?"

"He said eleven." Celine's voice was subdued. "I have a nasty feeling he's going to dump me at home and then take off."

"Of course he won't," said Cathie stoutly. She grinned at Celine. "Anyway we all thought you'd be going home with Caleb."

"He never asked me," replied Celine. "But I can tell you that until a couple of days ago, I'd have gone with him, and happily."

"Why didn't you? What happened?"

"Well, before the operation, he said that until I was ready to go home, he had to stay cool. He couldn't let emotions interfere with the kind of decisions he had to make."

"But he did, didn't he? He put his career on the line for you. If he hadn't defied that hospital committee, right now you'd still be in bed with tubes and IVs, trying to figure out where your insides had gone."

"Yes he did, and I'll never forget it. But once I was better, he said, it was going to be roses all the way. He kept watching over me, he held my hand, sometimes he held more than my hand. He's a very sexy person, you know."

"Yeah, I've noticed."

Cathie settled into the chair.

"All this time we had lots of long, cozy silences. Then when I was getting better, I wanted to start filling them." Celine grinned at Cathie. "Well, the awful thing is we had nothing to fill them with, aside from how I felt and how his work was going. We had nothing to say to each other. He doesn't read books, and I don't know about immunology. It didn't seem to bother him, but it bothers me. A lot."

Celine reached for a Kleenex and blew her nose, hard. "I don't know what's happening to me," she said. "I'm really getting soft, or something."

"You could use some softening," said Cathie. "I remember what you were like. This is an improvement."

"Then Maureen Spark came in and told me what I guess I'd known anyway." Celine rolled up her sleeve and examined a red area on her forearm where an IV had been inserted. "Anyway, after I thought about what she said, that's when I knew for sure that it couldn't ever work." She rolled down the sleeve and buttoned it, but her fingers were not steady. "And today's the day I have to tell him."

Caleb came out of the operating room and hurried toward the Harkness elevator, excited and apprehensive at the thought of seeing Celine. The whole atmosphere of their relationship seemed to have subtly changed in the last couple of days, and he didn't know why. Caleb wasn't used to feeling confused about anything, and he didn't like it. Maybe Celine was feeling the restraint of being in the hospital, or else it was the delayed effect of all that surgery. Whatever the cause, a space had appeared between them, and he was afraid it was getting wider.

Now, Caleb thought about Celine with a possessive sense of pride, and he laughed at himself for it. "You're feeling like a kid who's put a new motor in his first car," he told himself, wishing it could be as simple.

His pager went off, and Caleb stopped at the nurses' station to pick up the call. It was the Saudi Arabian embassy in Washington. A Very Important Personage who lived in the palace at Riyadh had developed an inflammation of the pancreas, and would Caleb come out immediately to consult? Caleb told them he'd have to check his schedule and would get back to them within the hour. Ever since his TV appearance, Caleb had been swamped with requests to see patients, to give lectures and interviews. *Time* magazine was going to do a feature on him, and the "Today" show wanted him to appear the following week.

Caleb turned his mind back to Celine and felt daunted by the practicalities of the situation. She would be going home, presumably, with her husband. Then what? Would she want to wait until she was stronger before joining him? What about Charles? Where would they live? How would he handle it if she got sick again? Who would take care of her? Caleb felt acutely uncomfortable with these problems, which seemed to increase logarithmically in size and complexity even as he considered them. Normally, problems of all kinds and dimensions were meat and drink to Caleb, and he couldn't understand why these seemed so huge and unresolvable.

He paused at the door of Celine's room, and his anxiety vanished in a surge of optimism and excitement. Everything was going to work out, he was sure of it.

When Caleb came in, Celine looked up quickly. He seemed full of his usual assurance. He closed the door behind him and smiled at her.

"You're looking wonderful," he said. "Are you all ready to go?"

"Yes, Caleb, I am," replied Celine, and something in her voice alerted him.

His gaze fixed on her, instantly questioning, uncertain. "We can talk while I examine you," he said. "But I can't check your abdomen with you all dressed up like that."

Celine loosened her skirt, lay down on the bed, and pushed her clothes down to expose her tummy. She was healing nicely; Caleb had closed her incision using a plastic surgical technique.

"In a few months, that'll hardly show," he said.

His hands felt cool and precise on her; as usual, they probed and pressed, and he watched her face. Celine could feel his unspoken questions as he examined her.

"Life isn't going to be the same without you, Caleb." Celine had trouble keeping her voice steady.

"Right," he replied, watching her carefully. "This was just an unpleasant interlude in your life." He smiled, but his eyes didn't waver. "You'll have forgotten all about me in a few weeks." His tone turned the statement into a question, an urgent one.

"*No, Caleb Winter, I will not.*"

The hands stopped.

"You know that I fell in love with you," started Celine, in a strange voice.

There was a pause filled with an almost painful intensity, and across Caleb's face came a look that Celine had never seen before. His hands came slowly up, and he gently held her face between them and stared into her eyes.

"And, oh my God, how I fell in love with you." Caleb's voice was barely a whisper.

Just as gently, Celine disengaged his hands.

"I've learned a lot," she said. "More than I could ever explain, and I thank you for everything you've done. You've saved my life, not just in the obvious medical way, but also in other ways that are just as important."

Caleb stood up slowly, his eyes fixed on hers with an unfathomable expression.

"I have an old friend," went on Celine, "Didier Franchet, who saw very clearly how I felt about you when he visited me here. '*Loving your surgeon is like having the mumps,*' he said to me. '*Hard to ignore at the time, but it's usually over in a couple of weeks.*' I didn't believe him then, and I don't believe it now. Caleb Winter, I will love you for ever for what you've done. I hope that you and Charles and I will be able to get to know each other outside the hospital." For a second, Celine wondered if she still had the right to include Charles in her plans.

Caleb's expression had subtly changed, and Celine could feel him receding from her at the speed of light. He looked exactly the way she'd first seen him, when she'd barged past Cathie Allen: cold, appraising, clinical.

"That's all right," Caleb said, his voice showing no sign of shock or disappointment. "You're right, falling in love with your surgeon is part of the treatment."

He straightened up and turned away from her toward the window, feeling suddenly sick and light-headed. His lips tight-

ened in self-directed anger. But falling in love with your patient certainly is not part of the treatment, he told himself.
Any doctor who does that is a fool, and only demonstrates his
own weakness. Caleb Winter, you deserve everything you're
feeling. He took a deep breath and turned back to Celine.

"Now why don't you get dressed, and I'll tell you some
things I think you should know, and then we'll go over what's
scheduled for the rest of the morning." One the surface it
was the old Caleb again, brisk, back in control, confident.

He went to the window, his back turned to Celine, and
thought fast, putting everything together in his mind with his
customary precision, arranging the facts in the way he wanted
to present them.

Celine pulled up her skirt, fastened it, and sat on the edge
of the bed.

Caleb came back and sat in the chair. His voice was calm,
didactic. "If you remember, I told you my lab had been gear-
ing up for years for our first pancreas transplant."

"And I came along with the right problem at the right
time," said Celine, smiling at him.

"When your diagnosis became clear," he went on, and Celine realized that he hadn't even heard her, "I had to decide
if you would be a suitable graft recipient. You can understand
how important that decision was; the future of our work depended on it."

Celine heard the clatter of trolleys in the corridor. They
were picking up the breakfast trays. Life was still going on
out there.

"But the first imperative, of course, was to make sure you
got proper treatment." Caleb shook his head. "And that
wasn't easy, I can tell you. You were facing a life-threatening
situation, Celine, but your attitude, your resistance could have
killed you." His mouth smiled just perceptibly, like the first
time Celine had confronted him in the outpatient building.
"I quickly realized how you felt about doctors and hospitals,
your mistrust and dislike of the system."

"So I *did* make it clear."

Caleb smiled. "Getting you ready for your operation was
like getting a high-strung racehorse into the starting gate."

"Are you saying that you *manipulated* me, what I was thinking and feeling?" Celine's mouth tightened fractionally.

"No, certainly not," Caleb said, quite relaxed now. "That's not what I meant. I guess you could say we helped you focus your energies in the right direction."

Caleb paused, staring at her. "Now surely you must see that if I'd allowed myself to get emotionally involved with you, I could never have been sure I'd made the right decisions?"

Celine could hardly believe what she was hearing. Now he was denying that he'd even let himself get involved. And he was clearly denying it to himself as much as to her.

Caleb's voice changed, and he was back to the present, all business.

"Now," he said. "Let's talk about something different. When you leave here there's going to be a fair amount of press and TV coverage. You made medical history, I'm sure you know."

"Like Laika the space-dog," said Celine.

Caleb ignored the comment. "The hospital administration and the networks have arranged for you to leave here at eleven-thirty, in good time for the one o'clock news." Caleb was tidying up; in his meticulous way, he was making sure that every last little detail of this problem was taken care of before tackling the next one, whatever it might be. That's what Maureen had meant when she said, *"Right now you're his work."*

Just before leaving, Caleb went over her medication and follow-up protocol with her; he gave her a typed sheet with all the information on it.

"Celine," he said slowly, as if reluctant to close the case, "I think that's about all. I truly believe that you are cured, but of course it'll take time before I can be certain."

"I'll be seeing you for the follow-up visits?"

"Yes," he said. "The dates and times are all on the sheet I gave you."

"One other thing," said Celine. "Is all this going to interfere with my having a family?"

Caleb froze for a second, then his voice was as businesslike as ever. "It shouldn't. But it might be a good idea to wait until you've got all your strength back."

"Thank you. It'll be back by tonight. Now, Caleb, you promise you'll come out and visit Charles and me?"

"Of course." Caleb smiled, and she smiled back, although they had never been further apart.

· · · · · · · · · · · *42* · · ·

After Caleb had gone, Celine sat down on the bed, sad, relieved, and emotionally exhausted. She looked around her
room, happy to be saying good-bye to it and now very anxious
to get out. She picked up the few small items she hadn't
already packed, put rubber bands around the two manuscripts
she hadn't finished, slipped them back in their envelopes, then
lay down for a little while. By ten-thirty she was feeling in-
creasingly apprehensive about seeing Charles again, although
she would know how things were the moment she set eyes
on him. Feeling that she was about to reenter a world that
had totally change in the last two weeks, Celine went over to
the window. The air had cleared after the thunderstorm, and
she could see the wooded hills to the north of the city set
against a clear blue sky. The picture matched her mood, and
she felt a great surge of confidence and determination. She
knew what she had to do to make it all work.

She stood up, feeling the optimism flowing back into her
spirit like a spring tide. She went into the bathroom to tidy
up. In the mirror she could see she'd lost weight. Celine put
her thumbs inside the waistband of her skirt and pulled. Not
bad. Maybe Caleb Winter should open a weight loss clinic—
nothing like cancer and major surgery to make you lose a few
pounds. She laughed at herself in the mirror.

Charles arrived on the dot of eleven, bringing Dan Carfield
with him. Dan was dressed as usual in his brown woolen suit
and walked with tremulous determination, helped by a thick

ironwood cane. He seemed exhilarated by the adventure. Charles was looking extremely fit and healthy, and Celine watched him apprehensively when he came in, unable to tell how he felt. He kissed her rather formally, then left immediately to settle with the billing office, leaving Dan with her.

He carefully sat down in the chair and looked at her quizzically. "You look well, young lady. Now, before Charles comes back, I have quite a number of things to tell you."

He settled back into his chair. "First, Charles came in fourth in the Trials, and as they selected the first five to go on to the next round, he's in."

"Oh, that's wonderful!" said Celine. "I'm so happy for him." Her voice was tight with anxiety. Next Dan was going to say that Charles had left her for Marion Redwing, and had already moved out of the house. But Dan was calmly telling her that everything was in readiness for her takeover of Fortman and Carfield. When he told her about Didier, at first she couldn't believe it.

"Oncle Didi," she whispered, after Dan had unfolded the entire story of Didier's villainy, "I can't believe he would do that."

But somehow Celine was able to absorb that information without the kind of despair she would have felt a few short weeks before. Didi and his machinations belonged to the old world she had already left.

"While you were in here, Charles did a couple of clever things," said Dan, leaning forward and sniffing the gardenias. "First he figured out what that rascal Didier was up to, and then he outsmarted Didier's Arab friend, Al-Khayib." Dan told Celine about the telephones and the air-conditioners for her office.

"There's one other point." Dan looked faintly uncomfortable. "I have to talk to you about you and Charles."

Celine felt the blood draining out of her face. Here it comes, she thought, it's all over.

But Dan didn't drop the axe on her. On the contrary. "The two of you make a great team when you're apart," he was saying. "How about trying it now you can be back together?"

Celine wanted to say there was nothing she wished for

more, but she couldn't get the words out. Dan watched her from under his thick eyebrows. "Charles has been terribly upset about you, you know, and—"

The door opened, and to Dan's obvious relief, Charles came in. "Here he is," Dan said. "He can tell you himself."

Charles came into the room, looked anxiously at Celine, then smiled. As he came toward her, Celine said, in a tone so heartfelt it made Dan smile, "Charles, am I happy to see you!"

After a few moments Dan made a loud hurrrumphing noise. "Would you mind keeping all that stuff until you get home?" he grumbled. "Charles, tell Celine about Anwar."

"Anwar? Ah, yes. Funny you should mention him," replied Charles. "There's a bit about him in the paper this morning. Apparently he was all set to pull down your old building, all his heavy equipment was there and everything, then somebody put an injunction . . ."

"Charles, you didn't! I made a deal with him." Celine was shocked.

"*Moi?*" said Charles, putting his hand over his heart. "Certainly not. That would have been most unethical." He grinned happily at Celine. "By the way," he went on, "did you know that Dan here is on the New York Board of Historical Monuments?"

It was time to face the media. Four aides came in, one with a wheelchair for Celine, the other with two trolleys for the flowers, which required an elevator all to themselves. Porky appeared, flushed and excited, looking smart in a fresh white jacket. The little procession trundled along the corridor and was joined at the elevators by Etta Pringle and her nurses; Charles found a wheelchair for Dan, but he wouldn't take it. He didn't want to be mistaken for the patient, he said. They all ambled along at his speed, Celine holding on to Charles's hand as if her life depended on it.

A small crowd had gathered outside the main entrance of the hospital, attracted by the throng of reporters, mobile TV trucks, and cameras. Celine, blinking in the unaccustomed sunlight, felt a new pair of hands take over the wheelchair behind her. She didn't need to look around to know it was

Caleb. Maureen joined them, looking very pretty, her hair sparkling in the sunlight. She walked very close to Porky, and Celine wondered if Porky was the "somebody else" she'd hinted at. Looking ahead again, Celine could see Trevor over by the curb with the car door open. She waved to him; he was smiling broadly for the first time she could remember.

They paused on the hospital steps while the cameras clicked and rolled. The surgical team was all there, and there were hugs and laughs all around. They gathered like family around Celine, the operating room techs and nurses, the nurses who'd taken care of her in the ICU, the lab assistants and technicians. A tired-looking man came over to shake hands; Caleb introduced him as Marshall Prince, the hospital administrator. He was followed by a big, handsome black man with a huge grin and a leopard's canine tooth on a leather thong around his neck, who smiled cheerfully at Celine. He put a friendly hand on Caleb's shoulder when the cameras started turning.

After the official pictures had been taken, reporters swarmed around Celine and took pictures and shouted questions as the group slowly trundled along the sidewalk toward the car. Charles walked alongside the wheelchair, one hand protectively on Celine's shoulder. A slim young woman reporter pushed her way through and walked backward in front of the wheelchair. She had a waiflike prettiness, and looked a little scared, but called out a question that Celine had been asking herself all morning.

"What did you learn from your experience, Celine?" she asked.

Celine stopped the chair by putting her hands on the wheels. "This is what I learned," she said, and smiling up at Charles, she reached her arms out for him and kissed him on the mouth. That was the photo that appeared in the national papers the next day.

Porky had to go back to his patients, so Maureen went over to rejoin Caleb. She stared at him for a moment; he seemed to have aged suddenly, and Maureen knew why and felt sad for him. They stayed at the curbside until the gray limousine had pulled away, then the two of them walked back into the hospital, both thinking their own thoughts. In silence they made their way through the maze of corridors back to the lab. Caleb, for once, walked at Maureen's speed.

From the window of the lab they could see the TV technicians putting their equipment back in their trucks; for Caleb, they symbolized the end of the case.

He drew himself up and took a deep breath, as if he were wrapping up all the events and all the emotions of the past two weeks into a tidy package and putting it firmly away into the files of his mind.

"We have a lot of rebuilding to do," he said, surveying the quiet lab. "We've lost Collie, and we may have lost Milo. They won't know for a while whether he'll be able to come back."

Maureen didn't say anything. She was thinking about Porky. It was going to be great having him working in the lab. Porky certainly wasn't a Caleb Winter—but maybe that was one of the things most in his favor.

Caleb gave her a hard, questioning stare. There was a look about her, a glow that reminded him of something.

He drew himself up and took a deep breath.

"Okay, Maureen," he said, turning away from the window. "I guess the excitement's over for now. It's time to get back to work."